Long Time, No See

Long Time, No See

DERMOT HEALY

ff

faber and faber

First published in 2011
by Faber and Faber Ltd
Bloomsbury House
74–77 Great Russell Street
London WC1B 3DA

Typeset by RefineCatch Limited, Bungay, Suffolk
Printed in England by CPI Mackays, Chatham

A CIP record for this book
is available from the British Library

ISBN 978–0–571–21074–9

2 4 6 8 10 9 7 5 3 1

Acknowledgement

Chapter Forty-Three and part of Chapter Forty-Five of this novel were first published in 2002, and displayed in the Chester Beatty Library in an exhibition by the Graphic Studio Dublin, titled *The Holy Show: Irish Artists and the Old Testament*.

BOOK ONE

Bang!

Chapter One

First Call

I headed down the townland of Ballintra in a Force 8 to light the fire towards the beginning of August.

Ah hah! said Joejoe, opening the door a fraction.

She's windy, I said.

Oh it's you, he said.

It is Uncle Joejoe, I said. He was my granduncle but sometimes I called him just Uncle and some times Grandda.

Hold her.

I have it.

Right now!

OK.

OK, go! *Tar isteach*, he shouted.

I took the handle and slid through with a couple of newspapers under my arm. He stepped back as I stepped in, the table cloth rose, Timmy the dog done a turn and I swung the door shut. Joejoe studied me with his back against the shaking panels.

I was expecting my dear neighbour Mister Blackbird.

Sorry about that.

And I said to myself that's him.

And it was me.

It was you, but it was his knock, you see a knock can carry anyone's signature on a day like that. I could have sworn. You know what it is son – memory is a stranger who comes to call less and less.

Aye.

And sometimes he's not welcome, if you know what I mean.

He could be anyone.

But not you.

He turned the key, let down the latch, pulled back the curtain on the window and looked out.

Is it the north-west?

It is.

The worst! But not as bad as February ninth in eighty-seven, he said as he came back from the misty, drenched window to the table. I don't like the look of it. The worst is at the filling-in of the moon, he said, handing me the leather-handled knife and then he put a plate of un-boiled bacon before me. You're just in time. The Bird will not stir that day, I'll warrant you, he'll stop above in the bodience, that sorry auld bed of his.

I began to saw off some of the raw fat and he threw the first slice to Timmy who nursed it up against the bedroom door, then Joejoe brought the remainder of the bacon joint into the kitchen and set it into a pot of boiling water filled with parsley and chives. He put the small slices of fat onto a saucer on the middle shelf of the dresser, out of the reach of Timmy, and alongside the Wayward Lad.

They were for his rat trap that he would set last thing that night.

Now, he said, how is the form Mister Psyche?

Not so bad Grandda.

Are you fit for dealing with a bad-tempered cratur like me?

I am.

He stood back and looked at the dresser, then lifted down one of his prayer books and handed it to me. Read mister, he said, from the Psalms. The Bible he always called the Psalms.

I picked a page at random, and, as always, it fell open at one of the texts where he had turned down the corner of a page from past readings.

And, behold, I said, *the Lord passed by, and a great and strong wind rent the mountains, and brake in pieces the rocks before the Lord; but the Lord was not in the wind.*

4

He was not, he said.

And after the wind an earthquake; but the Lord was not in the earthquake; And after the earthquake a fire: but the Lord was not in the fire; and after the fire a small voice.

Amen, he said, quietly. We're in this together, Mister Psyche.

He blessed himself; prayed washing his teeth and studying the dresser, then he came to a decision and replaced the Psalms by the picture of the thrush, lifted the pink shoehorn and sat it on a green tin of Old Virginia. He stroked the copy of *Moby Dick*, shook the rusted bell from the drapers to summon the spirits and Timmy barked, rolled in a circle onto his back and bared his stomach. Then Joejoe sat next the window and began to clean the oil lamp. He cleaned the wick. The oil lamp was his main source of light despite the fact that he had electricity. This was done very carefully. The globe, he'd say, should be bright as day. Did you ever see a gypsy face, he asked me, in candlelight? No, I said. They have very fine features, he said, and he turned to watch me as we moved on from prayer to yesterday's daily news. I read out the headlines, then rolled the sheets of newspaper into crisp tight logs and started to build the fire.

I lit it every morning, that was my job ever since I left college, to read the prayers, then the news, and light the fire, and then go on wherever I was going.

The newspapers I collected from all the houses where I had started doing jobs this summer. The timber came from trees felled in Dromod estate. The turf came from above on the mountain and up the Bog Road. And every day for the work I did, I got paid. This was my day-to-day life since college ended – cutting lawns, and hedges, driving tractors, digging gardens and building walls, and looking after Joejoe and taking in his lobsters from his pots out the rocks.

I struck the match, she took.

How is the beautiful Anna?

She is fine.

You're a lucky man.

All the news – the traffic congestion, business and financial affairs, houses for sale, wage and pension increases, obituaries, racing and soccer pages – shot up the chimney. We sat back and watched the flames, and then when the fire was at full tempo, he set the oil lamp on the window and studied the storm. He sang the song of the dog. Rain pounded the asbestos roof. We stepped out, slamming the door behind us, and he took the rusted spade to dig up some onions. The stalks were bent low and swinging in a frenzy of wind.

Let me, I said.

No. The one good thing is Mister, is that when there's a storm coming a body gets a build-up of energy, he said. The man that sleeps in beyond a certain hour suffers. You get a pain just here – and he tapped his skull – and you can see it in their eye. Yes, indeed.

He pulled a head of a blue cabbage and shook the earth from the roots. We stepped against the gable. The sea was leaping like a suicide over the lava rocks then scattering across fields of foam. A Mitsubishi Carisma drove by the gate, pulled in back of the beach, and a few souls went over the bank with cameras. Then a van, marked Sky TV, slowed to a stop, and the two men in the front sat eating sandwiches as they watched the waves. Lastly came the Mercedes, same as usual, with the little teddy bear, stuck fast to the back window.

We waved to them.

They did not acknowledge us, just a nod, but sat there watching the ocean; then seeing the height of the waves they drove away.

Two girls on the pier stood looking out, one behind the other and we went back through the door and he trimmed the cabbage and I cut the onions. Then all of a sudden Joejoe stood up straight, and shot a hand round the back of his neck, leaned forward, and scratched ferociously. He squeezed his shoulders together, and blew out of his lips a sense of burning.

What's wrong?

Nothing, he said. He looked at me a moment then he went over and leaned forward with his elbows on the window sill each side of the lamp.

I often wonder is it possible to see the world through new eyes, he said, but l have my doubts. That's the story. You go on, you do.

You see, look out there, you see him, here comes the bollacks, look at the gimp of him, and he pointed, but I suppose you can't be held to blame for the cut of your neighbours.

Outside the Blackbird who lived just up the road, arrived in teeming salt on his bike, heeled it against the stone wall and humped up the path and straight into the house as I turned the key. Gather unto me, said the Blackbird. The Bird sometimes claimed he was a far distant cousin of my granduncle because we all shared the same name Feeney, but as Joejoe often said *That man is no blood relation of mine.* As he stepped in the wind swept through the kitchen, the dog grumbled, the trapdoor rose above in the ceiling and the polythene sheet in the attic shook. He heaved the door closed. Neither man spoke. He sat into the other armchair, lit up and sneezed. Then sneezed again and wrung a long lookey from his nose, and as he leaned forward a beautiful exotic smell – as always – reached me.

Bless ya, I said.

Mister Psyche?

Yes.

When do you get the results?

Sometime soon.

So what are you going to be?

7

I don't know. It depends on how I did in the Leaving.

The *Leaving* is a sad word for an exam, said Joejoe.

It is that, said the Bird, looking at me, and nodding.

Now, said Joejoe, you know what you might do?

What is that I wonder? I asked.

He got carefully up and stood on Timmy's chair and took an envelope out from behind the radio.

There is a certain item needed.

Right.

You know what I mean?

I do.

A valuable item.

OK.

Cuckoo! said the Blackbird, with his mouth curved into an O, we are headed out to the Caribbean.

On you go. Don't get the small one; get the big one you hear me, never mind what the tulip says –

– I hear you –

– Here's a twenty and a fiver. The last few euro is yours, so do what you will with it –

– Thank you, sir –

– Not at all –

– Myself and Mister Blackbird will be waiting now.

You're right there, said the Blackbird and he tossed me a five-euro note.

Patiently, added Joejoe.

Good men, I said, facing the door.

I headed up the road head-down. A bag of turnips, and a bag of turf, shorn in the middle, was dumped to the side of the road. A For Sale sign was down and bucketing outside Keating's ruin. The spray was scattering over the meadows. Salt was raining and the bent grass was burnt black at the tips as if there had been frost overnight. Lyons cattle were eating from a trough with steam rising from them. The sun was high and squeezed into a blazing knot above the storm clouds on the horizon.

I looked back and saw the pier was deserted except for a small Fiat that stood with its boot open. There were a few boxes of groceries sitting there beside it. The tide was huge. Mrs Tingle, who had a holiday home up the road, was standing, her hair in curlers, looking down over the end.

She turned, saw me, and waved and waved me back, then drew me over with her forefingers.

Could you give us a hand here, she asked.

Sure.

I'm sorry to have to ask you this, she said, but we have a wee problem, and it's a big one, then she turned away, and pointed down.

Her husband who was a Leeds soccer fanatic was standing in a blue anorak below in our trawler hanging onto the cabin. Their boat was tied alongside ours. On the far side was the Conans' boat where Anna used come to read surrounded by all her old primary and secondary schoolbooks. There was a line of bags of groceries laid at intervals in both boats.

You're not thinking of going out?

No, she said, thanks beta God. We packed the groceries on last night for a journey out to the island, went home and did not listen to the forecasts.

It's wild, I said.

We were going to go out, but the journey is abandoned and we are taking everything back up again.

It's near the full moon.

It is and to tell you the truth, she said, I can't manage any more. Will you give us a hand?

I will.

Mister Psyche will get it, she shouted down.

The bird watcher, with the binoculars round his neck, roared from below something up in the wind, but when I looked over

9

the top he smiled and positioned himself at the bottom of the ladder. He lifted a bag in greeting. I said all right, and climbed over, swung out on the rope to the right over the edge to get my first foothold and started down. The choking wind tore at my chest. It must have been about fifteen feet down. I went rung by rung very carefully, holding on tight in between.

He stood looking up at me with one hand raised in the rocking boat.

I reached the bottom of the ladder, and he tapped my shoulder and handed me a bag of oranges. All right mate, he called. Up I went through the gusts and handed them to her. Thank you boy, she said. Then I shot back down for a transistor. No bird-watching today, he said, then up I went with a bag of cornflakes, and down for a bag of provisions. Towels, wine, her binoculars. Then we reached the last item I started up holding the black bag. He started to climb up behind me.

It was a long climb. The bag said Blankets. Their boat said *Gertie*.

Are you all right? came a shout from above.

I'm with you, he shouted from below.

I reached the top, clutched the top rung in my left hand and threw the bag over. I stood a moment on the fourth rung of the ladder.

Are you all right son?

Yes, I said.

I climbed up and reached out to grab the rope to the left to haul myself up and over onto the pier. I suddenly found that the rope was attached to nothing. I fell back out holding on to the top rung with my right hand. Jesus, shouted the woman, and her husband screamed and reached a hand up tight against my legs. It was a long moment. Only for I was holding the rung with my other hand I was gone. I got my feet, and reached again for the second rope that hung there to the right. I gave a strong tug and it held. I climbed over.

That was bad, the woman said.

I got a fright, I said.

Someone done that deliberately, she said.

I saw that, said Mister Tingle, climbing over, I saw that. Someone should have a word with the authorities.

I'm all right.

Nobody should leave an unattached rope there, he said and the hair in the wind stood on his head. Jesus. The blokes that are using this pier should be hung.

It's my friend Anna mostly uses this pier, I said, more than anyone else.

I know, I know. By the luck of God, I pulled the right rope each time I came up. We were lucky. You were lucky.

I was.

You were.

That's the sort of thing happens in the worst dreams, said Mrs Tingle. Are you all right?

Yes, I said. Is that everything?

It is now, he said. I helped them pack the boot of their car. A newspaper blew off down the shore and he waved goodbye to it.

Thanks a lot, she said again. Tonight I'll be thinking of you.

Goodbye, I said.

Thank you again, he said. I was about to walk off and then I remembered. I remembered *Anna*. Jesus, I thought. This evening she could have swung out on that loose rope to reach the first step. Jesus Christ, I thought. I went back to the head of the ladder on the pier and leaned down and tied the loose rope securely to one of the metal rings jutting out of the slabs. I gave it a long sharp pull with all my might. Went off, came back and pulled it again as if I was reining in a beast, a mad mare pony that was just being trained in.

Then my mobile rang.

Hallo, I said.

Where are you, Anna asked

I just saved your life, Lala, I replied, and then her voice disappeared.

The Tingles had driven off, now they stopped, reversed, and pulled in beside me.

I don't believe it, we were going to drive off and leave that rope untied, said Mister Tingle, only for you remembered.

I was thinking of my dear friend Anna.

Oh dear God, it was all my fault, said Mrs Tingle suddenly.

What do you mean? he asked.

She looked at me. I untied that rope last night, she said, to tie on some of the provisions and drop them down to my husband. I had forgotten.

What! said Mister Tingle, and he grabbed the steering wheel.

Please forgive me, she said.

It's all right.

It's shocking, he said.

I know, said Mrs Tingle.

Please let us bring you wherever you're going.

No thanks, I'm grand.

Please, he said, let us try and make up for the mistake.

I like the walk.

Mate, please.

Reluctantly I got in. The windows were thick with salt. The wipers were going like mad. I dug my feet into the floor as they turned around the For Sale sign. As we hit the blinding hail Mrs Tingle poured out a cup of coffee for her man out of a flask, and handed it to him just as we had to suddenly pull in for a truck, marked McNiff's Transport, to pass. It was filled with a load of motorcycles. It never stopped or slowed down but drove on straight by within an inch of us. We jerked back out onto the road, fast, and Mrs Tingle said John? And he slowed down. She filled a coffee for herself. The truck must have lost their way, for when they met the end of the road and saw the sea ahead, they turned and shot up right behind us as we waited at the small crossroads for a Shell Oil lorry to pass.

We waited. The lorry in front passed, and behind us the truck flashed its lights, and revved loudly but Mister Tingle did not budge as there was a bicycle coming in the opposite direction. He just raised his paper cup and laughed with his head back. Mrs Tingle politely dribbled sugar, piece by piece across the full cup of her latte. She lifted it to her lips like a child, and sucked in as she took a sip.

Nice? she said.

Very, he said.

Joe Donlon, straight as a soldier on parade gave a downward wave in greeting as he passed, as if he was petting a dog. Hi, said Mrs Tingle, waving out the passenger window. And Mister Tingle lifted his cup in greeting, and said it's a small world, we were lucky, and leaning forward, cup in hand, on the steering wheel, he looked both ways, and added He is a rare gentleman. Behind us McNiff's man blew the horn. We sat a moment longer as Mister Tingle held the pupils of his eyes up to the rear-view mirror, and his hand on the gear stick. The lights of the truck flashed and the horn blew again, and suddenly the truck, with a loud swerve, pulled out to the right to pass us, but at the last minute my buck shot into gear and we took off with a sudden jolt and roar of the exhaust up the hill.

John? Mrs Tingle said.

Yes, he said.

Please.

As he slowed down, in the back seat I got the sensation again of falling, and I reached out to the handle of the door. Being in a fast car was driving me back in time. We shot up past the Wishing Well and the quarry in fifth. Mister St Patrick was standing with his cows in the Long Acre. Then we hit the spot at Mannion's shed where Mickey died in the crash over a year ago. It was marked with tubs of flowers.

You can drop me here, I said.

I understand, he said, but I can wait and bring you on wherever you want to go.

I'm fine here, please.

If that's what you want, and he swerved to a stop, and the lorry passed us blowing its horn in one long scream of sound.

I got out and blessed myself.

Bye, said Mister Tingle.

Forgive me, said Mrs Tingle.

I knelt and went on.

I could hear a mouth organ playing in one of the county council houses, and over my head, tied by a blue string to a Stop sign, was a single purple balloon blowing and tossing like mad. It was still hanging there to mark the shortest route for strangers to take to the wedding in St Mary's Church that had been held a year and a half ago. That day there'd been a row of balloons and ribbons hanging from trees and signposts the whole way down from the main road. They'd all been blown away and this was the last balloon.

The balloon was tough.

It had survived many a storm, and now was entering another. And every time I looked up at that balloon I'd wonder to myself: Are that man and woman still together?

Then suddenly McNiff's lorry appeared again, this time coming back in my direction down the hill.

It pulled up alongside me. The driver let the window down and looked at me in exasperation.

He asked: Where are we?

Templeboy.

He looked at the map in his hand.

Templeboy! Templeboy!

Where are you headed? I asked.

Matty Gilbride's.

Go on down to the T-junction, turn left, and take the first right, then go on straight.

Turn left, and take the first right, and go straight?

Yes.

Thank you, he said and the lorry took off with a roar.

Chapter Two

Malibu

It was a Saturday.

A woman power-walker strode by. In the field beyond, a magpie stood on a sheep, on the middle of her back, looking off into the distance, and the sheep had her head a little off the ground, wondering. Pa O'Rourke passed in his tractor with a load of bales of hay. The General in his good suit was standing at his gate waiting and then Stefan stepped out of the foundations of an abandoned building site.

He shook himself.

Excuse, he said, frowning, I have a problem.

Go ahead.

Where you go?

To Mister John's.

For a drink?

Yes.

Hm. I think I join you, ah, he said and pretending to be drunk he fell sideways, put his two hands to the side of the face, and reached out to balance himself, then, with wide eyes, he snapped again into a correct stance, chest up, and sure-footed began walking alongside me.

Do you mind if I walk with you?

If you want.

Are you sure?

Yes, chest.

I am not Polish, and it is pronounced *czesc*. If you want to say hallo to me it is *labas*.

OK, *labas*.

You have plenty of money?

Yes, I said.

My boss is gone somewhere. Good. But, it is no good. Today the machine I work with is . . . and he opened his arms wide . . . is breaking down again. It is inside, and I have no key. Then he swung one arm in a wide circle. I am looking for Meester Doy-al. You know where he is?

No. Is he gone missing again?

Yes. He said to me yesterday that he was going to the bank today. But . . . !? And he threw out his hands . . . Who is Bob Geldof, please?

He is a singer.

He shook his head in puzzlement.

Irish?

Yes. Have you never heard of him?

No. Time it is an experiment in this country, Mister Side Kick, and he winked. I hear his name on the radio.

Ah!

I understand. Have you heard of Tomas Pekinoff?

No.

It is no problem. Neither have I.

We arrived at the small unmarked garage surrounded by wrecks on one side, and well-polished second-hand cars on the other.

You see I knock, I knock many times, but there is no reply.

I'm sorry.

It is a disaster, no? And I shouted Hallo! It is OK, I wait. Again. Hallo! shouted Stefan, and he threw his arms in the air, as he walked to the closed galvanised door. He turned. It is always good to meet you. You will take a look for me in the . . . pub, yes?

Yes.

Goodbye.

Goodbye, I said.

*

At two on the dot I stepped into Mister John's.

I was taken aback to find a crowd there. There were four men and a woman around the fire playing Twenty-Five with an old pack of cards. They all turned and nodded. The racing channel, with the sound down, was on TV. The horses were going round the ring. Mister John threw a sod of turf on the fire. Frank Morgan was sitting in the corner playing the accordion music on the radio with his eyebrows. When he saw me he held his nose with his thumb and forefinger and nodded at the toilet. The coalman back from Australia was asleep by the fire cradling a glass of Guinness between his knees. Michael Doyle was sitting alone before a pint. Daft Punk was on the juke box with the sound turned down.

Your deal, said Mrs Brady.

I'm only saying, said Frosty, I'm only saying.

Yes? asked Mister John, and what can I do you for his nibs?

A bottle of Malibu, please.

Fine.

The big one, I said.

I hear you. The uncle on the raz? he asked, turning away.

He will be.

With the Blackbird? And he bent forward to look at himself in the mirror.

The very man.

My, my, how do they do it?

Hearts is trumps.

The Blackbird is tough, said Frosty, tough out.

Mister John parcelled the bottle and let it down on the counter. He stroked his chin and said briskly: That'll be twenty-five euro –

– The last time it was twenty-three –

– Was it now? –

– It was surely –

– Is that so? –

– And the time before –

– He has you there, John, the boy got ya, said Morgan –

– Your deal –

I'm joking of course, said Mister John and he gave me the two-euro change and I put it in my back pocket, then I went over and put it in the slot machine, and spun the wheel.

Hard luck, said Michael Doyle.

I guided a gentleman to your door just now, I said, spinning the wheel again.

Did you?

Yes.

Well, that's very kind of you. I'm after hauling a broken-down jeep from Limerick. I went down and up this morning and I can't see in front of me. He'll have to wait.

I think he has been waiting a while.

Oh.

What is he driving?

Nothing.

The plot thickens. Who is it?

Mister Lithuania, I said, and I spun the wheel again.

But he's not due in today. I told him it was a bank holiday.

Out clattered a brace of coins and I started laughing.

Ah now I understand, I said.

I'm only saying, said Frosty.

What's he doing in today, Mick Doyle nodded and then he shook his head. I don't know. What does he want?

He wants to work.

Fuck. Are you going back up the road?

I am.

Tell him I'll be with him in half an hour.

Good luck now men, I said.

Before you go, tell me this, said Frosty, did you ever call any woman by the wrong name?

Oh never, I said. Well maybe the once.

Well you're forgiven, if you did, he said, for I did it myself at the door of a wrong house, you know, late at night, after a crash.

Let's not talk about crashes, said Mister John.

Your play, said Mrs Brady.

Now for you, said Morgan, holding his nose.

The coalman Mister Awesome suddenly fell and Morgan and Frosty and myself lifted him back up off the floor and into his chair. The card players rose, then seated themselves again, and played on. Mister Awesome woke up and eyed me and said: Hi you Feeney, you think the whole thing is a joke, don't you.

No, I said.

Well it's not.

I am not laughing.

Excuse me, said the coalman and he closed his eyes and Morgan's eyebrows swung on into the next tune.

You see the ghost has a body, said Frosty, same as you and me, and he dropped his head, sadly. And my heart goes out to him, the poor cratur.

Stop it, snarled the coalman. You're doing my head in.

I'm only saying, I'm only saying.

Stop it, said Mister Sweet John.

I made my way to Doyle's garage and found Stefan sitting quietly and correct in the passenger seat of one of the Volkswagen Golfs outside the garage.

Labas! I shouted.

He reared up in sudden fright, till he saw it was me, then a smile came, and went, quickly. He sat still without speaking. There was a look of humble sanity in his serious eyes. I came up to the window of the car and I turned my hand round and around in circles on an imaginary handle, and slowly, in time with me, he let the window down.

Yes?

He'll be along soon, I said. You see it's a bank holiday.

Excuse?

And Michael Doyle . . .

Oh, Meester Doyle?

. . . He will be here in half an hour.

Oh. He come?

Yes.

He let a roar of laughter.

Would you like to go to Bundoran? and then he jumped out of the car, winked, and indicated that I get in, but I pointed ahead down the road and lifted the bottle into the air; Ah the cursed drink, he said in a loud Irish accent; and he closed the door with a polite tap of his fingertips, and shook his head in dismay; lit up a cigarette made of yellow paper rolls and stepped aside like a gentleman and sat to the side of the shed in the roaring wind on a huge torn tractor wheel; kicked out, and shook himself viciously, then went perfectly still, in his leather jacket and Yankee baseball cap, with his two fists sitting one on top of the other on his left knee.

Goodbye, I said.

Grand, he said, looking straight ahead like a question mark in the wind blowing up from the sea. Next thing a taxi passed with the General sitting up in the back and he waved.

The Blackbird lifted his tumbler and filled it again, and then he filled my granduncle's. The kitchen was filled with the smell of boiling bacon.

Any news, asked Joejoe.

The pub was full for a change.

Well who was there?

Mister Morgan, Frosty –

– Frosty, said the Blackbird –

– And Mrs Flynn, the coalman Mister Awesome, Barney Buckley, Jim Simpson, Terence MacGowan and Joe Conan.

And Mick Doyle.

So it was like old times. And Mister Sweet John?

Yes, he's behind the counter.

And Frosty is there, nodded the Blackbird.

Yes.

That man is let in and I am not, and the Bird's voice rose.

Well he won't last much longer, said Joejoe. We all get our turn. Anyway going into that pub would only make you lonely. Oh by the way . . .

Don't try changing the conversation.

. . . I'm not. What I wanted to say to the young fellow is, if I'm allowed, is that your mother got me a new electric kettle.

She did, agreed the Blackbird.

And every time I switch it on a plane flies over the house.

I haven't heard that one before.

Well there you have it.

I have indeed.

Says I to myself every time I want to make a cup of tea the skies are fierce busy.

And why wouldn't they be.

True.

– So out I went one day to see the plane and found none –

– You did not –

– So I said to myself they must be going over fierce fast –

– Just like that, said the Blackbird, and he snapped his fingers –

And from then on whenever I put the kettle on and heard the drone of a plane I shot out and was there a plane?

The Blackbird studied the question.

There was none.

There was not.

I thought so.

And what was it do you think?

You have me there.

It was the kettle, I said

The kettle, by God. That's a sight.

Damn right, it was, said Granduncle Joejoe.

It certainly was, agreed the Blackbird.

They bought me a fucking jet to make tay in.

They did. Are we finished the joking now?

We are.

I'm only saying, said the Blackbird, and he bared his teeth imitating Frosty. Good luck.

Good luck, said Joejoe. I like Malibu I do.

Chapter Three

The Rooster

Is the Bird below? my mother asked.

He is.

Dear God. I thought I saw him.

She was nibbling a cheese-cracker at the kitchen table and going through a photograph album. All this week she was working nights.

You better keep an eye on them.

I will.

You see in this house they always leave it up to the nurse. I need a break. Look at your Aunty Eilish. Isn't she something else?

She is Ma.

Oh beautiful. But will you look at the hat. Who in their right senses would be seen in such an outfit. And that's George Wilson behind. George was gamey. A coy boy I may tell you. What was it I wanted to tell you?

I don't know.

It'll come to me. And I don't know what became of George. She flipped a page. There's Gerty.

And Da.

And did you hear?

Hear what Ma?

There was a robbery last night in Flynn's. They came in with a gun and emptied the till. They put the gun to Sara's head. And said: The lot. Do you hear me we want the lot.

Christ.

The lot, they said. She was taken into emergency about twelve. Shaking like a leaf. Wild-eyed. I held her hand till the sedation took. And she kept saying Bridie, Bridie, don't go. She was so shattered she'd forgotten my name.

Ma stood.

I'm going up to lie down for a while. You keep an eye on those boys below. And will you put the poor cat out please.

I went out to the shed for turf and when I came in the Blackbird turned his troubled eyes on me.

Just before you came in, he said, the room was full.

Full of what, I asked.

Why, he says, the ghosts of hens. Did you ever get that?

Never.

Nor me, said my granduncle. I saw no bucking hens.

Well they were here.

More fucking madness.

Well let me see – the Blackbird explained, sitting up. The rooster, he said, comes first cockadoodleooing and screeching with no sound. It's a terror to hear a sound that is not there. Have you ever heard a sound that is not there?

No, I said.

Well you will. In time.

Definitely, nodded Joejoe and he rose his eyes to heaven.

Now, the Blackbird explained, he – the rooster – stands over there – and he indicated the far corner of the room. On the bookstand that has no books. That's where the rooster stands – you know – cockadoodling. With the neck back. And a run of blue temper from his bill to his head feathers – the comb on the top of his skull oh bristling, and dreadful black eyes I can tell you. Cockadoodleooing. Say cockadoodle!

Cockadoodle.

Say it louder.

Cockadoodle! Cockadoodle!

Very good. Now you have it.

Now you're cockadoodleooing, said Joejoe.

I am.

You are, and you're listening to a mad man.

Cockadoodle!

And I can hear you, said the Blackbird –

That's right.

– But I can't hear him you see. That's the problem.

Oh.

And there – over there – he stands raising one claw a little, just very slightly – and the Blackbird stood and raised his right foot ever so quietly just a fraction off the floor, and then he put it down and then he lifted it again like the rooster did, and he held back his head and said to me – Go cockadoodle!

Cockadoodle! said Joejoe and me together.

He straightened up.

Then do you know what happens?

No.

In come the ghost hens.

Indeed they do, said Joejoe, and it's something shocking.

They come flocking from everywhere. Through the walls, the doors the windows the ceiling the fireplace. And are they busy?

They are very busy, said Joejoe.

And what do they start doing sir? – and the Blackbird signalled in my direction.

Cockadoodleooing!

No.

So what do they do?

They go chuckawkchuckawkha!

Oh.

Right, said Joejoe, the birds have changed their tune.

Dead on. But they're not, no, not as loud as the rooster when I think of it, but loud nevertheless. Then all these ghost hens start their chanting. A chanting you can't hear. Flocking round. Raising their wings. Then the rooster jumps down out of his perch and starts chasing them round the room. The hens go mad.

Then what happens?

Well they are likely to land anywhere. On your head. Anywhere to get away from him. And he chases them faster and faster. Faster and faster.

And then?

And then faster.

Yes.

Then – bang!– one of them lands in my pocket.

He clapped his pocket.

Then another.

And he clapped his pocket.

Then another.

No.

Yes.

Jeepers.

And once this happens the next hen jumps into my pocket. And another and another. Till there's only one left. Just the one. And the rooster is left chasing the last hen round the room and what does she do? She jumps into my pocket with a screech and now there is no one but himself and what does he do? He lets one last –

Cockadoodledo! said my granduncle.

And – bang! – he goes into my pocket.

And then what happens?

You came into the room, and he wiped away a tear that was not there.

Oh.

And so here I am, he said, and he pulled out the lining out of his pocket, shook it and pushed it back in, left with a pocketful of ghost hens.

Chapter Four

The Shot

Sunday morning I got up at seven with a shot of pain across my eye. I thought if I can get out from under the thump I'd be all right. In some sort-of bad humour that comes with repentance I stole through the sleeping house and found myself eating porridge and banana at the window.

By me was the ticking clock and a glass bottle of shells I had collected down at Shell Corner when I was young. Then Ma came down the stairs paddling in her pyjamas. I saw her feet, then the middle of her body and finally I saw her head come below the ceiling. She stopped suddenly on the steps and looked at me, I might have waved, but she didn't notice, just stood with her hand on the railing.

It was like as if she had heard something in the distance and was waiting to hear it again. To identify it. So we both waited. A long time, then once again she continued on down the steps in her bare feet, and seemed to walk by me or into me, looking at me she moved slow toward the kitchen at the back.

I heard nothing for a while but I could feel her in there mooching around.

And then she reappeared with a banana and she sat down opposite me, just eating, slowly.

I waited. Nothing. She floated there taking small bites, and all the time her eyes never left mine. Then she looked to where she had been standing on the stairs and gave this quaint satisfied nod to herself. Then she swung her head round to find me there, and she got up and carefully folded her banana skin and placed it by mine and went up the stairs looking back at me.

It's the work, she said.

First I fed the donkey and the horse, then at nine I headed down the road and stepped out onto our boat, then across to Conan's. Anna was sitting by the table reading a book on cats. Every Sunday and whenever she had a day off there she was, if she wasn't off running, she was in the boat looking through a magnifying glass at wildflowers. She'd left school to work in a garden centre.

Philip!

Girl.

What do you mean you saved my life?

Do you see that rope on the top of the ladder, well it was untied by a certain lady.

Jesus.

Aye. And I near took a bad fall.

She gave me a hug. Thank you Philip. You look moidered.

I had a bad night.

You should come out and join the gang sometime.

Maybe.

Ah Jeremiah, please.

In time, Lala.

OK. Are we going for a walk?

We are.

Just a minute. Did you know that cats were first domesticated in Egypt around 2000 BC. The export of domestic cats was prohibited by Egyptians because they were worshipped as goddesses. Now for you.

You should give that book to my mother to read.

I will.

And we headed off across the boats, up the ladder and down the shore.

At eleven I went to Joejoe's to light the fire. I knocked on the door.

Who's that, he called out.

It's me, I shouted.

Be careful! he screamed.

The door opened a fraction, I came in, he slammed it shut, turned the key and crawled over behind his armchair.

Get down, he said.

What do you mean?

Get down I said!

So I got in behind the other armchair and squatted there.

What's wrong?

Sh!

I looked up.

Keep your fecking head down!

A few minutes passed.

Do you hear anything?

No.

Go over easy and look out the window. The front window. Just take a dekko and drop.

I crawled over to the window, looked out and dropped.

Anyone?

No.

You sure.

Yes Grandda.

All right.

He moved his armchair back a few feet out of the trajectory of the window.

Quiet Timmy, he said to the dog. Now look at that window again. Closely.

I looked.

Do you see top right?

Yes.

Do you see a hole by any chance?

I do, I said looking at the small star-shaped hole.

Well that's a bullet hole.

Jesus.

Now do you see!

You mean someone shot through the window.

Amn't I telling you! At seven this morning. I was pulling on my trousers when fuck me – ping! It winged by me. The dog leaped out of his skin. And I've been here since afraid to move.

It must have been someone out hunting.

Like fuck. It was the General. He's had it in for me since we were young.

Ah Jazus Joejoe.

After a while I got him back into his armchair, went out looked around, saw no one, reported back, and then he made me to search for the bullet. I searched the entire kitchen but found none.

It has to be there somewhere, he said.

I started all over again, inched across the carpet, emptied the grate, went through his dresser, his boxes of clothes, the trunk, felt across the beauty board, opened the shoe box, searched the bucket of turf, the woodpile, emptied his cutlery, felt the armchairs, looked at the holy pictures, but found nothing.

Anything?

No.

Is there a dent in the wall itself?

No.

It would make a dog think.

It would.

He went quiet a while.

Well tell me this, he asked, is there a hole in the window?

There is.

And how did the hole get there.

I don't know.

Well I do – the General took a pot shot at me, and missed me. The fucker. He head-butted me once above in Nancy's because I asked Theresa Cawley out. He waited for me outside to knock the shit out of me but I sprinted by him. That's all of fifty years ago. And he's still trying to catch up with me. Can you imagine that?

It's hard to believe.

Well there you are – he's still gunning for me. Men like that never forget. You'll find one like that on your way through life. You will surely. Yes. They'll haunt you for something you didn't do.

He stared into my eyes.

Can I tell you something for nothing?

Do.

He looked out the window gathering himself.

There's a lot of spite on this planet, he said.

Right, Joejoe.

He continued to look out.

And Theresa went off with Hughie and had no time for the General. And the fucker is over there feeding on his hurt the best part of his life.

That's bad.

There's worse.

He brought his eyes again indoors.

Last thing last night I set up my saucer and went for the fat. And was there fat? There was not. The Blackbird ate my rat trap. I let him out the door last night after feeding him bacon and cabbage and found the fucker had ate the uncooked fat while I had my back turned. While I was in the scullery he was helping himself. Do you understand – how could a man do that? My own neighbour ate my rat trap – Jesus!

I dropped down onto *The Ostrich* – Conan's boat – after stepping across *The Oyster* – our boat – and made my way down into the cabin where Anna had moved on from the cats to a book on fish.

You will have to paint me a fish, she said sometime.

I will, Anna.

She turned pages and pages of photographs.

The fish, said she, gave his name to Jesus.

I didn't know that.

There you go. She tapped the book. I'm learning, she said. These books bring me abroad. The cat brought me to Egypt, the fish to biblical times. You see Jerusalem is an oasis in the desert. What are shrines now were wells back then, and what are holy places now are where the wells have gone dry.

Wow.

Water was sacred; it saved life. We don't know what the people there go through, even today. And so each tribe had their well, and that's how the fighting started. And when they reached the rivers and the sea the fish saved their lives. And now here we are centuries later fighting over dry wells.

When you mention the words fighting I better tell you that something happened in Uncle Joejoe's last night, I said.

Something bad?

I think so.

I dabbed my finger onto the blue of a tropical fin.

You don't have to tell me, she said.

I should tell my Da.

Do.

The boat rocked.

It'll cause hell, I said.

Do, she said, what you have to do. She turned the pages, then stopped out in the tropics. I began working my way into a fish's eye on the page. The fins spun each side of the face to form a shape I recognised. I stopped, and all of a sudden I was looking for a second at the star-shaped hole in Joejoe's window.

Philip!

Yeh.

Are you all right?

I am, I am, I said.

Chapter Five

When Whack!

When the father came in late that evening and was halfway through his dinner I told him that someone had shot a bullet through Joejoe's front window.

He said, you're joking.

I am not, I said.

God above! Why was I not told this before.

He jumped up and we went down the road in blinding hail. Night had fallen. The globe was lit on the sill. And the window pane that the bullet hit had been taken out. The fire was burning and the dog in his chair. Then my granduncle let us in and the father ran to the window.

Jesus, he said, Joejoe.

First thing this morning, bang! and he sat.

Where is the window pane?

I took it out.

Why did you take it out for Christ's sake?

Cause I could not stand looking at it.

Where is it?

In that box over there.

We looked into the cardboard box that once held Chiquita bananas. Inside the pane of glass was in smithereens.

You've broken it up.

Yes. I had to when I was taking it out.

Jesus Christ. How are we now going to see the bullet hole?

Why do you want to see the bullet hole?

To know it was there.

So you don't believe me. Well ask Mister Psyche. Did you

see a bullet hole?

Yes.

So you see it was a fucking bullet hole.

What are we to do?

You tell me.

Is all this really happening?

I think so son.

You better come up with us to the house.

I will not.

Get his things, he said to me.

Touch nothing I say, nothing!

You'll have to go up to us Joejoe.

No.

You can't stay here.

I'm not budging.

Christ! Should I get the guards?

Let the guards be. But you know what you can do?

What's that?

Would you put in a new pane of glass, I'm sitting here with the wind whistling through me.

The father went over and lifted the oil lamp and moved it over and back looking.

I can see no glass on the sill.

He shot clean whoever he was, said Joejoe.

There should be glass. Shards and splinters of glass.

I cleaned them up.

Where's the torch?

It's in the drawer.

Get the torch, the father said to me.

I got it.

Hold that door, I'm going outside.

I held the door against the wind, and he darted out with the torch.

Now what is the fucker at? snarled Joejoe.

We saw the father going to and fro outside the window. He shone the torch this way, that way, then he went out of view, reappeared again, studied the sill in the light. He stood there like some sort of illuminated spirit then he thumped on the door.

I let him in.

He set the torch on the table, sat down on the armchair opposite Joejoe and looked at him.

What happened Joejoe?

I told you what happened.

Tell us what really happened.

I'll say it again and I'll say it no more. I was pulling on my bucking trousers be the remains of the fire at the crack of dawn when whack!

Whack.

Yes whack! he shouted, and he slapped one hand onto the palm of the other.

And how come I found glass outside?

Did you now?

Yes, I did.

So what?

So how did the glass get there?

You tell me.

Where's your rifle?

Where it always is. There on the wall. Are you saying that I took a shot out through my own bloody window?

I'm saying nothing.

Well don't. He turned to me and tipped his cap. You hear what he's saying to me.

I do, I said.

This man is saying that I blew a hole in my own bloody window, and he stood and spat into the fire.

I'm not saying that.

That glass fell outside when I was taking out the pane. OK?

If you say so.

Go home with yourself, I'm going to bed and I'll bid you goodnight if you please.

Joejoe, said my father.

I'm tired, it's been a long day.

My father shamefaced stepped into the wind followed by myself. The door swung closed. We turned into the gale for home. Looking back I saw the oil lamp go out.

Now what, said my father, am I to do?

He folded his raincoat over the radiator and stood with his hands on the kitchen table.

A bullet no less. A bloody bullet. Jesus, he said, what next, and he hammered the table with his fists. I never in all my life met a more stubborn man. He'll be the death of me. What the hell went on in that house last night, that's what I'd like to know.

I don't know Da.

And of course the Blackbird was with him.

He was.

The bloody Blackbird. Whenever he appears you can expect the worst. Anything might have happened. Anything.

Yes.

Jesus. And I suppose they had whiskey.

They had Malibu.

And who got them the confounded Malibu?

I did.

Of course you did, and he glared at me.

He asked me to.

And the worst thing is I don't know whether someone shot in at him or he shot out. If we could tell he was shot at I could get the guards. But what does he go and do – he smashes the glass into smithereens. This is it you see, if the bullet hole was still there and I got the guards and they discovered it was him shot out the window it'd be him that would be arrested. Jesus. My own uncle, no less.

My mobile rang.

Philip?

Anna, I said. I can't talk now.

What's wrong?

Nothing.

You can tell her, he said.

It's just that . . . that Joejoe nearly got shot, I said.

What?

Honestly.

Oh sugar –

– Don't worry –

Look, I'm sorry, I'll ring you later.

OK.

The phone went dead.

Dear God, said Da.

And we stopped like that a while, in silence.

Chapter Six

The Blackbird's House

I'm going down to confront that man Tom, said the father and he put on his coat.

Can I come with you, I asked.

You might as well.

We sat into the car in the driving rain. The sky was bucketing and the car was shunted to and fro by the wind. We turned right down Cooley Lane and reached the Blackbird's. There was one bulb lit in the kitchen. A pile of timber against the wall, and a black plastic bag blowing. Stay you in the car, said the father and he went up the path and pounded the door. He stood there drenched to the skin. The water was running down his arms and his face was grim.

He pounded the door again.

The door opened a fraction.

Who in hell is that, shouted the Blackbird from the hallway.

It's me, Tom.

Who?

Tom Feeney, same as yourself.

Long time, no see, Mister Tom.

Tom, I need a chat.

Certainly.

What?

What do you want!

I want to talk to you!

At that the dog attacked the door from within and it closed.

The father backed away onto the street.

The lunatic has set the dog on me, he said to me then he went back to the door again.

And pounded.

Come here, he said to me. I came up beside him. Now you call him.

Tom, I said.

The kitchen window opened a fraction and the Blackbird appeared.

Yes, Mister Psyche.

Da wants to talk to ya.

Well let him behave himself.

Dad stood in front of the window, his hands on the sill and implored the Blackbird. Please, Tom, what happened last night?

Nothing happened.

Tom, I'm sorry for shouting. I just want a few words.

I can't hear you.

It's me!

I know that.

Open the door, Da shouted.

You can't get in the door because of the fucking dog, roared the Blackbird.

Well then you come out.

I can't let the dog out.

I said: *you come out!* screamed Da.

What?

Come out!

No. I will not.

What happened last night in Joejoe's?

What do you mean?

I want to know what happened!

What happened! What happened? We had bacon and cabbage and that was what happened. Do you hear me?

Yes.

Bacon and cabbage!

And is that all?

We had a drink.

I can't hear you.

We had a drink!

I know you had a fucking drink. Isn't the drink is causing all the fucking problems.

Stop the bad language.

Stop the shite. Were you arguing?

I was not, the Blackbird thundered, but I am now.

Tom, listen to me, something happened in that house last night and I want to know what.

Come back when you've settled yourself.

I'll break down the bloody door if you don't tell me what happened.

Nothing bloody happened.

Something happened!

Nothing, I tell ya. Psyche! he roared.

Yes.

Take your father home!

The window snapped closed, the curtains went across and the light went out in the kitchen.

My father hammered the door, then he kicked it. He ran to the bedroom window as the light came on.

Come out, shouted me father, you long black bastard.

The curtains were pulled and the light went out.

Come out, I say.

He came back and kicked the door.

Jesus Christ!

He drew back and stood in the middle of the street and stood looking at the darkened house in the rain-split lights of the car.

Blackbird! he yelled.

*

Blackbird, he yelled again.

Yes, came a quiet voice.

Where the hell are you?

I'm in the letter box.

Oh.

My father leaned down and spoke into the opening.

Come out a minute for a chat, he said quietly.

No.

Just a few words.

No.

I just need to know a few things.

No. Say what you have to say then be on the road.

What I want to know is –

Yes –

How come there's a bullet hole in Joejoe's window.

A what?

A bullet hole.

The door of the letter box slapped shut.

Do hear me in there, roared the father.

The box opened.

There's a bullet hole? asked the Blackbird.

Yes there is.

Did you see it Psyche?

I leaned down.

Yes, sir.

Now begod.

Then the father's roared: And I want to know how that bullet hole came to be in Joejoe's window.

I wouldn't know about that, the Blackbird said. That's beyond me.

Well, said my father quietly into the letter box, we need to talk about this. This is serious.

The dog suddenly crashed up against the window raging.

You better go away. You're making a mountain out of a molehill.

I'll stop here till I find out what happened.

Suit yourself.

Open the shagging door.

No, he said, the dog might ate you. And you should be ashamed of yourself annoying an old man at dead of night.

Jesus help me, said my father. Have you a gun in the house Tom?

No.

No?

Take him home, Mister Psyche!

The letter box slapped shut.

Blackbird, yelled my father.

He slapped the door.

Blackbird!

The place went quiet. Da looked at me fiercely, then we climbed back into the car, closed the door and we sat there with the headlights on for all 60 seconds watching the rain fall through the beams onto the roadway, then he hit the ignition and with a giant rev he pulled out, and turned, and shot down the road like what he would have called a boy racer. A hundred yards down he cut the lights and coasted in outside Mary Joe's, and sat with his hands gripping the steering wheel.

Right, he said.

He raised a finger to his lips.

You stay here.

Right Da.

I'll be back.

He cracked up his mouth and opened his door, and closed it with a little click. I could see the rain tumbling down on him as he turned back towards the Blackbird's. I sat there waiting. I'd been here before. The rain drummed on the roof and away off in the distance was the sound of the sea. I snuggled in tight against the belt. I looked in the rear-view mirror and saw the same darkness that was in front of me. I might have turned the radio on without knowing, but I remember turning it off. There was no sign of Da. I began to feel afraid of what was happening up the road.

I got out and looked, and closed the door quietly.

I stepped out onto the tarmacadam and saw nothing but the rain blowing towards me.

I skated along the hedge on the edge of the road back towards the Blackbird's. Stopped, and listened, and went on. Above my head were great black boulders of rain. All was black ahead of me. Then suddenly in the distance the Blackbird's chimney spat sparks and my heart went crossways. I ran like mad along the drain and the muck, then reached the low pebble-dashed wall at the front of the house. The cottage sat there idling in the dark. There was no light, and no sign of anybody.

I crouched a while there in the rain then got on my hunkers and moved along the wall as far as the gate, and found the father sitting against the further pier, with his back to it, out of the wind.

Da, I whispered.

What?

Come on home.

The bastard is hiding on me, he said.

He peered over the stone wall, then settled down again. We waited. There was no stir. The rain grew more fierce.

Please Da.

I could not see his face.

Please, I said.

Just call him, again, the once . . . for me.

I went to the door and knocked it quietly.

Tom, I said.

There was silence.

Tom, I said.

Yes, came a faraway answer that at the same time drew nearer, as if the Blackbird was approaching the door.

It's just that Da is worried.

Mister Psyche, take him home. He's wrong.

I walked down to the father.

Please Da, let's go.

Yes. OK. You're right.

He touched my shoulder, and went by me. Bending low I followed him along the wall, then he stepped onto the street and we walked back down to the car. I saw someone swinging a torch ahead of us outside Mary Joe's and as we came forward the light caught us both.

Hallo! shouted a voice. Who's there?

It's just us.

The light went up and down each of our faces.

You gave me a fright.

Sorry Mary, said my father.

I saw the car, and she shook her head, I saw the car outside the house and didn't know what to make of it.

We were chasing a beast, explained my father.

Oh, and she shone a light up the road.

It's all right. We got him. We put him in behind the Bird's.

Ah very good, very good.

Mary Joe swung her torch around to light us up as we got into the car. Then as my father started the engine she ran the torch from my father's face to mine, and back again. Da let down his window.

Sorry for the inconvenience.

Oh think nothing of it. You gave me a hop. Wild night.

Tis.

She gave a great wave as we pulled away. Sheets of water went up each side of us. I could see the rain pelting the face of my father as we took the road to the alt. He swung in front of the lane to Joejoe's house and stopped. The shock from the sea went under our feet.

The window, Da, I said.

He went to wind up the window. Then the handle came off. He tried twice and both times it came off. On the third it took.

Round one, he said.

For three hours we sat at the gate in the rocking car, lights off. Beyond us the thrashing sea. No one came or went. Suddenly my father's head fell onto the steering wheel.

Where are we! he shouted, wakening.

At six in the morning Da shook me.

Go down and take a look, he said. If he sees me there would only be murder.

OK.

I'm sorry for asking you to do this after what you've been through.

It's all right Da.

I'm losing it – the paranoia is growing – forgive me.

See you in a few minutes, I said.

The night was not over yet. I got up and dressed and took the lantern and started walking. It was eerie. I was holding the lantern in my right hand by my thigh, and as I walked the shadows of my two legs grew huge to my left. I was taller than the hedge of tall olearia. Another huge black version of me was walking the beach like a mad colossus. The gates were frightening as they shot by, swinging in the beam.

There were a whole lot of us walking abroad by the big sea.

I reached Joejoe's gate and saw his lamp was lit on the window.

As I came in the gate I could hear the music. I got as far as the window and there he was in his chair, hat on, playing a reel on the single accordion that was full of off-notes, as he looked into the dead grate. By his side, propped against the chair, was his rifle. I got a shock. He looked somehow like a wounded soldier. Then he suddenly turned towards the window. He seemed to be looking directly at me. He stopped playing. I backed off and went to the gable and doused the lantern. I waited. In a few minutes the music started again. I went out onto the road and stood in the dark wondering what to do.

It was not what I expected.

A rifle by his side.

I turned for home and soon the shadows were walking across the fields alongside me. The shadows seemed even darker now. I let myself into the house and found the father sitting at the bottom of the stairs.

Well, he said.

Oh, he's there.

Is he all right?

Yes.

Is he up?

Aye, he's sitting there playing the accordion.

At this hour?

Aye.

Christ. I do not know what to make of that man. Well I suppose we should go back to bed. Thanks Philip for that.

Next thing in bed all I saw was endless piles of naked people.

Every shape turned into naked people.

If I closed my eyes there they were.

If I opened them I was terrified.

I saw a man chasing me out of this hostel.

He snapped this buckle of his belt at my face.

Out, he shouted. Liar!

Out!

BOOK TWO

Visitors

Chapter Seven

Fixing the Window

When I woke the sun was up.

Men from Latvia, Lithuania and Poland were out the rocks fishing.

I went down the sand and nearly slipped on the seaweed. It was black wet rock after the storm. The beach was scoured clean by the high tide. The air was warm. The hawk was over Donlon's. Mary Joe was down on her hunkers on the sea shelf picking winkles into a plastic bucket. I went on round the alt through piles of small blue mussels blown ashore at Shell Corner to find what damage had been done, I checked the lobster pots, then I came upon this old wall set into the bottom of the cliff that had not been there before. The storm had dragged down the boulder clay and uncovered this ancient stone wall, about twenty foot long, cemented with sandy clay.

It was the same rock that built our house and built the walls in the fields. It was everywhere around me, but had never been there, under the cliff, stone on stone, until the sea hoked it out.

I said to myself have I seen you before, but I hadn't. It was a wonder, about four foot high, hidden for maybe centuries. Who was the man that built that? And why? It formed a kind of half circle then stopped at both ends in clumps of sea thrift. I sat in against the wall and looked out to the sea. Now, beyond me the island was floating in sunshine and I said to myself this must have been a look-out. If a monk got sick beyond they'd light a fire and the man in the look-out would see the smoke from the island and send out a boat. The monks were not oarsmen.

No, said my father.

They were not, said Joejoe.

I often heard them talking about the monks. I was a happy man to have found something that no one else had seen in years. That was a good start to the day. I came back up to the house, went into the studio and started drawing from memory the fish I'd seen in Anna's book.

Myself and Da carried water in a tall milk can into the North meadow. We poured a few drops onto the lips of a sick cow. Then filled the stone basin. Lying on her stomach with her hooves to the side she looked off into the distance. He patted her down.

I like that animal.

The cow continued to stare ahead.

He stared into her eyes.

Get better soon, he said.

We took off down the field.

Da, I said.

Yes.

He keeps saying it's the General shot at him.

Ah come on, come on.

That's what he says.

That's madness. Why in fuck's name would he take a shot at Joejoe?

Because of a woman.

Oh yeh? He sat on a stone by the sheugh. Tell me another one. Who pray?

I think it was a Miss Theresa . . . Crawley.

Theresa Crawley. Who is she?

I don't know.

Well neither do I. The only Theresa round here that I know of is married to Hughie Currid.

Well that might be her.

He told you that.

Yes. He said she married a Hughie.

Did she now?

Yes.

Good for her.

She was going out with Joejoe and the General head-butted him.

This wasn't yesterday.

No.

They have black fucking minds, do you know that. He's telling you this in all honesty?

Yes.

That the General shot at him.

Yes.

Why did you not tell me this before?

I tried to, but you wouldn't listen.

Did he see him?

No.

Shit. Shit. Fuck me. Are we to go down now and interrogate the General? We'll be had up for defamation of character. You should have told me this before.

Da, I tried ta.

Now what . . . Am I to head to the General next and ask him where he was at the crack of dawn on the 2nd? Do you know what reality is – it's a joke.

We walked across the field followed by the calves.

Go down you to Joejoe's, said my father.

OK, I said.

Go down you, said my father, and I'll follow you. First I have a visit I have to make.

Are you going to start arguing?

No.

I came to the front of the cottage. He was sitting outside on the wooden seat in the sun surrounded by lobster pots as he knitted one on his lap.

Sh! he said, raising a finger to his lips.

What now, I thought, what's happened now?

Then I saw the robin on the toe of his boot. I stood and watched. The bird looked my way, then turned to him. It lifted one claw and looked at it, scattered its wings, closed them and brushed its breast with its beak. Then it looked off to the left as if remembering something, bowed quickly, hopped onto his knee, fidgeted, then back again to the toe of his boot. Good man, said Joejoe smiling. The bird, shifting itself, lifted its head up and let go with one tweet then swung away back to the woodpile.

Did you see that?

I did surely.

Watch – *Ch! Ch!* he said.

The robin reappeared and hopped towards him, stopped, came on, stopped on one lobster pot, looked back, came on to another pot, and sharpened its beak on the knot of blue twine that Joejoe had tied to the arc of timber.

Good man, whispered Joejoe.

Then the bird flew off.

Ah, he's had enough for one day maybe, said Joejoe. I've been training him since the 12th of last March but that's the first time he's done it. He landed on my cap first, then down to the toe of my boot. He must have been on me all of ten minutes. Isn't that something?

It is.

I sat down on a log beside him. He put down the finished lobster pot, lit up a Woodbine, coughed and tipped his cap.

I have my own bird now, he said.

And I have my own wall, I said.

You have not.

I have.

Well good on you.

I found a wall under the cliff.

You did.

The storm took off the boulder clay and there it was.

Now.

I think it was a look-out.

Be jingo. A wall out there. On the edge of the flaming sea.
Damn it.

A wall, I said, nodding. And tomorrow I have to start
building one for the new garden.

We sat there considering the wonders. Then I saw that Joejoe
had pasted a bit of cardboard over the missing pane of glass in
the window.

I set the fire and made him tay.

Is your man coming down? he asked.

He is.

Now?

Soon.

Jesus. Well if he starts that crack again, be God, I won't take
it.

He toed a piece of turf, then broke a stick neatly into equal
pieces with the heel of his boot.

It's a strange world, he said, and threw the sticks into the
fire. Have you any news?

We were out there in the car for hours watching your house
last night.

For what?

To see if anyone came.

And who would come now that the damage is done?

How do I know? Anyone, I suppose.

Well you should have been home in your bed.

And we went to the Blackbird's.

You went to the henhouse, did you now. You were busy. And
what had poor Tom to say.

Nothing. His dog went mad. The father couldn't get in and
the Blackbird wouldn't come out.

At least he's good for something, the crature. I didn't think he had it in him.

The father got some drenching.

Good enough for him.

He was frightened for you.

Let him mind himself, and leave me be. And can I tell ya something. Ya were outside the wrong house when you went to the Blackbird's!

We were.

Yes, you should have spoken to another man entirely.

I see.

Leave it now, son.

The father came in with his bag of tools and a couple of panes of glass wrapped in newspaper. He took down the bit of cardboard over the break. Not a word was said. Da began whistling the wrong tune. Joejoe watched him like he was looking at me, his eyes softened, then he answered himself with a nod and went into the scullery. The father stepped outside. There was a crash of a drawer and a loud spout of tap water from within. Then Joejoe stood a while in the doorway with his chin in thin suds looking out at Da looking in as he brushed down the sill, then the auld fellow shaved in the small mirror on the dresser, emptied the basin, came back to the dresser, took down the china ornament of the Wayward Lad and replaced it with a phial of thumb tacks.

Stood back.

Moved the little boat made of reeds next to his copy of *A History of Ireland* with no cover.

Then he moved the book to the window. Placed the Brigid's cross where the boat had been.

Da ran a tape across the jamb and blew away a spider's web. I heard Joejoe say to himself for no reason: *You were some bird when you left Raspberry Hill, you were, you were*, then he went into his bedroom, came back, sat and changed his socks, *You were, you were*, scratched, put on his boots again with each lace perfectly tied, then as the window pane was tapped into place he set off again to the scullery whispering.

Then back again, down into the armchair, cap poised, legs crossed, ready.

The father thumbed in the last of the putty onto the pane of glass then came in and said, That's that.

A neat job you did there now, said Joejoe.

Oh.

Very tasty I must say.

Thank you.

Then Joejoe got up and peered out.

Be God, I think it lets in a better class of light than before.

That's good.

He turned and bent down and looked at Timmy. I can even see the colour of the dog's eyes, he said.

They went silent a while. I could see my father summoning up the strength to question Joejoe again and I was wishing he wouldn't. There was more small talk.

The weather is mighty.

It is.

More silence.

And the lad found a wall beneath the cliff.

You did not?

I did, I said.

Now.

Centuries old.

More silence.

Talking about centuries old I was draining Legget's field with the digger, said my father, and came upon a fairy fort.

You did.

And I said to Legget I'm not taking her down. What do you mean, he said, am I not paying you? I'll not take a fairy fort, I said.

57

You would not, said Joejoe.

I'll not take a fairy fort down, I said, a place that's been built all that time ago. So he said he'd get someone else to do it, and I said, go ahead, get who you like and I finished what I was doing, and left it at that.

You did right. Fuck him.

This was about a month ago and I went by there yesterday and it's still there, and it was still there this morning.

And it'll be there tomorrow.

And it will be there for all time. No man will touch it.

No, said Joejoe. They won't.

Joejoe lifted up the newspaper that the panes of glass had come in, he patted it out flat and began to look at the pictures. The father stood. Now I thought he's going to start. Don't do it Da.

I just wanted to say . . .

Aye . . .

Joejoe eyed him from under his cap.

. . . We'll say no more about the other night.

Right.

Not another word.

No.

It was like it never happened.

That's good enough by me, said Joejoe. But you see it did happen and that's the problem.

Oh and by the way –

Yes?

I ran into the General.

Joejoe looked at me, hard-eyed.

Did you now?

I did.

And how is he?

He's fine. The same General is just back this morning from Luton. He's been away for a few days.

Is that so, said Joejoe, staring into my eyes.

It is. I just thought you'd like to know, said Da.

I see.

Da looked at Joejoe, then he looked at me, and stood.

We'll leave it, he said, at that.

But there's one other matter outstanding, said Joejoe.

I could see the father grow grim-faced.

Yes? he said.

An apology.

Yes?

To the Blackbird.

The father looked at me.

I see the news gets around. An apology?

If you would.

Right. All right then, Sorry Mister Blackbird, I'll tell him next time I see him, OK. I'm off. I have a job above on a site at Lenihan's. He put on his blue woollen cap and pulled it down above his eyes, We'll leave it at that.

We will.

Good enoughski, Da said, and he took off out the open door with his bag of tools and down the path.

Then Joejoe let out a whoop of laugher.

He thought he got me. But I got him. Did you see him back down? Did you see that boy!

I did.

Hohoho, and he slapped his thighs, upped his fists to look at them, and made the mad eyes. I got him! I got him! He hammered a fist into the palm of his other hand and bared his teeth. I got him! he grinned, and he kicked out one foot then the other. He backed down! And you turned informer.

Joejoe, I was thinking the General was not here the other morning. I saw him go off by taxi – that must have been when he was leaving.

So if it wasn't the General, who was it, he asked me.

I don't know.

Then the exuberance left him, and slowly he put the reed boat back where it had been on the dresser, then the Wayward Lad, followed by the *History of Ireland*. He handed me *Moby Dick* and I turned the pages till I reached where we had left off the last time.

No, put him away, he said.

All was then put back as it had been.

Including the gun.

That I had mentioned to no one.

Chapter Eight

The Fairy

You know what you'll do for me today.

What's that.

Go you over to yon Blackbird, and tell him the kettle is on. Have you got that?

I have.

The kettle is on, right?

Right so.

I heeled in the bag of turf, and swept round the kitchen.

Don't enter into words with him.

I won't.

No don't. He is a strange creature, the same Blackbird. He had it tough when he was young, you see. I never know with him what's going on. He's a bad actor. Betimes. And while you're at it mind me bucking shoes.

I brought a can of ashes across the yard and dumped them in the rock. Timmy was rolling in the grass. He jumped high as my shoulder. A flock of ducks landed on the pond where a swan was studying its reflection.

It's a grand class of a day, I said.

I'm leaving you this house, and this world, do you hear that?

I do.

I'm leaving you a quandary. You're welcome to it. I never got to work it out myself.

Thank you.

For nothing.

Is there anything you want in the outside world?

No, good man, I'm fine. The Bird when he arrives will do. He will answer the question I need to know.

I headed off down Cooley Lane. The sea was flat calm. The bushes burnt by salt and wind. I was afraid to have to knock on the door what with the mad dog but the Blackbird was outside pumping his bike.

Are you going someplace?

Who's asking?

Me, I said.

What do you want?

Joejoe has the kettle on.

Has he now.

He has.

Is that so?

He straightened up and tapped the tip of his nose with the index finger of his right hand.

We'll see, he said.

At five the Blackbird arrived, heeled up his bike, sat into the dog's armchair. Long time, no see, he said. Joejoe dispatched me to Mister John's for a bottle. On the way I saluted Stefan who was wheeling a tyre round the back of Doyle's.

Aha, Mister Side Kick.

Stefan.

You are on the way to the pub?

Yes.

Again?

Yes.

Wow, nearly every day.

Not every day.

And you walk.

Yes.

He sat into the passenger seat of a Toyota, opened the driver's door, and said Sit in. Mister Doyle is down in Kerry.

There's no need.

You can drive, sir.

I don't mind walking.

But it is good for me to talk to someone. I like to talk to you, please, and so if you will not drive I will walk with you to Mister Sweets Johns, and he went to get out.

OK, I said, and I sat in.

Drive on sir.

So I took the wheel for the first time in a long time and we drove down the road talking of Cadillacs, Saabs, Jaguars, crabs, Aston-Martins, mussels, Land Rovers, how he loved Irish mushrooms and why did Irish drivers wave at people on the road that they did not know; Rolls-Royces, winkles and Triumph Heralds, Ladas and Volgas; how to say goodbye in Lithuanian, then I stepped into Mister John's and ordered the usual Malibu and twenty Major.

How are things, said Mister John.

Grand, I said looking round the empty bar.

I see you have company outside with you.

Yes.

Is he not coming in?

No.

Now, he handed me the bottle. I looked at the pool table, paid over and took one go at the slot machine, and won two euro.

Iki, I said to Mister Sweet John.

What, he asked.

So long.

Then I drove the Toyota back to Doyle's and said goodbye.

Drive on, Stefan said.

No, I'll walk the rest of the way.

Iki, he said.

Goodbye, I said. On the way home I said my prayer by the fresh bunch of blue geranium and red roses in the tubs at the cross at Templeboy.

When I got back they were sipping glasses of milk with poteen to coat the stomach.

Joejoe poured out two tots.

I had a visitor the other night, said the Blackbird.

You did.

I did. Are you listening Psyche?

I am.

Yes. Some visitor. A giant of a man. He came battering on me door at dead of night.

Now for ya, said Joejoe.

A man that was not right in the head, I'd swear. There was prolonged abuse and bad language.

And what did you do?

I kept the head and took it mild. I looked through the keyhole. He was like a shook fox. Go home and settle yourself, I said, my good man, and call round tomorrow. And be God he began battering the door again.

He wheeled round in the chair and looked at me.

Roaring and shouting he was like a madman.

Is that so, I said.

Said he'd bucking shoot me.

No.

I said I'd flatten him. Then he stopped and went off.

And that was that.

Certainly.

He put out his glass for another drop.

Oh a complete madman. I don't know where they get them. Good luck!

Good luck! said Joejoe.

And I'd swear, he said, turning to me, that he had a certain accomplice sitting out in the car –

– No –

– Aye. A certain wee gentleman waiting to finish me off.

Weren't you lucky, said Joejoe.

I was, he said slowly.

The Bird got up and went to the window and studied it. Then he looked out the back window. Then back again to the front.

Get out of my light, snapped Joejoe.

What ails you?

You're blocking me.

Oh.

Do you know you are in my house.

I do.

Good, I thought you were lost.

I know where I am, thank you.

Well make yourself at home. Are you expecting someone?

No, said the Blackbird.

So what's bothering ya?

Just checking.

Checking what?

There was talk of a bullet hole about these parts.

Was there? And Joejoe's eyes floated across at me, then over to the window. Well I don't see any.

But then on the other hand I see you have a new window pane in.

That's right.

Was the last lad draughty?

She was.

Very good. He sat. His elbows came up onto his knees. It's tight to get a craftsman so handy. So now, Mister Psyche, tell me truly, is this business finished?

Yes, I said.

Well it's a while since I've had to call in the law. The brown eyes pierced mine.

It would be a while back, Joejoe agreed.

And I don't want to be the one to call them in. Do I?

No, I said.

But sometimes a man is driven too far, do you know what I mean.

Yes.

So you might let a certain gentleman know that if there is any more dragging of a man out in the middle of night for talk of summary execution I'll be driven to have a word with the Sergeant. Have you got that?

I have.

You'll tell him.

I will.

Are you threatening the young fellow, asked Joejoe.

I am.

Do you remember those hens? I asked.

What hens?

The hens that were here the other day?

Good morning yourself, he said to me then he turned to Joejoe. What's Mister Psyche talking about?

Me not know, said Joejoe.

Well neither do I.

So I stood on one foot and went *Cockadoodledo!*

He looked at me astounded.

I clapped my pocket.

You have me, and he stared wide-eyed.

Cockadoodle!

What's he at?

Cockadoodledo!

Is yon fellow all right?

Hold it, said Joejoe. Go again!

I went up on one foot and sang Cockadoodledo!

I have you, said Joejoe, and he smacked his knee, them's those ghost hens you were talking about, you half-wit, the other day when you were out of your head.

The Blackbird watched him keenly.

Ghost hens?

That sing, I said, and you can't hear them.

Oh, he said uncertainly, the ghost hens. Oh yes. Just give me a minute. Ghost hens? He closed his eyes, sunk his chin onto his chest, and squeezed his shoulders in. Ah . . . now, who are those boys I wonder?

Then they land in your pocket, I said.

Ah Christ. He opened his eyes. Those boys? He looked up. Are them boys about? Jesus they're early about the place.

Are they fairies, I asked, them hens?

No, they are not indeed, he said, the fairy is gone. He left this part of the world a while back –

– Ah! –

– Gone –

– All gone, said Joejoe. The poor soldier has gone back into the woods.

Yes he has. He's gone, said the Blackbird. You don't see him any more. Have you seen one?

No, I said.

Me did.

Of course you did, said Joejoe guffawing.

I saw him first on the island after a drenching.

The very place.

The storm had come at the filling in of the moon and the sea had done a murder. Now at the full moon I mind the fish coming up for air in the floods. The worst time. Sara Cassidy was in our house. I believe she was two. I took her hand and we walked the street. My father was on the step. Be careful, he says. The sea was boiling. The gulls were pitching on the rollers. So we took it handy. We stepped down to where there was this big pipe that had come from the mainland the summer before to drain the land. It was a huge affair that a child could walk upright in. In the big winds she'd roar, in the breezes she'd whistle. And in the storm she'd become stuck, but the men had freed it of stones and sand and the floods were flying by. It was something shocking to see.

I bet.

Then there must have been another blockage because the water stopped and out stepped the fairy from the pipe.

What did he look like? I asked.

Why he was a small buck in green.

The very thing, said Joejoe.

He walked out, took a look around him and that was that. He turned back into the big pipe and headed on in. Is the man gone, said Sara. Man gone, I said. What was he doing? she asked. Me think he must have been checking the weather, I said. We stood looking at the dark pipe but he didn't reappear. Not long after that the men found the source of the blockage and the floods flew by again. I stood and watched to see if the water had caught him, but there was no sign of the gent. Just a powerful rush of water.

What size was he, I asked.

Why he would have been the size of my hand, well tanned, with bright blue eyes.

And you really saw him?

I did, said the Blackbird. I saw him all right but the question is . . . did he see me?

Now for you, said Joejoe.

You didn't think of that.

I did not.

Now. You see, what you don't believe in might believe in you.

That's a hard question, said Joejoe nodding.

The Blackbird turned to me, fastened his brown eyes on mine and called me in with his finger.

Well did he? he whispered.

I don't know, I said.

It might have come as a shock to him, said Joejoe, to see the like of you about the place.

It might, indeed. The Blackbird drew away to look into the fire. Anyway that was the last of them. They've left the country. And not long after that we left the island. First the turf went, then the sugar ran out during the war. Without the sugar we couldn't have made the poteen.

And I suppose, said Joejoe, without the poteen you couldn't have seen the fairies.

But I saw the buck before I had ever tasted a drop, said the Blackbird. You might say I had it in the nature. Anyway that was then. If you saw one now you'd be put behind bars.

You would.

They are not allowed in, he said, shaking his head.

Why? I asked.

They've had their day, he said. They were fighting on the other side – the wrong side.

There's a whole different creature abroad now, added Joejoe.

We lost the war, you see.

Oh.

What we saw then they don't see now.

No, said Joejoe.

And what they see now I'm blind to.

You're right there.

Aye.

But the thing is – what about the pipe? and the Blackbird sighed.

Aye what about the pipe, I asked. Where did it go?

I don't know.

I was out there last year.

You were.

And there was no pipe.

No. It was a great vessel to roar. It's the pipe is the mystery.

It is surely.

And the fairy is gone, said the Blackbird, he's left this part of the world.

I think he didn't like the sound of the radio, said Joejoe.

Something put him off anyway, agreed the Blackbird. That's for sure, and he nodded gravely. Then he clicked his fingers. There's another thing we forgot.

What was that? asked Joejoe.

The storm.

Ah.

It was the storm started it. Without the storm there would have been no pipe.

No.

And without the pipe, no fairy.

No.

Tom Feeney saluted the wall and Joejoe Feeney saluted the fire. Never miss a storm, young fellow, said the Blackbird. You see it's the purest form of music.

Chapter Nine

Visitors

I brought a can of fresh water over the meadow to the sick cow and started shovelling at nine.

I was digging out a path for the foundations of a wall. A plastic bucket flew round the house in the wind. The father came up from the beach with a few loads of stones, then he went off to draw a few from a shed that was being levelled for a house a little inland. As he drew the stones the iron on the digger roared. This Northern buck who used to park his car at our gate and walk his children along the beach came up alongside me alone, and started carrying stones across to me; he said nothing, just stood by rock in hand, then when I gave a nod, bit by bit he'd drop the rock on the wall and I'd put her in place.

Soon we were at it together.

I held one end of the string, he took the other, and we made a straight line. The wall was good.

That will do for today, I said.

Have you an interior life, he asked.

No, I said.

See ya boy, he said.

I took a lift with Da at three up the road past Mister St Patrick who was back standing with his five cows on the Long Acre, meaning the grass that grew along the public road; past Mickey's funeral flowers where I said my prayer; past Mister Doyle's, and I called out Grand day in his accent to Stefan who was rubbing a spit into a car tyre; past Sweet John's where Guinness barrels were being unloaded, on past Dromod; and on to the Judge's house, where Da dropped me. The Judge's wife, in a cap of feathers, was sitting reading *The Life of Napoleon* inside the glass-covered front porch. She looked up, looked down, then put her book away, and said Come in.

I'm afraid, she said as she put on the kettle, that the mower is not working. It's corroded with salt.

Ah Christ, I could have got the lend of one off my father.

Never mind, she said, and she put a plate with two eclairs in front of me, and then handed me ten euro; he left you this.

Thanks.

You want more work, don't you?

Yes.

Well I'm sorry.

Never mind.

Do you know what, did you ever try Miss Jilly?

No.

Do.

I didn't know she was looking for someone.

I met her this morning in the post office – she was in great form. The postmistress had taken her to a musical last night. Do you know what she said – she said it was the first time she had been out in years.

Ah.

That lady is nearly eighty and she is very independent minded but I'm sure she could do with someone to help her. You know she has a few gypsy lads come about the place sometimes.

Yes.

And the hippies did the garden for her.

That's right.

So why don't you go up there and knock on the door of that great house?

Maybe I will.

She'd welcome you. Go on.

I will.

And say I sent you.

You sent me!

Yes.

Do you mind?

I don't know, I don't know whether it will help you but maybe she can be swayed. Cheer up, what's the harm in trying?

Thanks for the tea, I said.

I rose and went to the door. And here's the second ten-euro, she said, he said to give you one ten when you arrived, and then when I told you the bad news, I was to give you the second ten when you were going.

Tell the Judge thanks.

I will. That's the way he operates.

I know.

Oh forgive me.

Chat you, I said smiling.

Get in, she said opening the passenger door of her car, and we drove along the coast road. I'll take you to the gate.

Besides sitting in with my father, this is my second time to take a lift with a lady today.

Oh, so I am not the first. Did the first lift with the lady bring you any luck?

Not really.

Sorry to hear that.

It was in a dream, but it did the job.

Good. I hate driving. I hate it, she said, I always imagine I am going to end up in court in front of my husband.

I never thought of that.

Bye, she said as I opened the door, and the best of luck.

Chat ya, I said.

I came through the gate of the estate, and walked up the avenue, past the surfers, to the door of the house. It was raining.

I rang at the tradesman's entrance down the steps in the basement. There was an old rocking horse standing inside the coalbunker. It badly needed a coat of paint.

I rang again. Away off in the distance I heard a wary voice calling *Yes?*

I went up the steps and looked the length of the building. On the third storey to the front Miss Jilly's face was looking out a tall window, with her hand to her head of hair.

What do you want?

I'm looking for work.

Where are you from?

Up the road.

What?

Ballintra.

Oh. I thought you were from somewhere else.

Mrs Keane sent me.

A nice lady. Come back again.

When?

Next week, maybe, and she pulled in her head and the window came down. On the way back a stray ass came out of the forest and followed me. He'd step up and bite at my sleeve. He had huge deep eyes and his hooves were bad. They were long and painful. At the road he jumped as motorbikes flew by. I spent a long time looking into his eyes. I turned back to the house with him at my side. He liked to put his chin nearly, but not quite, on my shoulder, then he'd tug at my elbow.

Settle son, I said to him as he butted me quietly. He bubbled his upper lip.

We passed swans in the bare reeds that looked a brilliant white. I arrived back up to the house and hammered on the tradesman's entrance, then stood on the steps.

The window came up and she looked down.

Oh it's you again.

Yes.

What is it now?

Your ass's hooves need cutting, I said.

What are you talking about?

Your donkey! I shouted.

Yes?

His hooves.

Yes?

Need cutting. Badly!

Oh.

The window came down and I stood there, with the ass at my back pushing up against me. I sat down on the step and spoke to the ass and he put his snout in my pocket. Then the front door open, and Miss Jilly stepped out.

She went by me.

Are you saying I'm cruel? she asked the donkey.

No, I said.

I'm not.

I didn't say you were.

But I can see his hooves are long, the poor fellow.

They need cutting.

But you see, said Miss Jilly, and she came and sat on the step beside me, that is not my donkey.

Oh shit, excuse me.

There you go. Can you cut hooves?

It's a science, I said.

Is that so?

I know a man who does it well.

Well get him.

Now?

Yes.

Right. I stood. She waved, and I went to go and the ass moved off with me. I'll have to tie him.

Then tie him.

Where?

To the pillar.

Have you a rope?

She went down the basement steps and came back up with a lovely long embroidered rope.

He might eat it.

By then you'll be gone.

OK. So I got a rope and tried to tie him to the pillars of the big house but I ended up tying him to the railings, and petted his snout; and just before I went off down the avenue he gave a roar and she tipped me on the elbow.

What's your name?

Ah . . . Feeney.

Feeney I believe is a surname. Correct?

Yes.

And your first name Mister Feeney?

They call me Psyche.

Indeed, and she waited a moment, then said, Thank you, and as she walked away she appeared to totter sideways.

I went up onto the main road and raised a thumb and the Mercedes that always parked down by our pier passed me by, then I went on walking till along came the old faded blue Volkswagen with Miss Jilly at the wheel. She pulled over. I sat in.

My conscience got to me, she said.

Good.

Right, she said, you give me directions.

On ahead, straight.

She tossed her scarf, dipped her head and hit the accelerator. We trundled down the road. She now looked like a pilot because of the black helmet she wore. Her grey hair was clipped close to the right ear. Right, I said. The radio was playing a station out at sea. The ring on her right hand shone. A car came towards us and Miss Jilly slowed down till it passed, then she felt her ear drum, and brushed something away like a bad thought.

Now what? she asked at the crossroads, bracing herself.

Turn right.

You are on holidays?

Yes, you could call it that.

What are you studying?

I have just done my final exams, the Leaving.

And what have you applied for in university?

Nothing.

Why?

A few souls outside Mister John's watched us pass and I waved.

Take another right, I said.

Why? And she flashed a sharp smile. Did you not want to end up as a stereotype?

I don't know.

She smiled with another quick flash. It was hard to know whether it meant friendship, but then her eyes meowed, and softened on the spur of another question: Where are we?

Tunadaley.

You should return to college.

Why?

Do you know that mothers give false information to their children to keep them quiet?

This is my third lift today in a car with a lady.

I see. The untruths are mounting up.

Yes; now straight on down the road.

Thank you.

Just here, now. Stop.

I knocked on the Blackbird's door but all I got back was the bark of a dog. Then we pulled in at Joejoe's. White turf smoke was blowing across the field. I went in. The two men were sitting eating ham and oranges.

Ah Mister Psyche, sit down, said Joejoe.

I can't.

Oh a busy man.

I have something to ask himself. Could you cut an ass below at Dromod House?

Dromod House, indeed, said Joejoe.

Is she bad? asked the Bird.

The hooves are turning up.

Where is she?

Tied to the railings outside the house.

Very good, and he bit into an orange.

And I have a car to bring you, if you want to collect your blades.

Right sir but I think I'll go on my bike.

Are you sure?

Certain.

I went back out to Miss Jilly and explained the Blackbird would make his own way. She foraged a sigh. And what will I do with you, pray?

I don't know.

Get in.

I suppose I can go back with you and wait to give a hand.

Good.

I sat in.

It's strange, is it not, she said, that he would not take a lift?

No, he goes everywhere by bike.

Now. She flipped her eardrum and nodded to a question she had set herself. That last house we pulled in at – I think I remember that place from way, way back.

It's my granduncle Joejoe's.

Feeney, she said to herself and she looked at me. I think I'm getting to know you, she said, and she nodded, and nodded, and then looked to the side for a long time.

Chapter Ten

Hoof-cutting

I would invite you in, she said, but the place is in a shambles.

Will you bring out any scraps a' food you might have.

I will.

She brought out a bucketful of scraps and went in to change her clothes. I went for a walk in her orchard under the apple trees. Along the stream three Chinese ladies were cutting watercress for the takeaway in Drum. Inside in the woods very quietly the General was secretly sawing a fallen tree. Eyes down he watched me pass without a word. I gave the ass an apple out of the bucket. Miss Jilly reappeared wearing a beret with a tassel and small green wellingtons. She had a bag of green peppers, pasta and scraps of bread. I fed the donkey a little.

Will he really come, your friend?

Yes Ma'am, he will.

He is very reliable.

Like clockwork, Ma'am.

A while later the Blackbird, sitting upright like a priest, came up the avenue on his bike with a sack hanging from the handlebars. Miss Jilly stepped down to greet him but with an indignant nod he passed her by.

Good lad, he said to the donkey and tied a rope around his neck and head. He's a very good class of an ass.

Do I know you from the post office? asked Miss Jilly.

Maybe.

I go up there to get my pension.

And I go to get me dole.

Your dole? At your age?

Well it is the pension.

It's extraordinary how ordinary life is.

Hand me the shears.

Here, I said.

Right Psyche, you take one ear.

And I'll take the other, said the woman of the house. She put her nose next to the Bird's neck. My God what a wonderful smell!

Now twist the ears.

I will, she said, as she twisted, that is not after-shave I smell.

No.

Is it a class of wild mint?

Psyche, haul him stronger.

Isn't it great that you have a friend like this lad here, says she.

Now twist the other ear.

I will, she said, as she twisted, I said isn't it great that you have a friend like this lad here.

Ma'am, to this day I never thought of Mister Psyche as a friend, not till this exact moment.

So I nodded, and as the donkey reared I put another apple in his mouth.

Yes, he is a friend, said the Bird, and he lifted the donkey's right foreleg, threw the leg over his knee and bent to cut and clip the hoof.

Twist.

We twisted.

The file, Psyche.

I handed him the file, and as he shaved nail filings fell at his feet.

Right, good man, he said to the donkey, you'll be the better after this, and he moved onto the next leg, and the donkey tried to drop to his knees. An old trick, c'mon son, said the Bird, and he grabbed the next leg, and so we went through all the hooves as Tom went round in circles and the donkey reared and then bit food off the palm of my hand. With each cut his eyes widened. No you're not upset, said the Blackbird, we'll be there in a minute. The ass just stood and took it. Next thing it was over.

We untied him. I emptied the bucket of scraps at his feet. He looked at the leavings then moved towards the trees. I got the spade and buried the nail shavings.

I'll make you a snack, said Miss Jilly and she went in.

We sat on the steps.

Cuckoo, he said, but she's a stayer, that lady. Cuckoo, but she is. And she has strength. Yes, she'll hold up against the odds for a while longer.

Mister Blackbird.

Sir.

Keep down your voice.

And she's on the pension, he said as he looked around him in wonderment at the huge mansion.

At the edge of the woods a deer stood. I had seen him very few times in my life. At first I took him to be the donkey but then he materialised into a deer. He looked at us a long time then turned away as if he had grown tired at looking at us humans. Miss Jilly came out the hall door with grapes and apples in a wicker basket and two glasses of cider. This cider I made myself, she said. She had a basin of warm water and a bright red towel. And a purse. The Blackbird beat his hands in the water till the foam rose.

Thank you, Mister Psyche, for bringing me a wonderful man, said Miss Jilly.

Watched by the Bird I drank the cider.

I see you like it, son.

I do, you know.

He turned to her. You could have just brought us in through that door to wash our hands. Inside that door – and he nodded to hall door – to the left there is a washbasin.

Yes, there is.

Aye, and he chewed the grapes.

But you see it has no hot water.

Ah. And to the right is a picture of a Red Indian –

Correct, said Miss Jilly.

– Before you enter the drawing room. I often walked that house – all fourteen rooms – in my dreams.

You have been here before, I take it.

Years and years ago, a neighbour of mine worked here.

In the good old days.

I used to come down with him.

And who was he?

Mister Joejoe Feeney.

Joeyjoey, she said and she looked at her feet, then she stared into the Blackbird's eye, and said questioningly: – Joseph?

Aye, the very man, Joseph.

A small man with red hair?

Once upon a time.

And he had a whistle. Yes. He dug Tonto's grave. He played the accordion once in the drawing room then he stopped, Joseph stopped yes, because my father took off his hearing aid and said: I think you might be out of tune there, sir. Your neighbour took great umbrage.

That is Joejoe.

Who was Tonto? I asked.

My dog.

She went quiet.

Didn't Joseph's girlfriend die?

Yes, said the Bird. Bridie.

She went to speak again, but words were somehow hard for her. Then she seemed to carry on a private conversation in her head. She was like a woman in a queue, with the round basket hanging from the left hand, and in the right hand her purse.

How much do I owe you?

Nothing, said the Blackbird, that ass was a timid cratur.

We can't have that.

That man there asked me to do him a favour and now it's done, so there's no charge. Mister Psyche is the boss.

Forgive me. What do I owe you?

Thirty euro, I said.

But that is a pittance.

A lift home would help.

Of course I can drive you home, and she handed me four tens. Do you want to see my pets, she asked. I nodded. Come with me. We followed her through the hall door into a porch with the sink and the Indian with the tomahawk and feathers, then into a reception area filled with armchairs covered in sheets. Shelves of tall illustrated books. She indicated that we follow her up the dusty stairs. A full-length Arctic explorer stood waiting us on the third floor. Old embroidered tea cloths were pinned to the walls, and everywhere there were photos and pictures of soldiers in a desert. Then drawings of angels. She lifted a box of cat food from the window ledge and stood outside the final room in the passageway.

Tell no one, she said, opening the door.

Not a word, I said.

We stepped over the threshold. Inside was a long wide carpeted room with a large yellow sofa. Pillows and cushions were thrown everywhere. Then the cushions began to move, and turned into white-cheeked ferrets lying sleeping. One looked up from the carpet. Another climbed out from under an armchair. They clucked. Hallo thieves, said Miss Jilly as they turned their heads and then waddled and hopped with a nip over to her like a group of butlers and altar boys.

She emptied raisins from the box of cat food into a tray.

Cuckoo, said the Blackbird as the ferrets gathered in a ring to eat.

*

Do you think he could put it onto the roof rack? she asked.

The Bird tied down his bike with the rope he'd brought to harness the donkey, then without a word he got into the front.

I have not had another soul in this ancient jalopy for years, she said, forgive the untidiness, and she leaned back and pulled a duvet cover off the back seat to let me in. The Blackbird had his knees to his chin. She let his seat back and he rose his bag of tools onto his lap. We took off down the avenue like ghosts.

Why did you bury the parts of the hooves, she asked.

Because, he said, they would stick in the throat of a dog and choke him.

Oh.

We reached the opening onto the main road. She drew in tight to the ditch on our left, stalled as she peered to the right. All clear, he said, and as she swung round she hit the button of the radio, and we were back out at sea again. Only for this car, she said, tapping the steering wheel, I would be lost without the car. I can go for a cup of nourishing soup in that café on the main road. I can watch the children playing round the school at eleven. I can get up the post office. And the night before last I saw *The Pirates of Penzance*. I want to thank you gentlemen for all you've done.

A nice donkey, said the Bird.

And he's not mine.

Right here, I said.

She leaned over and smelt the Blackbird's neck.

My God, she said.

The mountains were covered in white cloud. We pulled up at Mister John's after going a steady pace through the wind, marking time at some spots where she'd take a look at the trees and the birds; then as we approached the Long Squares, she stopped suddenly and said Where to?

Straight on Ma'am, I said.

We drove onto the next crossroads.

It's desolate, she said.

At the pier the sea was bucketing. The black Mercedes that passed me earlier was parked as usual facing out to the alt. Sprays of fume flew.

Have you guests, asked Miss Jilly.

Fishermen, I said.

I beg to differ, she said, they are not ordinary fishermen.

You can stop here, I said.

The Blackbird stepped out of the car, unhooked his bike from the roof, and without once looking behind he headed up the path to Joejoe's with his cloth bag, rose one hand in the air when he reached the door, and stepped in.

Would you like to come in and meet Joejoe?

She looked at me with an amazed smile, then glanced toward the house and touched her ear. Another time, perhaps, she said. I gave her directions home. She drove back up to the pier, turned and – head-down – shot off. I walked up to our house, and the pony walked alongside me on the other side of the fence then Timmy stepped out to accompany me to the door. All of a sudden I heard a car behind. It was the Volkswagen.

Miss Jilly pulled down her window.

I'm sorry, she said.

Are you lost?

No. I'm sorry – if perhaps I need you again will you be available?

Yes Ma'am.

And how do I get in touch?

I wrote down my mobile number and our landline phone number into her notebook, and she handed me a small calling card. She read my numbers back to me twice and rewrote them in her own handwriting. She stepped back, swung round and turned for home again. She shot fast between each pothole, skirting stones that had come over the bank with the tide, and then she stopped got out and lowered her head to the pony.

The two stood facing each for a time; then she looked through the four windows of the Mercedes, and drove off.

My mobile rang.

Where are you? asked Anna.

At home, I said. I am just after spending the day with a lovely lady.

Who?

Miss Jilly of Dromod House.

Oh my, *notre mère la Terre*, she whispered. And I am about to run a few mile. I will see you later.

Bye, Anna.

I stepped into the studio and began another fish – this time one closer to home. I drew the shape of a sea trout, then added the grey silvery back and the yellow eyes. I tapped in his spots, and opened his mouth a fraction. I rolled up the canvas and brought it down to *The Ostrich*, took the key out of its hiding place, went in and there on the table sat books on experimental science, stone circles, catalogues of plants and flowers, a book of caves, a book of waste management, all opened in a circle in the table around a single copybook, a pen and an atlas.

I stood and glued the drawing of the fish to the wall of the cabin, then wrote *Philip* in the bottom left corner.

Chapter Eleven

Saturday Morning, the Mercedes

I was out first thing next morning feeding the donkeys and horse some scrap when I saw the Merc with the foreign number plate was parked down the road from Joejoe's. As I got closer I saw the fishing rods sticking out the back window and one man looking sadly into the engine.

I came up the beach and stepped over the sands.

Hallo, I said.

Chest, he said and then I knew he was Polish. Even though they came sometimes twice a week, we had never really spoken to each other. One of them might have given the odd wave. It was like we all thought being too friendly was bad manners. Or that being over-friendly was an intrusion. He looked towards me with a shameful grin, and snapped a smile, and beckoned at the engine, downward, with his thumb.

Are you in trouble? I asked.

He threw a hand in the air.

It is possible, he said.

Let me look, I said.

He was leaning down in front of me, I touched his shoulder and he jumped, and smiled shyly. He looked back across towards Joejoe's, then opened his palms outwards, and leaned back against the wall, in his long wide shoes, and shook one hand down, fatalistically.

It's OK, he said, one minute, my friend will return, he will explain, and he lifted a single finger, and he pointed towards Joejoe's.

I looked in at the battery, while behind me he breathed out heavily. I tugged the plug leads, then took out the dipstick, dried it with a tissue, tipped it back in and out and looked at the coating of oil. There was plenty. I checked the water. There was more than enough. I stood back.

A beautiful car, I said. Do you mind?

I sat in, turned the key and turned on the lights. Then I went to the front and saw that the lights were on very low. He leaned in and turned off the silent engine.

You see, he said, we have done all that.

Sorry, I said and he pointed with one finger up the road, then put another finger behind the first, and let one finger follow the other, then fixed both fingers in a line and snapped his thumbs.

Aye, I said, I think I know your problem?

A problem, he laughed, yes, and he made a slopping sound, then made a tying movement, pointed ahead, pointed at the battery, said chug! chug! and let one finger lead the other again.

Got ya, you need a tow!

Excuse? he said, and his eyes widened.

Aha, said Joejoe, as he came up the lane from his house with a second man who was carrying a pair of pliers, Mister Psyche has landed. Tell me this why did Miss Jilly not come in yesterday to visit?

She will another time she said.

Tell her I'm expecting her.

I will.

Good man.

We need a translator here, I said.

I can speak English, said the second man, no problem. He was dressed in a yellow duffle coat with huge buttons.

Well then explain why you did not give me a lift yesterday?

Please, I do not understand.

I lifted my thumb and hitched.

88

You drove by me yesterday, I said, on the road. The two men laughed amicably, and nodded, and nodded, and shook their heads to and fro, then they both lifted their thumbs and started hitching.

I waved to you, I said.

I waved and they waved back to me.

Settle down, will ye, said Joejoe. This man gave a knock at my door, and I told him I had no television, I thought he was looking for licences; and then he asked me – and he made a cutting motion with his fingers – for what I took to be a set of pliers.

Excuse me, I said, as I got down on my knees.

Certainly, said the man, and as I leaned forward I saw that he was in purple wellingtons that reached his thighs. I lay down on the ground under the engine and steered myself in with my heels.

He knows what he's doing? came a voice from above.

Yes, my uncle answered.

I am looking for a petrol leak, I said.

There is no petrol leak, said the voice.

Anything? asked Joejoe.

No. Could you pull me out, I said.

The second man took my feet and slowly hauled me out. OK?

Let her sit a while, I said, I think you need a tow.

You understand engine?

Not really, I said, but my father does.

He shook his head, then the first man looked at the second man who translated then the two turned to Joejoe.

He says you need a tow, said Joejoe.

No, said the first man.

I'm afraid my friend thinks it's not necessary, the second man said, and shook his head, he thinks it will not work. The first man took the pliers and adjusted the battery plugs while his mate sat into the driving seat. He turned the key.

Nothing, and he slapped the wheel and got out.

You need a tow, I said, and I imitated a man pulling a rope over his shoulder as if he was hauling a great weight.

I need a tow? they repeated together; and the two men beamed, then immediately lifted their shoulders in misunderstanding and inevitability and what-can-we-do, it's-beyond-us, and my man spread his hand at the isolated landscape and made a low whistle, then he indicated the sky above, tutted! and leaned against the wall.

Excuse, he said.

His friend sat into the back seat of the Merc and pulled the door closed and went on his mobile.

Now Psyche, said Joejoe, what's next in your plan?

You have a rope? I asked my man.

My English, the first man said, and your Irish, I don't understand. We wait, yes? he said, and he pointed at his friend. So again I put the imaginary rope over my shoulder and pulled, then I tied the imaginary rope to the front fender and pulled, and pulled grimacing, and he yelled, Ah! Ah, he said, yes, yes, and now he made the same tying movement to the front fender, buckled his knuckles but then pulled away from me in opposition.

I suddenly realised we were saying the same thing with our bodies but now we were going in different directions.

I dropped the rope that did not exist.

It's what I think, I said.

No, he said, and he shook his head vehemently, no good; and, all of a sudden, he shot his two arms high in the air and cracked both thumbs and middle fingers. Cracked them again like a conductor starting an orchestra, then opened both palms to me to see if I understood, then he pointed at his foot and laughed, next he pointed at the battery and slapped the Merc.

The second man got out, they exchanged a few words; I am Theo, said the second man, who spoke English, and we shook hands, thank you for your help. Dido, said the first man and we shook hands, then they both shook hands with Joejoe. He's my granduncle Joejoe, I said. Dido pointed at me; Psyche, Joejoe said; they nodded, spoke again, and then they agreed, in some sort of acceptance prayer to open the boot and take out a tow-hitch rope.

Now, Dido, we turn the car around? I asked.

Hah, said Dido.

He closed the bonnet and went to get into the driver's seat of the Merc, but Joejoe politely tipped him on the shoulder, pointed him towards the back of the Merc and Joejoe sat in and took control, and so the three of us pushed while he steered and gave directions. We wheeled the car round and got her facing back the way she came.

Then I tied the tow-rope to the tow hook of the Mercedes.

We stood there a moment.

Now what, asked Theo.

Just wait a few minutes, I said.

He looked up the empty road and opened his arms; then proffered me his mobile.

You know someone who can help? Theo asked.

I took his wrist and looked at his watch and tapped the watch face, let go his hand then lifted a single finger in the air.

Mammy is coming, I said.

Mammy is coming, he said he and he looked at me closely, and shook his head.

Soon, I added.

He nodded, and in his turn he rose a single finger in the air to Dido. Mammy is coming, he said, and he roared laughing, then he translated it, and Dido glanced a little disbelievingly to his side, nodded, beamed, and cupped his shoulders.

We sat against the wall and waited. Joejoe beat his shoulders, scrutinised his shoes, then took off a shoe and shook it.

I know nothing about cars, sadly, he said, and anything I know nothing about, I keep away from.

Like strangers? asked Theo.

No. I like to see the strangers about the place. Strangers are good for a community. They keep you on your toes. Like yourselves.

The clouds overhead passed by like more of the apostles on the dance floor.

I smiled to myself.

It is not a joke, no? asked Theo.

No.

We wait for your Mammy?

Yes.

The Irish they laugh.

Does it sound false?

Yes.

Like all laughter.

Yes, but the Irish they laugh a lot. It is strange, he said, but then . . . how you say, the universe . . . yes? . . . is large, no?

I nodded. And it is increasing, I said, by the minute. Look!

In the distance the Fiat appeared through the small flailing ash trees. Ma slowed up, and gave me a long questioning look.

Could you help us out – Mammy, I said emphasising a name I rarely used.

Mammy is it, oh certainly, she said. She looked at the two men. Oh good day gentlemen.

Hallo, they nodded.

Just a mo, said Ma.

She drove on by, turned at the gate and came back and passed the Merc, then reversed till the two cars were close to each other.

I handed the rope to Dido who reluctantly tied it onto the tow hitch of the Fiat.

You intend a Fiat to draw a Mercedes, asked Theo.

Yes, just for a little jaunt.

He shook his head. You understand that hopelessness often propels itself into science for no earthly reason?

I do.

Pray men, said Joejoe, what are you saying?

Your grandnephew is plying a dangerous course.

He is.

OK, now it is tow, yeh? Dido said resignedly and again shook his head from side to side, is that right?

Yes.

Joejoe raised a hand to begin.

Theo, and myself and Joejoe got in behind the Merc.

Ma started the car and we jerked and pushed forward, the rope went taut, and she pulled the Merc along in neutral gear till slowly we came to the first incline. Ma hit second, and went up into third. We pushed and pushed, and got to the top of the low hill, where she suddenly accelerated. Here goes, Joejoe said. All of a sudden the Merc with no sound drew the Fiat back. Ma stopped, and started and went into a fast third, and we pushed hard.

The Merc shot forward for a few seconds and died, without a sound.

Ma slowly stopped. Theo sat in beside Dido and the two men sat dejected in the car. They hoisted their hands, then smiled, and grimaced as myself and Joejoe approached.

It is no good, Theo said sadly out the window.

Don't lose faith, said Joejoe.

If you deem it so.

There must be something wrong with your battery.

That is what poor Dido has been trying to explain to you, he said and Dido closed his eyes.

I untied the tow hitch and pointed inland.

We will be back in a few minutes, I said.

Good luck, said Joejoe.

We drove off.

Where are we going, asked Ma.

Doyle's.

What for?

Jump leads, I explained. I have a headache, she said, from listening to this bitch going on and on the entire day. Was she sick? I asked. Sick, no, she works with me. She was at a hen party and this one said this and this one said that. A hen party if you don't mind I had to listen to all the livelong day, said Ma. Jesus I think I need a break from that job. I was nearly in tears, and she laughed. Did you know that if you are an ambulance driver you have to get a licence to drive a bus and a lorry. Now for you.

We drove down to Doyle's and I explained the story to Stefan.

What type of car? he asked.

Mercedes.

Is the car petrol?

I think so.

I think it is diesel, he said.

You think so?

Yes, he said, that is why it is slow to start on tow.

Ah.

But there is something else Mister Side Kick.

Yes?

Is the Mercedes automatic?

Oh shit.

If it is automatic, as you know, it will not start on tow.

I forgot to look.

It is OK Mister Side Kick. Here, and he handed me a set of jump leads.

Thank you.

If you need me, come back, he said.

I will, I said, and ashamed of myself I sat in beside my mother.

We came back up the coast road to find Joejoe seated at the wheel of the Merc on his own, and the two men standing to the side against the doors, looking patiently out at the rampant ocean and the blaspheming waves.

Ma drove up alongside them, so both engines were facing each other. Joejoe got out.

I have never sat in a Mercedes before, he said, till this very day.

Good for you.

I have important information, he whispered. It is a true car. Do you know who Theo is?

No.

He is the Russian ambassador.

The two men watched me with a sort of meek sadness as I went to the boot of the Fiat.

Is your car petrol?

It is not, it is diesel, said Theo.

And it is automatic?

Automatic? That is the word, ah yes, and he shook his head up and down, yes automatic!

I put a hand in the air and cracked a thumb and middle finger, leaned down and said Forgive me and took out the jump leads out of the boot of the Fiat and handed them over with a bow.

Ah grand, shouted Dido and he spun on his feet.

At last! Theo said.

He lifted the bonnets of both cars and Dido wiped the leads, began to clamp the leads on to the battery, then he tightened them.

This is good, Theo said. Very good. OK Positive. OK Negative? OK.

Fine.

Theo sat back in, turned the ignition and the Mercedes started immediately.

Eureka! shouted Dido and he took off the leads and closed both bonnets. Then he turned to me and hoisted both arms in the air and cracked his thumbs and middle fingers, and again I realised what he had been trying to say back then.

Sorry, I said. I cannot speak with my hands.

Thank you, thank you, he shouted in Ma's window.

Get back in, get back in, she said, before it cuts out.

You are my great friend, he said to me handing me back the leads. Theo, after giving the car a few strong revs, came over and we shook hands.

Will you give me a lift the next time? I said raising my thumb.

Ask my chauffeur, he said.

Will you go on, said Ma.

OK, shouted Dido, we go.

Ma reversed a little up the road, then in further to the side, and we waited, looking at the Merc. Theo sat in the passenger seat and Dido took the wheel. A few seconds passed as the men tied on their safety belts, and then unexpectedly sat without moving. A low rev. Another. All of a sudden they looked foreign, and strange, as if sitting in the car together, now that it was working, had changed their demeanour. They had taken on another air. They looked like they were sitting in a hearse waiting on the cortège to gather up behind. Only for the fishing rods we were at a funeral. Dido leaned forward. Theo joined his hands in prayer. The Merc suddenly shot out onto the road as if out of control, then straightened, and the men in a long swerve passed by us with inches to spare. We gave them the hands up. The ambassador waved, and waved madly, and his chauffeur shot an arm out the window and lifted a thumb and hitched, and continued hitching till they went out of sight.

That chauffer is some son of a gun, I said.

96

No fishing today, said Ma.

We dropped off the jump leads at Doyle's and Stefan held them a moment and said They work? Yes, thank you. No problem, he said, and we headed for home. The local boys were shaving grass in the Long Squares, and the Black Bales were at the top of the fields. It was another cutting time. The sun was shining. Ma stopped at Joejoe's and said I did more good out here today than I did in the hospital. What I need is a break, a change of job.

I got out at Joejoe's gate, and headed in.

He met me at the door.

The red army got away all right?

Yes.

They made off with my pliers, he said.

We sat down by the fire.

Miss Jilly, he said.

Aye.

Ah dear.

He lit up a fag.

She gave me her phone number.

Oh good. You see that Bible, and he stood and lifted it off the shelf, you know where that originated?

No.

I'll tell you. Dromod House. The same. I don't know how many years ago. That's why I always bless myself passing a Protestant church.

He passed the book to me.

I don't know how to speak with my hands, I said.

Never mind. The stranger always teaches you something. He sat down. Just read me a few lines, he said; and he topped his cigarette and threw it into the fire as I turned the pages and found the Pharisees and then began with the question: *Your witness is not true.*

BOOK THREE

Sightseeing

Chapter Twelve

Saturday, Playacting

Saturday, yes. Ma loved Saturdays when she could get the night off. She'd get high. Then when Anna arrived with the book on cats, a homemade apple tart and a loaf of brown bread, Ma was enthralled.

You thought of me, said Ma.

He did, said Anna pointing, Mister Jeremiah thought you'd like the book.

Thank you son. He knows I love cats. Are you off for your walk?

We are, said Anna.

We'll see you in a while, I said.

Enjoy yourselves, and she threw open the book. Myself and Anna headed off down the rocks to the old wall I had found and we sat looking out to the island. This would be great place for nooky, she said.

Indeed.

I love your fish.

Thank you.

Did everything work out with your uncle?

In a way. Yeh.

It sounded serious.

I don't know what to think.

Oh.

Ah not to worry.

We'll leave it. Could I ask you a favour?

Go ahead.

I'm off to a get-together with the girls tonight in town and wondered whether ye are going in as usual?

We are. You can have a lift no bother.

You could come with me to the Forked Lightning and go off on your own and we could meet up on the dance floor.

I'm not in dancing mode Anna.

Ah do.

Not yet, but soon, Lala.

All right, Jeremiah.

We sat there for an hour watching the cormorants pass in ones and twos. She took my hand and we headed off round the rocks that were covered in sea pinks, sea urchins and sea kale. Every weekend we'd take the same walk, depending on the weather, along the strand, down by the blow hole, the lime kilns, the battery walls. We took off our shoes and walked the rock pool, and as the high tide gathered it scooped and smashed the rock stones up onto the beach. In the sunlight the fossils bloomed. We headed back up to the gate. Inland the trees in the reeds began to float and looked like they might rise slowly into the sky.

We headed in. Ma was reading intently.

I am enjoying your book.

Good, said Anna.

I dropped safely into the father's armchair. He was away plastering an attic for the Germans down Poverty Row. I was watching the cat to start a row because Timmy the dog had started ceilidhing with her kitten in its cardboard box, but she just turned the once to watch them play, meowed, then faced away and settled her snout snug down between her orange shins.

I'm learning a lot. For instance, you see that cat there?

I do.

She is not really a pet, said Ma.

If she's not a pet, I asked, what is she?

She's a half pet.

What does that mean?

Well she's not a dog for instance.

Ma?

What I mean is she doesn't know us that long. The dog you see goes further back. In our memories. You see the dog has his uses, he was needed in the fields for hunting. She wasn't.

She kills mice, doesn't she?

Yes, she knows her mice. But you see she'll mice kill anyway – whether – hold it – she's a pet or not. So why bother training her. Leave them in the wild to fend for themselves is what I say.

The dog gave the kitten a long fatherly lick that lifted her clean into the air.

Anna threw out her feet and ruffled her hair.

And she became a goddess.

It's true, continued Ma. The poor Egyptian got lonely, you know. Out there in the desert. By himself. They still are. I never met an Egyptian surgeon inside in the hospital, she added, but he was lonely.

That's because they're away from home.

I wonder. There was a Dr Kempo. I had a soft spot for him. You never saw a lonelier man by an operating table. I used to think he was about to break into tears. You'd have more sympathy for him than the poor fellow stretched out on the sheet.

There was a display of feathers in a glass on the sill, and she picked out a pigeon's, and blew it.

On the other hand the lonely man is a proud man, she said. It's only after they're done praying that they look happy.

So if the people had lived in the forest, I said, the cat would have stayed wild.

Right, said Ma, I suppose.

So that's the cat's story.

And, she said nodding, it's not finished yet.

No, said Anna and she drew up her legs onto the chair, threw her arms round her knees, and faced Ma. The dog tapped the white stomach of the kitten and she hurtled against his claw like it was a rag. I let Timmy out the door and he ran down to Joejoe's. Ma lifted her book, blew a few pages apart, flicked over, and ran the pigeon feather along a sentence.

Now, listen to this children everywhere – it appears that man brings out the child in the cat. I could have sworn it was the other way round. She looked at me, and she looked at the cat and read on, petting the pages. Now there's something. Read that and she handed me the book.

The cat grew short legs so she could become a friend of man, I read out.

Now, said Ma. And she took back the book and read –The cat hasn't proper eyes. That explains it. She has mirrors in the retina.

Indeed – that's why they shine at night, said Anna.

Because, I said, they're picking up the moon.

Right, said Ma.

Or the lights of cars or whatever.

Right.

If there's no lights on they don't shine.

No Philip, they don't shine in the dark.

It's kinda sad, said Anna.

They eyed each other, then both women more or less simultaneously turned in my direction you'd think to some command I'd given, to check if I was I still there, the witness they did not want, or maybe the witness they did: they were always doing that, first the one, then the other, in the middle of a TV programme, or when Da spoke out of hand; I'd catch it out of the corner of my eye and suddenly find them simultaneously tossing their hair, and then turning at the same time to look at me, and as they did then, they did now – then they both looked away.

Anna brushed a handful of nothing onto the ground and stared down as she spoke.

Do you know what happens when I look into the mirror? she asked Ma quietly.

No.

I see the past looking back at me.

Well, you see, it's because of the good looks you inherited from your French ancestors.

And the two ladies, laughing, went off on a journey to the island off France, the Côtes-d'Armor where Anna's great-great-great-great-great-grandfather had come from in the French Invasion of 1798.

Some day I am going to go there, said Anna.

Do.

And you will come with me.

I will, I said.

Ah good, she said with mock sadness and handed each of us a slice of apple tart.

And Philip there is the cut of his father; he travelled up the Feeney side.

It's tough Ma, I said.

Oh, is it Philip?

Everybody looks like someone else, said Anna.

To begin with, corrected Ma.

Fair enough.

Then you grow into yourself. As you will. It's the same with friends. Things change. You have a friend and you think you'll be friends with them all your life. But you lose them.

Yes Ma, I said.

Sorry Philip, and she leaned over and took my hand, I did not mean it that way.

I know that. It's all right.

I'm really sorry.

It's OK. Carry on.

How is my apple tart, said Anna, trying to keep the chat from going dark.

It's great, I said.

Yes. Things change, said Ma. You start out thinking about getting on with people. Other people. You're thinking of who you get on with, and who you don't, and all that. And then, when it's too late, you find that the person you have not been getting on with, a lot of the time, is yourself. This is what I found out about myself, she added, and she looked at me, and she petted the pages again, firmly this time.

But you have to laugh, said Ma.

I'm glad to hear it, Mrs Feeney, said Anna and she opened her mouth and aped a tortured smile.

Anna stop, you're making me dizzy.

Girls, I said in my schoolmaster's voice, stop it!

Ma threw her eyes left and right, and up and down, and put a hand, palm out flat against the shape of Anna, then she lifted the book up to her eyes.

You know what the problem is, said Anna, sentiment is the same as cruelty.

True.

I pity the poor Annas of this world, said Anna fondly and a great flirtatious melancholy travelled through her eyes.

So do I, I said sadly.

You think it's funny my dear friend.

I do.

Did you ever watch the way men go on when they look at women, she asked Ma.

O I do, said Ma and she immediately went all floppy, and made a face all scrunched-up with puffed-out cheeks and said in a bass voice towards the ceiling, *well Geraldine*, and next with her mouth and eyes thrown to one side Anna whispered *how is it going Anna*; then she sat perfectly still, glanced down at my shoes and Ma's eyes travelled from my feet to my head, and finally stopped at my eyes, and then Anna with this big long half-witted flirt look, said hoarsely *You're looking lovely Anna.*

You've got him to a T, and Ma roared laughing. And now you look kinda . . . What's that word we're not supposed to say in front of this lady . . . ? –

Sexy, I said.

Anna stood with her eyes closed.

Don't say that word, she whispered. That word is banned.

And Mother pushed back the hair from her forehead, dropped into a starting posture in the chair, and with her arms out in supplication, said: Gone now, sadly, are the days of saying sexy.

It's a woeful pity to have everything reduced to that unmentionable cacophony of sounds, said Anna flicking her curls with a smile

Oh forgive me, Miss Conan.

Le réalité et toi, vous ne vous entendez pas, n'est-ce pas. It's disgraceful. Isn't it disgraceful you?

Yes, I said.

So why are you laughing, you jinnet.

Do I live here I wonder, said Da, and he came in as if he had been there all the time.

He left the front door ajar, peered about him, sat down with his back to us on the step and started to take off his boots. He was drenched in plaster-spit. The cat and kitten ran over to him. Good day, he nodded. Yes, I can recognise an odd cratur about the place. But I don't see anything funny do you? No, I'm sorry. I don't know what they are laughing at.

He stood.

No sir, I do not know what they are laughing at. Now who is here oh good evening Anna, he said as she handed him an apple slice.

Good evening sir.

Ye are enjoying yourselves as usual.

We are.

This is beautiful, he said as he chewed.

Before you go any further, will you step into the ring? I said.

OK monsieur.

Who do you see when you look into the mirror?

Oi, tough one, and he went all sad-eyed and French. Oi! Let me see.

He looked at me, darted a sharp glance at my mother who was oh absorbed in reading by the window, looked long and sadly at Anna; then he closed his eyes, slapped his thighs, upped his fists to look at them, bared his teeth, then shut one eye, dropped, jumped, and lifted an outstretched hand and head-down pointed an accusing finger at Ma.

Thank you, said Ma as if he wasn't there and she handed the cat's-story book back to Anna.

I know what I'm going to do, Anna said. When I get away from this part of the world I'm going to change my identity.

Can I go with you? I asked.

If your parents don't mind. She paused. Let me see. You can have the room at the front, Jeremiah.

OK, Lala. That'll do.

And we'll visit ye on Sundays, right Ma, said Da.

Whatever you say.

Are youse ready for town tonight, he asked.

Can I take a lift in with you sir, I am going to a girls' outing.

A hen party? Certainly Miss Conan.

He put on the idiot face and looked into his two fists.

Hold it there, I said.

Yes?

Do you know who you remind me of?

He closed one eye and bared his teeth.

Who?

I slapped my thighs, upped my fists to look at them, bared

my teeth, closed one eye and kicked out one foot then the other, then dropped down and lifted an accusing finger.

You got him, said Ma. It's him. You have captured Mister Feeney.

Da, spluttering, waved a finger in my direction.

That foolery has been noted Mister.

He wrote something into his imaginary notebook. Put a pen that didn't exist behind his ear and waved the game on.

Do you like sitting in that armchair? he asked gently.

Yes, I said, getting up.

See ya all later, said Anna and she headed off down the road running with the cat book under her arm.

Chapter Thirteen

Saturday Night

We pulled in at Joejoe's first.

He was seated by the fire, the small accordion deflated on the floor beside him, a patch of ointment on the back of one hand and another on his cheek, and Timmy the dog in the other armchair, curled up with one steady eye.

You're for the town.

Aye.

Sightseeing.

Yes.

I stroked the dog. He leaped up and landed at my feet.

Can I bring you anything back?

No. Yes. Twenty Woodbine. Here you are – I'll spell it out into your hand.

OK.

He gave me the money.

Right. Good night Timmy, he said to the dog, have a good time.

It was a broad starry night. The Scottish calves followed us along the ditch. With the steamed-up windows I could not see into the car. I looked back at the cottage, then felt round for the handle of the door.

I opened the door. Timmy jumped in.

Are we right, asked Da.

Yes, I said.

Is he OK?

He is.

Nothing will happen him, Tom; said Ma. Isn't that right, she said turning to me.

Yes, I said.

So let's not worry. Off you go!

Anna was standing outside the doorway of her house. She climbed into the back beside Ma. We took off. He drove the back way under the mountain so that we could have the lights of the town below us as we went.

When we hit the outskirts Da shuffled in his seat a little closer to the windscreen, eased the driver's window down a fraction and turned the radio low; this meant business; my mother looked left, then right, said Go; he drove slowly up various streets, Bridge Street, Cathedral Road, Pearse Street; taking his time at the traffic lights, guiding cars out from side streets with a sudden flash of his dims to full lights and a wave of his arm; we stopped for any pedestrian in sight to cross the road, sometimes not thanking you; pulled in for a pause along some dark side street where we sat looking round us at the locked door of the Mason's Hall, and beyond it, the broken-down Scout Den.

Philip? asked Anna, leaning forward.

Yes.

Did I tell you about the hummingbird?

No.

I'm lost, said Ma.

The hummingbird – she can fly backwards and she has to eat her own body weight each day to stay alive.

Oh.

I'm jealous of your knowledge, said Da.

We'll talk about her again, Anna said, and she sat back.

Then it was down the Hill; and into a short tour of the Market Square, squashing tomatoes and soft earth fallen that afternoon from the trays of Mister Organics' plants; twice round the roundabout; a long enough stop to read what was on in the Odeon for the following week; the Romanian woman squatting under the awnings of Tesco waved across at us; Go, said my mother; we crept through the huge new blocks of flats, looking up; he turned to full lights so that he could read how far the job had got and then he climbed out and shook a bar of the scaffolding; The Poles, he said, get there quicker than us; a short jaunt through the woods out to the Holy Well: No courting cars now, said he; None needed, said she. No, he agreed; Boom time, said Ma and Anna and myself got out to walk the stations under the trees; then, back into the car, and he began a climb up to the railway station then around the car park of the Great Southern where a band called The Blue Flares were taking their instruments and sound equipments out of a van by torchlight; then he headed in through one set of silver gates to the dark convent grounds and out the other.

Hold it there, something is coming. All right on the left, Ma said; he spun down Main Street for the first time, and slowed nearly to a stop as he looked closely at the people passing; Look at the bottle, said Anna, someone had placed it carefully on the pillar of the bridge; we got in the wrong lane at the lights and went round the town again; Blast it, he said, Why do I keep feeling that I'm doing something wrong; we dropped down the steep hill by the antique shop and the pound shop; There's the barber Quigley; There's Sheila Masterson, said Ma, I can't stand her on the phone – Could I speak to Doctor James Masterson now! I said now! Tell him this is Mrs Masterson! Have you got that – Mrs Masterson! at the sound of the raised voice Timmy began whining; a small turn right in second, then with a jerk Da stopped at The Magic Glasses for tay, left the car running while Anna went in, came back; he drove down the docks with his bag of chips in his lap: we putputted to a stop and ate the takeaway with the headlights trained on the harbour, and there – with timber stacked sky-high at the pier – was the same boat that came in across the sea behind our house every month from Norway; That timber is some of the most expensive in the world, said Da; and next to the boat was a great pile of busted cars, engines of all sorts, wrapped round each other as if there had been some terrible crash – all bound for a scrapyard somewhere in Spain; It's hard to believe, said Da; It is, I said; I wonder how Joejoe is, said Da: on the radio we were in the deep South of America listening to Mrs someone sing Hum and Mister someone-else milking cows; this is not a salad burger, Da complained, this is a lettuce burger; Ma got out and threw the bags into a rubbish bin, sat in; gulls wheeled; Da adjusted the driver's mirror, patted the steering wheel, looked behind him and reversed; we went through the huge silent industrial estate, not a soul, then over the bridge and drew out into traffic again, turned down along the river; lads were leaning over the wall flinging popcorn to the swans; lots of folk yelling; the girls in tall boots and sailors hats and brown shawls walking arm-in-arm with each other or else barging ahead head down.

The cats grew short legs, said Anna.

They did, I nodded savagely.

I like it, she said.

Fellows stopped on the streets looking back behind them for someone they thought they'd lost; the east went west with cans in bags; fellows in black suits, bareheaded, shaven-headed, sauntered; Greed is in a hurry, said Anna; the cider drinkers were under the elm tree on their hunkers with a radio on a bench beyond playing Country and Western; On the next bench three men were keeping time; I could hear myself singing *You were some bird when you left Raspberry Hill, you were, you were*; I know every one of those people, said Ma, by their first name, those people sitting there on the bench, they're all patients of mine; music pumped from The Leitrim Bar; three Spanish-looking girls in blue coats were sitting on a step inside the bank door beside the cash dispenser with their bags at their feet; the Chinese man at Chino's was staring out the window of his café as he fed himself biscuits; Go, she said; I wonder how

113

things are in casualty tonight, said Ma; Anna in the back seat beside me fumbled, turned aside and took a look into her hand-mirror, snapped it shut and lifted her bag, ready for off.

So what will I call you? I asked Anna.

Hm? she asked

When you move change your identity.

Oh.

Anna thought long and hard.

I will continue to be Lala, I think.

Da slowed, flicked his indicator and pulled outside the disco at The Fork Lightning and looked back.

There you go girl.

Will you come with me, Jeremiah?

No, Lala.

You could go after me and the girls. Please.

Some other night.

She stepped out quick.

Ma pulled down her window.

Hi?

What?

You're looking lovely, Miss Conan, said Ma.

Oh thank you Geraldine.

Anna crossed the street to join the crowd of girls that had gathered outside. A cheer went up and the hugging began.

Will you look at the cut of the dolly birds, said Ma.

And they're all gardeners, said Da.

Then Anna turned to look at us, and mouthed something I couldn't read. I pulled down the window.

What? I shouted.

Come on Philip!

No.

And then came one obscene middle finger straight up in the air.

Hark at the environmentalist, said Da.

Chapter Fourteen

Sightseeing

OK? he asked, OK, said Ma, go, and Da budged out carefully behind Gyrums Transport – trading from Plymouth, and Edinburgh – who were picnicking on the pier and an empty Roadstone lorry, that was parked facing Gyrums; and we headed back into the centre of town. He turned round by the monastery into a small car park along the river, cut the lights, got out and put a cap on his head.

See ya later, he said.

He pulled his jacket tight, walked up the lane that led to High Street and crossed the road to the jewellers opposite where Mister Mayo stood, in a coat that reached his boots, selling *The Final Issue*. He put a few coins in his tin, they had a few words and the man on crutches shook with laughter, then Da disappeared into the shadows under the clock that always said 9.

Soon I saw a match strike, he came out, turned left and went from sight down the street. He was followed by a line of girls in vests to their knees. They looked like parcelled apples. We pulled down both front windows a fraction to listen to a bell ring ten times. A man came down the archway and had a piss with one hand on his cock and his other hand holding a mobile to his ear. There was a sudden whoosh of crows down from the monastery walls. I began studying the stone work. I counted the stone layered from the window above to the ground below; the curve; the weight and the lift. A young lad in pumps and tweeds went by with a pup on a lead and Timmy rose on the back seat and followed him carefully with his eyes.

Coriander, evening primroses, and one Corsican mint, order a shelf for the glasshouse, what's all that about? said Ma, studying her shopping list. Oh that's from last summer. She turned a page. Sage, matches, she looked up, then back, and said: There's a good crowd.

Students.

Aye.

Onions, she said.

She checked the mirror to see who was coming behind us, and fixed it so the world behind could stroll directly into her line of vision. There were plenty of them tumbling into the reflection. All the night people used the car park to go from one street to another. Along came an African lady with a two-tiered pram; a white-haired business man hopping a tennis ball, and four tall middle-aged ladies, in woollen hats, nibbling scones, with big haversacks on their back, speaking what sounded like German. Ma put her shopping list away. Under a small street light a few East Europeans stood silently in their leather jackets and caps looking over the gate into the monastery. They took the odd mouthful from a small vodka bottle, while we ate peppermints. Gangs would pass, mostly ladies, in slim white boots, sipping cans. A policewoman, with her elbows pinned to her hips, stood a while on her own under the archway, then lifting her mobile she walked away, looking back. Ma put on the radio and sat into the driver's seat, and I climbed into the passenger seat.

The exit is at the entrance, I said.

I see. Yes indeed. Is it too warm in here, asked Ma.

No.

Well I think it's too warm.

It's not.

If you say so.

She let the two front windows down slightly and spun the dials of the radio.

I was thinking of having my hair dyed, and waved, she said, and she flew past blasts of rap and Mister Beethoven looking for the station that played on Saturday night the music she loved to listen to on a Sunday morning. Yes, that's what I'd like to hear, she said. By this time Da would be on Main Street in the doorway of Molloy's the drapers, and Anna would have trotted out onto the dance floor to go tunnelling into the circle. Yes, sir. We sat there for maybe half an hour watching folk that didn't know we were there watching them. We were invisible till a girl in a yellow vest and white jockey's cap fell against the bonnet of the car, and righting herself she came to the driver's window and stared in at Ma as if there was no one there. It was like she was looking through a spider's web, then she suddenly darted back in mock surprise, lifted her hands to her cheek and waved her fingers in at us. She had a huge pair of eyes.

Hallo, said Ma, letting down the window a fraction more.

Hallo, she said softly.

Are you all right?

Excellent, the girl said. Absolutely.

Ah good.

Hallo in there!

Hallo, I said.

Is that your dog?

It's my granduncle's.

Nice dog. I was in the *Gazette* last week.

Were you? asked Ma.

On the fifth page.

Isn't that something?

Yeh. And I was supposed to go to Maynooth this evening, she said across to me, but they went on without me.

That's bad, I said.

Oh no bother. I can go next weekend.

Fair enough, I said.

Were you going to a party? asked Ma.

Oh no. I'm allergic to orgies.

Jazus, said Ma.

Who's the dog?

Timmy.

Hi ya Timsum. No, it was my brother I was going to see. It's not too far from his gaff to the shops. She plucked at her vest and asked my mother: Are you his Ma?

Yes.

He's nice. I said you're nice.

I said, Oh, thank you.

She put her head in the window. Do you mind me asking like, but what are youse two doing sitting out here all alone in the dark?

We're waiting for my father.

Oh is he doing the shopping?

No.

Ah, I know, he's in the pub.

No.

It's kinda mad. What's he doing?

He's walking about, looking round him.

Oh. And you just like sit . . . like . . . here?

Is right, said Ma.

Yes, every Saturday night.

And Christmas Eve.

That's weird.

Is it?

Anyway, sorry about that, chat you later, she said, and took her head back out, sucked in and waved, and with a sly grin and popsy eyes, went on.

The crowd kept coming, this way, that way. Alone, together, scattered. After the first hour we hit ceilidh music. Then horns blowing in jazz. And on to a programme about the First World War. I'll take a look at the shops, she said. I'll go with you, I said. The Hill was full of Northern bucks wrapped in shawls. Three girls, dressed as barbers, were singing in the Glazed Oven. Ma bought three slices of tongue, a bag of paprika, almond nuts and yes, sage, she said. At the monument a woman was screaming into her friend's mobile. Ma strolled over to Molloy's the drapers to see the style. She passed my father who was standing outside Currid's the chemists. She did not look at him, and he did not look at her. We went on up the street and into the Tesco Arcade, and then across to Dunne's. She strolled through the clothes, pulling the odd sleeve out of the racks.

We ate a crêpe outside the cinema.

Upstairs, next door, in the Yoga Parlour, a line of girls were lifting their arms beyond the windows. The Romanian lady was sitting on a rug outside Cawley's solicitors with a tray of coins on her lap. Ah Geraldine Feeney, a voice called. It was a man in a light blue suit pushing a trolley. He took Ma's hand. Thank you Nurse, he said. Mister Anderson, she said, I didn't know who it was, and you look so well. I'm getting better, he said, thanks to you. And he joined us to listen as the minister from Northern Ireland took up his position outside the old community hall and began praying into a microphone. And sometimes the prayers were from the Psalms. A few people would gather, others took not a blind bit of notice of him, or the older man who always came with him, someone like an uncle who lay against the window of the Investment Company, waiting his turn.

He's a brave man, I always think, said Ma.

He is, said Mister Anderson, and he went on pushing his trolley. I'll see you back at the car, I said, and I hopped into the Internet Café, and sat down in a chair between a Polish girl on my right who was laughing at her boyfriend on the screen, and a dude who was eating an apple. I emailed Fran in New York and told him his fly was open. The place was laughing out loud at something that was painful. One euro. I went on up the street.

I went up the escalator of the new shopping centre, and crossed the balcony into the diamond-shaped hall and looked across the river.

On the way back it was my turn to pass Da. He was standing in the doorway of Maguire's the newsagents. He watched me pass. We made no signal. He pulled his head in the air and stepped into the arcade alongside a few hard men and a few tired men. He yawned, nodded at a passerby. He was like a guard on duty observing the flow of life.

Standing to attention among the skinheads in business suits, and the shoppers in corduroy.

I stopped at the monument for a line of cars to pass. There was a couple arguing fiercely by the telephone booth under the monument. It was the exact place we'd seen the girl screaming earlier into her friend's mobile. A taxi driver, stalled in the traffic, was watching them.

Hi, he shouted out the window, keep it down.

But they didn't bother with him. They went on arguing. He blew his horn. Then the driver of the car in front of him got out, and turned around.

What the fuck is wrong with you, she shouted at the taxi driver.

Then the man who was arguing with the girl roared at him: Yeh what the fuck are you blowing your horn for?

The couple went off, and the driver got back into her car. The taxi driver, who was eating a Magnum, looked over at me.

Did you see all that? he asked.

I did.

Well thank you, he said, for not smiling.

I went down the archway. Met Pete the buck who was on his way to a stag and wanted to bring me with him, and when I said I didn't want to go, he asked me when I'd be coming back among them. Soon, I said. Poor Mickey, he said. Aye, I said. You all right? Yeh, I said. Chat ya, buddy, and he tapped my shoulder and off he went. Ma was back in the driving seat eating Mexican crisps. The car park was half empty. We sat there a while. I took the dog for a pee around the walls of the monastery. As he walked he kept right behind me, and with each step I took he tapped his snout off the calf of my leg. It was his way of walking in town. He lay down. Three swans came up the river, climbed up the bank and stood in a group under a tree. Their young were standing below on stones on the far bank out of the light of the new cafés.

A few fellows crossed the bridge and came over and stood by me. They looked down on the water a while.

Grand night, said one.

It is, I said.

Timmy sailed into the back of the car.

We sat on. A helicopter flew over the town. The local news was on the radio, then came the weather, followed by ads for holidays abroad in Florida, St Petersburg and Monaco. Ma put on the Dubliners tape that Da always kept in the car, along with CDs by Johnny Cash. Hmm, said Ma, humming. She bit into a mint. Up the alleyway came the same woman shouting into her mobile.

Who's that, said Ma. She had her eyes shut.

She looks like Catherine Tate, your one on the TV.

What is she saying?

I don't know.

The arguments you can't understand are the worst, said Ma. I hear them everywhere in the hospital. The problem in there is you can't take sides. She opened her eyes and looked at me. She switched off the tape. What is going on in Joejoe's?

I don't know.

You can tell me, she said quietly, You can tell me the truth.

I don't know, honestly.

I think you do.

All right. I came down the other morning at six and he was sitting by the fire playing the accordion.

So?

And he had the rifle by his side.

Dear Christ!

Across the road the shutters went up round the Central.

We'll have to do something, she said. Something will have to be done. He'll start locking himself away again and we can't have that. Jesus. There was a silence. I know you don't want to, but you'll have to tell your father what's going on.

You tell him.

In the dark I could feel her turn. And look at me a long time. And look away.

Who is your granduncle afraid of?

Ma.

What?

I looked at the words in my head.

I don't know.

I took a stroll up the Mall, and down into Main Street I met a few of the lads and lassies from out our way all trooping between sessions. Everywhere shutters were going up. You could hear the drone of music from the nightclubs. I did a small dance by myself on the bridge, and a young fellow crossing gave a few footsteps back in reply and then I did another few steps and turns outside The Fork Lightning where Lala was inside rocking.

I headed on and then I saw him.

Da was standing next door to McDonald's with his back to the wall watching the traffic stopping at the lights and the people crossing. I dropped into the bank doorway on my hunkers to study him. He was in his favourite spot, pretending to be waiting on someone, the hat low so you could not see his eyes, the two hands in his jacket pocket. The legs crossed. The odd time he'd nod at someone and look up at the sky. A look to the left, a look to the right. He was still on duty. I crossed with the lights. The hat rose as I passed. He smiled, but without any attempt at recognition. More like a warning – keeping going buff! I came back over the bridge and across the river into the dark side of the car park and came up behind my mother who was sitting looking ahead of her into the passenger mirror.

I was thinking, she said.

Yes.

We need to get him out among people.

Aye.

Or get people in to him.

How?

I'm working on it. Did you see his Highness?

I did.

Yes, she said, a party would be the thing.

The place was emptying fast. Soon we would be the only car there.

Anna will definitely get here, asked Ma.

Yes Ma.

She's quite the young lady.

Then there was a tap on my window.

The girl in the cap was back.

I let down the window.

Are you still here, she asked.

We are.

You're very patient.

You know yourself.

Well I got good news, like. I did. I have a lift up to Maynooth tomorrow.

Well enjoy yourself, said Mother.

But I'm not going to go.

Oh, why?

It's the principle of the thing. I just wanted to see them act sincere. You know what I mean. That I got asked anyway; like that was the main thing.

I see, said Ma.

And your father is still out there?

He is, I said. He's at McDonald's.

Wow. Cool. Chat ya. Thank you for listening, anyway. She turned to go, stopped and looked into the back. Good night Timmy, she said, and she tipped away.

That girl has a great memory, said Ma.

We saw the swans drop down into the river. The street light against the monastery walls seemed to glow. Soon Johnny Cash went quiet as the tape ended. We let the windows down and listened. A stray sound of a single guitar came across the river as someone opened a door in The Mint. One of the chefs from the Chinese stepped out the back of the café, stood under a tree for a smoke and suddenly he was whipped by the wind. Paper blew. The people walking through looked very alone, and strangely familiar. I tried to walk by in their place. I found I was down in the monastery lighting a fire for breakfast. I made porridge and brought some out for the crows. I climbed the round steps up and looked down out of that V-shaped window. Underneath the souls in coats strolled in a medley. Even as they talked together, squinting to the person on their left, or right, they looked like animals entering new territory; and those who knew the place, and walked ahead through the dark with great confidence, were more alone than the strangers. I waved, but no one saw me.

He'll be back soon, said Ma.

Yes.

Will Anna make it?

She will Ma.

OK.

Look, I'll ring her.

I rang Anna and got no reply. I texted Anna and got no reply. We sat a long time in silence. Then, a small man, Daddy, on a walking stick made his way very slow, slapping the tarmac in a circle with each step of his old loose pointed shoes. Passing he raised his stick to us. How are you, Daddy? said Ma. The same, he said, going on, and stopping, every few steps, to look ahead.

A caravan backed into a place by the river. The car cut its lights but no one got out. Paper blew.

Then on the dot of eleven forty-five Anna appeared. Some girls behind her in the alley called out Good night, see ya! after her. She walked towards us, looked round her and with a quick skip, opened the door and jumped in.

Hi, she said.

You've great timing.

Any crack, I asked, Lala?

Oh all my mates were there, lepping. But I kept looking round to see if you would appear.

I was outside on the street dancing I said.

Ah if only I had known.

Were you loyal, I asked.

Philip!

I was only asking.

She handed us both a a packet of crisps and left another on the dashboard in front of the driver's seat. A few minutes late at twelve o'clock Da came whistling into the car park.

I climbed over into the back, and Ma climbed into the passenger seat.

He sat in.

Busy enough night, he said as he turned the key.

Oh Jesus, I said, I forgot Joejoe's fags.

Don't worry, she said, we'll get them in the all-night, said Ma.

*

I looked in and there Joejoe was, seated, with his head in his hands, looking into the fire. I gave two knocks on his window, he replied with two quick smacks of a coin on the arm of his chair, then he rose his hand and saluted with his index finger without looking up from the fire.

I opened the door.

The dog shot up into his armchair.

Hallo Timmy, said Joejoe, you're welcome home.

How are you?

I'll tell you this – this is between us, you hear. The hair on my head is stinging my scalp.

Oh.

I'm destroyed. I might as well have a bunch of nettles on my head.

You had no visitors.

No I had no visitors, only this fucking stinging. I was expecting the Blackbird, but he never came. Your man out in that car drove him away. And no call for it either.

He suddenly leaped up.

Jesus. I'm destroyed. Will you do me back?

I hoisted his jacket and tore at his back.

Up! Up! Yes, there. Oh Christ.

Next thing Anna came in.

Ah Miss Conan, said Joejoe, you're welcome.

What are you doing?

I'm getting scratched.

You what?

Scratched.

That all right? I asked him.

Fine. Fine.

He sat.

He eyed me.

Well?

Well what.

There's a certain item outstanding.

Yes.

Me fags.

Oh Christ I forgot.

He shook his head sadly and squeezed his eyes closed. I put the packet of fags on the table. He lifted up a finger and pointed it at me.

You –

Ya little fucker ya, he said when he saw the fags. I was about to explode. You're some trickster. Isn't he Miss Conan! You see I was down to my last. Thank you, Mister Psyche. I won't forget you, ya fucker you.

Good night.

Good night.

And myself and Anna stepped into the night.

Chapter Fifteen

Sunday Dinner

I brought water to the sick cow who was lying in the meadow looking out to sea, did three lawns after Mass, the teacher's, the banker's and the German's, then I went to the wall at the back of the house. I was out there building stone for three hours. I had been at this dry-stone wall for three weeks, on-and-off, and it was good work. All you needed was a length of string, a few rocks and a sense of balance.

Sometimes I'd be building walls in my dreams.

Some of the stones I used had come inland in storms. But today I started to haul from an old ruin up on the bank overlooking the sea. I got an awful bad feeling as I pulled the rocks out of the ruin. I had to tell myself over and over that they were going back into another wall. The ruin was supposed to have been a henhouse way back, but it was the strongest-built henhouse I ever came across. There were massive stones in her. I could have been demolishing a small church, and sometimes I thought I was.

A beehive hut it might have been.

A monk's chamber.

I could even feel the sense of balance of the man who had built it.

He drew the stone from the coral beach by ass and cart to the spot I was taking them from. As he built alongside me, I was pulling his work down. As he dropped a stone into place, I lifted it and carried it away. He built towards me, and I built away from him. I could feel the way he carried himself. He could have been a great-great-granduncle of mine. In his wall

I came across chaffs of wheat that were still dry. The bones of coral. White marble. One clay pipe. I was over and back with the barrow, then I began to build. And he came with me. Fit in, stand back, put in a small stone, and follow the twine.

Good man.

He stood to the side watching me work.

The light was going and coming. And there were sudden gusts of wind coming from the north-west. An empty bucket went flying across the field. A heave of salt flew across. Then up went a puff of sparks from the rusted transformer on the electric pole next the house. The gust passed. The sky darkened. There was the one faraway cackle of seagulls. The island drifted out of sight.

Good evening, said my father.

I got an awful shock to find him standing behind me, right where I had placed the stone man.

Time to call a halt, he said. It's getting dark. And we have a visitor for dinner mind you. I am trying to take a weight off your shoulders Philip.

I put in a few more stones, and stood against the wall, then sort-of took cover, ducked low, and turned for the house.

Joejoe was seated at the head of the table. He was in his Sunday best. I could not believe it.

How is the man? he asked me.

I'm grand.

You did not expect to see me.

I did not.

I only ever eat in my own house, but I was coerced from below be a concentration of mind from that woman there, Miss Geraldine Lockett, your mother, and I couldn't say no.

Joejoe was mad to chat. And the chat was mighty. The wine was out, and the whiskey. I was allowed one glass of white and I drank it in a very old-fashioned way. Like in an ad. Rain was lashing against the windows.

Ma was about to carve the leg of lamb that was doused in wild mint leaves.

Good luck, said Joejoe.

Good luck, said Da.

Then the lights gave and the house suddenly went black.

This is grand, said Joejoe.

For a moment we sat there in the dark by the table as the storm raged round us.

Here, said Joejoe and he struck a match and handed the box to Da.

What the hell – Da cracked a match.

Buck it, he said, the shagging salt has eroded the insulator again!

The match went dead.

He lit another and got up on a chair and looked up at the fuse board. No good, he said. We're out.

The search for candles began.

I have two boxes below, said Joejoe.

I meant only yesterday to buy some, said Da.

Blast it, said Ma.

You know what, said Joejoe in the dark, we could have the dinner down in my house.

Joejoe, will you stop. Why did this have to happen?

There were no candles to be found except one tiny Christmas candle that Ma had in her room. Da struck another match and went looking for the lamp. No lamp.

Where did you leave the torch, he asked me.

I don't know, I said.

I headed round the dark house looking and found nothing.

This is bucking disastrous.

Everything is going cold, said Ma.

We'll find a way. I knew I should have got them to install a new generator, said Da. The salt has it eaten.

That's the third time this year, said Ma.

It's shocking.

Well now, said Joejoe, you know what you'll do, go down and get my oil-lamp.

Right, I suppose, said Da, eventually.

And remember the candles are in the kitchen-table drawer.

OK. Yeh. Yeh. The shame of it.

When he opened the door the wind blew the candle out. Feck it, he said.

Then he stood looking round him.

The whole country is in the dark, he said. They are all out.

He closed the door, stepped in and lit the candle again, left us the matches and went out the back. We sat there in the dark by the one fluttering butt. Our faces swam. We disappeared from each other. Then Ma served the meat and spuds in the dark. It was touch-and-go. Thank you very much, said Joejoe, you could be feeding us anything. She was a shadow. You could not see the plates. Then the little candle went out. For good.

Good luck, said Joejoe in the dark.

Good luck, I said.

Whiskey tastes better in the dark.

Is that so?

Oh yes, said Joejoe and he put a glass into my hand.

Then Ma's hand touched my shoulder.

What's keeping him, I wonder, said Ma.

We were there for ages. Rowing. Going over and back across the same wave. In the distance my mobile rang. It was like a firefly. I lifted it to my ear. What's happening, said Anna. I'm sitting down to a very pleasant dinner, I said, by candlelight. Ah so your lights are gone as well. Yes, I said. Chat ya, she said. Now we were back in the time of the stone man that built the henhouse. He was having his revenge. We ate with our hands. You felt round the plate and took whatever came handy. Then Da came back at last with the lamp. I got lost, he said, in your house. I had no matches. I could see nothing. Joejoe lit the lamp and placed it centre of the table. Soon candles were blinking everywhere and slowly we could all see something of ourselves. We were a funny crew. We kept going and coming.

All around us was the dark.

And the dark was frothing.

It's like old times, said Joejoe. Good luck.

Good luck, said Da.

I'm glad you asked me up. This is the way I like it. Thank you Miss Lockett for your kindness. We forget what we owe to what we've forgotten till we encounter it again out of the corner of the eye, in passing.

We were sitting by the roaring fire when Joejoe said: The mind is a terror.

It is that, said Ma, and the body is something else.

True for you. I didn't know I had a body for a long time.

How come?

Me body was a sort of a ghost. Coming behind me. But I knew from the beginning that the mind was there. Take the Blackbird, he has a fierce mind. But he has only a slither of a body like myself. Do you think a lot?

– Who are you talking to? Ma asked –

– That fellow over there –

– Me? –

– Yes, you –

– I do, I said in his direction, I think a lot –

– But you don't tell us what you're thinking, do you, though I can see you at it all the time –

– Anna thinks out loud, I said –

– That's because she's an honest person –

– The mind is never asleep, continued Joejoe. I was in bed the other night and I spent hours trying to get back into my old house. I was haunted. I was down on the beach there looking for the gate, and eventually I found it and came up to the house and went round it and round it looking for the door, but was there a door, there was no door.

That's terrible, said Ma.

Anna had a dream the other night, I said, that she was trapped in a coffin, and she began to shout and shout for them to let her out.

But they didn't come, said Joejoe.

No.

They never do. That same dream goes back in the Conan family. I remember her grandmother telling me she used to wake screaming thinking she was in the grave. And her father before her. One of them a long time ago must have been buried alive back in France –

– I didn't know that–

– It's true –

– Jesus, no one ever told me that before –

– And it's stayed in the memory.

– This is rare talk, said my father –

– It is. You'll get that. The mind is a bad actor. Good luck –

– Good luck –

– Christ, I said.

Joejoe drew on his fag and he tapped sparks into the grate.

We were still sitting by candlelight and the oil lamp at midnight when things went wrong. Ma had just filled out another round of drinks, when Da suddenly said Sure you might as well stay the night.

No thank you, said Joejoe.

But we have your lamp.

I have more candles below. I have all I need.

The bed is there, made up, and ready for you.

I don't want to stay.

There's no need to be angry.

I came up here for the dinner, do you understand.

Joejoe, I was just offering you a bed.

You were trying to trick me. To get me out of me house below.

No I was not. Was I Geraldine?

No.

I'll go now thank you.

OK, I'll get the car.

There's no need for the car. I'll walk.

Across my dead body.

Joejoe stood and his face went into the darkness.

You can bring me my lamp tomorrow. The young fellow can walk me down. Isn't that right – you.

Yes, I said, though I could not see him.

Hold on there, hold on everyone. Look I can drive you.

No. But there's one thing you can do. You can say you're sorry to the Blackbird.

I will.

Are you right? he said to me.

His shadow grew on the back wall.

You can't walk on a night like that. And if are going to walk, said Da, you'll need a blooming lamp.

I'm walking.

God help us.

I need my independence. Where's me coat?

Ah dear.

Where's me coat!

Just then the electric lights came back on.

It was like someone had suddenly taken a photograph of us. There was the three of us looking at Joejoe and he was standing with his arms out reaching in the wrong direction for the door. He turned and looked back at us as if struck. We seemed to have leaped back into existence. Next door in the kitchen the radio started talking about Baroque music. In the corner the

TV came on speaking of a new rise in wages. We had been in the black without faces, just a nose or a mouth, then suddenly we were in colour, and the whole face was a surprise; before there had only been the voices, then suddenly there in front of you was the face and the body that accompanied what was being spoken. We had gone in one evening from darkness to a single candle, then to lamplight, then back to electric light.

And into an argument.

I was sorry we were back in the known world.

This is all wrong, said Da. You're taking me up all wrong.

Forget about it.

Sit down now for a while.

Are you right, said Joejoe, turning to me.

Yes.

Take the lamp with you at least, said Da.

No, bring it down tomorrow.

He took my arm and we set off across the yard with Ma and Da standing behind us at the open door. We took a right down the lane, stopped, and tried to let our eyes adjust. I felt out for the small wall with my foot. His fingers dug into my arm. I could not see a fucking thing. The hedge of olearia had disappeared. The wind from the north-west struck my left ear like a knife. Over the rocks the sea pounded.

Do you know where we are?

No, I said.

We went on a bit further.

We'll be straight into the rocks.

Steady.

We stood a minute.

I heard the car start back up at the house. Then it came on down behind us till the full lights bounced over our shoulders. And that's how we walked, being shepherded by the Fiat down the lane, like folk being driven from some town for wrongdoing, it was like walking on the moon, then onto the road, two long bustling shadows ahead of us, till we reached the gate, and I walked him to the door while the car stopped out on the road for home and lit up the front of the house. It was blinding. Joejoe said nothing as he unlocked the door. I lit a match and he took out the candles and lit four, one for the window, one for the bedroom, one for the toilet and one for the mantelpiece.

Ma came in with Joejoe's lamp in her hand.

Here you are, she said.

There was no need.

No bother, she said.

He followed her out to the gate.

Thank you Nurse Lockett, he said to Ma as she sat in behind the wheel. You are a lady. That was one lovely Sunday dinner.

I'll see you, she said, Joejoe.

Goodnight.

Goodnight!

I sat in and Ma turned round on the road, flashed the lights as Joejoe waved, and we crawled back to the house.

Why did that have to happen? said Ma.

Don't worry.

Da was seated inside by the fire looking into the flames.

The cursed lights, he said.

We sat round for a while, then the phone rang and Ma answered it.

Yes, OK, she said.

I have to go in, they're short of staff.

A few minutes later she took off. I sat with Da a while, then said good night.

When I went to my room I found the missing torch to the left of my bed. I got in beneath the sheets and started building stone after stone after stone into a wall.

Chapter Sixteen

Working the Beach

I went down to feed the pots and took home eight lobsters. As I worked on the wall I saw the Fiat pull in. Later I came up for a cup of tea and tiptoed through the house for fear of waking Ma. Then I heard the TV on in the living room. I found Ma in a white sheet lying out on the sofa trying to change stations with the father's mobile.

Ma, I said, that's the mobile phone.

Is that what it is?

Yes.

Can you believe it!

The item you need is the remote.

Thank you, I know that. There is no need to be so condescending.

This is the lad, I said.

No, you do it. Get me something nice. Something where everything is light and airy. I've had enough of tragedy. There was a football final in town yesterday, and so in they came, all night, one drunk after another, and they flutered.

I found her a black-and-white movie on TV 4.

At least there was one bit of crack. Owney Brady came in and he says I'm after stout in Clarke's and it's fastened to me lips, then he fetched down on the bed. The mother laughed. And he says, You know it's only five-thirty in the morning in New York. Now that's casualty for you, she said. There was pure enjoyment in her voice. Is that Greta Garbo I wonder? She watched the box a while. Turn it off, she said, I'm so moidered I can't follow it.

I turned to the news.

No thank you, she said, I've had it up to here.

I switched the TV off.

Thank you. Good, some silence.

She undid her shoes.

It's a strange life. By the time I get in, he's gone. And by the time he's back I'm on my way out the door. I'll be glad when nights are over.

So will he.

And what will we do with the auld fellow. Bullets through the blooming window. I'm losing touch. If anyone hears what's going on we'll all be put away.

She stood and wiped down her skirt.

Then paused.

I saw the saddest thing as I was coming off duty. She lifted one foot then the other to look at her heels, and pointed a finger toward me. About a month ago the gynaecologist died. And his dog seemingly comes up to the hospital every day looking for him. So I'm told. She rubbed her eyes and forehead, lifted her head as if to concentrate on the sentence she had just finished. I never saw him till this morning. A fox terrier. And there he was being walked round the grounds by one of the patients at the crack of dawn. And this happens every day. Leaping in the air, she said, chasing the ghost of his master.

With her toes she traced semicircles on the tiles.

I'll go up now, I think.

See you later, Ma.

Aye. And there we were standing around an agitated man in the nude and what were we nurses talking about – community hours, overtime, planning permission and the days off that we are entitled to – that sort of crack, and then she mounted the stairs shaking her head.

The thing now was to stay quiet. I boiled the lobsters and left them out to cool down then I got a book by Grisham and sat in on a shooting downtown. I heard the father's car coast to a stop in the early noon. He took off his boots at the door, came in and heated a can of Heinz spaghetti and had it with toasted soldiers.

How's things, he whispered.

Grand.

The mother all right?

She's fine.

Good.

Jesus, so that's where it was, he said lifting his mobile. Do you want to take a break from the wall and come with me in the bucket for a while?

I'd love to.

He washed the dishes, dried them, made ham sandwiches and a flask of tea and left a note for the mother, then we drove to the next beach where his digger stood on the dunes. We put on our ear muffs. The beach looked like it was inhabited by aliens. Piles of small rocks had come in with tall pods of seaweed flowering from them. The roots clenched the stones with a drowning man's grip. There were hundreds of them, standing up straight, going this way, that way. It was like a demented garden. I climbed into the bucket and we drove down toward a crowd of huge rocks brought inland by the storm. Then I got into the box behind him. It was freezing and full of draughts and the loud noise of bad memories.

Now, he said.

I leaned forward, turned the ignition and shot back in time.

He pressed down with his foot.

We started forward, then I grabbed the handle to lower the bucket and we tucked in under the first rock. He pushed forward, tipped, let her weight carry her in, the iron roared, then he lifted the bucket high and we turned back to the sea wall and dropped the huge rock into place.

Now, he said. The trick is to imagine that there is always an electric wire running over your head, just up there, and if you touch it you'll blow your self up, so that's how you teach yourself that you should only go lifting to a certain height. Right?

Right, I said as he pointed up at where there was only an open sky, and said Do you see it – the electric wire?

I do.

Good.

What you imagine soon becomes a law. Isn't that so?

Yes.

Good lad.

He got in behind me and I sat into the seat. I let in the pedal and we took a jump then hurtled forward.

Now, take yon one!

We jumped again, I turned the tracks, the digger braced itself.

Lower her.

I did.

And went in nicely underneath but when I swung the bucket up the weight of the rock carried it out over the lip.

Buck it, I said.

I backed and screeched forward into the sand an inch at a time, got well underneath and swung her up.

Aisy, he said.

The bucket swayed dangerously.

Remember the wire, he shouted.

I will, I shouted.

Easy son, easy!

I levelled. Turned. She was a great weight. I throttled forward slowly, then when I reached the sea wall I held her a moment, this way that way, then dropped her clean onto his rock, and she shivered, then held. I nudged her in with the bucket. Then he took over, the box warmed up, and for a couple of hours without talking we took turns to traverse the beach and the lane like moon men going through the tall shoots of seaweed, pulling out from inland the debris from the storm, screeching in under one rock after another, all soaked black and blistered with fossils, the sand heaved and fell, the tracks screamed, we lifted, swivelled and trundled in.

At last he switched the engine off. I took off my muffs and heard the sound of rocks and steel and the roar of brakes still screeching in my ears. He turned on his transistor. The Pogues were singing. We sang along. He broke open the sandwiches and we sat in the box eating and drinking the tea. You could tell that he had spent a lot time in here. It was another room from home.

Beyond the sea was panting white, spuming across the lava and flurries of salt blew by.

Further out on the horizon there was this great darkness gathering.

The plastic window of the box rattled.

It's not finished yet, he said. He hit the ignition and swung back towards the stones.

So, he shouted, he wants me to say I'm sorry.

A flock of gulls rose. The talking stopped. I took the wheel, and then he took the wheel. Till near dark we were there going to and fro, swivelling along the cluttered beach. The sea wall grew. The tracks of the machine dug deep into the sand. Sometimes when he'd give me a go, I'd watch his eye; but now when he took over, he went on by himself, working as if I wasn't there, foot in, foot out, pulling on the handle, lowering, then at last he'd stop a moment to see what we had built, look back to see what there was left to do, then he'd turn a complete circle on the spot swinging the bucket high as if to say we're done and we went back along the beach, leaving a deep trail behind us, up onto the dunes, onto the road, he lowered the bucket, and cut the engine.

A sore day, he said.

The box shook, the digger settled down.

The sea won't come in there again for a while, he said. We sat there a while watching the next storm come racing in with threads of rain. Soon the shower was pelting the box.

Then he said Light drizzles expected. Sunshine at intervals. Showers turning to rain. Yes. We got into the car and sat there for maybe an hour being lashed by the rain and the wind. He never stirred. The tide was going out. A calm descended. All of a sudden the Blackbird appeared out of nowhere on his bike carrying a bucket. He set off down the beach to pick winkles followed by his dog. Da got out and followed him, and out the rocks they faced each other, and shook hands in the drizzle, then the Bird bent down and began to pick.

The dog sat in front of him watching his every move.

I took the mother a cup of tea in bed. She was sitting bolt upright looking into the distance.

Ma.

Who is that?

It's me.

Yes?

Tay.

Oh.

She took the cup and turned to me.

Where were you? I asked.

On the other side.

And how are things there?

I'm sad to say things there are the same as here. Just the fecking same. She laughed. Thank you.

No problem.

She looked round the ceiling.

I loved beauty board – the old panelling on the walls – but they've done away with the beauty board. The risk of fire, mind ya. If you had beauty board you could find strangers looking down at you from the whorls of wood. All classes. People you hadn't seen in years.

See ya.

Yes. I've been thinking. I've been thinking of holding a party for your Joejoe. In fact I've contacted the priest. I think a bit of religion might settle his mind. So we're going to have the Stations below in his house.

When?

Soon.

He'll like that, I said, and I headed out to the unfinished wall.

That night both houses feasted on lobsters. I went up to the pub for the bottle of Malibu and a bag of cheese and onion crisps. Only Frosty was at the bar. Alongside him were all the stools and chairs without a soul sitting there. Liverpool was playing Chelsea on the box. Mister John's daughter Sara was listening to Johnny Cash. I put the fifty-cent in the slot machine and lost.

That's the way, said Frosty.

I walked down to Ballintra where the two men were seated by the fire and told Joejoe that Ma was throwing a party for him.

Of late there's being a lot of talk in this house about fairies, said Joejoe. The fairies are like old relations.

She means it.

But then I suppose we all spend a lot of time talking about folk we never met. It's like when you read out the newspapers to me. The car crash, the court case, the get-together.

Except Joejoe you might run into someone you know in the newspaper, said the Blackbird.

True.

And not only the living.

Explain.

That's where you might find the dead.

Oh aye. The obituaries.

In living memory of.

The same.

He passed away on the first of May.

Got you. Thank you. That's enough for now, Mister Blackbird. The head can only take so much, amn't I right Psyche.

You are.

He poured out two dots of Malibu.

Ma said she is going to hold the Stations, I said.

The Stations! said the Blackbird. Where?

Here.

Here in this house?

Yes.

Who's coming?

Well for a start – the priest.

Who else? asked Joejoe.

The whole crew.

Meaning?

Everyone.

The Blackbird came to his feet.

Well that man there will be my main guest, and Joejoe pointed at the Bird who suddenly bowed out through the front door with a lit fag in his mouth like a man on a journey.

Chapter Seventeen

The Photographer

The day before the Stations I headed down to *The Ostrich*.

Anna was singing with her earphones on *It's murder on the dance floor, but you'd better not kill the groove.*

Hallo, I shouted.

Ah!

Are you coming over to Joejoe's tomorrow.

I will of course.

Great.

By the way, she asked, did you notice anything strange on your way down.

No.

Nothing?

Nothing at all.

Well when I arrived there was a funny crowd down the beach, all dressed up like. I thought I was losing it.

I didn't see anyone.

One of them had a straw hat on. And a mask.

And?

The others were like balloons. She paused and tucked back the side of her hair with her fingertips. Hallo! I hollered, Hallo! I thought I was seeing things, but they never even looked in my direction.

We went up on deck.

She gawked about her.

Then we climbed up the ladder and went down the beach.

He was standing just there where you are now, said Anna.

Well he's gone now.

You don't believe me.

I do.

He's somewhere.

What are you on Anna?

I saw him.

We stood there a while. Myself, Anna. In the slanted light. A red lorry of gravel pitching forward on the graveyard road. On the low wall the long shaft of a magpie.

Hallo! Anna hollered.

No one appeared.

Hallo, she shouted again. We went back to *The Ostrich* and stood on deck looking down the shore.

It's funny the things you remember even as you make them up again, she said, Mister Jeremiah.

We went into the cabin. A few minutes later, we heard these footsteps and there was a knock on the cabin door. Anna opened it, and there stood a cameraman, and he says do you mind if I film from your boat?

Go ahead Anna said.

We followed him out on deck.

He waved.

And a second later round Shell corner came a man in white hat and white face and each side of him two people dressed as animals, and next came the folk in balloons with the sea-spray shooting up behind them and to the side stood the sound man with his long mike held aloft.

Now, said Anna, there they are. I'm glad they reappeared. I was beginning to get worried.

Sorry about the intrusion, said the cameraman as he looked into the lens.

Not at all. I thought I was having hallucinations.

We went in and sat in the cabin.

Now Philip, she lifted one of her tomes, ran through the pages, stopped and said: Now answer me this what bird does not kill?

Hold it – let me think.

Anything?

I don't know.

Read that.

I took the book and she pointed with the tip of a feather –There!

Only the vulture does not kill, I read out loud.

Now for you. But it doesn't stop them eating.

No.

You see the thing has to be dead first before you can eat it, therefore someone has to kill it.

True.

Unless you're considering eating it alive.

Stop.

Anna took back the book and looked at her feet.

That's the story, she said.

Then that evening back at home the phone rang. Ma was just in the door from shopping and she took the call out in the hall then came in and sat down.

Who was that?

Your Uncle Joe.

She shook her head.

He's away with the fairies, she said.

What's wrong?

He's suffering from delusions. He said that he had seen lights. Fireworks, said Ma, and other things.

Oh Christ.

That he had imagined that there was a cleaning force due to tidy the shop – meaning the house – but he could not see them. I said the troops would be round on the morrow.

It's the film crew Ma.

What film crew?

I started to explain but then a few minutes later the phone rang again but by the time I got to it, he'd rung off.

I rang back on my mobile but he didn't answer.

Ma was going on night duty to the hospital. She brought a saucepan of soup with her, and bread rolls. She placed a few items in the boot. I took a lift with her down to Joejoe's and as I stepped in the gate with the hoover I met the Bird coming up from the house with a tall sack, wrapped round something, over his back.

What are you carrying?

You don't want to know, he said.

He climbed onto the bike and headed off with the sack over his shoulder. I watched him go wondering and stepped in, with Ma following me with the soup and bread rolls.

Was the Bird doing a bit of tidying for you? she asked.

He was, he said, yeh, that's right – he cleaned out the whole shop.

He looked at me sharply.

You're not going to start that yoke tonight, he asked, pointing at the vacuum cleaner.

No, I said.

Thanks beta God.

Then Ma brought him in a blue airman's shirt, with two breast pockets, his Christmas jacket, a tin of snuff and a copy of the daily newspaper, and took off to her night shift.

He stood by the fire ironing his tweeds and a white lace handkerchief.

Well? You have the bad look in your eye, he said to me.

No, I haven't.

Yes you have, what is it?

Nothing.

What are you saying?

Nothing. You saw fireworks?

I did.

I missed them.

We'll not talk about it.

OK. I could explain, Grandda.

I don't want to know . . . Are you all right Mister Psyche?

I'm just tired.

Settle, he said, you're making me nervous. He ironed on. Will you do me a favour? I didn't answer. Give us a reading from the Gospels, he said.

Now?

Aye, if you don't mind.

No bother. Which one?

You pick.

Psalm 102.

The very thing.

Hear my prayer, O Lord, and let my cry come unto thee. Hide not thy face from me in the day when I am in trouble; incline thine ear unto me: in the day when I call answer me speedily. For my days are consumed like smoke, and my bones are burned as a hearth. My heart is smitten, and withered like grass; so that I forget to eat my bread. By reason of the voice of my groaning my bones cleave to my skin. I am a pelican of the wilderness; I am like an owl of the desert.

Say that again.

I am like an owl of the desert.

Yes.

I watch, and am as a sparrow upon the house top. Mine enemies reproach me all the day; and they that are mad against me are sworn against me. For I have eaten ashes like bread, and mingled my drink with weeping, because of thine indignation and thy wrath: for thou hast lifted me up, and cast me down. My days are like a shadow that declineth; and I am withered like grass.

Like grass, he said.

Aye.

Like grass Psyche.

Yes.

I closed the Bible and sat opposite him.

He laid out the flat handkerchief very carefully on his knee. There would be no trees for him to land on, out there, would there, on the sands, the poor owl, he said. I never saw one in my life. He carefully folded in the four corners of the handkerchief, and patted it, and went back with a hum to his ironing as if his spirits had lifted. I went walking the sour path. I saw that the rifle had been taken off the wall. I read him of a bank robbery, the discovery of a golden torc – an ancient Celtic necklace – in a wardrobe, and how a male librarian delivered a baby for a woman who gave birth in a back room filled with antique books written in Latin.

We climbed Croagh Patrick on a television programme, then headed down a side road in Baghdad behind a line of soldiers. As we watched the news Timmy crouched between Joejoe's knees and he petted the dog, over and over, leaning down sometimes to whisper in his ear, then when I turned off the telly the animal went back up into his chair.

I took all the newspapers and turf and timber and put them in a heap out in the shed, leaving only what was needed for the fire on the morrow. I sat looking into the embers till near one in the morning, and he brought me tea, and, then, suddenly a fire-rocket shot up into the sky past the window. We opened the door. Another shoot of rockets went off down the beach, and stars were spilling into sea, and Timmy was shaking.

What's going on?

They are shooting a film on the beach, I said.

Where are you going?

I'm just going outside, I said, for a minute.

Watch yourself.

I stood by the pier of the gate watching the stars. My mobile rang: Did you see that? asked Anna. I did, I said. I'm glad, she replied. More sky rockets took off and the Audi again suddenly careered off the road again in my head. I took a deep breath.

150

Down the road from the beach came a man dressed in white, with a torch. He had on a stiff white mask, and a stiff black beard and wide black boots laced up the ankle. Would you have the loan of a euro? I asked him. He shook his head and stared straight ahead. He did not speak to white trash like me. After him, out of the dark, came a Leopard with a lantern walking very coquettish on its back legs. Good evening, I said, are ye training for Halloween? He bowed. The very thing, said the Leopard. And lastly along came a young girl all in black, with a tiny snip of light pointed at her feet, carrying the fireworks. Then the cameraman and the soundman called out goodnight as they passed by.

It's busy, tonight, I said to Joejoe as I sat down.

In here as well, he said, and he tapped his head.

I feel fierce low, I said, and he gave me a shot of whiskey in honey for the road.

Was it the lights?

Maybe.

The lights did it, I think Mister Psyche.

They did.

Say a prayer, he said.

I thank the sea, I said.

You do.

And I thank the Bird.

Good man.

And the dog.

When he heard the sound of the name of his species Timmy got up and nodded. Then he and me stepped out the door together. I looked towards Templeboy. Good night, Mickey, I called up the road in a whisper in my head. The dog started shaking. The moon was in its third.

I got into bed and sailed off in the boat-house. The road snapped and the house came free and we went out onto the waves.

Then the oars overhead began moving. And the roof came in and out like an accordion. We fell to one side then the other. The wind was deafening, the house groaned and soon there were huge fish swimming by the windows. I saw a big yellow shipwreck rusting at the end of the garden. There were all these fish snapping at bright blue flowers that grew out of its walls. An octopus clung to the window and he looked in at me.

He moved his arms in slow motion like a bush in wind.

Who are you? he was saying over and over.

But I could not say my name. It would not come to my lips. He got closer and blacked off the window so that you could see nothing. The room went black as ink. I held my breath. I could hear him tapping gently on the window. Tap-tap. Tap-tap. Who are you? Let me in, he was saying. I could hear him breathing. It was a long slow breath. A heaving. Then we seemed to take off in a hurry and somersaulted and there we were on the top of the boiling water again. There was no land only water.

The rain fell harder and harder.

Down the chimney it came.

Then we struck something and came to a standstill. I looked out the window to see we were on an island, with the flood waters flowing. The cow was strolling with her calf in a further high field. The grey Connemara pony was standing looking at the grey crow. I read the cuttings from the newspapers. How the wind had shot down and taken a baby out of her cot into the sky.

That's her, that'd be it.

Eventually we hit the calm waters.

Chapter Eighteen

The Stations

How is the Nurse? Joejoe asked me next morning.

She's fine.

Good. I was told we were having a hooley, next thing I hear it's the blooming Stations.

I put the plug in the socket.

Don't, he roared.

I have to.

Don't!

I turned the vacuum on. As the volume rose he held up the palm of his hand. He roared something I couldn't hear. I switched it off.

I hate that yoke, he said.

I turned it on again.

He came across, and placed his hand on mine to force the handle down, then shouted into my ear I'm going! He tiptoed off in his stocking feet and long johns to the scullery. I pushed the vacuum cleaner into his bedroom and started at the foot of his two-poster. Some tobacco and a few grey hairs and one clot of toffee. Outside Timmy was barking like mad. Against the skirting boards I sucked up a few shivers of plaster that had fallen from below the weeping stone on the wall. Otherwise the room was clean. He'd placed a stiff wooden-armed chair that usually sat out in the woodshed to the side of the window for the priest to sit into, with a cushion on the ground to the left for kneeling purposes when confession started. I brought down spiders' webs from overhead. And from under the bed I cleared an old spill of sawdust, and crumbs. Then, below his pillow, fallen onto the bedsprings, I found a St Anthony's medallion on a black string and I put it back for luck on his mantelpiece. I came into the kitchen and plugged in. Ash from the fire, and plaited hair from Timmy flew into the bag with a growl. I cleaned round the grate, below the dresser, along the walls, and reached the back window when suddenly I heard the sound of something hard shooting up the pipe.

I switched off, and knelt down on the rug to see if there were anything else solid down there, but there was nothing. It was spotless. I switched on again to see if the tube was split, then I hoovered on, but again there was an almighty rattle, and the hoover went up into a high whine. Joejoe appeared in the doorway.

What is that? he roared.

I don't know.

Shut it down, he roared pointing, then pointing again at the socket.

I hit the button. The kitchen went down to quiet.

I think, I said, that a stone shot up.

Stone, my arse, empty it! Empty it!

We went outside. He watched me as I took the bag and emptied the soot, and plaster and hair into a pile on the footpath. He got down on his knees and felt through the dust, and then suddenly paused. He lifted whatever it was into the palm of his hand – a single euro. He got up, leaned down and stirred the dust, then went in. He put the coin on the kitchen table.

I thought it was the fucking bullet, he said.

I didn't think of that.

Because you don't believe me!

He lifted the coin and put it on the dresser. Money does not travel far these days, he said, and damp-kneed he headed back toward the scullery, then at the door he stopped, turned, twirled a forefinger, returned and moved the ship and sails to the left of the plates on the dresser, stood the plaster dog on a thin box of plasters in the upper shelf, then shifted the photo of himself and Grandda and Grandma to the centre of second shelf, stepped back and nodded.

What's needed Mister Psyche?

I don't know.

Christ's tears, he said.

Ah, the fuchsia.

Correct.

I'll go get the flowers when I've finished here.

I hoovered on under the table and over to the mat inside the front door. There was a sudden squeal of brakes, and Ma arrived in with lilies and wild daisies. She put a pot in every window, then washed the table down. I hung the mat on the washing line and beat it senseless. The dog turned and looked at me a long time on the doorstep. We lugged in the cups and plates and green doilies. Next thing Anna arrived with two apple and rhubarb tarts and a few dozen sandwiches.

Joejoe came in from the scullery in his tweed jacket and the airman's shirt.

Ah Miss Conan, he said.

Mister Feeney, said Anna, how wonderful you look.

He dusted his bum, then dusted the seat of his chair and sat down. He pulled up the leg of his trousers and scratched.

There's fecking perfume in the soap, and he scratched again. I told them not to put it in but they do.

It's shocking bad taste, she said.

Cruel out, he said, it would not be right on the night of the Stations.

Have you all your sins off, she asked.

Every last one, he said.

Good, I'm off to pick the last of your peas, sir, she said, and went.

Ma cleaned the holy pictures of the Virgin and Child. Re-hung the polished rosary beads on its nail. Took down the mirror and shined it, and hung it back on the wall, righted the fiddle and then looked round her: Where is your rifle?

He hesitated. I put it away for safekeeping, he said.

Oh.

He took up his boots and began polishing them.

Give me your shoes, he said.

I took them off.

He went with his brush from boot to shoe, and shoe to boot, and back again like a man sawing. Then he spat on the tips and drew a rag tight across for the final polish.

There, he said, and I began threading the laces back in.

At seven my father and mother arrived with a trailer-load of chairs from Mister John's. We stacked the ones with armrests against the walls, then placed two plain rows before the small wormeaten table that Ma took in from the scullery. She draped the white linen cloth over the table. Sweet John arranged three trays of glasses in the visitors' room where my father was raised as a child, then plonked a bucket of ice in the fridge.

She cut lemons and parsley, and chopped wild celery.

Joejoe sat bolt upright in his armchair, legs crossed, hair up in a tuft, supervising.

Da brought the whiskey and gin into the third room. There was the loud pop of a cork, then another.

Now, said Ma.

Very good.

Is that everything, pray?

Lachrimae Christi, he said.

Excuse me, is that a prayer?

The fuchsia, I said, Christ's tears. Sorry Joejoe, I forgot.

You forgot the monk's bush?

Forgive me.

Never let it be said, announced Da, and he went off with a scissors and came back a few minutes later with a handful of early dripping red flowers from a bush up the road, and Joejoe took them, emptied one of the pots of lilies, then carefully arranged the young branch of fuchsia into it instead, watered it, and set the pot of Christ's Tears on the worktop of the dresser between the alarm clock and the plaster cast of Jesus.

Alert the troops, he said. Da went out the door and Ma went into the scullery to shred lettuce and parsley. Beside her Anna was making pea soup, with hoards of wild mint and coriander. Beside her Ma started to make a second fish soup with mussels and lobsters and mackerel I'd collected that morning. I fed a log onto the fire. Then Joejoe called me in with his forefinger till he had my ear to his mouth, and he whispered, looking straight into my eyes, Tell me this Psyche, do you ever tire of being a servant?

No, I whispered.

Are you lying? he asked, widening his eyes.

Yes sir, I said, with a bow.

I locked Timmy outside in the car just before the parties started arriving. He was to be the alarm signal.

Da took up his position at the door.

Anna went out to the gate.

A few minutes later came the first bark, and through the door came the Dunleavys. Joejoe stood and took their hands. Another bark. In came the two Carters in shining black. He rose in welcome. Mister and Mrs Tingle stepped in with a box of daisies; then Frosty arrived and went by Joejoe and took my hand, and said: I was baptised too, you know. In came Mrs Flynn, J. D. Moffit, the coalman Mister Awesome, Barney Buckley, Jim Simpson, Terence MacGowan, with old Mister Bree. And Mick Doyle with Stefan who was dressed in green.

Mister John went out the back door and came in the front with a bottle of Sandemans port. Thady came in a grey suit, with the image of a grey hurley stitched onto his tie, and sat at the back, wiping his knees, and hummed. The widows spent a long time turning their car to face back the way they'd come, then they entered, gravely, nodded at Joejoe, and sat alone smiling in the centre of the front row. Mister and Mrs Conan stepped in with Anna and they immediately asked if there was anything they could do to help. Joe Currid came with fresh-cooked mackerel stuffed with prawn. You won't take exception, he said, to me bringing a lock of food into the house for afterwards, and he laid it on the side table. Joejoe suddenly took a portion, downed his chin onto his chest, and chewed sharply, lifted his head back and was about to swallow when I said: You will not be able to receive communion.

He spat it into the fire.

Was it any good? asked Joe.

The business, he said.

The Blackbird landed, parked his bike down by the reeds, then came through the door, with his eyes narrowed, looking from side to side.

Oh, he said speaking to no one, and he stepped by Joejoe quick, as if they were strangers, and sat into a chair along the back wall. Joejoe gave him the thumb, then his eyes swung back to the door.

With each bark of the dog, he was on his feet to greet all arrivals. But in between all the small talk, I could see his eyes were trained on the window, and there was a note of warning in them. He was watching for the General. Madam Adams and her husband, the artist, who lived at the Cross arrived with begonias and blue cheddar, and the widows introduced themselves and began explaining to them the meaning of the Stations. It's a Mass said in a house, said Bridie, who held a hanky to her mouth, and there's confession beforehand.

There is, agreed May.

And you are –? asked Madam.

We are the widows, said Lilly Mannion.

You lost your husbands? she said astonished.

No, we never married.

Oh.

Claus and Ingabore came with doughnuts and nut bread, then turned to go again, without explanation.

Hallo, shouted Joejoe.

Goodbye, said Claus. We go now.

Hallo, shouted Joejoe, higher this time.

Please, said Claus, we shall return, sometime again, and he gave a quick smile and stepped out with his wife who stiffly waved the fingers of her right hand. And then Mister and Mrs Brady – Mickey's parents – entered. Mother squeezed my shoulder. They looked round the room, then immediately came over and took my hands. The place went silent.

I'm so glad you came, I said.

Philip, my heart goes out to you, said Mrs Brady and she kissed me on the cheek. We miss Mickey a lot, and I know you do too.

It's all right son, said Mister Brady. It's all right.

Ah Sean and Patricia Brady, said Joejoe, come in and sit down. You are very welcome.

I led the Bradys by the hand to two armchairs in the middle of the room, then I returned to Joejoe's side.

Good man Mister Psyche, he said, and he tapped both of my knees and put his shoulder against mine.

As the people of the townland gathered they sat against the walls or in rows, chatting; no one ate or drank; then, at last, at 7.30 the priest ducked in, shook himself, went over and put his chalice on the small table, breathed out with a shake of his shoulders, who have we here, he said and he wandered off to meet the stranger as the locals came up and shook hands with Joejoe, then Father Grimes sat forninst my granduncle.

I'm sorry to be taking you out, Father, said Joejoe.

Not at all.

You see I'm not able to get to the church these days.

Say nothing.

But if I am able to get to the pub, I should be able to get to the church. And I'm sorely tempted by the pub at times.

Always give in to temptation, said Father Grimes. Isn't that right sonny?

Yes, I said.

There is one good sign Father, said Joejoe.

Is that so?

Yes, I've stopped telling lies to people I know, said Joejoe, but there's a down side, I've begun telling them to myself.

Now.

And that's worse.

Indeed, Mister Feeney.

Joejoe, Father.

Joejoe.

Have you ever met the owl in the desert Father?

I have.

The sparrow on the house top?

Yes.

And the pelican in the wilderness?

The priest looked at him.

I have Joejoe, but only on paper, he said, with a slight trace of stubbornness, or was it irritation. Then came the smile, and he jerked his shoulder, and worked his arm, then he took off his coat, nodded to the gathering, and said: Who have we here? as he tapped the Adamses on the shoulders.

Father, said the lady.

Your first time at the Stations? he asked.

Yes, said Roberto.

He shook Stefan's hand.

I see you in the church, he said.

I go, yes.

And I see you singing.

But I do not know the words.

Ah, and he clapped him on the shoulder. Then he spoke into Mrs Brady's ear and shook her hand and then her husband's hand. And then, having greeted a few other souls, from other religions, Father Grimes sat down in a chair by himself for a while to study his missal, looked round, got up, put the missal on the table, and sat down again; looked at his hands and then at his watch and closed his eyes; and went at last in and sat in the bedroom, head-down, with only the light of a candle on the window sill fluttering behind him.

Joejoe jumped to his feet.

Right, he said, I won't be long.

He left the door open behind him and went in and dropped to his knees on the cushion facing the priest, and immediately began to speak out loud like a man on a street talking into a mobile. *I cursed, I swore,* I –. Just a minute, said Father Grimes, please can someone ... One of the widows got up and closed the door. It is very interesting, said Mister Adams, in the silent kitchen. Very interesting. No one spoke as through the thin wood panels Joejoe kept up a loud litany of sins: what was left to him was not right, it was not right, and then the voice went low and seemed to rev into all kinds of obscurity, *someone killed the pups that wished his enemies harm, they tried to shoot me! There is not a soul there now;* then he recited the Act of Contrition in a loud marvelling voice.

There was a huge wallop of sea down the shore.

Extraordinary, said Mister Adams; then a few minutes later Joejoe reappeared, got into his armchair, and clapped his hands.

I'm done, he said. It's your turn now.

And in stepped J. D. Moffit, with his cap in hands. People moved along a line of chairs that had been placed next to the bedroom door, and as they stepped in to confess, talk in the room started up to cover the sound of confession. As the door opened it stopped. Then when the next person entered the talk was of animals and houses and timber, the Celtic Tiger and building then buildings, then silence. During the next confession it was Volkswagens and rust and growth and Where is Declan, then baling; then silence as a widow came out and a bachelor entered; and schooling and what's-his-name-married-to-Yvonne and dying and Where is Declan, those houses and more houses going up in the village, can it last, and so many bachelors and spinsters living by the sea, drinking and driving, and the fast cars and silence, and I looked at the Bradys who smiled back and Mrs Brady put a finger to her lips; then the talk went to empty bars and huge salaries and the price of old slates, and blocks, and cement and I prayed to myself.

I prayed long and hard.

Anna went in to tell her sins with a smile in my direction, then a few more people arrived, were greeted and still Joejoe looked beyond them, out there, past the candles, for the enemy he was seeking.

The Bird stepped into the confession bedroom, and pulled the door gently behind him.

There was not a sound from within, or in the kitchen. For once as a confession was being made the conversations stopped momentarily. It was like everyone was listening to find out what went on his head – this local man that everyone saw and met and passed on the road or the beach but no one really knew, because he was a loner who really spoke to no one, except Joejoe; but all we heard was silence before the talking started all over.

Then it was my turn. I was the last penitent. I went in and closed the door behind me and went to my knees forninst the priest. I blessed myself and whispered. He reached over and his hand came down on my shoulder.

Is everything going all right tonight? he asked.

I hope so Father.

How are they out there?

Fine. Possession is ended.

What did you say?

Excuse me, I made a mistake, I meant to say that confession is ended. I am the last. Everyone has been heard Father.

Except for myself, he said.

Oh.

Now will you listen to me?

I will.

Things are not good with us now, unfortunately. The church is adding to our lot I am sorry to say. I am ashamed of what is going on out there in the world, with the priests. Do you hear me?

I do.

It's difficult.

I understand, Father.

Good. Tell me this, are things all right with you?

Not so bad.

And the pelican in the wilderness. Pray tell me how does that man Joejoe come to know the Bible?

I read him the Psalms, sometimes.

Indeed. Well now. I'm glad you have someone to talk to. By the way will you come up to cut the hedge soon?

I will.

Good man.

He rose out of his seat. He gave a great wide gesture, and made the shape of the cross in the air, and I blessed myself, and he turned and blew out the candle leaving us in the dark. I opened the door and waited expecting him to follow me, but he waved me on and knelt down on the cushion in the black room to ask himself for forgiveness. I left the door open behind me. I sat back in my chair. The kitchen went quiet as the priest took a few minutes to himself alone. It was a long eerie silence as everyone stared at an angle towards the ground, then again towards the dark space beyond the open door.

In the silence this mad fit of barking started, Joejoe rose a finger and Da went back and stood guard by the door, then eased it open.

The General dressed in an immaculate blue suit and shiny hair suddenly entered, clapped his hands, and sat down immediately inside the front door, and stared at the floor.

You're late, whispered Joejoe.

The General looked up.

Sorry, he said.

I believe you were over in Luton for a while?

For a couple of days.

Aye.

And I saw people over there that we both knew.

Joejoe started stepping towards the General like a child without getting out of his chair. His feet worked crazily on the flags as he stared at the General's white bristling face. Up came the arm, the finger out pointing.

And did you enjoy yourself?

I was at a funeral.

God forgive me, said Joejoe retreating, I did not know.

What's wrong Joejoe, asked the General.

I'm sorry, he replied. I am deeply sorry.

What is wrong, asked Mrs Adams.

Ma and myself placed our hands on Joejoe's shoulders.

The General rose and looked round the room. The people looked at each other. I could feel the convulsions in Joejoe's body travelling up my arm.

Let me up, he said.

He went over and took the mirror and turned it round facing the wall.

This is the Stations Joejoe, begged Ma. Not a wake.

We will remember the dead, he said. Forgive me, he said again to the General. He went back and stood in front of his armchair. You see the other night . . . The other night a bullet came through that very window, Joejoe said slowly, and he pointed at the window, and he sat.

There was consternation.

A bullet? asked one of the widows.

Yes, said Joejoe, a bullet.

Stop! said the Blackbird.

What?

Joejoe turned and looked at the Bird. Excuse me, said the priest entering, in his vestments, with one arm out and one arm in. His white hair was askew. Anna got up and tried to pull the surplice over his head. The General sat back down into his seat.

It's true, said Joejoe

Stop Joejoe, said the Blackbird again, directly and quietly. Leave it.

The voice this time was not expected. We all thought the crisis was over. Neither was the tone expected. It was a far-off thing said casually and quietly. It was the Bird's voice brought calm back into the house. Father Grimes straightened himself, and looked round the room as he worked his right shoulder. The candles flickered round the room.

Are we all here? he asked.

Yes, said Ma.

And are we ready to start?

Yes, said Da, indeed we are.

Thank God.

The priest stood with his hands crossed on his stomach, and his eyes cast down. Joejoe turned slowly and looked at the Bird, but Tom Feeney had his eyes fixed on a small tiny dot away out there. The priest rose his hands, and flattened his palms. Da sat down in despair, and beside him the General breathed in slowly. I could hear Ma whisper something to Anna as she knelt before the makeshift altar. Thady fixed his tie and smiled. There was a long silence.

I'm only saying, said Frosty quietly.

I ... think ... that ... is ... everyone, said Joejoe, and he nodded to Father Grimes.

The priest turned his back, stepped up to the small table, leaned down and kissed it. The congregation dropped to their knees in the small kitchen. Joejoe closed his eyes. He mumbled something but the voices in prayer drowned him out.

Chapter Nineteen

Go in Peace

The priest came up off his knees, turned and blessed us, and hauled off his surplice that Mary Joe deliberately hung on a hanger over the dreaded window where the bullet hole had been. The Mass was ended, go in peace, the priest said; the wine was handed round, the soups arrived, Anna's brown bread appeared. The General sat very still in his chair, accepted a drink, the priest sat by the grate.

The cat, said Frosty, likes to have his milk by a nice fire.

He does, said the priest.

The cat can do without people.

He can.

Yes, said Anna. The cat is a funny person.

Not so bad, said Frosty. What are you going to be?

An environmental manager.

Good. And what about him, he said pointing at me.

I don't know, said Anna.

Neither do I, I said.

Mary Joe went round with the teapot, the pea soup was served; the sponge was cut, Joejoe sipped his Malibu and stared at the General. I brought sherries and ham-and-cheese toasted sandwiches to Mister and Mrs Brady. I sat by their side for a few minutes talking. At the third whiskey the widows started singing 'Take me home again Cathleen'. J. D. Moffit sang 'The Old Triangle'. The Blackbird stood and recited:

> *The crows are alive on the trees*
> *Like a hive of honey-Jack bees,*

Then they begin their squawking
It must be the weather
Starts them talking.

All of a sudden Joejoe stood up and took the euro off the dresser, flipped the coin with his thumb and threw it through the air like a dart and it landed at the floor at the foot of the General. There was silence a moment. The General studied it and laughed.

Is there luck in it, he asked.

There is, said Joejoe.

Thank you, said the General, and he picked up the euro and put it in his pocket.

We are all savages, said Mrs Dunleavy. And this soup is beautiful. Beautiful!

The chat started again. Ma and Mrs Conan went round with buttered scones and homemade blackberry jam. Sue Ferrid, who was ninety-three, took an apple tart that was still warm out of her bag, and fell to waltzing with Mick Doyle. There must have been about thirty people in that room, eating and drinking, and maybe five men in the scullery, downing bottles of beer and eating ham. Da leaned down and whispered into my ear.

Keep that man occupied, he said.

I went over and sat again by Joejoe.

He lifted a finger to answer a question to Owney Burke, turned and smiled to someone else, then he shot back his eye to the General, said Yes, that's true, spat, and shuffled his feet again, as if he was trying to frighten a dog; then he looked at the window where the surplice was hanging and gave it the thumbs-up, and turned to me.

Another small one, if you please.

And don't forget me, said the Blackbird.

Certainly gentlemen.

And one for the priest.

Thank you, said Father Grimes.

And Frosty shuffled over and proffered his glass.

I poured out two Blackbush and two Malibu. The men saluted each other. Where did you encounter Malibu, may I ask, asked Roberto. I would have thought it would have been – how do you say – exotic for this part of the world?

Above in Mister John's, said Joejoe, forty years ago, in April of sixty-six.

In the days when I was let in, said the Bird, and he looked at Mister Sweet John.

A certain German ordered a round of Malibu at the bar for us all, and I was smitten, said Joejoe.

Mary Joe shook her frock and made it dance then continued on. Ma, without taking a drink, went to and fro, sitting, talking and serving. I'm only saying, said Frosty. You are, said Mary Burns. The thing is what became of Robert Emmet? Did he get married? he asked. And did Wolfe Tone? Hah?

Stefan came over and sat on the floor by my side.

Are you enjoying yourself? I asked him.

I am, Mister Side Kick. But being happy makes me sad, somehow . . . I think . . . I think . . .

Here, said Anna, and she handed him a cushion.

This is Anna and this is Stefan, I said.

Hallo, she said.

Labas, he said. I see you running on the road, and I see him walking. No? You are always going in different directions.

It is true, at times, and she went off with another tray of meringues.

I am Joejoe, and my granduncle promptly poured him a shot of Malibu.

Nice, said Stefan, settling onto the cushion. This is a holy party. I am glad to be here.

Good, said Joejoe.

I hear certain talk of bullets, but I do not understand.

Neither do I, said Joejoe, neither do I.

It is strange, no? said Stefan as he looked at me.

Yes, I said and I winked.

I will say nothing, he whispered, and he gave a loud laugh as if I had told him a joke, and I smiled in return; then we both sat there as beside us Joejoe conducted the scene with his hands.

The General started whispering in one of the widow's ears. Not at all, she said. No, not at all, and she sang 'I Wish, I Wish in Vain'. Mrs Brady lowered her face into her hands and listened, and when we all thought the song was over, the widow finished with a verse that the old folk said they had not heard before.

> *Come all you maidens*
> *I pray take warning*
> *And never heed what yon men do say,*
> *For they're like a star on a frosty morning*
> *When you think they are near you.*
> *They are far away.*

True, said Mary Joe. The priest recited a poem that brought down silence on the house. I put the accordion in Joejoe's arms.

I say did Wolfe Tone get married? asked Frosty.

Now, now, said Mary. Keep such questions to yourself.

He eloped with Matilda, said Father Grimes.

And did they get married?

They did.

I see.

He was a very honourable man.

And then Frosty stood and sang:

> *I wish the queen would call home her army*
> *From the West Indies, America and Spain,*
> *And every man to his wedded woman*
> *In the hope that you and I might meet again.*

Joejoe hit a couple of notes to the air then dropped the box at his feet, and Stefan very carefully lifted it and carried it over and put it on the window sill behind the surplice.

Good man, said Joejoe, will you read for me, Mister Psyche.

Later, I said.

OK, son, he said; then he suddenly stood and shot a hand round the back of his neck, leaned forward and scratched ferociously. He squeezed his shoulders together, and blew through his lips.

Dear God, he said.

Are you all right, asked Ma.

Yes, yes, he said, pulling his elbows tight against his ribs.

The priest took his surplice off the hanger and waved his missal.

OK, said Da, getting to his feet; before you go Father, I'd like to thank everyone for coming, especially you Father Grimes.

Good night everyone, called the priest.

And slowly the place emptied. Out the front the dog Timmy kept up a rampage as Roberto and his wife and Adams and the Tingles and Mister Awesome headed to their cars. Stefan stood and placed his hand on Joejoe's shoulder, then Mister and Mrs Brady came up to me and we walked out into the night together to their car.

I enjoyed myself, said Mister Brady, no end.

And so did I, said Mrs Brady. Thanks for looking after us.

No bother, I said.

They drove off.

Mister Doyle and the other remaining men took all the pub chairs out to Mister John's trailer where he sat waiting in his car, and when the last was on board, he hurtled off to the pub. Stefan stamped each empty tin of beer with his boot, and collected them into a pile. Goodnights were called. The widows shook hands with everyone, then off-headed into the night.

The General came over and stood in front of Joejoe.

Joejoe, he said, and he tapped him on the shoulder. Good luck.

Joejoe stood.

Good luck.

The General was one of the last to leave and he was followed by Frosty who gave the Bird a final punch on the shoulder.

Good man, he said, we miss you above.

Ma and Anna and Mrs Conan cleared the food off the table, took down the altar and Da and myself took the bottles away, leaving only a half-finished bottle of Malibu and a full bottle of Blackbush on the table. Mister Conan took the confessional seat back out to the turf shed.

And Anna landed a kiss on my cheek.

Ah, I said.

Myself and Ma walked herself and her parents to the gate.

Thanks a lot, said Ma, for all your help.

No problem, said Mrs Conan and they took off walking.

When the place was cleared, and we were about to go, the Bird and Joejoe were sitting side-by-side at the fire.

Will ye men be all right?

We will, said Joejoe.

Goodnight, Da called.

The Bird came to his feet walked over and took Da's hand and shook it.

Goodnight Tom, said the Bird.

Goodnight Tom, said Da. I'm sorry for intruding on you that night.

Good night, Joejoe, said Ma.

Thank you nurse Geraldine Lockett for everything, said Joejoe, I thank you from my heart.

And as we went up in the car Da said: Would you mind taking a look at those pair in about half an hour?

Done, I said.

I think the drink is getting to them.

In the house Ma sat into the armchair and closed her eyes

For a minute there I thought I was back on night shift, said Ma.

You're not, said Da.

What a relief to step back into peace. That was a trial, she said.

But in the end it went well, said Da. Philip got to see the Bradys and the Bird calmed the uncle.

We were blessed.

Now, will you have a drink?

Yes, she said, spreading her arms and her fingers touched my ear.

Sorry pet, she said. I'm so glad you got to speak to Mickey's parents.

So was I.

It was good for you. We are all here for you, she said.

Thanks Ma.

So last thing that night Da drove me down to Joejoe's and then headed on up to Mister John's for a last pint. I came in the gate and knocked.

Who's that?

Me.

Joejoe opened the door.

You're welcome as the flowers of May, he said, and felt his way along the table and dropped back into his armchair. The Blackbird was still in his coat, two black sausages on a plate on the floor at his feet, and he had a lap full of crumbs. I heaped up the fire. They rose their glasses. I emptied the bottle as I poured out two last glasses of Malibu.

We're discussing women here, said the Bird.

Are we? asked Joejoe.

Indeed we are.

If you say so, you gallot.

I do.

I can recall fairies but not ladies.

Well we were.

All right then.

Now tell me, Psyche, he said turning to me, is Anna your girlfriend?

I think so, I said.

So you're going on a journey.

I am.

My heart goes out to you. Let us know when you get back.

I will, I said.

Good for you. You better hold on to her. I had one once and lost her. You see the way it is. It's a cross –

– Too true, said Joejoe –

– That you have to bear.

Indeedy.

Recently I've took to noticing women.

Boys oh boys – and mark you on the night of the Stations!

At the beginning I thought they were people I wanted. Now they are people I look at.

He's past it, the auld bastard.

The way I see men and women is, well some fit into each other and some don't.

You'll get that.

Yes. You will. I had a chance of a woman once and she had a chance of me but it didn't work.

No belly bumping for poor Tom, said Joejoe.

No, sadly.

Didn't stop you trying.

Nothing wrong with that. But look at yourself.

What are you saying?

See that man over there, your poor Joejoe; he was a terror for the women. You couldn't pull them off him.

Stop the blather.

Oh into the best of clobber, small and quick, the shoes shined and away with him on Saturday night, and Friday, and Tuesdays, the small talk, and the blarney. He knew the sweet bush and the sour bush, did your Joejoe. Oh yes. And me? Not a bloody one. No. He tipped his glass into his mouth. So you see for me women grow more beautiful every day.

Do men? I asked.

I don't know rightly. That's a strange question. He looked at me oddly. I'll have to think about that.

I think I'll put the bottle away, I said.

Do what you must, said Joejoe.

You're right, you're right, said the Blackbird, but maybe you'll countenance one for the road.

Just the one, mind.

I got up, opened the bottle of whiskey and poured them each a stiff one, and poured myself a shot, and then put the Blackbush on the high shelf, out of reach, and sat again.

There was a long silence where the mood seemed to change as if the men were heading off in another direction. They lifted their glasses simultaneously and drank, then Tom Feeney turned quietly to Joejoe.

Do you think of your old girlfriend often? the Bird asked.

Joejoe poked the fire.

Bridie?

Yes.

I do, he said. But she was like myself, not lonesome, so I don't miss her. If I missed her I'd only hurt her. And I don't want to hurt her. Bridie is where she is. She passed on. She was like the hare, enchanted. The hare has a lot to answer for. Filling you with the gra then going down to wash her clothes and hair at low tide and leaving you here be yourself. That's all I can say, it skips through your mind, all men's mind, so I'll leave it.

Aye, said the Blackbird and he studied the Joejoe a long time.

175

Then he stood and said: A lady she was. God grant her rest. Now. I'll hit the high road, I will. He leaned against the inside of the door, lit a fag and pulled the door behind him with a loud bang.

Stop there a while, said Joejoe, till I get my bearings.

He got up and turned the mirror on the wall so that it faced back into the room. He looked at the reflection of himself for a long time.

The sea pinks are dying, he said, and so is the sea thrift. The year is moving on.

It is.

Read now, he said, sitting into a chair by the window.

I lifted down the New Testament and turned to Psalm 45 and read:

Oh my God, my soul is cast down within me, therefore I will remember thee from the land of Jordan, and of the Hermonites, from the hill Mizar.

Deep calleth unto deep at the noise of thy waterspouts; all thy waves and thy billows are gone over me.

Yes, Joejoe said, and I put the book away. I lit the candle in his room and led him to his bed.

He sat on the edge of it while I undone his laces.

Good man, good man, I'll be fine now. Let yourself out and throw the key in the post box.

I let myself out, locked the door, dropped the key in then looked in the bedroom window. He was sitting there, poised, looking off into the distance in his stocking feet.

BOOK FOUR

The First Fall

Chapter Twenty

Waiting on a Lift

I came onto the road, and that's when I found the Blackbird sitting in the ditch beside his bike with the lamp shining up into the dark sky. He was smoking a fag.

What's wrong, I asked him.

Nothing. I'm waiting on a lift.

I see.

I brought his bike into the yard.

I'm not in the mood for riding home, he said.

I'll go get someone.

Good man.

Wait there, I said.

I will.

I phoned the house. Ma immediately sat into the Fiat and drove down. The Bird watched all from afar. In the beams from the headlights she stepped out and looked into his eyes.

Tom.

Yes, he said.

Do you know what's happening?

Indeed I do.

So what happened?

Tell me this where do you put the questions marks when you are not asking questions Mrs?

Please, said Ma.

He came onto his knees, laughed, put his two hands on the ground, brought up his behind, and stayed there like a runner about to begin a race, and then shot straight up, and stood perfectly poised.

179

I'm getting there, he said and he laughed.

Oh, she said, I thought you were drunk.

No, not at all.

I opened the passenger door.

He sat into the front seat like a policeman, head back, eyes wide, elbows tight against his ribs, and the two hands braced out like choppers. Then as we drove along his head started to swing in circles, and when we pulled up outside his house he nodded and said Drive on.

No, Ma said, we're here.

He looked out the window at his own door, then faced forward and pointed with the tip of his index finger.

Go on, he whispered ghost-like.

No Tom.

If you leave me here, I'll never be heard of again.

Out Tom.

We took his arms and led him to the door of the house. Inside the dog charged.

Have you the key, asked Ma.

I have.

Well open the door.

Just leave me here and I'll head on in when you're gone. He sat down with his back to the door. You hear me, go on. Then he closed his eyes and his head fell forward.

Search him, said Ma.

I went though his coat pockets, then his trousers, and there was his limp mickey against the lining but no key.

Inside the dog lunged against the door.

He must keep it someplace.

I unearthed all the stones and timber and went round and across all the window ledges looking.

What are ye at? he said without opening his eyes.

Where do you keep the key?

In the same place.

Where?

The same place amn't I telling you. Now go on. You're hurting me head.

OK, said Ma.

She nodded at me. We walked down the path. We got into the car and drove down Cooley, she stopped at Mary Joe's and we walked back up the road just like the night with Da and crawled along the low wall. The Blackbird was still slumped against the door. A light fall of rain was gathering on his shoulders. We waited a quarter of an hour but he did not stir.

He'll get his death, Ma said.

We waited another while. There was no change.

We better bring him up home, she said.

We lifted the Blackbird. He was like a rake. There was not a bit on him. And he smelled, like always, of all kinds of strange perfumes. Again he sat tight in the passenger seat tight up against the safety belt. The eyes saw nothing.

Who are you, he asked Ma.

You know quite well who I am.

You're not Eileen?

No.

I thought so. Well fair enough.

At the house when she opened the car door it was the safety belt kept him upright. He fell to the left, then tumbled out, then he went to his knees; then shot to his feet and straightened himself in her arms. I led him towards the wooden studio in the garden where there was two beds, a place I used sleep in some summer nights and draw; and it's down there Da would go some nights and read, and garden, and sit out till all hours alone, with a glass of orange juice and squeezed lime. It was where I would head out to draw. Now Tom Feeney entered and looked round in wonder at the paintings and drawings on the wall; the books on plant life and aliens. I took off the Bird's

181

jacket, and unlaced his boots and he kicked them off. I laid him down. Ma put the sheets about the Bird and brought out a radiator and we plugged it in. He pointed over his head and said: What's that? He looked round the cabin and said Agh. She took his temperature, felt his wrist and looked into his eyes.

Well Madam? he said.

Do you feel sick?

Not at all.

Get a pail and put it by the bed, said Ma. I got the pail and as I came back in the Blackbird sat up and vomited into the air. By chance I caught it all clean.

He lay back.

His face went white.

What was that?

You got sick.

Oh.

Show me your tongue? she said.

He put out his tongue.

All right, she said, and then she took his temperature again, and felt his forehead. She went out to get some hot water.

Is that you, Psyche? the Blackbird asked.

Yes.

Is there many of them?

Only a few.

Good.

He reached for the sheets and pulled them to his chin. He smiled to himself. Not long after Ma arrived with a bowl of tepid water and he offered his face. She washed his cheek and forehead. He gave his hands to her like a child then again he pulled the sheets to his chin. This is a grand place, he said. I'd like to bring it home with me.

*

We sat watching him sleep.

The minute he sat into the car the drunkenness came on him, did you see that?

I did, I said.

What brought that on I wonder. Did they have a lot to drink?

I suppose they had a fair share, but I put the bottle away.

I thought the Stations would quiet them. Would quiet us all. Were they arguing?

No, not at all.

I think your father is right. The drink is getting to them.

Maybe.

So what were they talking about?

They were talking about women.

I don't know whether to laugh or cry, said Ma.

She looked at him, and laid a hand on his forehead. Tom? she said.

He did not stir.

The Blackbird, I said, was talking about how women in his eyes are growing more beautiful.

Heaven forgive me for asking, but why did his nibs think women were growing more beautiful?

Because he lost the girl he had.

The Bird made a slight groan and said: It's true. Hens.

What, asked Ma.

He did talk of hens a few days ago, I said.

Tom, she said touching his forehead.

Yes.

Why hens?

I was reared under their wings.

She looked at the man in the bed.

Tom, are you there?

I hear youse, said the Blackbird with his eyes closed. I hear youse.

Then he started into the litany.

*

We sat in the garden shed for maybe half an hour while the Blackbird travelled though the galaxies. Up Cooley and across Poll an Baid. Pocawokatche. Culleens. Culleens. Poll and Saggart. Through the Bent. The Night Field. The raven. Dromod. Through the willows. Take a left. Onto the New Road. Into the quarry. Out the island. In among the Hens. Ballintra. Ballintra. Cooley. Hens. I was reared under their wings. Sea holly. The long squares. Christ's tears. Sally Anne. Culleens. The blooming General. Culleens. Cooley. The fox gloves. St John's Eve. Cooley graveyard. Childer, Childer. The long awns. The moon. Joejoe, Miss Jilly. The urchin. The rake. That was some house I believe Mrs Feeney. The one I grew up in. Me sister and brother slept in the one bed, hens flying in the rafters; a goat would push in the door at any blessed hour of the day. Sea pink. Sea pink. *Cnoic! Cnoic!* he shouted. And the daft heads of the sea urchin. He lashed out at nothing and smiled.

He patted the sheets.

Then suddenly Da came through the door of the shed.

What the hell –

Shhhh!

The fucking Blackbird, he whispered astounded. I thought it was Joejoe. What is that man doing here?

We could not get him into his house.

I thought I was looking at a visitation.

You are.

Is he all right?

Yes, I think so.

Da walked over to the man in the bed.

I'm sorry Tom, he said.

I hear ya, I hear ya.

But you couldn't tell if he did hear Da.

The three of us sat a while, then he fell asleep and eventually we went to bed. And during the night I saw Ma cross the yard to the shed where the light remained on. Then again I saw Da going with the lamp. They were like sleepwalkers.

Then came the strains of the song I could not make out as I saw Lala in a dream start poking my shoulder.

Lala, I said.

Philip, will you get up, said Da.

Right, right!

It's your father, here. Are you all right?

Yes, OK.

It was seven o'clock. Ma and Da were setting the table in the kitchen.

Will you go, Ma said, and give the Bird a shout.

All right.

It was still dark in the garden and the light from the shed fell through the olearia like an aura. I came in the door and patted his shoulder. Mister Blackbird, I said. His big brown eyes opened in terror, the top half of his body shot forward, and then he recognised me.

Ah Psyche is it you.

You can get up now, I said.

What time is it, he asked.

It's just after seven.

I don't rise till eight, he said and he closed his eyes and immediately went back to sleep. I returned to the kitchen.

Is he on the way? Ma asked.

No.

Why?

He said he doesn't get up till eight.

Hah?

Yes.

He doesn't get up till eight?

That's right.

I've heard everything now. She called up the stairs to the father. You want to know something.

What's that?

Mister Blackbird does not rise till eight.

She began making breakfast as she chewed a banana. The morning went on. The three of us were at the table eating when just as the hand of the clock reached the hour a shadow crossed the window.

What was that, asked Da.

That's him, said Ma.

Look at the time, I said.

He's punctual, said Ma.

He's a blooming mystery, said Da.

I think he's OK, said Ma, I'll head to work.

I went out and watched him go. His walk was wiry. His motion thin-shouldered. He took to the beach. Ma drove by me, then Da passed by on his way to a new building site by the Yellow Strand. The Bird came back up from the beach onto the road. He walked quick by Joejoe's gate, then stopped, looked round him, leaned down and laced a shoe, then went to his knee on the ground and laced another, beat his knees and looked out to sea, picked up his bike, thought about it, came back up to the head of the pier and stood on the blue bank of gravel, tossed a stone into the water, turned and went from view then reappeared, opened Joejoe's gate and went in, wheeling the bike.

Soon after that I saw a column of smoke rising from the chimney.

He was doing my job.

I collected four lobsters out the rocks and carried them to the gate where I stood waiting for the Judge to come and collect me. I stood looking across at Joejoe's, wondering should I go over, should I go in and see were they all right, but then suddenly the car appeared away in the distance and the horn blew.

Chapter Twenty-One

The Judge

Morning, said the Judge.

Morning, sir.

I have a few jobs for you, he said, today.

And I have a few lobsters for you, I said. And they're getting less and less these days.

Good man.

I got into the car and he drove first inland to his sister's house on the edge of the lake where we had muffins and fed the ducks, then while the pair sat talking I did her lawn, cut up a lock of timber, and dug out her drain; then we went on to the Judge's house.

I took out his lawn mower. As usual it wouldn't start. I near took the arm off myself. But I got it started. They called me for tea. He was inside at his table doing the *Daily Express* crossword with his wife. She was wearing a Mexican shawl.

Plenty of late growth, I said.

Who laughed at original sin, she asked.

Wait a second.

Was it Stalin? she asked.

No. Shaw. Shaw, he replied.

And she wrote in the answer.

Thank you so much for the lobsters, she said.

I started from the tool shed and worked my way around the front of the house in circles, minding as I went the blasted swinging New Zealand flax and the wild blue rhododendron. I flew along the sea stones, thinking of what they might look like painted blue-and-yellow in a window, and when I turned I saw the Judge waving from the window. I cut the engine.

– Hi sky hawk, he shouted –

– Sir –

– You wouldn't happen to now what gunfire at dawn is?

Me not know.

Thought so.

He pulled the latch partly to, and with a pen in his mouth, considered the lawn. Soon both of them were standing there. She pointed at something I could not see. Then they started to laugh for no reason. I pushed on and rose a family of frogs in the grass. From next door the two girls – Daisy and Sheila – came over. They sat up on the wall talking away. I stopped at last to take stock of what there was left to do, and Daisy said: How are you Philip? Love you too, I said, Good, good, she said, and they roared laughing and waved goodbye as I headed round the side to sweep away the grass from beneath the sycamore. I sat a while on the seesaw before pushing the lawn mower back into the shed and began axing logs of beech and pine.

At dinner time the Judge landed me into the car and we drove to town to eat in McSharry's. I had me a steak and chips and he had two fruit salads and bubbling water with tablets for the stomach then some wee pill to lift the depression as he said it was getting late very early these days.

A man landed at our table, glanced in the Judge's direction, and sat down with his hands propped on the bag on his lap.

He nodded quietly to himself.

Do you know why we get depressed Mister Feeney? the Judge asked me.

No sir.

Well I'll tell you: we are old for far too long. Now if I was born at the turn of the century I would be dead by now.

If you were born at the turn of the century sir, I said, you'd be only six years of age.

Sorry, I'm talking about the last century. If I was born in 1900 I'd have died in 1928.

Oh.

He finished his coffee.

You see it's now 2006 and I'm sixty and still here. I should not be. A regular man in those days gave up the ghost at thirty. Now we're given an extra sixty years to regret that we were ever born. This tells on a body. Hence the depression. Hence the pills.

He called for the bill with his forefinger. He looked around him. The stranger sat stock-still in his chair. He never budged as the waiter took away the bill and the cash. Then when we stood, he stood, and followed us across the dining-room floor, through the front door and past the wedding guests that were gathering on the hotel steps. The three of us stepped aside for the bossy photographer to take a picture of the groom in his kilt. Then avoiding the bridesmaids who were posing in tiered hats we crossed the forecourt to the car. A waiter with a tray proffered glasses of wine and whiskey at the gate. The two men helped themselves, then the Judge opened his car door, sat in, leaned over and unlocked mine. The silent man stood looking away from the car. The Judge turned and unlocked the back door. The man sat in, and propped his bag on his lap. We took off round the town and suddenly stopped at Spar.

The Judge went into the shop.

I waited with my companion in a long silence. I could see him in the driver's mirror, looking straight ahead. He was indifferent to everything. He laughed at nothing, no matter what the sounds said. I thought his soul might burst at first, or maybe mine, I was so mad to say something, but I didn't. I thought of the Bird. We watched the shoppers stacking their boots and the fellow in yellow washing the Toyota with a jet of spume. When a lorry backed past us only inches away the man behind didn't budge as he fell into its dangerous shadow, in truth he was very easy in himself, and when the Judge appeared with four pots of pansies, the stranger took them and placed them neatly on the back seat.

We turned out the road to the city.

Strafe it was, the Judge said, and smiled.

Ah, what is strafe, I asked.

Gunfire at dawn.

Oh.

Now what was the other one? he said to himself.

At Baker's bridge the Judge stopped the car and rang in to back a horse called The Hard Yoke, fifty each way, then we went on. Not a word spoken. The Judge tried various stations on the radio and we listened in for a while to stories about nothing I could follow. Then we got the racing station and heard mention of The Yoke, in a blare of static and police alarms, getting beaten on the line. Two across, said the Judge. Words that imitate sounds. Words that imitate sounds. What in God's name is that? The leaves of the trees were thrashing. Gravel shook like mice. I had forgotten all about the man in the back as we passed the burnt gypsy caravan to the sound of an oldie called 'You've Lost that Loving Feeling', the huge quarry under the mountain with more gravel scattered across the road, and every few miles the signs for Cross Winds and Black Spots, the rows and rows of newly built, unlit, empty housing estates when suddenly a voice from the back seat shouted Here!

The Judge braked and slewed into the left.

Onomatopoeia, said the Judge.

The man settled the overturned pots of parsley in the back seat and lifted his bag out onto the towpath, then he got out tipping the door ahead of him open with the toe of his boot, then he clicked the door into place quietly, tapped his forehead and turned away, bag in hand. The Judge went up into second and pulled out into the traffic.

That man never spoke to me, I said.

And neither did you speak to him, said the Judge.

Chapter Twenty-Two

The First Fall

We were approaching Ballintra when I saw the bike down at the corner of Cooley Lane.

Hold it, I said. The Judge stopped the car.

It's a neighbour of ours.

My God.

I got out. The Blackbird was sitting in the middle of the road with blood pouring from his nostril.

Gather onto me, said the Blackbird.

I gently took his shoulders.

Psyche, he said. What are you at?

I'm taking you in off the road.

Will you leave me be.

You fell.

What do you mean I fell, I never fucking fell.

You did.

I did not!

You did.

I did not! he shouted. But if you say I did, then I did.

He stood uncertainly in my arms. His left arm hung lifeless down his side.

Don't move, said the Judge.

Do I look bad, your honour?

You're bleeding. Are you in pain?

I am not indeed.

Ma should be back from work, I said, she should be in the house. I rang but her phone was on silent. Would you please go up to the house for Ma, sir.

Yes, yes, the Judge said. I'll be back in a few minutes. He drove off.

Psyche, said the Blackbird.

You'll be all right.

I will.

He took my hand.

Upsa daisy, he said.

Aye.

He sat into the ditch.

So I fell, you think.

You did.

I'll have to be careful in future.

You will.

Good man Psyche, you were always a decent skin.

I sat in the ditch with my arm round him.

Psyche, he called.

Yes.

Nothing.

Then he began to shudder. His legs went straight out. He swung his head to the side.

Tom, I shouted. Tom!

The shuddering got worse. I put an arm under his head. He thrashed as if he were fighting someone, then he went still and slowly his eyes opened.

Ma rushed from the Judge's car and threw a blanket over the Blackbird.

Oh God, she said. I called an ambulance. Ah Tom.

She looked into his eyes.

Tom.

Aye.

This is terrible.

She leaned down and wiped his face.

This is all my fault, she said as she teased the blood from his nostrils into a tissue and spread ointment over his face.

It's not Ma.

I was foolish not to have brought you into the hospital last night.

You are not to blame, said the Judge.

It's me is to blame, I said.

No one is to blame, said the Judge.

You're right, you're right, said the Blackbird, you're right there, your honour.

Not long after we heard the siren come across the fields and the ambulance arrived.

Geraldine, said the driver.

Johnny.

Is he all right?

He hit himself bad.

What's your name? the ambulance man asked.

Tom Feeney.

Hallo Tom and how are you?

Grand.

Where do you live?

Above in Cooley. He hesitated. With a dog.

You were lucky to have this lady Nurse Feeney here to mind you.

I was.

One two three, the man said, and they lifted him onto a stretcher.

Aisy, he said, take it nice and cushy.

Then slowly he went aloft and was wheeled into the back. Ma got in beside him. He sat up again like he had the night before, the eyes looking rigidly ahead, and the hands stiff by his ribs.

Lie down, Tom, she said.

He pointed at me with his right hand and tapped the side of his forehead with his index finger.

Lie down, Tom, she said again.

He put his head on the pillow. The doors were pulled closed. They reversed up Cooley, came out and turned for town.

Now what, said the Judge.

I'll have to find Da I suppose.

Well let's find him together.

So I rang his mobile but it just rang out, then myself and the Judge drove the few mile out to the Yellow Strand where Da was working but the JCB was sitting empty on the site of the new building, and there was no sign of his Volkswagen.

Where to next? asked the Judge.

I don't know.

I rang Da again but there was no reply.

We headed past Joejoe's.

Down to Mister John's.

I went into the pub. It was empty except for two strangers sitting on a bench together watching a film. We went over to the French house. Then out to Culleens, and as we passed the graveyard I saw Da's car parked among a few others. Stop, I said. When I got out I heard his mobile ringing in the car. I opened the passenger door and went to take the call, then it rang off. I looked at the number. It was Ma. I got out and ran over to where there was a group of men standing holding shovels to their chests by an open grave. They watched me approach. Da was not among them. Then I spotted him. He was down in the grave digging alongside Mister Awesome. It was their turn while the other men waited. Without looking up he threw a shovelful of fresh clay from the grave skywards. Then he dug deep again.

Da, I said.

What?

He looked up at me.

Ma's on the phone.

What?

Ma just rang you.

Hold on. I have a bit to go yet.

He continued to dig and throw, dig and throw, like a man demented, the sweat running down his dirty forehead, then he stopped as Mister Awesome called a halt; they both put their spades crossways across the grave and pulled themselves up. Another two men jumped in and took their place and started to dig. The father was handed a glass of whiskey. He drank then he turned to me.

Now, what?

Ma rang you.

He rammed the spade into the earth and reached for his jacket.

Is there something wrong?

Yes.

Jesus Christ, he said.

We started down through the gravestones towards the road. I handed him his mobile, he rang, and as we walked down the path, he cupped it to his ear.

Nothing, he said.

I heard it ringing.

What's the Judge doing here?

He was leaving me home and we saw your car.

What's wrong . . . there's something wrong lad.

Da, Tom Feeney fell.

No. Is he bad?

He was shook.

At the gate the Judge was standing.

And you were drawn into all of this, said my father, you poor man.

Is there anything I can do?

No thank you, Judge King. You've done enough.

Who is it that's passed away?

A neighbour that died in London. He's arriving into Knock airport this evening.

I wish ye the best of luck, said the Judge, and then he paid me what he owed me for the labour and the lobsters.

Thank you.

He drove off and we sat into the car.

Now what? said Da.

Then his mobile rang again and he lifted it up and nodded, then he said: Right, right, Geraldine, we'll go there right now.

Chapter Twenty-Three

There'll be Another Day

We drove straight to Joejoe's.

At the crossroads two strangers were hitching back the way we'd come.

Da stopped.

Killy-na-begs? said the thin man.

Sorry, said Da, we are going in a different direction. You'll have to make it back out to the main road.

OK, he said. It is all right.

We drove off.

Who are those boys?

I saw them in Mister John's, I said.

They're on a binge, he said.

The Bird's bike was lying against the ditch at Cooley. The door to Joejoe's was wide open. The wind blowing straight in. The empty bottle of Bush was on the table beside an empty bottle of Jameson. The fire out. Papers scattered. The chair empty. The place a shambles. Da walked towards the bedroom.

Joejoe, he called. Hallo Joejoe.

He knocked.

Joejoe.

Who's that? came a faraway voice from within.

It's me.

Well you're very welcome, sit down and I'll join ya.

Christ, said Da.

He shook his head and breathed out.

Jesus, he said, I didn't know what to think.

197

I closed the front door. We sat by the table. Minutes passed. Well I suppose we should be doing something, said Da. I got up and relit the fire. Da put the jet kettle on and began to wash the dishes left over from the night before. We tidied up. Then again we sat there watched by the dripping eyes and ears of the branches of fuchsia. There was no sound. In the distance the lorrying sea. Nothing else. Da looked at me then nodded to the room.

Joejoe, I called.

There was no answer.

Grandda, I called again.

Yes, came this small voice.

Are you coming out to us?

I am I suppose.

We waited.

It was a ghost house.

He's fucked, whispered Da. I'll have to go in.

Then suddenly the door to the bedroom opened and first the dog jumped out then Joejoe appeared. He had his cap on. He was carrying his boots. He was like a scarecrow in a field of geese.

Good men, he said.

He sat down and started to put on the boots.

And how are ye all?

We're fine.

It was a grand class of a day.

It was.

Any news?

Uncle Joejoe, said Da, I have something to tell you – there's been an accident.

Yes.

Tom took a fall.

He did not.

Off the bike.

God.

Joejoe perched uneasily with a boot in his lap.

Where?

At the turn for Cooley.

How is he?

He's in hospital.

He put on the boot and slowly laced it up.

He lit a fag. Then Da's mobile rang.

Yes, yes, he said, while we both watched him. I'm with Joejoe. He's fine. He's sitting here in front of me. How is Tom? Oh. The poor Blackbird. Right! Right! I'll see if I can get in. He put the phone away.

Well? asked Grandda.

He's in casualty. With herself. I have to go. You can stay, Da said to me.

You go too Mister Psyche, said Joejoe, and tell the Bird I was asking for him.

I will, I said.

Says you – there'll be another day.

He turned to the fire. Da took some lilies from a vase.

Right?

Right.

Do you have a key to the Blackbird's house?

I don't rightly know, here, try these, and he handed Da a number of keys he had in a box on the mantelpiece.

Are you sure you'll be all right by yourself, asked Da.

I will.

Well lock the door after us; there's a pair of go-boys knocking about. They're on the raz.

Joejoe waved us away out of sight as Da lifted the lilies to his chest. We drove up towards the Bird's. I got out and rode the fallen bike to the house. The bulb was lit in the kitchen. The dog barking. We tried each key in the front door but none fitted. We tried again and again. We tried the back door but there was no key hole, it was padlocked from the inside.

199

The barking rose to a peak.

We drove off.

That dog will have to be fed, I said.

We'll get something in town, he said.

At the crossroads the two men were lying back in the ditch. They did not raise a finger. Da drove by without stopping.

The waiting room was full of people sitting in silence. Inside the door to casualty we found Ma seated by Tom who was lain out on a trolley.

Ahem, said the Blackbird.

Well Tom, how are you, asked Da.

I'm all right. I broke my left arm to start with.

Da put the lilies on the bottom of the bed.

You bought me flowers?

I did.

Well now, thank you Mister Feeney.

I'm sorry.

For what happened to me or what you blamed me for.

Both. I'm sorry.

Here.

The Blackbird put out his good hand and my father took it.

He never once complained, said Ma, did ya?

I couldn't say, said the Bird. I never hear myself talk.

Ma pulled across two chairs and put the flowers in a plastic vase. We sat round him. The Blackbird was lying up in his vest against a pillow, with his right hand flat on the quilt. There were plasters running across his forehead. His left arm was in a sling. He was a thin man. There was no flesh on his shoulders, just bone. I did not know him rightly. The soul had flown up into the eyes and the soul was amazed. He watched all the comings-and-goings with his lips slightly open. The lips were on the point of a low whistle that never came. As the nurses and doctors passed his dark-brown eyes followed them with a kind of rare squint, his sharp chin went out, then the thin lips pursed.

He patted the quilt.

Right, he said.

And nodded.

Then he studied his broken arm. He touched the fingers of his left hand. Opened and closed his fingers of the right hand like he was trying to bewitch himself.

I cannot move the fingers of my left hand.

Are you feeling sore? asked Da.

No.

Is there anything I can get you Tom?

No.

He needs pyjamas, said Ma. We might soon head downtown.

All right.

But first I'll take you to chat the doctor, said Ma.

OK, said Da.

We'll leave you two boys together, she said. You just call the nurse if anything happens.

They got up and went off.

The Bird watched them go till they went out of a sight.

Were you ever in a bed that moved? he asked me.

No.

Well I'm in one. You could take off at any minute. You could bring me for a spin. Right. See that yoke below, that's it, now let it off. No you won't I suppose. This is where your mother works, said the Blackbird. Did you know that?

I did.

Very good.

He was like a tourist in some foreign part of the planet. He looked at a nurse going the other way. Then he looked at the man in the next trolley, the boy in the wheelchair beyond, the doctors that swept along past reception breezily with their white coats akimbo. He listened to the announcements.

Nodded. Stay clear of the doors said a faraway voice. He studied his broken arm intently, nearly as if it belonged to some other.

Nodded.

Then for a long time he looked at me, looked away, patted the quilt, mumbled something, then looked at me again with his head back as if was trying to recognise me. The eyebrows tightened. He went rigid. I thought he was going to have another attack. Then he suddenly called me in with his finger. The smell of whiskey and perfume hit me.

Psyche, he whispered into my ear.

Yes.

I knew that things looked bad the other day, he said. For you see the other day I had a shite. And when I looked into the bowl there was nothing there. No. Not a thing. I hate when that happens. It's a lot of work all for nothing. You understand.

I do.

Good. He nodded. See that woman there, in the next bed.

I do.

Don't look at her.

I won't.

Don't. She did a fair bit of damage to herself.

Oh.

And she has a sharp tongue in her head. She turned on me only a while ago. For nothing.

A nurse came over.

Are you all right – she looked at his chart – Tom?

I am.

Would you like some more tea?

The Bird nodded like a wound-up toy as she beat his pillow.

I believe you are related to Nurse Feeney.

I am that.

And you?

I'm her son.

Well now.

She smiled and went.

Were you talking to the boss? asked the Bird.

I was, I said.

And what had he to say for himself.

He said there'll be another day.

Aye, and he nodded, and then began looking around him again – to the left, to the right, and then up at the ceiling.

What are youse whispering about? asked Da.

Do you remember that song called 'Hallo Dolly'?

I do.

Well I was teaching him the words.

That's right, I said.

Ma and Da sat. She took the Bird's blood pressure.

You're still high.

I am, he said.

By the way you have two ribs broken, Tom. And that will put pressure on your lungs.

I see.

There was a sudden screech from behind a curtained bed down at the front. The Blackbird darted up. This was followed by another screech and another. A man pouring blood from his cheek was pushed past. There was a flurry of movement. Ma dressed the Bird's chest with bandages, then she lay the pyjama top, one arm in, one arm out. For you see the man is coming, she said, and we have to have you good and nice. Then as Da held the bed sheets up she pulled on the bottoms.

You're the bird with a broken wing, said Ma.

Aye.

The jugglers are coming, said the woman in the next trolley along, watch yourself.

Ma drew the curtain. This doctor came in and looked into the Blackbird's eyes.

You've done yourself some damage, he said.

What happened me?

You've had a minor stroke. I'm afraid you may be with us for some time.

Grand.

I can't get him a bed in one of the wards. Not as yet. Maybe tomorrow. You know yourself, sister.

Thank you, doctor.

She drew back the curtain.

The woman in the next trolley again called out.

Hi you.

Yes, said Da.

When is dinner coming?

Oh soon.

Well try and keep the men in white at bay. You hear me?

I do.

The Blackbird winked at me. The woman rose herself up on her elbows and looked at the Tom in his new regalia.

Why has he got a nurse all to himself? she asked, and I haven't.

We are related, said Ma.

That's no excuse.

She got up and sat between them.

I'm not on duty.

Do you know who you remind me of?

No.

Judge Judy. She's a fine class of a lady. She knows it all.

What happened you, asked Ma.

Well I got a toe off last winter. And since I got the toe off I lost my wind. You see they took the toe off on the heart side.

Oh.

That was bad enough but then . . .

Yes?

. . . Then this juggler.

Juggler?

. . . Yes, that doctor, and she put out both her hands as if she were juggling something in the air – yes a man who juggles life and death – he came along and said to me: Prepare to die.

He said that?

The juggler did, certainly.

He did not, said Tom.

Did he not?

No.

So what did he say?

The doctor asked you who was your next of kin.

By God you're right. That's the very thing he said to me. Thank you for that correction.

No bother.

Tell me this – will you be there when I wake up? Will you be in the next bed beside me.

I will, said the Blackbird.

Do you promise me?

I do.

Are you a witness to that Nurse.

I am.

He will be there beside me, no matter when I wake up?

He will, I promise you.

She studied me. I believe you do it different now these days, she said.

No I'm afraid we do it the same, I said.

I'm sorry for you, she sighed.

I never heard such dirty talk, said Ma.

Just then the porter arrived and as the lady was pushed away she cried out to the Bird: May we never be driven asunder.

At eight Ma's night duty started, and she left us to attend to others.

Drunks came through the door feeling ahead of them. I saw her disappear behind screens, look up at X-rays pinned to a light, take blood, read files, pause at Tom's trolley, go on. It was the first time I had stood in the hospital with her. She looked like someone else entirely. The Blackbird's eyes chased all that was happening. His pupils hopped through the ward. She stopped again by his bedside.

Will you not trying sleeping Tom, she said.

He nodded.

Will youse feed me dog?

We will, said Da.

I'll bring him down food from the hospital kitchen, said Ma.

He'd like that.

Where's the key? asked Da.

The Blackbird shook his head in despair, swallowed his bottom lip and sucked. He closed his eyes momentarily, then immediately opened them. He lifted his good hand as if to wave.

You don't need the key. Feed him through the post box.

Is that fair? The dog, said Ma as she tucked him further in, will need to get out.

He'll get out when I do. He closed his eyes. Yes. When I get out, right?

I will have to let your relations know you are in here.

Let them be.

Have you got their phone numbers?

They are all in the desk in me bedroom.

So please give me the key, said Da.

No.

Please.

They will not want to know, said the Bird. The lights began to dim. The beds and trolleys floated away from each other. I woke to a sudden cheer out on the corridor. Come and get me, a young fellow shouted to the guard that was holding him. There was commotion in the gents. A doctor entered. Then the lady was wheeled back in beside the Bird. The jugglers are coming, she said, and she pulled the sheet over her face.

Chapter Twenty-Four

Sailors and Trees

There was a ball of dark in the sky coming in from the sea, and she hit us at Barney. It swept over the road. We had taken the long way round. Sweet John was standing in the lit doorway of his pub on his own looking up the road towards the graveyard.

Should we get a bottle of Malibu, I said, the small one?

If you say so, said Da and we went in for a game of pool, but we should not be adding to the chaos.

The place was empty except for Miss Currid and Donald Bree. The balls shot out in the quietness. The sound travelled round the pub. Da ordered a pint of Guinness and I had a 7Up.

I'm glad to see you, said Mister John. How is the Bird, I hear he took a fall?

He's not so bad. We'll have to wait and see.

Well give him my regards.

I set the balls and broke, and found myself on reds. Then missed an easy shot.

I see there's few knocking about, said Da, tapping in a yellow ball.

There's no one going out these times, said Mister John, the Paddies are all at home sitting guzzling wine.

That's the way, said Da as he potted another.

The only people you meet in the pub these days are strangers. And by God I had a pair of strange bucks in earlier, said Mister John. Two Russian sailors. They were here for a few hours.

I think we saw them.

And a pair of lucky men they are.

Is that so? said Da, as he watched the white roll into a side pocket.

Yes, indeed. What I could make out from what they were saying is that their boat nearly went down off Donegal.

Jesus, said Da.

They were saved and brought to Killybegs where the boat is being repaired. The crew is being looked after by locals, and those pair of lads just stepped out onto the road hitching and ended up in Ballshannon, then Bundoran, and then here. They wanted to see Ireland.

And I drove by them on the way to the hospital, said Da.

I shot in three reds in succession, snookered him and took the next three, then faced up to the black.

I should have stopped and brought them out to the main road, Da said.

Maybe you did them a favour. Hitching on the main road at night when you're jarred could be dangerous.

Bottom left, I said, picking my pocket, and the black bounced off the hole and spun slowly across the table and fell into the middle pocket.

Hard luck, said Mister John.

OK, said Da, finishing his pint.

And, don't forget, the bottle of Malibu, I said.

Right, Philip, he said, and he called for a large bottle, paid over the €24.50, and we headed for Joejoe's leaving Mister John looking very lonesome behind the bar.

We drove by the castle, along the wall of gabions, by the handball alley, and then back by the Night Field. Then as we approached our crossroads there were the two Russian sailors sitting in a ditch, and as we approached they lifted the palms of their hands towards the headlights of the car.

We drove by, waved, then Da stopped. I can't leave them out for the night, he said and he pulled over, turned round and drew in alongside them.

Where are you going?

Killy-na-begs, no? said the orange-haired man and they both stood.

You'll not get there tonight.

No?

Get in, said Da.

Kill-na-begs?

No. Killybegs is less than an hour's drive away.

OK, and they sat down in the ditch again.

Get in, said Da, please.

Where do you take us?

A boat.

Boat, the tall thin man said smiling, and his hand dived up in a straight salute, we are sailors.

So I heard, said Da.

It is a small country, said his mate as they climbed into the back. Irish people are mean, you are not mean, here, and the orange man tried to hand a bottle to Da.

No, thank you, he said.

You take, please, he said. It the real Russian vodka.

No, said Da, but thanks all the same. The thin man took back the bottle. Look, he said to me, and his head came round the seat and he aped a quick shot to his mouth and winked, then all conversation stopped. I suppose we should get the animal out of the way first, said Da. Right, I said. Then he turned up towards the Blackbird's and drew up at the gate, left the lights on and we were back exactly as we'd been a couple of nights before.

Just a moment, Da said. We have a job to do.

No prob, said a voice from the back.

I got the bag of food from the hospital canteen out of the boot and went up to the path. Immediately the dog threw himself against the door. The bulb was still lit in the kitchen. We could see the dog standing on the seat of a chair snarling. Da came with a rope to collar the dog, and an empty spud bag to take up the shite. You take the front, and I'll take the back, he said, and we'll have another look. Striking matches I searched beneath the windows and under the door, around the gate, aware all the time of the two men watching me from the car with the window down, while the crossbred raged in the hallway, then began to leap at the window.

There was no key to be found.

This is bucking nonsense, said Da. We'll have to break in the door.

Da wait, I'll put the food in the letterbox.

And what about the shit that's piling up inside?

Excuse, said a voice from the car, and a hand proffered a lighter through the window of the back side door, the thumb clicked down and it lit, then it went off again, then he cracked down, and it burst into a tall flame. Good?

Thanks, I said.

We did one last tour behind the house with the lighter but found nothing except a medallion on a piece of twine and a few crates of empty Jacob's Creek wine bottles and Smithwicks beer tins out the back. He shouldered the backdoor, but it didn't budge. He tried all the windows. I caught a hold of a chicken leg and pushed it through the letter box. The bone shot out of my hand and immediately I shoved in the bag of leavings, of bread, wings, sausages and ham.

Wow! shouted one of the sailors.

There was a savage roar from the dog, then silence.

Well fuck me, said Da. I've seen it all now.

I wonder what those boys are thinking, I said.

They're watching idiots, he said.

We got into the car. The same hand reached out from the back, palm upwards, and I looked at it a moment as

Da turned the car, then I remembered and handed over the lighter.

Good, said the orange man. What you do?

We feed the dog, I said.

You feed the dog?

Through the letterbox.

It is strange, no? I have not seen before, and he laughed.

Da put the foot down and turned back to the West. A long hare stood in the middle of the road facing the lights. A hare, I shouted. Look, roared the thin man. They rose up between us out of the back pointing.

Hare, I said.

Hare, they shouted.

The hare moved a little to the left and then sat primly. Go to dims, I said. He dimmed, the hare drummed forward and stopped, bounced left right, left right, then strolled into the ditch like a person entering a shop. We took off. Da turned on the radio and it was ceilidh time on RTE. A hand came down on my shoulder and with his fingers the thin man played a sudden melody down my arm, then conducted us round Cooley corner, and with a swoop pulled his hand into the back.

We passed the lit house at Ballintra and stopped at the pier and he put on the full headlights.

We got out, and the two men sat on.

Hallo, said Da, leaning in, we are here, and he shot a thumb back over his shoulder. In the back seat of the car they looked at each other in the overhead light. Then they stiffened. The thin man drew his coat over his knees. I leaned in and said C'mon lads. They looked at each other. The thin man studied me and said OK, and they got out, and put their bags on their back.

They started to walk away.

No, said Da.

Please?

Hold it, said Da.

They waved sharply and kept moving.

Just a minute, he shouted.

They turned and looked at the ground.

You can sleep on the boat tonight, said Da. Sleep, he said, and he tucked his hands against his cheek.

Boat?

We led them across to the small pier, and he pointed down at the oyster trawler that sat alongside *The Ostrich*. Ah, us? Yes, you. Haya, shouted the orange man, and first I checked both ropes and climbed down the iron rungs ahead of them and turned on the outside light. Then they came after me at a trot and alighted on deck with great familiarity. This is good, good, said the orange man. They stood together looking out at the dark ocean holding each other's hands. I lit the lamp in the cabin and the sailors immediately looked at the map of the world on the wall

There, the thin man said, pointing at Serbia.

This way, I said.

I showed them the bare bunks below by the light of a match, then I threw the blankets on the bed, and put my head to the side and laid both my hands under my cheek and closed my eyes.

I found a little peck of a fingertip on my forehead, and I opened my eyes and inches away the men had closed their eyes with a smile and were breathing furiously as if sleeping.

They shook hands with me and then they shook hands with my father in the cabin.

The orange man took the bottle of vodka again out of his haversack.

Please, he said.

No, said Da.

It is very good.

No thanks.

Why do you lock the dog? asked the thin man, is it not wrong?

It is, said Da. Now it is time for bed.

The sailors bowed and went below. I stacked the books and we doused the light and we made our way across the deck.

I hope, said Da, that I am doing the right thing.

The father turned the key in the ignition but the car did not start. He dropped his head on the steering wheel. A few minutes passed. I thought he was going to fall asleep, then, without looking up he hit the ignition and we took off.

We went up Ballintra, and pulled in at the cottage gate. The house sat like a long moored passenger ship out there in the dark. Each window was lit with a candle, and in some there were three or four, stuck into bottles and salt-and-pepper tumblers. A small squall of rain blew by in a whirl of light.

I have been putting this off all night, said Da. I don't want to upset him.

Do you want me to go in by myself?

Yeh, maybe it's best if you go on your own. Think of the time it is. Yes, maybe it's best if I leave him be, said Da.

OK, but he'll be worried.

All right. Go on and take back these keys with you.

I walked quickly up the dark path. The front door was open slightly. There was a crack of light from inside going sharp across the stone paving.

I knocked. There was no reply. I pushed the door quietly open and Tim flew out. The door to the bedroom and the scullery were open. The back door was open. There was no one in any of the rooms. I put the keys back in their box on the mantelpiece. I went outside again to look, and suddenly at the gable end facing the sea I heard a bark and saw the lit end of a fag in the dark, and I realised Joejoe was sitting there in the open air on a chair against the wall.

He shot a beam of light from his torch onto my face. Was that ye down at the pier?

Hallo Joejoe. Yes. We were putting two sailors into the boat.

Good for you. How is my friend?

He was asking for you – . . . *Grandda.*

Now.

They are keeping him in for the night.

He's in good form?

Aye.

We stood a moment together. Is he all right, your father? asked Joejoe. What's he doing sitting out there alone?

I went up to the car and called Da. He came up and joined us by the gable. You have the place well lit Uncle Joejoe.

The lights will stay lit till that man – the Bird – returns, he answered. Did you get the door open?

No.

We stood each side of him. The moon was jutting out of a rain-filled cloud. Da dropped down into a squat. The sea tumbled. I went in and threw more timber on the fire, came out again and we stood there in the dark without talking a while.

You know what I was thinking of, said Joejoe, I was thinking of what it would be like to be surrounded by trees. I tried growing trees, I tried sycamore, I tried beech, I even tried willow over the years.

But no good.

No good, is right. Not one took. It would sadden you to look at them being torn asunder by the salt and wind.

It would.

A beaten tree is a sad sight. I wanted trees, but there again if I was surrounded by trees I would not be here.

You would not.

I'd be living somewhere else.

You would.

Still and all I'd like a tree to look at.

Will we go in? asked my father, and Joejoe immediately said: Will you do me a favour?

I will if I can.

Bring us for a spin to the woods.

At this hour?

I need to get away from here for a while. Somehow I always felt free among the trees.

This way, sir.

Lead on Mister Psyche! and he shot a beam of torch light towards the gate.

Chapter Twenty-Five

Hippies

It was near one in the morning.

We went to the woods in Dromod.

I have not walked these woods in years, Joejoe said as we turned in through the old high pillars of the estate, and drove up the potholed drive, and around through the side roads, then down to the old granite ruins by the sea. We got out and walked each side of him through a fierce head of hawthorns, through the beeches, the oaks, and the ash trees, and stood listening. By the light of the torch Grandda stroked the trunk of a sycamore, then taking his hand we dropped down onto the beach. The half-moon had come out and was going from pool to pool. Sand that had been driven from a further shore was piled high in heaps against the stone ramparts. Then we climbed up on the road and in through the gate and walked the orchard. The two men sat into a broken seat and watched me hurl sticks up into the dark unknown, hoping for fruit to fall.

Go on, son, shouted Joejoe.

I flung a stick with all my might, and, as if in reply, a nest of sparks rose far to the left on the second beach.

What in God's name was that? asked Joejoe.

We have company, said Da.

Let's go see.

This was not part of the plan.

C'mon.

On the little shore, by the abandoned boathouse, another bunch of sparks rose as we approached, then from a distance we stood still. There were three people sitting round a fire by a tent. Two of them, with their back to us, had a rug round their shoulders. It's the hippies, whispered Da. There was a smell of smoke and some sort of strange cooking.

Good night, called Joejoe sending forth a beam.

A face turned back to us out of the side of the rug.

Hallo?

Hallo yourself!

Christ! a lad shouted, as he looked the wrong way, who is that?

Over here, said Da.

The figure in a woollen hoodie leaped up and sent a torch round in a circle that settled on my father's face.

Hi, the lad called.

A brave night.

Are you all right? asked a girl coming out of the rug. Are you lost?

No, I said, we're locals.

Oh, cool. You gave me a fright.

The beam reached me.

Oh, sit down, please.

We levered Joejoe down onto a deck chair, and we sat down on huge round cuts of firewood.

You live near here? asked the lad in a woollen hat.

Just up the road, I said.

Ballintra, said Joejoe, and you're welcome to call any time.

Thank you, we will.

I used to work above in that house – Dromod – when I was a boy.

No.

Yes.

Wow.

She turned the beam on me again. I know you, I think, she said.

I seen you in the shop, I said.

You like Magnums.

I do.

Here, said the other lad, who had glasses and curls, and I heard a squelch; then he shook a big porringer and reached back to me with a paper cup, Here, he said, you drink that, and this is for you, he said to my father, and this is for you sir and he placed one in Joejoe's fist.

What is it, pray?

Blueberries and apple in the young lad's, and homemade cider for the senior gentlemen.

Cheers, said Da.

They drank and I drank.

It's lovely and warm, I said. I felt this light burning sensation.

Why are you out so late? asked the girl.

We're coming from the hospital, I said.

Oh. Is someone hurt?

The Blackbird fell.

The Blackbird fell? she asked astounded.

Aye.

That's weird.

Let me explain. A neighbour of ours, said Da, fell off his bike.

Yeh?

He fell but he's OK I said, I think. He has a bad shoulder.

So they tell me, said Joejoe.

Are you cold down here, asked Da.

No, but the lady of the house is. She can't light a fire. Her chimney is blocked, like, yeh.

We could clear her chimney, I said.

Tonight? asked the girl.

Well not tonight.

Oh right.

Dead on, keep it in the family, said Joejoe, and you'll want to have a sight of brushes to take on that job. I pushed more brushes up the chimneys of that house over the years than I did in my own fireplace at home.

That's random, said curls.

Homemade cider, said Joejoe.

Yes sir, from the lady in the house.

Very nice.

Thank you.

Because of the dark I'll never know you for again, said Joejoe, and tell me this, and he shone the torch into the face of the silent lad, what about you, what kept you up till this late hour?

We were expecting something. We are waiting to see the meteors going along a ley line.

Did they come? asked Da.

Not yet.

We all looked up at the sky that was like a map of knitting needles. There was a whoosh as a new log took. Sparks flew onto the forest.

We are all on a mission, said Da.

We are son.

Here, said the lad with the curls, and he filled out all our cups again.

C'mon, said Joejoe.

Jesus what next.

C'mon.

And we got up and followed him down the beach, through the open gate and up the avenue to Dromod House. There was one light on in the basement. Through the railings we could see the lady sitting alone on a couch in front of a fireplace. Miss Jilly had a rug draped round her shoulders and another draped round her knees. A one-bar electric fire was at her feet. A deer stood perched on a hillside in a painting on the wall. The hearth was black.

Thank God it's not cold, said Da.

Let's call on her, said Joejoe.

I don't know about that, said Da. Think of the hour it is.

We walked round the house and back again. I went up to the window to look down into the room below. Miss Jilly was still seated on the couch. Her eyes were closed. She was feeding strands of her hair through the fingers of her two raised hands. All of sudden Joejoe threw a handful of gravel at the window. Miss Jilly rose immediately, waved and ran out the room.

Jesus! Joejoe, what have you started, said Da.

We waited, wondering. A light went on in the porch. Soon the front door opened. She peered around her. You – who are you, said Miss Jilly, who are you?

It's me Miss Jilly, said Joejoe.

You? Who are you?

I knew you years ago.

I thought you were the hippies.

You know my son, said Da.

It's me, Miss Jilly, I said.

Oh, Mister Psycho, she said looking into my face.

Psyche, I said.

Oh forgive me. I'm hallucinating. I woke up and thought I was sitting a law exam. I don't know any more.

This is my granduncle Joseph, I said.

Who is he?

Joejoeing, said Joejoe.

Joejoeing? She came forward and looked closely at his face. Joseph; my god, is that you?

Yes, ma'm.

I don't believe it.

And this is my nephew and his son.

Come in, she said. The two of them stood looking at each other. Come on in, please.

The hour is far too late. I took a chance in wakening you at this late hour because –

– I'm glad you did –

– These lads might be able to help you out in the morning –

– Indeed? –

– We just came to call, explained Da, because you see we met the hippies down the beach, and they said you were having trouble with your chimney.

I certainly am, and her voice grew nearly bad-tempered. I'm afraid the place might go up in flames.

Well let's hope we can be of help, said Da.

This is the plan – these pair of boys will come here first thing in the morning and do the chimney for you, said Joejoe.

Oh Joejoeing, do you mean it?

We do, said Da.

Good night now.

Don't go, please.

I have my orders Ma'am, and Joejoe touched his cap.

She stood looking after us as we walked down the avenue to the car. Myself and Da sat in. My granduncle stood looking back at the big house then up at the sky for a few minutes, then he went into the bushes with his torch shining, came back and climbed in with a handful of broken sticks.

And now home, he nodded, along the ley lines.

BOOK FIVE

The Curve

Chapter Twenty-Six

The Watch Room

At eight in the morning my mobile rang while I was breaking a saucer in a dream.

Hallo?

It's the 16th, ye have a job to do later today, Anna said to me, and rang off.

I got dressed and stepped into the kitchen.

Are you ready for the heights this morning, said Da.

I am, I said.

I got my pin and examination number from under the radio, and placed them by the computer.

What are ye at?

There's something I have to do this afternoon.

Take your porridge, said Da.

I will, I said.

We ate and he came to his feet.

Will we head?

Sure.

Yes, we better check the sailors, Mister Professor, said Da and we got our chimney rods and drove down directly to the pier.

We climbed down the rungs not knowing what we might find. The deck was empty, but inside the two sailors were sitting by the wheel. The thin man was retracing their journey across the sea in my atlas and the orange man was looking at the pictures in Da's photo album

I'll bring you out to the main road, Da said, and you can catch a bus.

Thank you, they said.

They waved to the sea, and got into the car. We stopped at Joejoe's and took his chimney rods, then we stopped at the Bird's and threw food in through the post box while the animal within raised a murder. In the back of the car the sailors looked on in puzzlement, then as we took off the thin man leaned forward.

Why no let the dog out?

We have no key.

The orange man shook his head in wonder.

Can we do something for you?

Da looked at him.

Maybe. Yes, you can help me clean a chimney.

Oh yes? he replied puzzled

Instead of going on to the Donegal, we turned in at Dromod. The sailors looked in astonishment at the big house. Our ladyship was weeding the dead flowerbed.

Good morning, gentlemen, said Miss Jilly. She was dressed in a shop coat, short yellow boots and a fisherman's cap.

Good morning, said Da, I have brought some lads to help me, and he opened the boot and unloaded the brushes in plastic sacks and a load of empty cement sacks. The men took their haversacks off their laps, got out and each of us took a bundle.

I don't believe this is really happening, she said.

She led us into the drawing room that stank to high heaven of smoke. Da looked up the chimney.

You're in trouble all right, he said.

Each day I've had to fight off the desire to light a fire.

It's good that you did. That chimney is badly blocked. He tore off a bit of ash from the chimney, and looked up again into the heights. Now I could brush from here up but that could be looking for trouble so I think we'll do it from above and brush straight down. OK?

Whatever you say, Mister Feeney.

Right.

I have a feeling that my past life is soon going to go on display.

Well, first, it would be best to cover up all here, and he looked round the room. Now have you sheets and newspapers?

I have, she said, myriads on the ready, and she showed us a pile of newspapers and bedclothes behind the settee, but you see I did not want to cover the room in case you did not arrive, and she shot a sheet out from her two hands and landed it over the settee. I am gravely superstitious.

The sailors grabbed the other sheets and covered the armchairs, the window ledge, and we spread the newspapers that went back years and years across the carpet. She lifted a vase off a small table and held it to her chest, then replaced it, on a sheet of newspaper. The drawing room had turned white. Now it was in keeping with the armchairs in the entrance hall.

Could you boys bring in a few stones? asked Da.

The sailors arrived back with stones. Da placed a tall box in the grate to catch the spill, and to stop the spill of soot spreading into the room he hung about half a dozen plastic bags pulled tight across the front of the fireplace, held in place at the top under the weight of the stones he placed on the mantelpiece against the weight of the stones he placed on the tiles.

Now, said Da, will you stand here by the grate while I'm above, he said to the orange man.

Yes.

When you hear the brush getting near the grate you yell to him.

I yell to him.

He'll be out there. And he brought the other man out into the yard and placed him at a spot that faced up to the chimney. Then he came in and opened the window. You yell to him, OK.

I yell, said the orange man.

Then we all gathered again in the living room.

Now how do we get out onto the roof? Da asked.

Have you ladders? Miss Jilly asked playfully.

No, replied Da, but a certain gentleman said to ask you to take us to the Watch Room.

She looked at me. Then she nodded to herself.

The Watch Room, she said, announcing the words very slowly.

Aye.

Joejoeing?

The same.

I have not stood in that room in years. This way, she said, gentlemen. The four of us heeled up the rods. I will certainly bring you to the Watch Room, she said, I have not heard it called that name in a long time. We followed her up past the men in the North Pole and the room that housed the ferrets, past the sheets of embroidery, and the sailors looked at every passing picture in wonder; along a corridor with old photos on each side to a final door; she opened the door and we went up a set of steps boarded on all sides towards the top storey, and reached another door, she turned the handle, but it wouldn't open.

I don't believe it, said Miss Jilly, and she swung the handle again.

Aisy, said Da.

It's the rust.

I have the very man. Have you got it, boss?

I have.

I looked through his bag of tools, Miss Jilly steeped back and Da took the WD40 and he shot a spray into the keyhole and round the lock. He turned the handle.

The door opened.

Miss Jilly led us into a small blue room with a glass roof to one side.

A telescope, on a pedestal, stood facing skywards.

The orange man stared at it. The walls were covered with old maps of the sky. A few stars had aged, and one of the sides of the moon had grown dank. Lists of names were everywhere. Stars near the Ecliptic, 1842–1849, said the heading.

My great-grandfather, then my father, said Miss Jilly, spent some time up here scouting the heavens.

It is like being out at sea, said the thin man.

As if they had rehearsed this a long time ago, and many times since, she opened a window in the roof and Da immediately placed a chair on a table, stepped up onto the table then onto the chair, pulled himself up, slid out onto the slates, held for a moment, then disappeared.

He is good, said the orange man.

I climbed up onto the table, then onto the chair with the first of the rods. My head just reached up over the roof. Da was slithering up across the pitch of slates, then he rode the ridge across to the chimney. He pulled himself up, looked around him at the courtyard below and the sea beyond, and gave me the signal. He was about five rods away from me. He had the first rod with the brush head tied to his back. As the lads handed me the rods I screwed up four and pushed them in a straight line up across towards him, then I screwed in the fifth, and it reached him.

Now he began feeding the first brush down into the chimney, followed by the others.

The soot rose up into his face.

Is everything all right, Miss Jilly called up.

Fine out, I said.

The sailors handed me the next set of rods. I screwed another five, edged them across the roof to him, and he took them slowly up into the air, loosened them, screwed them together again, then in turn fed them down the chimney. He turned, signalled me to stop and pointed to the yard.

You had better go down now, gentlemen, I said, and Miss Jilly led the two Russian sailors downstairs.

Da stood on high waiting for a few minutes with a couple of spare rods in his hand.

All right, he shouted down to the courtyard.

OK, came the call back.

He fitted in another rod and pushed, and turned, and pushed and turned.

Suddenly the thin man in the courtyard roared, in answer to the roar from inside the house.

Go on below, Da shouted, we should be nearly there.

I found my way back down to the drawing room. The orange man was on his knees holding the plastic bags against the fireplace. Grains of soot were shooting out onto the tiles and some were coming from the sides.

I am getting frightened, said Miss Jilly, and again she lifted the vase from the table.

She looked at me with terror in her eyes. Just then another belch of soot from above made the plastic bag billow out, but the brush had not reached the fireplace yet.

Hold it, I shouted.

Hold it, yelled the orange man.

Hold it, the thin man shouted up to Da.

I laid out a large black roll of plastic in front of the grate, took the stones off the mantelpiece, and the orange man slowly let the plastic bags down and a shower of soot fell out of the grate onto the plastic. I took the box out of the grate. It was full to the brim with the debris of nests, dead birds and soot. The lads rolled the plastic sheet into a balloon, then we carried the box and the plastic outside, and emptied them into the cement bags, came back and I looked up the chimney, but I could not see where the brush was. It was pure black. I put the box back into the grate, then myself and orange man drew the plastic bags across the fireplace, put the stones back in place, and drew another sheet across the bottom of the grate to catch the fall.

Ok, push! I shouted.

Push! shouted the orange man.

Push, shouted the thin man.

Da hauled up and down. A little soot loosened and fell, then there was another great fall into the box, and against the bags.

Hold it, I shouted.

Hold it!

Hold it, shouted the sailor outside.

It was dancing in the dark led to contrition, said Miss Jilly, and I could see tears in her eyes as she held the vase to her breast.

Again we took down the bags, emptied the box and plastic; then set everything back in place.

Push!

Push! shouted the sailor.

Yes, came a distant cry.

Go! I shouted.

Go!

Go!

Away up above them Da attached the next rod, and rowed down, and I looked at the grate, then when the next rod plunged down the sailor jumped as the brush head gave a dunt in the grate and just then Miss Jilly came with one hand in the air towards us as the plastic began to tear.

Hold it Da, I shouted, you're there.

Hold it, shouted the sailor.

Hold it! shouted the other sailor. Hold it!

The brush spun, then stopped.

Myself and Miss Jilly and the orange man stood listening as the last of the dirt thrashed down into the grate from above. It might have been coming from way back down the centuries. The hard ash from coal, timber and turf. Thousands of pages of newspaper. Through slits in the plastic spumes of black spread.

Oh dear, said Miss Jilly as the last ash spilled.

Da began to haul the brush and the rods up. I took away the bags lightly. The box was half filled with soot.

Ashes, said Miss Jilly, nothing but ashes.

Aye.

She replaced the vase on the small table in the corner.

It's disgraceful, she said. That chimney has not been cleaned in years.

Never mind, Madam, it's done now.

Soften the pain, oh Lord, she sang.

Excuse me?

Yes?

What did you say?

It's a line from *The Pirates* I think.

It's all right, I said.

I don't know. I have no control over my talents or my failings. How is your neighbour who cut the ass's hooves?

He's in hospital.

Oh dear.

Out we went to empty the soot, and my mobile rang.

Well, asked Anna.

I have not looked in yet.

What? What are you doing?

Cleaning chimneys.

Ah Philip, see ya later.

See ya.

Then we all went up the Watch Room. Out at the chimney Da was hauling the rods up, unscrewing them, and letting them slide down off the roof into the yard below. When Da was done he rode the ridge, then let himself across the slates, and slowly worked his way to the window. I helped him climb back inside. He was black faced. He stood in the Watch Room looking down at his body. It was strange to see him beside the old telescope.

Somehow they looked the same.

Do you want to look up at the sky, Miss Jilly asked.

Please.

I took one look into the telescope but all I saw was a reflection of my own eyes.

What do you see?

Myself.

Then a cloud swam into view, then another and another, then my eyes returned into the frame.

Some night maybe you can look up at the stars, she said. Then the two sailors, speaking in another language, took a turn looking up at the sky. Lastly Da took a quick peep at the heavens, then carefully we followed him down the stairs. Miss Jilly winked at me as we passed the ferret room. In the living room Da scraped down the last of the hard ash with the brush into the empty box. We had filled nearly three cement bags with soot and stacked them all in the trailer; then Da stepped out into the yard to beat his clothes and put the rods into the boot.

And finally we all stood under the Indian in the entrance hallway and washed our hands and faces in the sink while herself stood by with towels.

I am indebted to you, said Miss Jilly.

It was Joejoe, dreamed up this job last night, said Da, when he did something he should not have done and threw the gravel at your window.

It gave me a fright.

I know.

Give Joseph my sincere thanks. I have to tell you this, when

I heard the noise at the window I went out to ring the police station.

Jesus.

Then I said to myself when I had the telephone in my hand maybe it's the hippies. Or maybe I'm just hearing things.

Thank God for that.

Here you are, and she handed me an envelope addressed to Mister Psyche Feeney. I hope it's sufficient. What hospital is your neighbour in?

The General.

Is he all right?

Not so bad, I said.

A thousand thanks gentlemen, she said. We have not spoken at all, she said to the sailors. I am Miss Jilly.

Petro, said the orange man.

Sergey, said the thin man.

It's good to meet you. Thomson House is gone. Heather Castle is gone. One is a hotel and the other a health farm. This house will not go.

It will not.

Not while I'm alive. You all must come to dinner sometime.

We will, said Da. Right, and we sat into the car, and drove off. I opened the envelope. There was a handwritten cheque for one hundred euro in it and a small photograph of the ferrets posing on their couch. And a note *Thank you, Mister Psyche, and please forgive me for misspelling your name this morning, yours, Miss Jilly.*

Da drove first to the graveyard where the man from Luton was buried. The two sailors and myself sat in the car outside the graveyard in total silence. They looked towards the gravestones and the mourners gathered by the new grave. Then Da reappeared, and drove the five minutes out to the main road, turned north into Bundoran, and out to the far outskirts.

Here will do, please, said Petro.

Goodbye, Da said, and he handed each of the men twenty euro.

The two sailors thanked us graciously in another language. All morning I had wanted to ask them what happened that day out at sea but now they were taking their story away with them as they gave myself and Da a great hug, and then Petro and Sergey started walking away towards Killybegs, with the haversacks on their grey backs, and their thumbs up in the air.

Would you like to take a walk round Bundoran, asked Da.

No, I said, not today.

Is it because your father is covered in soot?

No.

So where would you like to go?

Home, I said.

Well now, he said. That's a new one.

I have certain business to do.

Whatever you say, son.

He waited on a crowd of surfers to cross the road, then slid out into the traffic. I counted the cars and lorries in the back of my head. When we got to the house I sat down by the computer, went online to www.examinations, and tapped in my pin and examination number.

Up came my name and the results of the Leaving. I trawled down the list like I was going down the rungs at the pier, and when I reached the bottom, I climbed back up. I sat there a while.

My mobile rang.

Well? asked Anna.

I passed, I said, with three honours.

Congrats Philip, good man. I'm glad you made it.

Thanks Lala.

Bye-bye Jeremiah.

I printed the results out and stood in the kitchen drinking a cup of tea. After taking a shower Da appeared in a clean set of clothes, sat down and poured a cup.

I was destroyed with soot.

You were.

What's that, may I ask?

I handed him the print-out.

He read it like a man reading a list of debts, then as he came to the end he found that he owed nothing.

Jesus son, he said.

He stood and shook my hands and ran out to ring Ma and give her the news, then reappeared a few minutes later and said, She asked me on her behalf to send her best wishes to the Professor, and then he stared at me, grinned and lowered his head.

Chapter Twenty-Seven

The Curve

When we came in at visiting time that evening the Bird was fast asleep. In the next bed the man was sitting doing his crossword. He had the pen clenched tight in his hands and the magazine bang in front of his face. Behind the large glasses he wore his eyes never stirred as he stared at the clues.

I put the dudeen I'd brought with me on the side table.

Tom, said Da.

Tom, copulation is a mere habit, said the Bird opening his eyes. We should live alone.

And then the world would come to an end.

Exactly, meaning our part in the world.

You are obsessed with sex.

I am. How is my dog?

Locked up, I said, but fed.

Good.

Will you not give us the key to the house?

No, I'll be out soon, and everything will be put in order. So what's happening out in Ballintra?

Fishermen, I said, and sailors and hippies.

The same old story.

Aye.

Where did this come from? he asked lifting the dudeen.

Out of the old shed at the back of the house.

Don't put it in your mouth, for God's sake, said Da, but the Bird with his left hand promptly sat it between his lips and drew hard.

Nice one, Psyche, he said. It's great to get a good old draw. But there's no feeling in my left arm, and he patted the back of his left hand as if it belonged to another person.

We left the hospital at nine with more provisions from the hospital kitchen and turned up Cooley to the Blackbird's house. The small bulb was still lit in the kitchen. To the side of the house the cattle were gathered, staring steadfastly across the road.

The sky was a dirty black.

This is a lost cause, said Da.

Against the front door the dog pounded and leaped up towards the window in a frenzy of barking.

Shut up ya fucker ya! Now watch yourself.

With a stick he pushed in the flap of the post box. I got the bag of bones and meat, and shoved it in as the dog tore at it.

This is scandalous. It's fucking pagan.

The dog threw himself against the door.

Jesus. This can't go on.

Hold it.

I'm holding it. Are you done?

I'm nearly done.

Shut up! Jesus. The flap closed. Da stepped back from the terror shaking his head. This is fucking terrible. The dog leaped again to the window and stood up on his hind paws barking with no sound. A spit of blood flew onto the glass. Down, shouted Da. The dog ran out of the kitchen back to the hall. He's a demon, said Da. The barking echoed down the path. In the garden the cattle drew closer together. We went into the shed and tossed them hay.

If I was to break down that door, said Da, the dog would kill us.

You'll need to get a vet, I said.

I need a miracle, said Da.

*

238

The oil lamp and candles were lit in Joejoe's.

He's still up, said Da.

He pulled in at the gate. We sat a while listening to the radio, then he switched it off, and stayed there still without talking, then we made our way up the lane and stood against the gable listening to the sea.

What next I ask you? he said. He lay against the wall and put his forehead into his hand. The Bird is not well.

No, Da.

Are you right?

Right.

We knocked and Joejoe came and unlocked the door.

He sat and crossed his legs and as he poured nuts into the dog's bowl Timmy kissed his hands.

You're up late, said Da.

I am. Any word?

They're keeping him in.

They are. I thought so.

You should get some sleep.

I'll sleep in the chair.

Whatever you think.

Psyche.

Yes . . . Grandda.

Sit down. I like when you call me Grandda.

I sat.

You look like you seen a ghost. Was there a fellow at the gate?

No.

There's lemonade beyond.

I'm not thirsty.

No? This boy is upset.

Yes, said Da. He just got good news this morning from St Martin's College. He passed with honours.

Joejoe levered himself onto his elbows.

Good man. Do you know what's wrong with me?

No.

What's wrong with me, he said, is that I never went to school.

You never went?

No, sadly, he said. And . . .

Yes?

You have your chance, so take it; go on and do something with your life. Send him on to the big college . . . to do what is it called?

To do a BA.

A BA? Right, fuck me. Bring him on up to bed. One of us should get a night's sleep.

OK, said Da, and what about you?

I'll sit here.

Will you come in over the next few days to see the Bird.

Joejoe shook his head.

Will you be all right?

I'll be fine.

Could you not lie down for a while?

Leave it.

Good night, Grandda.

Goodnight son.

Poor Afghanistan, he said switching on the TV, then he flicked over and the screen filled up with whales.

I think that man is in deep grief, said Da as we drove home.

I mind to see a hare as we walked down the path to the car. I mind the stairs to the room. And the pillow under my head like a cave. And a queue of shadows forming behind the shadows on the far wall. The last shadow was me watching the others gather.

And then I found myself in a dream at these crossroads well removed from the torrents. The man beside turned into Joejoe and then into the Bird. He was not looking but talking so much he missed his footing and fell and hurt his eye. We bathed it in a pool.

240

Then we went on.

We crossed a field and he approached this red cow and calf he said was his. Are you all right Sissy, he said to the cow. He put his hand round her back leg and then Sissy kicked him in the other eye.

Now he had two bad eyes.

I'm ashamed of myself, he said. He hit the beast a slap. Bad Sissy, he said. The bruise from his fall grew huge. The other one from the kick of the cow sweated red. Blood poured from his left nostril. We went to his house. He got onto his sofa and stretched out under a pile of newspapers. He found these tea leaves and put them in a wet cloth and soaked his eyes.

Bad cess to Sissy, he said.

He fell back and slept. And slept. I did not know rightly what I would do. I should go out and build. The radio was telling bad news over and over. So I travelled through the rooms of the house. I came into this big bare white room filled with the white bones of animals and white timber taken from the sea. There was a key turning and turning in the door. One wall was plastered with cuttings from newspapers. And then more maps. Maps of stars. Instead of beams in the roof overhead there were oars. Four sets of oars pinned across like we were in a boat. The boat was sinking. There were seashells on the window. I sat down on the floor and waited.

A cat walked across the sill then stood on her hind paws, looked in through the windows and meowed and scratched. Behind her the storm was coming. So I opened the window and let her in just before the winds and the rain struck. She went by me.

The man pointed at the fire.

You see that flame standing straight up, he said.

Aye.

That's a sure sign, as he wiped the blood and tea leaves from his eyes.

*

241

That's a sure sign, he said, as the helicopter coming in from the ocean woke me as it thundered across the roof.

All that Thursday and Friday afternoon I worked the wall, pushing the wheelbarrow to and fro, lifting; looking; standing back and then heading off again. I was trying to get the curve right. The curve had to be gradual. The thing to do was let each stone find its place; this was the rule that went through my head. Every time I lifted a rock I heard the command from somewhere in the past – let the rock find its own balance, let it sit on its own weight, and when it does, only then push in the slanted stones to right the position.

I have rules for everything.

If the rock does not fit, wait; every rock will find its place in the wall. No stone should be proud; and stand out from the rest.

It is the small stone that no one sees gives all the balance.

I had nearly taken down half of the small monastery; stone by stone; and moved it an acre away to shield a garden that did not yet exist. All that was growing in there now was whins and nettles and thistles and wild grass. Da was on the look-out for top soil.

I was trying to repeat the pattern of the old stone work in the new wall. I lifted out a rock from the old shed and there in an empty space I came across a child's shoe surrounded by chaffs of wheat. It was small, made of leather, and still unharmed. I brought it up and carefully placed it in the drawer in my room. I took the chaffs of wheat and found places for them in the new wall. The wall grew along the curve. A choir of starlings stood feeding on the seeds of the New Zealand flax that stood over my head in the next flower garden. Hallo, I called. Hallo, they called back. Then they began the flirty whistling. A stonechat spun by, then the wren, with a tipped-up tail, hopped along a branch of olearia, keeping time to a questioning song she sang alone.

242

There was no reply.

Then Timmy appeared, and started pulling himself to and fro against a low tough hanging branch of olearia, all for a scratch on the back. I thought of the two sailors heading up the road as I saw the Lithuanians make their way with their fishing rods along the beach. Then along came the Japanese fisherman who always parked his motor bicycle in our drive. A year ago he'd asked for permission, and some days he'd arrive, shout a greeting, and drop out of sight behind the alt. The gulls were thrashing around Tingle's boat as it sped outside the bar. Beyond that a trawler was headed towards the island.

The thing was to lift, put in place, let sit.

Then gather.

Push.

Wait, while across from me, the clothes that Ma had hung out that morning on the washing line blew like the front line of an army of empty ghosts. The sea thrift was losing its white leaves. The heads of the sea pinks had faded to grey.

It was Saturday morning. I saw the curve. I could not get out of the bed. By the time I woke the next time I had finished the wall. Then when I really woke I knew I hadn't. Everything was there for me to do in the long future. I felt this terrible sense of loss. I was thinking of Mickey. I felt humbled at having drawn stone from the church. It was Saturday again and the mother and father would be going to town to take in the sights. Each time Ma looked into the room I kept my eyes closed.

It's a beautiful day, Ma said.

I said nothing.

I know you're in there, she said, listening.

What?

C'mon with me, she said.

I'll be with you in a minute. How was your night in the hospital?

Well I lost no one, she said.

Good.

C'mon.

I'll be with you in a minute.

That's what you said before.

I have a dizzy head.

Do you want me to get you something?

No. How is Tom?

He's doing well.

I turned over. She sorted out the sheets round my neck. Dusted down the eiderdown.

She brought me throat lozenges and lemon drinks.

She felt my forehead.

I'm all right. I just want to stay here.

Do as you please.

She went off about house again. My soul started getting bigger. Downstairs I heard an argument on the TV. I had the long hands again. In another dream I threw my mobile in the ocean after I received a text from Mickey. Then they put the paper in front of me and I knew none of the questions. Please, said a voice, please take the isosceles off the triangle. I thought I should know something, some small thing, but I recognised nothing. I moved the stones. I looked down the straight line. The teacher smiled at me. I smiled back.

Then myself and Mickey took the corner at Templeboy.

Are you coming or what?

In a minute, Ma.

I went out onto the landing in my pyjamas. She was at the front door with Da.

Well?

I'll stay.

Why?

I don't know.

She looked at me in the way I didn't want.

But I'd like if you came.

I'll go again, next week.

They left. I sat on the top step of the stairs doodling then eventually went back into bed and looked down at the exam paper I had to do. Then I was in the church looking at the altar. Then I got up and opened the drawer and looked at the child's shoe in wonder. I heard the car pulling back in. They had not gone to town.

I stayed in bed the entire day and the day after. I do not want to mention people or where they came from. I might mention that tomorrow. Dad was in and out. He might talk politics, or maybe how the digger was fucked. I think Mammy opened the blinds once, for there was a big surge of light, then it became darker. I saw a toy face in a frame among tens of others. Then the toy spoke.

– It's me, Anna, she said –

– Hallo, I said, but I felt I was imagining her –

– Lala take you an orange –

– Sound –

– It is good for you –

– Yes –

– Do you mind me being here? –

– No –

– Talking –

– Do –

– And afterwards you'll be all right again –

She must have sat there most of the evening reading about the planets. How our food chain was breaking down. Over-fertilisation is the enemy – that's why we are growing obese. We are feeding doses of chemicals into the earth. The fields are like trays of pharmaceuticals, she said. The poor cow is ridden with toxins to make her grow fast, and then what do we do, we eat her.

245

Silence.

We eat her, Philip.

Yes.

Then she headed off again round the world and the food chain then onto and into beds and beds of flowers.

I tried to fit her in but found it hard.

– You were born one year and a week after me –

– That's right –

– I saw your Miss Clarke the teacher today –

– And how is she? –

– Well –

– Yes –

– She was asking for you – Tell him to go to university, she said. Philip? –

Yes.

Do you know what's between your brain and whatever?

What?

A parrot.

Thank you for telling me.

All space is crooked, nodded Anna. Did you know that?

I do now.

Good.

I saw a curve among the shadows.

Get better soon, she said, we need you. Woof! Woof! And look, she said, what I found down on the deck of *The Oyster* in a paper bag. And she lifted out the bottle of Russian vodka that the sailors had left behind as a present in the boat, and she gave me a tipple, and she took a tipple; then Lala said Oh my God!

Chapter Twenty-Eight

The Tent

Next morning I went and gave the sick cow a drink of water then I was at the wall from dawn.

I nearly had three sides done and began the fourth. I was wheeling and judging distances as the stones were finding their place. I weeded the onion bed and squeezed the caterpillars off the cabbage till my hands were green. From inland there was the continuous drone of a strimmer. Then I saw the gulls landing out to sea. I fed the pots with scraps of bacon fat, and got three lobsters. I took the rod and cast off the alt. In the distance I heard the cheers as I came down the road with a few mackerel. There were about fourteen men playing soccer in the Night Field. Around the fences women and children sat watching with haversacks and cloth bags at their feet. There was a line of cars up to our gate. Then I saw the tent that was perched in Joejoe's back garden and the coloured campervan was in the driveway. I thought – what's that, then when I stepped into the house the hippies were round the fire all lit up by the flames, and on the kitchen table were two huge bags of oranges and apples.

Come in sunshine, said Joejoe, this is Mister Thomas that you met down the beach the other night, and this is Miss Angela and Mister Aaron.

Delighted to meet you again, said Thomas. Those fish look really excellent.

Hi, said Angela, we don't know your name.

He's Mister Psyche.

OK, said Aaron.

That's weird, the girl said, that's really weird, like. Why do they call you that?

Ask him, I said.

Joejoe rose and took the fish. I don't know, he said, someone called him that and it stuck.

OK, enough of that, hallo all, I said.

Oh hallo, great. Sit down, said Aaron.

Now for you. These gang here asked to perch a tent out back and I said go ahead, come in, you're welcome.

Your uncle is a lovely man, said Thomas.

He is absolutely, said Angela.

Absolutely, said Aaron handing me a paper cup that he filled with apple juice. And I heard Stefan mimicking the Irish accent.

Do you ever notice that people in Ireland say the word absolutely an awful lot? I asked. They looked at me waiting for me to go on.

Like?

Never mind.

I just don't get you, said Angela.

We are repeating a word we never said a few years back.

We are repeating ourselves?

Absolutely, I said, giving it a great flourish. Then I said Gorgeous. Then I added Grand. And ended with At the end of the day.

Blimey, said Aaron.

Where are you from?

I'm Drogheda, said Thomas.

The Boyne?

The path of the cow is right.

And we're Dublin, said Angela.

Would you like a tincture? asked Joejoe leaning up to the shelf where *Moby Dick* sat, and he hoisted a small turf-coloured bottle of poteen into the air.

Yes sir, said Aaron.

You're very kind, said Angela.

If you're kind to yourself, you can be kind to others, said Joejoe. Then he lifted up *Moby Dick*. Have you read it? It's a great book. My father used to read it every night over the winter months. So each night round nine we'd head out to sea. Then we sold the sea to the EU.

I gutted the mackerel and threw them on the pan. Then I boiled the lobsters. Tommy alongside me washed up the few dishes and put the radio on. That's Jethro Tull, he said. He had small rimmed glasses, and he sang along as he inspected each plate by holding it up to the light. Outside the soccer ball rose in the sky.

You want onions?

Onions'd be nice. Do you mind, I mean would he mind if we smoked some marijuana?

No.

I went out to the garden to pick from the last of the carrots and potatoes. A few wild cheers came over from the Night Field. Tommy smelt the carrots as he washed them under the tap, then he squeezed an orange into the boiling water. I made myself a cup of tea. Joejoe appeared in the scullery with his bottle of poteen and said, Look at the curlew! Where, asked Tommy. Over there, out beyond, and as Tommy looked out the window the old man shot a drop into my cup.

I see him, said Tommy.

Indeed you do. Good luck.

Good luck.

The five of us sat round the table and out came the cider.

This is the nicest fish I ever had, said Angela.

Psyche is some boy.

To Psyche, she said.

They lifted their glasses and tipped them off each other.

Can you remember your dreams? asked Tommy.

No, I said.

Are you sure?

Just very rarely.

Who are those lads kicking soccer in the field?

Latvians or Lithuanians and maybe Poles.

Do you know them?

No, except for the odd nod.

Or when he has to fix their automobiles, said Joejoe.

And those Germans we met down the beach on horseback – are they local?

Oh yes, they live up the road.

The wife, Miss Ingabore, said Grandda, made that St Brigid's cross there on the wall. Yes, that one. She made that last May.

It's beautiful, said Angela.

Is it not strange to be in the centre of a tourist area, said Tommy. Do you not feel kinda threatened?

The young, said Joejoe looking at his plate, are very old-fashioned.

You mean bad-mannered.

No, I mean old-fashioned.

I don't understand.

Backward.

Conservative, I said, I think is what he means.

There was a silence for a few seconds.

Is that a joint?

It is.

Mrs Puff, said Joejoe, is some boy.

Would you like a blast?

I will thank you, and he took the joint. Ah Mrs Puff can leave you a long time on the road coming home, he said, cracking a match. I mind being above at the bridge one night for a long time, and this girl from Sweden led me home. September of seventy-two. He drew a pull. She slept in there – and he pointed at the spare room – and next thing's it's five in the morning and in she comes into my room –

– Oh dear, mumbled Angela –

– And said someone was trying to come in her bedroom window.

What?

I would have taken a look but she wouldn't let me. I'm too gallowsed, she said. Gallowsed, by God! So what did she do, she climbed in behind me.

– Oh.

– Oh yes, and he took another long pull. It was like sleeping with a feather. The dog was put out. He was fierce jealous. And next morning after she was gone I took a look out the window of the room she had slept in, and who was looking in at me – the blooming ass.

An ass, said Angela, somehow horrified.

Oh Mrs Puff, she has a lot to answer for, as he tapped the ash into the fire and handed on the joint to Angela, who accepted it very graciously.

You want to see that German lady Miss Ingabore nip the reeds into place, and he pointed again at the cross. Psyche?

Sir?

I want to give an order – pour us another drop of the crature.

I poured a drop into his empty glass, and then he handed the glass back to me. Check it, he said.

I smelt it and nodded.

Try harder.

I did with a little sip.

All right?

Yes.

Good.

Nice one, said Aaron, I like it.

Do you come down here every night Psyche? asked Angela, smiling.

– Mister Psyche, said Joejoe, correcting her –

Yes, I said. Nearly every day.

You seem like old buddies.

We are.

Far out, she said.

He's my minder, said Joejoe.

And he's my boss.

Here, check it again.

Thanks . . . Grandda.

But he is not your granddad, right? said Aaron.

No he is not, but sometimes he is, and I downed the shot.

Weird, said Angela.

Good man Mister Psyche, God bless you, he said, as he took back the empty glass. Now young girl –Miss Angela – I want to give another order – will you do something for me – will you take the brush and sweep the floor.

I don't understand – you want me to sweep the floor?

Seashells, geese eggs, he hummed back.

That means immediately, I explained.

What are you laughing at, she asked me as she walked round to get the broom. I was just like Oh my God wondering where will I sweep?

Anywhere, I said.

Is there two of you giving orders?

Well, you see, that would be my job usually.

She let go with a broad stroke across the flags and as she did so the dog rose up instantly onto his rear end, faced the ceiling, shook and shivered, and let go with an O. She stopped. Timmy settled. She made a quick scratch with the tips of the twigs. He shot a leg up to beg her to stop. She swept past him across the room and Timmy found the note for a long moan that travelled up inside his nose to the upper chambers.

– I'm stopping, said Angela –
– Good day, said Joejoe –
– Holy fuck, said Tommy –
– Down, I said to the dog –
– I never in my life, said Angela –
– Now do you see, said Joejoe, we're motoring. If only the Bird could come through that door.

The bird? Ah yes, your friend in hospital.

If the Bird came through that door there'd be fireworks.

I didn't think this was going to happen, like, said Aaron, all this. Straight up like. Yeh. Mister Psyche?

Yes, I said as I took a long draw of the joint.

Have you ever slept in a tent?

No.

Just then there was a tremendous knock on the door. The joint was quenched and went into the fire. The bottle went back up by *Moby Dick*. The knock came again.

Come in, said Joejoe and he patted dust off his knees, then – Come in will ya! he shouted getting to his feet.

Councillor Mister Townsend, in a bright green jacket and winnowing light trousers, opened the door and looked in.

Mister Feeney, he said.

Is it that time again, said Joejoe, come in, you're welcome.

Am I interrupting?

Not at all. You have my vote. Now lads and lassies I'd like to introduce you to Mister John Townsend, the elected representative in this area.

Hallo all here, I'm sorry to butt in. I'll just sit a minute; I can see you have a full house. John, he said, offering his hand to

Aaron who took it with a backward smile as if he was putting his hand surreptitiously into a drawer.

How are you, said Aaron.

So what part of America?

Castleknock outside Dublin.

Oh pardon me, you are looking well Joejoe, and he took Angela's and Tommy's hands.

There are three stages of man I was once told, said Joejoe, youth, middle age and –

– And?

– And *You're looking well*, he said aping Townsend's voice.

There was a slight pause.

You never lost it Joejoe.

Pour Mister Townsend a drop.

I lifted the Malibu off the dresser and poured him a drop, then a drop for Grandda.

Is this a party? asked Mister Townsend.

Yes.

I know you son, don't I, go handy, I'm not looking for a vote, young Feeney, there's no election in the offing, I was just passing by and I saw a soccer match in full swing in the next field and I thought *what's happening* and then I thought I'd look in to ask you how your neighbour Tom Feeney is –

Just then his mobile rang. Hallo, hallo yes – where am I – down by the Atlantic Ocean in a certain house, where are you? Where? He looked at the mobile and rose the face to the dim light. It died, he said, then it rang again and he stepped outside to get the signal, and pulled the door after him.

A poor class of an actor, the same man.

Malibu, said Angela.

The same, said Joejoe, sipping it with his eyes widening.

I rang Anna on my mobile.

I'm in Joejoe's at a party – why don't you come on down?

I will.

Then the front door opened again and Townsend looked in and said: There's a man here wants to talk to you.

Send him on in.

A hand came through the door with a pair of pliers.

Hallo, came a strange voice from outside.

Now what? said Joejoe.

Chapter Twenty-Nine

The Death of the Ass

This gentleman stood on the doorstep and said nothing. Timmy went to the man's feet as if he knew him. He was wearing a long orange jumper. I stared at him but his face remained strange till he saw me and lifted a thumb in the air. Suddenly I realised it was Dido the chauffeur. I stood up. He handed me the pliers, looked round the room, then stepped back with a smile onto the doorstep.

Hi, said Angela.

I want speak to the old man, please, he said.

I'm here, said Joejoe.

Oh excuse me. I do not see you Mister Feeney.

Where did you get me pliers?

Forgive my English, and he petted his ear, then he petted the dog. I am Dido.

Well come in and welcome. Sit down.

I will not stay. Please I also bring you this. He stepped forward very daintily and put a package on the table. He pointed at me, and then he pointed at Joejoe.

Have you anyone with you? asked Joejoe.

My wife.

Bring her in, sir, bring her in and let her sit her exams.

Dido lifted the package and handed it to Joejoe who handed it to me, then he stepped out through the door, waving.

I opened the package. It contained a new pair of shoes.

The very thing, said Joejoe. The day is starting all over again. Here Psyche, these shoes are for you. And get chairs from out the bedroom. Tommy please put on the kettle. I feel a good time coming on. Now boys and girls relax, we will take it as it happens. All the politicians are on the move today.

In the bedroom I put on the shoes. I arrived back in my new footwear carrying the auld-fashioned chairs that looked like a pair of young people that had aged prematurely.

Are they coming? I asked.

They are standing at the gate, said Aaron who was at the open door.

Give them a wave.

Come on in, called Aaron.

The minute Dido reached the house he and his wife kicked off their shoes on the doorstep, and carried them in. Both were wearing white socks. He had a purse on his chest that hung from his neck. He looked like he had his hair freshly cut that morning. They crossed the room very quietly and sat by the table.

Going from right to left, said Joejoe, we have Aaron, Tommy and . . .

– Angela –

And Angela, he said nodding. Thank you for the present sir. You like?

I do.

And did they fit? the lady asked me.

I stepped forward in the new shoes.

Ah good.

I am Barbara, the woman said, and my husband is Dmitry Beria, but called Dido.

Psyche, look after our guests.

We are strangers, said Barbara.

So are those crowd, he said pointing at the hippies.

Do you not feel exposed with so many strangers in your house?

Once the strangers talk I don't mind.

Please?

It's the ones who don't speak mean you harm.

I do not understand.

Strange, said Angela.

Dido said something to Barbara. She nodded and translated. Theo was driving back to the henhouse, yes – when Dido saw the pliers . . . on the back seat, and Theo asked him to return them. Sometime.

The henhouse? How does a henhouse get into the story?

It is where we work. With chickens.

I thought Theo was the Russian ambassador.

Oh no, she laughed.

And Dido was his chauffeur.

She shook her head, No, no, she said, laughing, excuse me, did Theo say that?

He did.

She spoke to Dido who grinning bowed his head. He is very honoured, he said, and would like to know that he also came . . . to say thank you on Theo's behalf. You see we live off the fish they catch here in your bay.

You will have a drink?

No, said Barbara so Angela poured out cups of tea for the pair.

You are – Barbara asked – Psyche?

Yes, I am.

The ambassador told me about you. He said you would make a very good fast bowler.

Is that so?

Do we intrude?

No.

Are you interested in psychology? You see, I am Polish, she said, and my husband is the enemy. He is Russian.

Dear God, said Joejoe.

He knows very little English. If you speak slowly he will know what you are saying perhaps. But never mind, we find you. You help my husband. He is very grateful. You thought the

Mercedes was not automatic, no? He enjoyed that day with you. He said it was like being back on stage. He used to be an opera singer but one morning he lost his voice. He was sad. So we come to Ireland, and she made a strict sweet smile. We leave you now.

You will not, said Joejoe.

I drive.

Aye, but let Mister Dido have one drink.

But we come to bring *you* a present!

And now it returns to you, said Tommy and he poured the gentleman a glass of cider.

How did he lose his voice? I asked.

It is a problem. She sat a moment. She spoke to her husband. He nodded. I will explain. He lost part of his throat. It is very sad. I meet him in Warsaw. She moved her scarf slightly. Yes, she said. Then she looked with fond isolation off into the middle distance, and for an instant she picked at a fingernail, scrutinised it, picked a tit-bit, then faced us again.

You like music, and she pointed to the fiddle hanging on the wall. You have a violin.

And it's out of tune.

It is? When did you play it last?

Twenty-five years ago.

Oh. She took it down and he handed her the bow that was hanging from a nail on the dresser. She smiled that stern smile, fitted the fiddle under her chin, turned to her husband and drew the bow across the strings with a quick sour flourish. He kept his eyes steadfastly on her, as she turned a key and gave another dart across the strings.

You play now? she asked Joejoe.

No, thank you.

She spoke to her husband and he said something and looked at me. He had a boy's face with altar boy's eye, a nose that was young and huge hands.

He likes you, she said. Please say yes.

Yes, I said.

And she went to hand me the fiddle.

No, I said, I can't play.

The fiddle went back on the wall, and the bow to the dresser.

Tommy arrived to Miss Barbara with another cup of tea and a few carrots soaked in orange. I brought Dido and herself fried slices of potato.

I would have loved to hear him sing, said Angela.

Maybe, said Barbara, it is possible.

Maybe?

Yes, my husband will sing.

I thought he lost his voice, said Joejoe.

Have you a CD player perhaps?

No, I said.

We have one in the tent, said Aaron, it works on batteries.

You don't mind, sir, she asked.

Call me Joejoe.

Joejoe.

Not at all, said my granduncle, go.

Aaron went out to the tent, and I put on the kettle in the scullery. I stood looking out at the footballers playing seven aside, when all of a sudden behind me an orchestra struck up. I was in two worlds at once. In came a cheer from the field, while at my back another voice called out to a lover. I went into the parlour. Everyone was sitting quiet. Barbara looked at her husband who stared straight ahead as the disc played; sometimes raising his eyebrows as if questioning something in the sound of his own voice, then relaxed he'd look to the side; now Mister Townsend came in the front door, hand in the air about to speak and explain his absence, and the dog growled, but Joejoe rose a finger to his lips and so Mister Townsend entered the quandary, and sat; and then the question Dido was asking himself would turn his whole face and eyes into a shy attempt to answer as his voice travelled round on horseback; he'd smile over at his wife; then the smile would disappear abruptly; the voice went outdoors again, and grew distant; a cheer went up in the Night Field; Dido signalled the violin and Joejoe listened without once averting his eyes from the CD player and urged the voice back in with a little shuffle of his fingers; there was a single deep cry from someone shouting something that could not be explained; the cry was repeated, and now Joejoe and the singer locked eyes; the hippies seemed to have shrunk into their seats, Townsend's toes began to move and Barbara petted her knees as her husband's lips moved silently.

The door opened and in came Anna in her shorts and runners and coloured jacket. She was carrying the same shopping bag that held the vodka.

Joejoe rose a finger, Aaron switched off the CD player, got up onto the window sill and Anna sat into his chair.

Hallo, said Aaron.

Hallo, said Anna.

And you are?

She is my good friend, Anna, I said.

And, said Miss Barbara, she is very beautiful.

She is, nodded Joejoe.

Now Anna I said, listen to this . . .

Aaron pressed the button and we went back into the song again where the lovers were quarrelling; the walls grew on every side; the singer was rushing round his prison, the waves came in, then the flute, and as Dido opened his mouth a fraction to form the shape of the next sound, suddenly the singing abruptly stopped.

Oh, said Angela.

Oh Christ, said Tommy.

Shit, said Aaron, do you know what, the battery is gone.

261

It has happened again, nodded Dido.

Who was that singing, asked Anna.

Him, said Joejoe, that man there sang that song.

You're joking.

Am I joking Psyche?

You are not.

That was powerful, said Anna. Are you sure the batteries are gone?

They are, said Aaron.

What a pity, and she purred.

Aaron handed the disc back to Miss Barbara.

Can I congratulate you, said Mister Townsend.

Jesus, Mister Beria, I said, and I got up and shook his hand.

Thank you, he said, and then he said something to his wife.

He said to thank you again for starting the car, she said, and he wants you to have the disc as a present, and she placed it on the dresser.

Tell him it was nothing.

It was nothing, she said, and she translated it.

He stood and shook my hand again, and tipped his glass off my cup, it was nothing, he said, repeating my words in the accent exactly as I had spoken them.

In fact it was a friend of mine up the road, Stefan, who got your car going that day –

Thank you, Stefan, said Dido.

A Merc is fallible too, nodded Joejoe.

You are Polish? asked Mister Townsend.

Yes, said Barbara.

Ah Lech Walesa.

Yes.

Dido nodded vigorously and took a drink from a pretend cup, up and down to his lips, then looked at his wife and Barbara looked at her husband and nodded as if understanding a complex cry for help, then she lifted an unseen cup to her slim jaw, tasted whatever it was, closed her eyes and suddenly gritted her teeth at the imagined taste.

Jazus, said Joejoe, that's a sour cup of tay you just had.

Oh, she said. I think my husband would like a . . .

I think, said Anna, that I have the very thing and she took a bottle of 7Up out of her bag, poured him a thimbleful and he looked on amazed as she put the glass on the table in front of him.

Please? he asked.

Drink, she said.

7Up, he said shaking his head.

Yes.

Not me, he said laughing.

Please.

Oh well, he smiled, lifted the glass and downed the liquid in one go, froze and threw out his arms in wonder.

It is beautiful he shouted, Beautiful! Beautiful!

Aha, shouted Joejoe.

Wonderful, shouted Dido.

What? asked Aaron, amazed.

Russian vodka, said Anna.

I don't believe you.

And she poured another shot into his glass.

Thank you, thank you, said Dido.

Very good Anna, I said, you had us all fooled.

Are you all right Philip?

Yes, Anna.

Oh she cares for you, said Angela.

And I have just run four mile. Tommy headed off to the kitchen with the dirty delft and began washing. You have a lot of servants in the house today Joejoe, said Anna.

I have, girl.

Aaron produced a bottle of their apple cider, and poured out a glass for me as Anna entertained a drop of 7Up for herself.

Please, said Dido. This is a nice house. I see you every morning sir that we go to fish, and I see you outside with your dog, and he petted Timmy, and you're – you are – an old man – how do I say it – and he spoke to his wife.

And you are lonely, she translated.

And you are an old man and you are lonely, said Dido, I think, yes you look lonely but you see I am wrong, and he opened his hands wide and nodded at all the souls gathered.

Joejoe got up and clapped Dido's knee and threw his arms around him.

You have me, said Joejoe and the two drank then touched their empty glasses.

I love Smirnoff, said Anna and she said the word again with a long, long f-sound.

– Hallo there, said Joejoe –

– Hallo –

– You say Hallo very often in Ireland, said Dido –

– We can't help it –

– It's why we have put on so much weight, said Mister Townsend. I think it might rain.

Slainte, said Anna, downing her vodka and aiming the empty glass at me with a flirty eye. Do you know what Mister Psyche's real name is, she said.

What is it? whispered Angela.

– Doras, whispered Anna –

– No? –

– And I'm Fuinneog –

Doras is door in Gaelic, said the Councillor to Barbara, translating from the Irish, and *fuinneog* is window.

I see, said Barbara.

– And you see the door is closed, said Anna, but the window is open –

– Yeh? –

– Psyche, asked Joejoe, are you there? Did you hear that? The girl is saying the window is open –

– I heard her –

– And your man said it might rain, he said chuckling –

– He did, indeed –

– Are you enjoying yourself? –

– I am –

– Good. You see I lie to myself ever so often –

– The trick is I think if you could break out laughing when making love, said Mister Townsend –

– Is that it? –

– I think so.

– Go on, said Tommy. Have you tried it? –

– No, said Townsend, I would not dare. I'd be shown the door –

– Weird –

– And Doras, continued Anna, is making a special garden for his mother –

– He is –

– So that Fuinneog can bring myriads of vegetables and flowers from the garden centre next year –

– Anna will not step into a supermarket –

– What, asked Angela –

– Never, said Anna, you see I work in one –

Extraordinary!

Overhead outdoors the save-and-rescue helicopter flew by. Dido looking perplexed, said something to his wife who said Dido would like to share a secret, would you like to hear it? We all nodded. With a long sad face he repeated to her what he had said earlier, and lowered his head in sorrow. She turned to us with furrowed brow and lips puckered. My husband thinks there are too many foreigners in Ireland, she said, and they both broke out laughing, and looked round at us and laughed again.

I like it, said Tommy.

Psyche?

Yes Joejoe.

You're very quiet.

I was nearly going to say I'm cleaning my hooves, but what I'm really doing is timing my moves.

Tell us what you're thinking Doras, said Fuinneog.

– I was thinking of . . .

– Don't make it up . . .

– I won't . . .

– Go on . . . But first can I share a secret, said Anna, can I tell you all something?

Of course you can daughter, said Joejoe.

Please do, said Barbara.

Is it one of your dreams? I asked.

Yes.

Ah.

OK, explain to me this – and this will always be with me – Last night I dreamed I gave birth . . . to an ass. OK, that's normal you say. That's funny, you might think. But here's the strange bit – the calf was dead.

Jesus, said Aaron.

Dead? said Tommy and he looked at Anna a long time as Barbara in a hushed tone translated for her husband.

That is sad, said Barbara.

And your granduncle, said Angela, what's weird is that Philip's granduncle Joejoe slept with a Swedish girl who thought the ass at the window was a man.

What?

It's getting fairly intense this conversation, said Mister Townsend.

Oh tut tut, said Anna, I'm all for the ordinary. But if it's not in my head what can I say. You see I think dirty. I may not talk dirty, but I think dirty. The truth is I feed our donkey every morning. I know him. Did you ever look into a donkey's eyes?

No, said Tommy.

Do. If you do you travel far back in time. Yes. And I woke, and felt an awful sadness for the poor dead ass.

That's hard, said Aaron.

You're brave, said Tommy.

So I say to myself, say it, whatever it is.

Nice one, said Angela.

Here's to Fuinneog, said Tommy, raising an empty fist.

To Fuinneog, we all said raising our glasses, and then Joejoe clapped and Dido broke out into sombre applause as if he was away at the back of an audience alone.

Extraordinary, said Barbara.

– Fuinneog –

– Yes Doras –

– When I was young I was told I lost my mickey in a bicycle accident so I would often inspect the place where my mickey used to be and it brought me great pleasure –

– Dear Jesus, said Townsend. What next? –

– Now Mister Psyche, said Joejoe laughing . . .

What is *mickey* please? asked Barbara.

The dowser, said Joejoe and he pointed at his loins.

The divining rod, nodded Tommy.

That's her, said Joejoe.

I think it's time to go, said Mister Townsend, thank you for the company, and just then Dido beat his knee and roared laughing as he heard the meaning of *mickey*, then everyone stepped through the door and followed the Councillor over to his car and we waved and waved, while Timmy flattened out on the ground ears up, then the Councillor got back out again and said he was only joking, he was not leaving, and we all walked over to the Night Field where the soccer game was ending. All of the cars had been turned to face the field and their headlights were blazing. Dido and Barbara spoke to some of the people watching. Angela went down the beach by herself.

Joejoe stood to the edge of the goals that were made of two bales of hay. He stood with his two hands gripping his walking stick. A local single tractor stood on the road. The ladies along the edge in large coats were sipping beer.

You know what I would like to have done today, said Joejoe, I'd like to have seen the Bird referee this match.

A man put his finger to his lips and whistled. The players took off their boots. The tractor went off. The Japanese fisherman shot by on his motorbike with a wave. Soon the cars turned, and took off with the beams heading inland.

Who won, asked Joejoe, I wonder.

Poland, said Dido, Poland was playing Lithuania and Latvia.

The Night Field grew dark as we headed back into the cottage.

We go now, said Barbara.

I have one last request, said Dido.

Fire away, said Joejoe. Everyone had sat down, including Dido, then he scooped a shot, rose to his feet and opened his arms. Please, he said and we all went quiet. I sing. Now please someone else sing!

Sing you, said Aaron.

I will, said Angela. She stood and sang what sounded like a prayer, and with each line she looked into a face, then the next face, and in between she looked at the floor, then suddenly finished leaving more words we did not understand hanging in the air with a swoop of her hand and a swish of her hair.

Aaron beamed and nodded. Angela made a perfect child face and sat as we clapped.

But what was that? asked Joejoe.

A hymn, said Aaron.

Barbara scrutinised a nail.

Now it's your turn, said Joejoe and the three hippies sang 'Help!' as Tommy hopped a spoon and banged the table with

268

his elbow, his fingers, his knuckles, and ended with a riff on the side of the turf bucket.

It takes a worried man, said Mister Townsend, to sing a worried song, as he lowered a shot of poteen.

We all clapped. The room grew dark suddenly and Joejoe lit the oil lamp. The dog made circles. The two lads began to clear all the delft and glasses away and starting washing in the scullery. Dido sat with his hands cradled on his stomach, nodding. Anna stood by the window looking out. Angela crossed herself, and lifted her bag, took out a needle and began to sew. I took a walk to the gate. Miss Daisy Currid, who had run third in the Dublin Marathon, went by jogging in the bright yellows of a high-visibility jacket. Then they all came out of the house behind me led by Joejoe and we stood in a group at the gate. The ear of the moon opened in a cliff on the mountain. No one spoke, as Anna said goodbye and went off running back up the road to home.

We go now, maybe, said Barbara.

Goodbye, said Dido.

We'll all go, said Townsend and leave you be.

The hippies got into his car to take a lift to the pub. Dido's Merc took off chased by the dog. Myself and Joejoe walked round the back of the house.

He pointed.

What is that, he asked.

A tent.

Oh.

And you never played a tune.

Ah Mrs Puff, he said and he shook his head. She has a lot to answer for. I'll go in.

He squeezed an orange into his last glass of Malibu and closed his eyes, opened them suddenly and saw me and nodded. I built up the fire and stoked it quietly, over and over.

Read, he said.

I lifted down the Psalms. It fell open at the Epistle of Paul, the apostle, to the Galatians 1:21–23.

Afterwards I went into the regions of Syria and Cilicia. And was unknown by face to the churches of Judea which were in Christ: But they had heard only, That he which persecuted us in past times now preacheth the faith which once he destroyed.

And they glorified God in me.

That's it Psyche, he said.

There was a silence.

Help! I sang.

Are you all right son?

Yes.

That's it then. It was a busy night. I think I'll hit the sack.

But first he lit the candles and placed them on the window sills and then with Timmy at his heels he headed into his bedroom.

I sat on my own till three o'clock. Every time I got up to go I found another excuse to sit on. I took the drawing book and the pencils over beneath the lamp. I started drawing the face of a man facing away from me in an old copybook. I drew his streaming hair. I tried to imagine what his eyes would see. I felt the tiredness. I drew a fish. I drew a bird. Timmy made a low moan in the other room. I heard a radio away off in the distance, so I doused the lamp, and saw a face –Angela's face – in the light of the candle stop at the window in front of me, but she did not look in, she just seemed to caress and pat the sill for a few seconds before heading onto the next window sill. Then onto the one after that. She was going round the house. After a while she disappeared, so I let myself out and found she had filled the outside window sills with sea shells. I went up the beach under the stars, and let myself quietly in the front door of home, and yet somehow the sound of it closing frightened me. It had a squeak that upset my head, so last thing that night I oiled the hinges.

Then out of the dark I saw the donkey looking at me over the gate. I looked into his eyes. Good night Chief, I whispered.

Chapter Thirty

Visiting the Bird

Next morning I was working on the wall from eight till eleven, then I took a break, sat down in the kitchen, and the house phone rang.

Who is that? came a distant voice.

Mister Psyche, I said.

Oh dear, this is Miss Jilly, I –

Just then the Search-and-Rescue helicopter flew over the house and her words disappeared in the boom.

– and I so desperately wanted to, you see, her voice was saying as the sound lessened and went inland, do you hear me? Then there was a knock at the front door. Excuse me, I said, there is someone outside, I will be back in a second. The hippies' van covered in painted petals had pulled in at our door, and when I stepped out Tommy gave me the thumb and said: – I think you are going on an expedition. I saw my granduncle sitting in the front passenger seat as Tommy climbed back behind the wheel.

The window came down.

Get in, shouted Joejoe.

Just a minute, I'm on the phone.

I went back in. Are you still there? I asked.

I am.

I'm sorry, I have to go.

Go on then. You are a busy gentleman. Anyway I am glad I spoke to him. Bye.

Bye.

I got my jacket, stepped out and climbed in beside Joejoe.

Who were you talking to?

Miss Jilly.

What did she want?

I don't know.

Oh, I see.

Dad came out wearing only his trousers and looked in at us.

Is there a peace demonstration?

We are off to see the Bird.

Good men, send him my best, said Da.

The van turned and took off.

Good morning Mister Psyche, came a voice from behind. In the back were Aaron and Angela sitting on a sofa bed. We passed by the pier with the radio turned to Country and Western and then Bob Dylan sang a number as we sped down Ballintra, and just before the cross we came upon the Merc parked under the oak. In the mirror I saw Angela breathe out smoke with her tongue. Tommy slowed down, enough for us to see Dido and Barbara fast asleep in the back seat under a bright yellow rug.

Will I go on, asked Tommy as he drove quietly by.

Let them sleep, said Joejoe and next thing we saw Timmy crouched in the hedge watching the Merc. Now do you see the fecker, said Joejoe, and he pointed forward, and soon we'd gone by the shop and were passing Dromod House, then hit the main road with a broad swerve, and after few miles I said Left, and we were pulling in outside the hospital.

They drove straight up to the front door.

You can't park here, I said, or you'll get a ticket.

The plan is to leave you here, you see, we're going on, said Tommy.

Oh.

That is Joejoe's plan.

I see.

Oh we can wait if you want, said Angela, it's no problem and then bring you home, yeh?

We will make our own way back, said Joejoe, never you mind.

They all got out and shook hands and embraced us.

I hope your friend will be all right, sir, said Aaron as he and Angela got into the front with Tommy. Thank you for everything Joejoe, said Tommy, it was a great night, and they drove off.

On the steps of the hospital we watched them till they were gone out of sight.

I would never have come to the hospital to see the Bird only for that crew talked me into it. I thought that in time it would be the Bird coming to see me in here. That was how I saw it. Yes. Lead on MacDuff, said Joejoe. *Wash your hands, wash your hands*, said a voice over the speaker as we entered the doors.

The Blackbird was sitting in an armchair by his bed with his cap on his head. The wrist of his left arm was still in a sling. He was gazing straight ahead of him with a quiet look. On the tray on the small bed was half a bowl of ice-cream. On the table the dudeen sat. In the next bed along the same man was doing his crossword puzzle. The male nurse was singing to a man he was feeding in another bed. The Bird saw these two people approaching him at the last minute.

Long time, no see, Joejoe, he said and he offered his right hand, and they shook hands. Mister Psyche, he nodded.

Sir, I said shaking his hand and for the first time in my life I did not get the faraway smell of mint and perfume from him, instead he smelt of sweat and soap.

How are you? asked Joejoe.

I wiped away a tear before you came in, said the Bird, it was my mother's.

Ah Christ.

You see, I go into the past because they have denied me the present.

There was a silence, and then his voice kicked in again.

273

I'm still living in that crevice. I don't have a story, Joejoe, because there is no story.

I understand you.

I can see everything out of the corner of my eye. I have a swollen gland in my brain. It's like a stitch of pain in the tooth. Now tell me.

Go ahead.

What is constipation?

Tell us.

A handbag full of waste.

Steady.

You see I'm going to get better, but they won't let me go home. And a whole lot of shite is piling up.

I see.

Aye.

The male nurse in a stiff white coat came over and leaned down and sang a couple of notes into the Bird's ear as he wiped his face with a wet cloth.

How are you? asked Joejoe.

Grand, the nurse said.

Where are you from?

The Philippines.

Is there many living there?

Eighty-eight million.

Jesus Christ.

On 7,000 islands.

I'm inclined to think that as regards sex, said the Bird, we should go back to the early days.

When was that? the nurse asked.

Back to when you made love to yourself.

A tricky affair, said Joejoe.

Indeed, it would be complicated now. But not back then 365 million years ago. They were more complex times. I don't know how it was done. Then we separated into two.

Like Shiite and Sunni, said the nurse, and Spanish and Chinese.

And man and woman. The last time I saw her she was wearing a cloak, and I was wearing a jumper, said the Bird sadly.

– You were –

– And we took a waltz –

– You did –

– Then she was not there –

– Lonesome is as lonesome does, said Joejoe –

– She walked out through the door –

– She did –

– And never came back.

No.

I'd rather live without the other sex.

But you do.

Not willingly. But you see the truth is I was always afraid of beautiful women. I could work as either a nun or priest when I get out, if I get out.

Touch wood, said Joejoe and he tapped the bedside locker.

The dark-haired broad-shouldered nurse sang to the Bird: *Dahil sa yo, dahil sa yo.*

What language is that? I asked.

Tagalog, he said, and then he sang in English: *Because of you I want to live until the end of time.* He stepped back. Now you look well, Aye. Grand.

You might know my mother, Mrs Feeney? I asked.

She is in the hospital?

Yes.

What ward?

Emergency.

Oh dear. What is wrong with her?

She is a nurse.

Ohohoh, very good, and he tittered, then roared laughing. Like us all, he said. Mrs Feeney? and he thought to himself. Is it Geraldine?

Aye.

A grand lady. Goodbye.

Goodbye, we said and he stepped off down the ward to another patient.

A gentle soul, said the Bird.

He's a nice lad, said Joejoe, friendly. A nice lad.

There was another silence.

Look, I said, I'll leave you two men to talk.

Just then a female nurse appeared and said: Are you all right Mister Feeney.

Where did you get the new shoes, the Bird asked pointing, did someone die?

Christ, she said, do you hear him?

See ya, I said.

I went from Medical North to Medical South, then down the stairs and by the Eye, How is things? a nurse in a blue top and black trousers going one way asked a nurse going the other. The same as usual, she replied; I went on past the Heart, all the blue-handled doors, and down the stairs into Emergency where a gypsy cornered me and asked was I O'Neill? You have the wrong man, I said; *Going up, Doors closing*, and I took the lift to fifth where a baby was crying like an old man giving a lecture on the inner self, Sorry pet, said a voice, you've got to stop; nurses in white uniforms edged with black and nurses in light blue swept by; and next door I heard the single voice of an old lady reciting a prayer I had never heard before; along the corridor an old woman in new black boots with long sharp heels came along swinging a bag followed by more women carrying flowers and their heels echoed on the tiles like hammers driving home nails; *Going down, Doors closing, Mind the doors*; I headed back to Emergency again and as I walked past the seats facing the office the gypsy's eyes followed me with an I-know-you look as he sat there among straight-haired girls with false brown faces who had their hands up their sleeves; I asked a man pushing a trolley where Nurse Feeney was and he said Who is asking? Her son, I said. That's sound, well now, she's out there, he smiled, smoking, and he pointed through the glass doors out to where the ambulances pulled in; Well wonders, she said; Joejoe is above talking to the Bird, I said. No I don't believe it, and she sucked the last of the drag, I thought he would never step into the hospital; this place can be very depressing, she said, very. What time will you be going home? I asked. At five, she said. At five we'll take a lift with you, I said. OK, now I have to go back in; two lads wearing tall green St Paddy day hats were sitting stoned in Emergency and Ma called out *Bertie Wilson!* and one of them stood, and said See you head, and his friend said It's mental. Follow me, she said to Bertie, and bade me goodbye; a baby girl with a bandaged arm shouted Mammy I want a colour! I want a colour, I want to take off my duckie; No, said the mother; Why? I never get to take of my duckie! she screamed; *Going up, Doors closing; This is the Sixth Floor;* I looked into Medical North and the two men were nearly face to face, and I saw the Baby Power go quick from one mouth to the other; I went back down the corridor where Indian doctors strolled and looked out the window onto the town and I saw a street full of newly built, empty buildings, empty bedrooms, empty offices; And the nicest looking building of them all is the asylum, said the man beside me; down in the hospital yard were piles of round see-through plastic bags of paper cuttings; a woman passed in a black suit with silver glinting on her buttons, zips and lapels; away in the distance two lads were kicking football on a small pitch overlooked by a weeping willow and a church; I looked in again and the two men were talking; I went on down past the Delivery Suite, and washed my hands, and sat in the empty church where a woman in a wheelchair sat before the small altar while her man stood watch behind her; I mind a lot from a child's eyes, she said; outside X-ray it said *Switch off your mobile; Going up, Mind the doors*; in the lift a woman was painting her lips; another woman was saying *Brilliant, absolutely* into a mobile, then she added: The problem is that the undertaker is on his holidays in Lithuania, Yes, I know, but there was a fair gathering, nevertheless; chat you later; doctors slouched along in white coats with spectacles and temperature gauges swinging like thuribles from their necks; Why not, shouted a boy; and when I looked in again the men had gone silent.

They were looking away from each other, thinking.

As I stepped in I found the ward was filled with the breathing of a man in a far bed sucking air through a plastic tube as he slept.

I sat on the edge of the Bird's bed.

Said he, you've been a long time away.

How is the man, I asked.

And how is my dog? Well?

He's fine.

Is he?

Yes.

Mister Psyche you don't sound so sure of yourself.

He's in your house. We feed him through the letterbox. We can't get into the house, and he can't get out.

Son, you can let the dog out.

We can't.

You can.

He might attack someone.

What did the dog do to you?

Nothing.

Who told you he might attack someone? he said, and his voice was rising.

You did. You said the dog would ate us.

He was only protecting the house!

278

Calm down, Bird, said Joejoe.

I'm worried about the madra.

I know you are worried about your dog Tom.

Cnoic! he shouted.

Cool down!

Now Psyche, this is what you do – next time you come to that door – by yourself mind – put the key in the door, turn it twice, then open the door a fraction and say Cnoic, Cnoic!

We don't have a key.

He reached over with his right hand and lifted his left hand and shook the lifeless fingers, then placed the hand back down in the sling, and then he reached down inside the bedside locker, lifted an envelope and handed it to me.

Inside it was a key.

Now you do, he said. So?

What?

Say it.

Cnoic! Cnoic!

Cuckoo! said the Bird.

The man in the next bed looked up from his crossword, then the answer came to him, and he wrote it in. Suddenly silence filled the ward when across the way the man's breathing stopped. I thought – God. Then he woke and looked around him. The female nurse took his temperature, and came across to us.

That man there – she said pointing at the Bird – had a visitor yesterday, did he tell you?

No, he did not.

He did. A very important visitor.

Who?

A certain lady, and she pointed at the card on his side table, lifted it up and opened it and handed it to Joejoe who looked at it and shuffled his feet.

Go on, she said, do you see who it is?

He shook his head.

I see an ass, he said.

But there's her name, she said pointing.

I can't read it.

Look, she said tipping the card with her forefinger.

He handed the card to me.

Oh forgive me, she said. You have not your glasses.

When a word is written down, sister, it loses its sound.

The card was stitched with thread and hand painted. On the inside there was a donkey with a hoof raised. On the opposite page was a handwritten note. I read out what it said: *Get Better, Miss Jilly Adams.*

You are some boy, said Joejoe.

Mm-mm-mm, mumbled the Bird.

You want to see them, said the nurse.

Poor Reverend Father Feeney.

And do you know what – she offered him a bed in her house if he needed someone to look after him when he got out of here.

I wonder, meanwhile would she take his dog.

Steady Joejoe.

The nurse leaned down, and the Bird offered her his face and she spread some cream below his eyes.

This woman here, this nurse, said the Bird, do you know who she is?

I do not.

She is Mrs Bridie Waters – a Carraway from Cloone.

I knew your mother well back in November of sixty-two.

Is that so, she said, turning to look at him in a different light. Are you saying I could have been your daughter?

No, we were just friends.

I know the story, she said and smiled, and she took Joejoe's hand and shook it, then she took mine, waved and went off.

Last night, said the Bird, all the people I knew died in my head. Then they woke up in their own bodies. They were themselves – not part of me. I had freed them of my control and I was grateful – I was – for the rush to the head. Mister Psyche, the thing about sitting in the third storey of a hospital is that the birds are below you, or just there in front of you – and he pointed towards the window as a seagull flew by.

Then he looked at his old neighbour Joejoe. I could not give a fuck if I died, he said. Then he looked at me. That's why I'm handing over the key.

For a long moment there was silence. Then Joejoe stood.

We'll go, he said.

Good luck, Joejoe.

The Bird nodded and flattened a sheet and righted his cap. The man in the next bed wrote in another answer, and then righted his glasses.

Bye, Mister Psyche, said the Bird smiling.

Goodbye.

We started to walk down the ward, when I heard the voice behind me ask What will you say to the dog?

Cnoic, I called back, lifting the key in the air.

Cnoic! Cnoic! came the reply.

He'd caught me. I was one word short. *Going down, Going down; Doors closing, Mind the doors.*

Let's go see the nurse.

We stepped into Emergency and stood a few moments till Ma appeared out of Intensive Care wheeling the child who had shouted for Colour! She waved, and said See you at five, and went on. *No smoking allowed,* said the voice over the airwaves as we went through the front door.

Please wash your hands.

Please wash your hands.

Chapter Thirty-One

The Walk

We stepped down towards somewhere in the town. Joejoe was walking fast like a man with a purpose.

Where are we going? I asked.

I don't know.

Will I ring Da?

No, please Mister Psyche, ring no one.

OK.

And with his mouth open he kept walking, with one arm slung through my arm, and his hand gripping the edge of my jacket. We stopped every twenty yards as he stared at the shop to his left and the shop to his right, then took a number of breaths and a long look to what lay ahead, then the nod, and we started again. He did not speak, but even though we were very close, he grew distant, and when he looked at me I saw sorrow that turned to blame in his eyes.

Do you want to sit down? I asked him.

He shook his head.

I just want to walk, he said.

He tugged at my jacket. We went across the Market Yard, and past the Theatre, and stood looking at the pictures of the actors and singers and musicians.

Let's do the stations, he said.

We slowly headed up Main Street into the doorway of Molloy's the drapers. We stood there a few minutes on guard, surrounded by models in suits and blue shirts with yellow ties, then we trooped down to Currid's the chemists, and read the names of the medicines. The next stop was the doorway of

Maguire's the newsagents where I bought a copy of the local *Gazette*. And the last stop was McDonald's where we stood like my father did – pretending to be on duty, or waiting on someone.

Now, said Joejoe. I used to walk your father when he was a young lad round the town. *Can we go do the stations Uncle Joejoe*, he'd ask me, about once a month, and so on the odd Saturday night and we'd set off from Ballintra for town on the tractor. On the blooming tractor. It took over an hour to get here. Then it was off on *the walk*.

He surveyed the scene from all sides. I brought him to the car park and he stared up at the monastery. I could feel his bones.

Will we sit now?

No, not yet.

We stood on the bridge. American couples were leaning over the wall looking down at the river where swans were dipping underwater, while other swans walked the grass at the edge of the river holding their skirts up for fear they might get sullied. The water poured furiously over the rocks.

At the White Horse, the Romanian woman in a great wide skirt handed Joejoe six blown-up balloons on a string. He handed her three euro and we headed back up Main Street with the balloons swinging, then he handed the string to a child in a pram who whooped and let them sail away into the sky.

I could feel my granduncle quivering.

At last he himself sat down outside an Italian café-bar on the pedestrian way.

I don't know where to put my knees. They feel they're not rightly there.

It's just the chairs.

Why is that thing turning into different colours? he said pointing at the flower in the jug.

It's not. It's not turning into different colours.

No?

No. It has different colours.

So what colours are they?

It depends what you use them for.

Pray?

I think it's red and green.

You are a rare boy. Are you doing everything right?

Me?

Yeh.

Do you think I'd be good for anything?

You have knitting fingers.

Thank you.

You'd make a good lawman, do you know that?

Sorry?

It's too late to say sorry now, and he looked at the ground. The chauffeur was some chanter, and those hippies are some boys, but I should never have gone to see the Bird. If anything happens him, I'm gone.

Grandda, please.

Sorry son, it's all right. Aisy now, I should keep my thoughts to myself, and he clapped my knee.

The waiter appeared out onto the street and started clearing away the other tables then he stood facing us.

Now, please, what can I get you? he asked.

What would you recommend?

The soup it is good. Coriander and carrot.

Two soups, then.

Would you like something to drink? We have good red wine.

Two lemonades, said Joejoe.

Thank you.

The waiter took off and we sat there watching the pedestrians pass; the shoppers from Tesco carrying plastic bags; the insurance men smoking outside their office; the fellows smoking outside the pub across the way, and the scatter of stubs of cigarettes at their feet; the accordion player drawing his box across his knee as he sat in a deckchair at the entrance to the Shopping Mall; the gangs came down the street all laughing, then stopping and going on, with the stragglers coming behind, twitching or speaking into the palm of their hands with an array of mobile phones and looking to every side watching out for the enemy and the friend; and suddenly Anna and Emer Waters and Vincent McSharry saw me and pointed.

There's Psyche, Emer shouted.

The gang stopped and Anna came over.

Hi Joejoe.

Anna, he said sadly.

Is everything all right?

We've just been to the hospital, I said.

Oh, is he all right? She whispered into my ear.

He's low in himself.

Look I'll leave ye in peace, she said and she kissed my cheek. See you later, Philip. Bye bye Joejoe and she took his hand.

Bye.

Chat ya, said Vincent, smiling, Emer waved, and they headed off.

The two lemonades and soups arrived.

Cheers, I said.

Slainte, said Joejoe lifting a glass in the air. I did not know from which eye the tear on my cheek is falling, nor which cheek. Did you ever get that? It's a curse. A curse! Did you hear what he said?

I did.

We ate. He then asked for a bowl of cheesecake with assorted fruit and cream. He spread the cream with great care. And then went silent, with his mouth open. I thought he'd be opening up, but no, he just went *Mister Psyche, Mister Psyche*, then looked away.

The poor Bird, I said.

Leave it.

Sorry.

Leave it. I don't want to go into that.

He tapped his lips with a tissue.

This is between you and me, do you understand?

I do.

He surveyed all round him.

It's strange to sit in a chair in the middle of a street, and he held both arms of the chair tightly. A man lifted a traffic cone and began to sing into it a song called 'Blueberry Hill'. A queue lined up at the pass machine opposite us like a line of communicants. Her face like an angry squeezed-up lemon a girl inside the door of the café-bar got change to go back and play the slot machine that she'd left a minute before.

Joejoe called for the bill. I asked the waiter for a bag of scraps if he had any.

Scraps, he said in great wonder and shook his head as he took the money, then a minute later he brought out a Tesco bag of waste held by the tip of his forefinger and thumb, and handed it to me on his tippy toes.

Have a nice day, he said, with a bow.

Good man, said Joejoe, and he put two euro as a tip on the table.

Ciao, said the waiter.

Slán, I said.

The walk began again.

The high tide was washing up the banks along the river.

Woe . . . be . . . tide, he said. Oh dear, dear.

Then suddenly his grip on my jacket grew tight and he swung me towards Collins Avenue. We walked twenty yards and stopped, then the next twenty, and then he propelled me across the road towards the railway station. The place was packed with taxis and cars. The Dublin train was just about to leave. We entered the station. There was a queue leading up to the ticket seller's office. He let me go.

Now, Mister Psyche, we made it.

Yeh.

The next move is up to you, and his eyebrows shot up.

Where are we going?

He looked into my eyes, then shook his head, as if he were giving up on me.

Nowhere, he said. I just want to see the train leave.

So I asked the attendant at the door could we sit on the platform to watch the train depart.

Certainly, he said.

We perched out there on a seat with the bag of scraps at my feet. Crows were flying overhead. Last cigarettes were being smoked. Couples speaking many languages and heading back to Eastern Europe dragged huge bags through the doors. Children in prams were pushed along; and following them along the platform came young businessmen with tight black hair, in striped black business outfits, and carrying briefcases and laptops.

There is nothing more awkward to look at, said Joejoe, than peasants in suits. They don't fit into them.

A man stepped along, stopped, and combed his hair with a horse comb, then stood with a hand on his case and read his mobile, lifted it to his ear and said Oh talk to you later, bye, and looked straight at us.

You had better get on, he said, it will be leaving soon.

Oh we are only looking, I said.

I see, he said and he opened his hands and buckled his mouth, and got on. Inside a man slept in his seat like he was trying to look close at what he wanted to forget. A woman dragging her bags tightened her belt. The train filled up, all the doors were closed. At the rear the railway man waved, then blew a whistle.

The roar of the engine rose to the roof. Joejoe suddenly stood, and took a couple of steps towards the closed door.

Grandda, I shouted.

The train took off and he stood like a soldier watching it till it was gone.

We should have taken it, he said and he spat on the sleepers.

I think it's time for home, he said as we left the station.

We'll head up to the hospital and get a lift from Ma.

No way. I don't want to go back to that hospital again, please.

What will we do?

I don't know.

Will I get a cab?

No way. We'll walk.

Joejoe, we can't walk all the way home.

I know that.

Let me ring Ma, I said, at least she'll know.

No. Don't be annoying her. We'll only go out a bit on the road and the nurse will see us and stop. All right?

All right.

And so we went along the river counting the swans and stopping every twenty yards till we hit the main road.

We passed the last traffic lights and walked out beyond the petrol station and the shop. His grip lightened as we trod the slow lane.

What time is it?

Five to five.

Now it's up to you, he said.

We went another few yards and stood. He looked with great wonder at the lines of sycamores and oaks that had begun the first light shedding of their leaves. I watched the cars and lorries approaching and looked out for the red Fiat. We were there fifteen minutes and there was no sign. We moved on and sat on a low cottage wall. Just then my mobile rang.

Are you all right? asked Anna.

Yes, I said.

Ring me if you need anything.

Will do.

I'm here potting away.

Away in the distance the mountain looked like a dark circus tent. And just in front of us a real circus was pitching its tent and the camels were feeding like mad off the hedges. The elephant was prodding the gate with his snout. A squad-car, alarm ringing, raced by. We headed out past the Fisherman's Inn, past the old fort, with Joejoe hanging off my jacket, and yet he would not stop walking. We must have gone three mile. I kept looking behind for Ma's car.

Will you promise us something son – one day, can we take that train?

I promise.

Good man. I need to get away out of here for a while.

We walked past the huge deserted building that was once a mill. On the other side of the hedge sheep followed us. My mobile rang. I looked at the number. It was Ma.

Who is it?

Ma, I said.

Don't answer it, please – we are on an adventure.

It rang off and I texted her: Ma we are on an adventure. We stood by the graveyard. The first blackberries were showing their grey heads. Then along came a garden of blue rhododendrons. A line of traffic went slowly by behind a tractor that refused to go into the slow lane. Soldiers, in a green jeep, blew hard on the horn. Grass from a mown lawn down the road lifted and fell like sympathy cards among the graves.

How long is the river Liffey, he asked me.

A good few mile.

Cool, he said, imitating Anna and he turned and raised his hand in the air like a bandleader. A line of cars and lorries flew by, then suddenly an old Toyota shot to the side, pulled in and screeched to a stop. Stefan stepped out and threw his arms out wide.

I am at your service Mister Side Kick, he said and he opened the back door and said Grand day, Mister Feeney, and Joejoe crept in and put his cap on his knee. I sat into the front seat beside Stefan.

Where to? he asked.

Dublin, said Joejoe.

You say, he said looking back . . . Dublin?

He's only joking.

I too would like to go to Dublin, said Stefan, but . . . it is not possible. Not today. Mister Doyle would not be happy.

Some other time, maybe?

Yes. No problem.

You promise?

I do.

Good man, good man, said my granduncle. Stefan, you are a gentleman.

Absolutely, said Stefan in a broad Irish accent. He turned the ignition on.

You were shopping? he said indicating the Tesco bag on my lap. I opened the bag and showed him the scraps of fish skins, spaghetti, and bread.

Phew! Oh, dear, he said, and he adjusted the mirror, turned on the indicator, and watched waiting for a break in the traffic. I do not understand you. You go on a journey to town to take home rubbish?

Yes.

It is a joke?

It's for a dog, Stefan.

The dog, you go to town to shop for the dog?

Not really.

OK, grand. So we are for Ball-in-tra, asked Stefan, yes?

Yes, but did you ever feel that you did not want to go home?

I know what you mean, Mister Feeney, that is why I am here.

Can I ask you a favour?

Yes.

Will you bring us the long way home, through the trees under the mountain. I want to see the trees before they lose their leaves.

I will.

Thank you.

And may I ask a question please? asked Stefan.

Fire ahead.

Why you are out in the middle of the country, hitching – at your age? he asked, as we took off to a wild burst of classical music from the radio and shot in behind a Guinness lorry.

It's a long story, said Grandda from the back. I don't know where to start.

Stefan turned the radio off.

I am listening sir, he said.

Chapter Thirty-Two

The Rifle

All of a sudden we were stepping down outside the cottage at Ballintra. Stefan took my granduncle's hand and helped him out of the car.

Thank you for all the stories, he said.

And thank you for the lovely jaunt; come on in, said Joejoe, for a small shot of something.

You think?

Yes, I said. Stefan walked up and started to spill the shells on the window sills through his hands as Joejoe unlocked the door.

They bring you luck, no?

Yes, said Joejoe.

But I must not drink too much, no?

One shot, said Joejoe.

One, said Stefan, nodding, and he threw himself into a drunken heap against the doorway, lay down on the path, straightened up, and we all trundled in, and Stefan looked round in wonder as Timmy sat in his chair on a beautiful new plaited rug.

Your house is beautiful, a beautiful tidy home, he said.

Take a look around, said Joejoe.

The house was impeccable, every corner had been tidied, the items on the dresser placed in perfect order, there were bundles of wildflowers in every vase and in flower pots; the pictures on the walls had been newly hung in straight lines; line drawings in colour had gone up on the walls; in the kitchen every dish was washed, and out the back every stitch of his clothes were hanging on the washing line. We went into the bedroom, his bed was made. I looked under the bed; I looked in the wardrobe, and came back into the kitchen.

The place is spotless, Joejoe.

Look, he said, the fire is set, and in a box in the corner the turf was neatly piled, and all the sticks of timber had been cut.

The hippies were busy, I said.

They were. They've saved you a spot of work son.

I took down the bottle of poteen and poured out two small measures.

It is?

Poteen.

Achiu, said Stefan.

God bless you, said Joejoe.

Thanks a million.

The Bird made it, the real thing, from his own spuds.

And they drank both glasses on the spot.

One more, said Joejoe.

One?

For the road.

The road . . .

I poured out two more.

Ah, he said smelling the glass, *Mister Poteen*. What will Mister Doyle think? Will he smell it off me? He shook the drink, lifted it to his mouth, and slowly drank it down and stood. I go now, sir.

If you must, said Joejoe. The two of us followed him out the door, and just then a hare came down the path, and Stefan rose his arms and aimed as if he had a rifle in his hands, followed the run of the hare, and went *Bedumb!* as his finger closed on the imaginary trigger.

You got him.

I did.

So you are a gunman?

In another life, I was a marksman. He looked around him, and put his fingers to his head pretending to have lost where he was, and then looked round in a drunken wonder.

Now where am I?

Ballintra.

Ah yes.

He took out his mobile.

Mister Side Kick, please give me your number and I will ring you.

086 78 35 713.

Thank you, he said as he repeated the numbers then pipped them in, and suddenly my mobile rang.

Hallo, I said.

Hallo, said Stefan as we stood face to face.

Oh it's you.

Yes. It is me. Now you know how to get me. Some day soon we can take your uncle for another spin through the trees.

We will, I answered.

Iki, he said.

Goodbye.

Cheerio, said Joejoe.

Kol kas, said Stefan. I will see you. We put away our phones and Joejoe and myself walked him to the gate. He sat into the Toyota, waved, and drove down away. As I lit the fire Joejoe placed an unlit candle by every window for the night ahead.

Then he stood by my side.

The shells look lovely, I said.

I'll sleep tonight, he said. One thing son, I will never stop in to see the Bird in that hospital again. Never, OK?

Got ya, I said.

Never, he repeated. If anything happens the Bird there won't be much point in me continuing on.

Is there anything you want?

No need son, it's all been done.

OK. I'll come down later tonight.

Do, then Joejoe studied me and said: But isn't there something important you have forgotten?

What is that?

He turned an imaginary key with his thumb and forefinger.

Oh sugar, I said and I felt the key in my pocket, I left the shagging bag in the car.

You what?

I ran outside. The Toyota was back at the gate, and Stefan was holding aloft the bag of scraps out of the driver's window with one hand, and holding his nose with the other. I took the bag.

I return your rubbish.

Thank you, Stefan.

No prob, he said, and he drove off smiling with his head bobbing and his eyes closed.

Good luck, Mister Psyche, muttered Joejoe as I set off for the Bird's house with an imaginary dog tearing at my skin.

When I reached the door the mad growling began inside. I emptied the pasta and old ham on the footpath, opened the envelope and took out the key.

Now, I thought. The barking grew worse. I said a prayer and put the key in the lock, and turned it a fraction.

I could feel him pounding and leaping inside against the timbers. The barking went up the scale.

OK, I said, here goes, and I turned the key twice, opened the door a fraction and shouted Cnoic! Cnoic! And then I drew it wide open. The dog rose silently onto his back legs, strutting with his ears up. He ran forward and rammed his snout into my shin. I could feel the weight of his body in his jaw, then suddenly he shot by me, and went straight to the food, yowling.

Cnoic! I said, Cnoic!

He went silent for a second as he took a mouthful. I was about to close the door, but on instinct stepped inside and pulled it after me. Now that I was inside, and he was outside, the barking stopped. Thank you Mister Bird, I said to myself. I had entered the Bird's house for the first time in a couple of years. I opened all the windows. Padre Pio still hung alongside a starfish on the wall of the little corridor. I looked into the living room, yes, the settee was sinking but the table was wiped clean. A single armchair faced into a grate of paper, twigs and turf, ready to be lit. Each side of the fire were chunks of timber and turf. Empty naggins of whiskey and brandy stood like a group of lost souls in an old glass cabinet, bottles that I had bought over the years from Mister Sweet Lucky John's. Above the cabinet was a photo of Joejoe and Tom Feeney fishing out on Loch Teo.

The carpet of roses was worn.

I headed towards the kitchen. Each step I took I expected to land in dog poo, and this is where I thought I would find lashings of shit, but the kitchen was cold and clean, with a kettle on the gas hob, and the remains of onion soup in one pot and the bones of mackerel in another. On the rack washed delft lay. A pile of winkles sat in a bowl on the floor. When I touched them a few moved and tingled. They were still alive.

Then I heard voices.

The voices went.

I started towards the toilet. The carpet was covered with dog hair, and there at the end of the corridor was a hole in the back door that opened into a small shed at the rear. I lifted the latch and walked in. It was a dark dusty place filled with tins and old newspapers going back to the fifties. There were teddy bears and nails and hammers. A pair of whale bones, and a picture of a small cowboy. There was a large aluminium basin of sand on the floor and this was the dog's toilet. It was ridden with shit and piss. I pulled back the bar on the back door and emptied

296

the basin into a drain and filled it with sand from a pile at the ditch. I locked the back door, placed the basin back where it had been, and re-entered the house itself, and stepped into the Bird's toilet.

I looked in wonder at the ledge under the mirror and suddenly understand where the exotic smell the Bird always exuded came from.

There was a line of perfume bottles on the shelf.

I squirted them into my hand and smelt the Bird. I did my neck and knees and elbows with Celine Dion. A towel on the floor had two black footprints. On the window ledge were coral fossils. I headed to the bedroom, opening windows as I went, and then I heard the voices again. They were talking in a mumble. I waited, and then went in. Inside the bedroom was a small single bed covered with an army jacket. From an old electric radio the voices were coming – and they were arguing for an increase in the dole. *We are entering a new phase*, the voices repeated. The dog reared up on his legs at the back window and was looking in at me. On a pillar of red brick sat a gold clock and a photo of an ancient lady sewing.

I leaned down to switch off the radio.

It was then I saw it, leaning to the right of the dressing table, a rifle that was the exact replica of the one Joejoe had. I stood and looked out through the window at the dog and as I reached up for the latch to open the window in the far distance across the fields I saw our house above on the cliff, and for a split second below to the left I imagined I saw Joejoe's house. I lifted the rifle and went through a fierce uncertain angry feeling. Jesus Christ, perish the thought. I saw the bullet hole in the window. I put down the rifle. I heard the Blackbird shouting *I never fell; what are you talking about?* I saw again the Mass begin at the Stations after he had called *Stop!*

*

Then I smelt the perfume on my hands.

I washed my hands in the kitchen sink and went in and looked in the drawers and found a list of phone numbers on a sheet of old ruled paper.

I sat in the armchair and read them. Folk in Luton, in Glasgow, in Mayo.

I looked at the makings of the fire and began to enter the Bird's head. I saw the child of Prague and the Buddha on the mantelpiece; the fishing reel on the table; the two bottles of Spanish Rioja placed in the corner. The small wooden ship on a shelf above the fireplace. I heard the shot in my head. Jesus, I thought, so I went out the front door and brought in his bicycle into the hallway, closed the door and sat on the wall outside. I waited. The dog came over and studied me.

Cnoic! I said, Cnoic!

He turned, went on, then turned again and ran on up the road. I called him, but he just sat looking back at me, saying *come on!* with his snout, so I went back in and closed all the windows, turned off the light, took up the basin of winkles, locked the door, pocketed the key and went towards home, with the dog following me at a distance, and something else was following him – a great shadow – a darkness. I threw the winkles down the rocks. I stood at the gate at Joejoe's and looked back at the Bird's house but I could not see it. I had made it up. I had imagined it.

Up overhead the clouds stepped out like three of the apostles out onto the dance floor.

Well sunshine, are ya coming in? a familiar voice behind me suddenly said.

Timmy and Cnoic faced each other, then rolled in the grass and chased each other down the beach without a bark, then ran back up side by side.

You got the dog.

I did. He's called Cnoic.

Good man, you're a good soldier.

I'm heading up home to do the wall.

So, you can leave the dog here. Is that you Cnoic, he said.

The two dogs followed him into the house and he closed the door. I went down the pier. Inside the cabin on The Ostrich I imagined I saw Anna reading, with her head in her two hands and her lips moving as she faced down into another language. Her ghost looked up at me for a second, and waved, and I waved back and said Love you and I went on, then turned back and walked up to the pub. It was empty. John's daughter was behind the bar playing Sudoku. I shot a game of pool by myself and then heading home I stopped a moment at Mickey's monument and blessed myself and said a prayer.

Eventually, I made my decision and headed to Mick Doyle's.

Stefan was lying under a BMW.

Hallo, I said.

Who is that?

Mister Psyche, I said. You understand guns.

I do.

Can I ask you something?

Yes.

Would you answer me this – there's a bullet hole the size of a euro in a window. Right?

Right, he said, pushing himself out on the low trolley so his eyes were looking up into mine.

Now did the shot come from inside or outside?

Good question, he nodded. Was the glass . . . how you say . . . shattered?

No.

So what was there, please, again?

Just a round hole with little shards.

Shards?

The bullet hole was shaped like a star, and I made the shape with my fingers.

Well Mister Side Kick if the bullet came from a long distance away the pane of glass would be in pieces.

I see.

Outside, you see, and he stood, and pointed towards the trees and the sky, you have to contend with the . . . elements, yes. The bullet would go this way, that way. Indoors . . . there is peace, no?

Yes.

Less . . . turbulence, right?

Got ya.

And inside the room is small, no?

Yes.

So . . . it is a short distance to the window . . . so it is . . . my belief that the bullet was shot from inside this house. OK.

OK.

That it?

That's it, I said.

Why do you ask such a question?

I needed to know.

Are these the bullets mentioned on the night of the Stations?

Yes.

You look sad Mister Side Kick.

Look, thank you, Stefan.

It is nothing, sir, soon we shall go for another drive, sometime. Right, and he rolled back under the car.

Chapter Thirty-Three

Away with the Birds

Outside the house the red Fiat was parked, and Ma was standing on the step as I came across the yard.

So you got here at last, she said, drawing on a fag.

Yes.

I waited at the hospital for over an hour but you never came back.

I'm sorry, Ma.

I rang you and you did not answer.

I know. It was just that Joejoe did not want to be putting you under any stress.

So you went on an adventure –

– Yes –

– And left me waiting. Who brought you home?

Stefan – who works in Mick Doyle's.

So you met him in town?

No, out the road.

I don't understand.

Ma, I'm sorry. Joejoe wanted to walk.

He wanted to walk home?

No, we waited out the road for your car to appear. He would not go back to the hospital.

Why?

I don't know.

So what did you do?

We hitched.

You hitched home.

Yes.

I don't believe it. Why did you not ring me?

He would not let me.

She sat down on the bottom step of the stairs.

Things are going asunder, she said.

I'm sorry Ma.

What is going on?

I don't know.

Did himself and the Bird have a row?

Not that I know of.

Not a cross word?

No. But you see the Bird more or less said he was going to die.

Oh Jesus.

And Joejoe was upset.

Ah Christ, she said.

So I went out to the wall and started building. As I lifted the stones my head grew heavy.

There was not too far to go. Then in my head I walked the Blackbird home the morning he left the house. He did not fall. I saw the guns raised, and I put them down. I made peace as the fossils in the wall grew. Some were shoes, some backbones, some a bird's wing, and one or two were leaves. I saw a saint's face. I saw a pair of lips in a round sea stone. The wall grew as the star-shaped hole in the window opened a vein in my head. I carried stone after stone, put them in place and stepped back to look.

The line was wandering. The curve was growing.

I got that run of the wall nearly finished. I went into the sitting room and turned on the TV low. Men and women and children were collected on a sandy area waiting on water. Somewhere else *The Bill* was just beginning. On the next station they were shooting pool.

I heard his car. The door opened and Da entered in his working gear.

You did a sight a' work outside, he said.

A bit.

Well I have good news for you, we have a new job starting soon.

What's that?

Miss Jilly has asked me to remove a small hill that's blocking her view. It will take less than two days. So are you right for a bit a' work?

I am.

He sat.

Well how is the Bird?

He was asking for you.

He stood looking at me.

They're getting to you, son, he said.

I'm all right.

You're in trouble.

Just bewildered.

I know what you mean.

Just then there was a rush against the front door and a burst of barking. Da got up and opened the door and shouted Timmy but Cnoic came in and lay at my feet.

Jesus Christ, Da said, is that who I think it is?

Yes.

You got into the house by God!

I did. And I handed him the sheet of phone numbers.

Fair deuce.

He watched the dog.

He trusts you, he said.

Do you mean the Bird or the dog?

Both I suppose. Good man, son. He sat into the armchair. We can bring up the top soil from Dromod and make your mother that garden for next year. There's great earth down there, it's black and fertile. We'll dump it in behind your walls. All you have to do tomorrow is tear up the ground and do a bit of excavating with the JCB so we don't end up feeding the weeds.

I like driving the JCB.

That's good.

He looked at the pool players on TV potting balls in silence.

Is there anything you want to tell me?

Today we nearly took the train to Dublin, myself and Joejoe.

Oh I see.

That's the truth.

Yes, son, there's a funny side to everything. But is there anything else you want to tell me?

Yes.

Go on.

I'm sorry we didn't go.

Well fuck me, and he roared laughing. Cnoic crushed in against my legs and I petted him. I reached down and Cnoic reached up and kissed my ear. Da, I said.

Yes.

I'm seeing things.

Settle son. Settle. Easy does it. I grew up like you once, taking sides. You know something but you won't tell me.

Ma appeared, and went over and petted Cnoic who followed her back to her armchair.

Dare I ask? she said. Is this the Bird's madra?

Aye.

I thought in the long run he might have to be put down. So you freed him. The poor cratur. Was the house a mess?

No, I said, pouring out a glass of still water.

Really?

It was all right, I said calmly.

Dear God, she said, will someone tell me what's happening?

Would you like glass of Sauvignon Blanc, Geraldine?

I would.

Da went off to the kitchen.

304

So, there was no dog poo?

No. It was all out in the back shed in a pot of sand.

Good dog, she said. It was unkind having him locked up. I'm glad he's free. Da came back with a long tall glass of wine in one hand, and a bottle in the other, then there was a polite knock on the door and Anna looked in.

Gentlemen and ladies, am I intruding?

Not at all, said Da.

Is this a party?

Kind of.

May I join you?

Indeed you may, and Da poured her a glass of white and she went round each of us touching glasses, then she stood in the middle of the room and lifted her glass in salute to me.

I have news for ye all, she said.

Pray tell.

This lad here, said Anna – I would like you to know – was sitting this afternoon on the street with his granduncle Joejoe outside one of the most posh restaurants in town.

Is that so? said Da.

Indeed we were.

With their own waiter standing by.

Aye, true.

And then – if I may interrupt – after their meal, continued Da, they had another plan.

Is that so?

They were going to catch the train to Dublin.

Is that right? asked Ma.

Yes, I said.

The plot thickens, she smiled.

But reluctantly, added Da smiling, they came home.

And the story does not end there, said Ma.

No, I said, give me a glass.

Jimminy! he exclaimed and he poured me a thimble of sparkling wine, and we drank together.

Oh yes, said Ma, and now I would like ye to consider the means of transport they took coming home.

Did you not bring them?

No, I did not.

So who did?

Silence.

They took a taxi, don't tell me, said Anna.

No, wrong.

Then how did they get back may I ask? Da asked looking at me.

They hitched, said Ma, grimacing.

That's mental, said Anna.

It's fucking daft, said Da.

It's what he wanted to do, I said.

You head into the hospital with a dose of hippies and next thing you hitch home?

That's the story, I said.

You're away with the birds, said Anna.

Exactly!

Settle.

And, by the way, it's not funny.

No, it's not, Da said smiling.

I said it's not funny!

Steady. Cool down, son. There's something he is not telling us but I have no appetite left for arguing with my uncle or my son. One day will you tell us what is going on?

I will. I promise.

He has the walls nearly done, said Da. The day after tomorrow we are going to start to make you a flower and a vegetable garden Geraldine for next year. I have a man who is going to be coming up with earth from Miss Jilly's and that boy there is going to help me. And we will buy all our produce from that girl there Miss Conan.

Thank you.

We will let the hare sit for now, said Da.

Cheers, said Anna, I think it's time I took off.

Right, I said, and I'll head out to finish that wall.

At this hour, said Ma.

Yes, I said and the dog got up and followed me, and outside Anna kissed her finger tips of her right hand and touched my cheek.

See you later, she whispered.

Bye.

It was growing dark. I lifted, stood and held. Then Da came out and wheeled over a few barrowloads of rocks from the small pile left. We did not speak. When we worked together we never spoke. He emptied the loads at my feet. Cnoic lay watching us. Da tapped me on the shoulder, and nodded towards the house.

OK, he said, I'm leaving it at that. I think there's enough there to see you through.

Right.

I'm going in to ring the Bird's relations, he said. He headed off.

I worked on. Ma came out to me with a cup of tea.

Take it easy now, she said.

We have to have this done for the morning.

You'll do your back in.

I'm grand.

I'm not getting at you, you know.

I know. Thanks Ma.

The golden rods were tossing. The dying buachalawns were bunched up in dry stacks of brown. The sun as it set out to sea was shining like mad in Grandda's window. The rays burnt like flames. Then the windows went dark and on came the candles. Two cormorants flew south. A wren was chiselling the question mark. A starling like a gent on a street corner was whistling at the ladies. The brown hare went down his track, bracing himself every few steps. Then going north came a lone cormorant, and dead straight overhead, he stopped his wings for an instant. The last stonechat talked in flurries on the wall. The sudden sharp bellow of a cow. In the far distance the sky above the town lit up. Lights appeared on further shores. I had reached the point where the gate would be. It was nearly done. I had gone round into the round. I was working the pillar to match the pillar on the other side. The curve had started again.

I let it be and put one of the last stones in place.

Tomorrow I would finish it.

The starlings rose into a mushroom in the sky. There was something else I needed to do before I went to bed. I looked into the living room and said I was off down to Joejoe's to say goodnight.

On you go, said Ma.

I rang all those numbers, Philip, said Da, and not one of them ever heard of Tom Feeney. And Geraldine has just told me what happened ye in the hospital. I'm sorry son.

And all because of this, I said and I lifted out the key, all because he handed over the key, I said, and I put it back in my pocket and headed for the door. With Cnoic at my side I went down the road looking at the stars. Joejoe let me in.

We sat by the fire with Cnoic and Timmy at our feet. I lifted up the Gazette and read him the news of local arrests, drunken assaults, lists of planning permissions, drug finds and details of an ongoing murder trial. When I reached the obituaries I turned to him.

Can I ask you something . . . Grandda?

Fire ahead.

Where's your rifle?

Why do you ask?

Just.

He studied my face.

I think you know where it is, he said.

Do I?

I think you do.

Silence.

You saw it in the henhouse above. Didn't ya?

Did I?

You did.

It's your gun?

It is. You see, the Bird took it away from me.

Silence. I bowed my head.

When?

He took it away the night before the Stations.

Why did he do that?

For my security, he said.

Silence.

You see he thought I might do myself or someone else an injury. Do you think I put that bullet through the window?

I think so Joejoe.

Well if you think I did, then I must have. I musta shot at my own reflection. To kill my ghost.

You don't remember?

No.

I sank the palms of my hands into my thighs. Then Joejoe looked at me and nodded.

You look lost.

I am.

Read on, Mister Psyche, he said, and so we hit the deaths.

BOOK SIX

The Protestant Earth

Chapter Thirty-Four

The Dig

First thing next morning Da had the mobile to his ear. He was looking to hire a local lorry to draw the clay from Dromod.

How much an hour did you say? asked Da.

Then he looked at me.

Forty euro? I'll ring you back.

He put down the phone.

He must be joking, he said.

He rang the next in line.

How much? he asked. Look, I'll be in touch, yeh, soon. They are all living in a different fucking time, he said to me. He rang around the drivers he knew then he hit upon a crew in town. They put forward a deal at twenty euro an hour, and that afternoon Da drove to town to lead the lorry out to our place. About two hours later he rang me to meet him at the gate. He pulled in with a convoy – a lorry and a van – following him behind. The lorry was parked at the pier, and then the driver dropped down to look out to sea. He was joined by the driver of the van.

This is my son Philip, said Da. And this is Gary, and this is Desmond. We shook hands.

I have never stood in this neck of the woods before, said Desmond.

It's awesome, said Gary who was wearing a wide leather Australian hat. He looked inland. Now that we are here I wonder how do we get home?

You go back the way you came, said Da.

I take that for granted, but –

– No problem, it's the same for everyone, now said Da, go
straight for a half a mile? –

– OK –

– Then you go left at the first T-junction –

– Right –

– No left, Da said –

– OK, said Gary laughing –

– Then on to the school, then right –

– Got ya –

– On past the fort –

– Past the fort? –

– Aye, and Da traced the journey back to town with his
finger in the air while the two men moved their lips quietly
repeating what he was saying to themselves. Just then the
Japanese fisherman rode out through the gate on his motorbike,
with the fishing rod tied to his shoulder; waved to us, and
headed off. Have you got all that?

I think so, said Gary in wonder.

I'll bring my digger over now to the site, and Philip will see
ye at eight in the morning, here at the gate, OK?

– Dead on. Sound as a pound –

– And you'll lead them to Dromod, right Philip? –

– Right, I said –

– Then I can start at dawn, Da said. Now, anything else?

No problem, said Desmond, that's it.

Here Philip, said Gary, I'll give you the keys of the lorry for
the morning.

Thanks.

See ya.

Gary took one last look at the ocean, and just then a sudden
gust of wind came and blew his hat into the sea.

Ah Jesus, he cried and it looked like he was going to jump in.

Hold it, I said, and I went down the steps, into our boat, and
got the fishing rod. The hat was going out with the tide. I spun

the hook and weight twice, then on the third time it caught the rim of the hat and I drew it in.

Gary took the soaking hat and pressed it to his chest.

Thank you, thank you, he said.

They sat into the van and took off.

They are a right pair of lads, said Da, and they're coming at the right price. The rest are just gone plain greedy.

He drove his Hitachi digger up into the low-loader and gave me the key of the Volkswagen.

You come and collect me in a few hours, all right? he said.

All right.

Just take it handy.

OK.

He set off for Dromod House. It was like looking at a circus leaving town. I dropped the keys of the lorry into a drawer in the hallway, and headed into the garden and started excavating with the small JCB.

Soon the small stretch of poor soil and weed and whin had been ripped asunder ready to receive the new clay.

For Ma.

About five hours later I went over to pick him up. It was my second time behind the wheel of a car in over a year. All of a sudden the road ahead of me blurred for an instant then reappeared like an hallucination. Fear shot through me. I took the long way round. Back behind me was a lorry. I pulled in to let him pass. Then another two cars came up behind my ass. I pulled in at the church and with a bad-tempered flourish they shot by. At last I reached the gates of the estate and drove in. Miss Jilly was seated in a deckchair, with a pile of picked parsley and rocket lettuce in her lap, watching Da at work. He had ripped the earth, and tossed it into huge piles. The clay was a dense black. I waited as he tore over and back over and back.

I looked at the red berries on the rowan trees tumbling over the old granite stone that looked like church walls. When I sat down I went back years watching workers and boats and choirs on the go. A place where wheat fields, books of wisdom, wars and beheadings mingled. I walked the orchards where the large apples of the season were hanging, and I ate one looking out to sea, then at last Da gave in, and left the digger off the road in the haggard. It stood there like an old tall toy, with arms and head bent, beside the dark house.

I will be here at first light, he told Miss Jilly. I hope the noise will not offend you.

Not at all, she said, I have had my fill of silence.

At seven next morning, I had the kettle boiling. Da had already gone at dawn.

I drove the dumper wagon into the garden ready to scatter the loads.

I fed the ass and the horse, and brought water across to the hurt cow. She was lying there dead. I rang Da and he rang the Dead Animal Removal Service. Ma took off at eight and I took the keys out of the drawer and went down to the gate to meet the men.

No sign.

To the south the blue turned dark, a black cloud gathered and miles away beyond the mountains there were threads of rain slanted west. There was thunder out there somewhere. I went back up and took the washing off the line, then walked down to the pier to the lorry, stepped up to look in the cabin window, then took the key, opened the door, sat in, and read some sort of Holy Words written in a language I did not understand beneath Christ's face on a picture that was pinned above the driver's windscreen. The rain came in a dense fast downpour. I waited there looking for half an hour, and still no sign. Not a soul. Then came the first text onto my mobile.

Where are they, said the first, *Where the fuck are they?* said the second, and *Where are you?* said the third.

I rang him back.

What's happening, he asked.

They have not showed.

Ah Jazus, he said. And I've been ringing their mobile and got no answer.

Look, give it a little more time, and I'll ring you.

I stood at the gate. No sign. I waited. Nobody, till Joejoe and Cnoic and Timmy came walking up the lane. What are you doing? he asked. Waiting on a pair of men, I said. You'll get that, he said. There was a faraway roll of thunder. The two dogs shivered, then flattened themselves on the ground, and Cnoic went up into a crazy whine as he dug his snout and paws into the earth; and then they both ran back to the house. I better let them back in, said Joejoe and he went home. I sat again into the lorry and put the keys in the ignition, waited, turned the key and the engine roared.

Should I? I thought. I turned it off, looked down the road and then rang Da.

Well?

No sign.

What am I going to do?

Well the lorry is here, Da. They have to come sometime.

OK, but when?

I sat into the lorry and waited. Then in the distance the postman George appeared in his green van followed by the two men in the grey van.

I stepped down.

The postman winked, handed me an advertisement for Tesco, and said in a whisper – I found them miles away at the far end of Downing's, they were in a panic, that's the third crowd I found missing out these parts in the last two weeks – then he turned and went off. The pair sat face forward in the

317

van for a few seconds, like they were stopped at the lights, then they got out at the same moment.

You'll have to forgive us, said Gary.

And you see the mobile had run out of shekels, said Desmond.

OK, I said, Da is waiting.

This is a terror, he said. You have the keys?

They're in the ignition.

He looked at me.

I see. You weren't thinking of going to drive it, were you?

I thought about it, I said.

Hmm. Gary sat into the lorry behind the wheel, and I climbed in beside Desmond and slowly we made our way up the road.

Where's your hat?

In the van, for safe-keeping.

– Straight ahead, I said –

– Right, said Gary –

– We tried everywhere, said Desmond –

– But every road looked the same –

– Now go handy, she's a bad corner –

– Will do, said Gary as he slowed down –

– We ended up at nearly six roads going down to the sea, explained Desmond –

– And none were right –

– No, they were not –

– Get ready to go left –

– Right, said Gary –

– And we knocked on a couple of doors but there was no one at home, said Desmond –

– No one –

– Then we asked that postman –

– And he laughed, kind of –

– Now at the T-junction go left, I said, blessing myself –

– Got ya, said Gary –

– We were rightly lost –

– We were –

– Now, right at the school –

– Jesus, the school, the blasted school, said Gary, beating the steering wheel. Is this country haunted? –

– Yes, I said –

– Jesus –

– Now straight on and then right –

– Right –

– We are nearly there –

– I'm glad to hear that –

And eventually, we came near the gate of the estate.

– Slow down –

– Slowing down –

– Now turn in here –

– In here? –

– Yes –

– Is this it? –

– It is –

– We must have driven by this gate a dozen times, said Desmond.

We made our way up the drive at Dromod and there in front of the house among a pile of felled trees Da was hurling earth in the air while Miss Jilly sat in her deckchair in a loose blue raincoat. He spun the digger round, saw us and slowly rose the bucket high up in the air, then swung round and dug up a pile of clay and held it aloft waiting. Myself and Desmond jumped out and Gary backed the lorry in and took the first load, and after the second Da jumped down out of the digger.

Am I glad to see ye, he said. I'd given up.

We got lost, said Desmond.

Oh.

Sorry, said Gary. Look, we'll make up for the lost time, we'll work late.

No bother.

OK, we'll head back.

Do you mind, pray, if I follow you in my car, gentlemen, asked Miss Jilly. I think I'd like to see the old earth from the estate safely delivered to the alt.

Of course, said Desmond.

You are not Russian?

No.

Good luck, Daddy shouted as the three of us sat into the lorry, and we took off with Miss Jilly tucked in behind us in the blue Volkswagen.

Is that lady who I think she is? asked Gary.

That would be her.

The famous Mrs Adams whose father travelled to the North Pole?

Yes.

And she still lives alone in that huge house?

Is right.

My God, I never thought I would get to see her in reality. Her husband rose through the ranks in the British Army, went right to the top, and then went on to become a famous IRA –

– Now left, I said –

– They say –

– And straight ahead –

– But I'm sure you know the story –

– Leave it Gary, said Desmond –

– Oh, got ya. Where's the fort?

– Coming up –

– Are you writing this down? asked Gary –

– I am, said Desmond –

– Watch for the pot-holes –

– I will –

– They are everywhere –

– Now go right at the end –

This is a strange country, said Gary, I have never in my life lost my way going to a job.

We passed the ring fort, the school, the new country homes plastered with blue stone, the gardens with solar lights, and met the tractors drawing trailers of newly baled hay. We passed the lines and lines of wild foxgloves and fuchsia and montbretia waving its thin arms, and I blessed myself at the flower pots, and eventually we took the final turn.

I got out at the gate, and there was Joejoe standing below on the battery wall. He joined me and Desmond as the lorry turned and began reversing up the sand-clogged lane to the headland, and behind it, facing forward, came the wee Volkswagen. As they reached the two stone piers they backed in as far as they could go, Desmond got out and turned the handle and the first load rolled into the garden. My granduncle went straight in to inspect the top soil. He burrowed through the pile with a fork.

He toed the earth and smelt it.

Chin lowered, Gary watched him through the side mirror as Joejoe spilled the clay through his hands, then Joejoe saluted.

All right? shouted Desmond.

All right, it's mostly top soil, but we're talking about some dab, I don't like to see too much dab. Tell him to keep an eye on what he's at below.

We will.

Good enough.

Good day, Mister Feeney, Miss Jilly called.

Oh, good day, Miss Adams, I forgot you were behind me.

Never mind, Joejoeing, look what I brought you – good Protestant earth.

Thank you, thank you. You're the last Irish woman in these parts. The rest have forgotten.

I am loath to see it go. Come for tea, sometime.

I will, I will.

Please do. Those are lovely stones in the wall. Have you any left?

Yes.

Could I have some one day?

Ask the lad.

Yes, I said.

Thank you Mister Psyche. I turned to the men. You know where you are going? I asked.

I do, said Gary. I know my way back to the site.

Well then I will follow you, said Miss Jilly. I like the idea of Dromod House being called a site.

She reversed back down to the pier, as the lorry followed face-to-face. At last the Volkswagen backed in safely, turned, and the lorry led the way back to Dromod. I got into the dumper and began to spread the earth.

Joejoe went picking winkles.

And so the day continued. The truck would land every forty minutes, empty the soil and some small yellow flat boulders, and return for more earth.

Joejoe stood as guide at the gate, watched the spill without speaking, then he'd nod and give them the thumbs-up and head off. I began taking out some of the flat stones to use them as the final top on the wall. At two Miss Jilly arrived alone with a meal for me and my granduncle. The other three were being fed at Dromod. She gave us salad and tomatoes, bread rolls and queen cakes.

Tomatoes from the house! said Joejoe.

Yes, she said.

Good woman, and he bit in with exhilaration like a child. I ate on the shore, lay back a while, then a while later heard the roar of the lorry reversing up the drive. It had started again.

Round three o'clock Anna on her half-day arrived in her running gear, took the wheelbarrow and started collecting the weeds, and told me that all that she could hear running through her head was dates, dates, dates and the names of endless groups of flowers. The lorry again arrived. Joejoe signalled the men then strode off down the lane.

The two lads waved to Anna.

Who is that man below? Desmond asked, if you don't mind me asking?

He's my granduncle, I said.

He has a ferocious pair of eyebrows, said Gary.

And he combs them.

My, my. Would he be kinda anxious? asked Gary.

Anna looked at me.

He might, I said.

I thought so. He has a slight corr.

What's that?

A sort of sad bedevilled look in the eye betimes, explained Desmond.

Oh.

And they took off.

Will we take a break for a few minutes, asked Anna and so we headed off down the beach, out to the blow holes and the mystery wall, while overhead the Search-and-Rescue helicopter shot out to sea.

All day we were swimming in mud.

Then Ma arrived and went with the rake into the garden before she headed to the kitchen. The truck was over and back till eight. And then Da rang to say the two men were going to join us for dinner.

Humming, Ma set the table.

Gary parked the lorry down at the pier after the last load, and went walking the beach. Desmond sat into a chair. Soon

Da arrived home in his mud-spattered Volkswagen and poured the wine, but Desmond refused a glass because he was driving back to town. And next thing Miss Jilly stepped through the door. Da and herself went to view the piles of black earth and rubble thrown among the whins, then she came back in and began excitedly talking to him about an idea she had to build a small tomb based on a drawing her grandfather had made in the last century. It had been unearthed by a scholar going through the family's records. The tomb, if it was built, was to have a single turret and a tall wind chime and be designed by a local architect, a friend of hers.

My mother listened as Miss Jilly moved on to other plans she had in mind then as the smell of the chicken grew she said: I'll be off now.

Won't you stay for dinner?

No, thank you.

I think I should go too, said Anna.

Ah stay Anna.

They are expecting me at home.

All right then.

Well then, said Miss Jilly, you will sit in with me.

But first I have a story for ye all, said Anna. After work in the afternoon I headed into the heritage office to look up records of the Conans and by coincidence this American lady came in to look up her family history but the records for the very year that the lady at the counter was looking for had disappeared.

Ah.

All her family for that year was lost. She was from Virginia in the US. And what was her name, Anna said turning to me.

– I don't know –

– Finney –

– Yeh, so? –

– And when she looked it up, she found Finney is a direct derivation of Feeney. –

– Meaning us, said Da –

– Yes, but also meaning soldier, or sometimes, in another sense, it has to do with trees –

– And so be Jazus, I said, that's why the Bird and Joejoe would talk about the fairies as soldiers that hid in the woods –

– So there you go, said Anna, I thought I should let you know where you came from Philip, and she touched my cheek –

– Did you tell her you knew some Feeneys, asked Da –

– I did and the lady took my hand and shook it, she was delighted, send them my regards, she said –

– You're a great girl –

Bye, and Anna stood smiling.

Please stay, I said.

OK, I just wanted to hear you ask me.

Da walked Miss Jilly round the scattered piles of earth in the garden, then she climbed into the car and was still talking out the window to Da as she drove away.

I went down the beach to get Gary. He was sitting on a rock looking out to sea.

Dinner is ready, I said.

Do you mind if I ask you something? –

– Fire ahead.

– Are you a religious man? –

No, I said.

You sure?

– Yes –

– OK –

Why do you ask me?

Did I not see you bless yourself twice in the lorry?

. . . You did, I said.

Yes – twice – and the thing is you did it so quickly.

It's at a spot where a friend of mine died.

Oh, I'm sorry to hear that.

That's OK.

Was it a crash?

. . . Yes . . .

Were you in the car?

I was.

Forgive me.

He was driving. I was beside him. It was a year ago. He had done his final paper in the Leaving, and a crowd of us were on the raz in the town and he said to me – Let's go out to Sweet John's, the local pub, for a breath of fresh air and that's when it happened. He hit the wall above in Templeboy –

– I see –

– That's it –

– It's tough –

– I could have driven, I was sober –

– Don't blame yourself –

– And a few weeks ago I got the results of my exam, and I thought of him –

– He never got his? –

– No, his parents did. And he passed, with honours.

We both sat there a while.

Sorrow is a hard load to carry, said Gary. I'll tell you my story later, about my mother. You see I'm trying to get my bearings. I'm watching that island, and then I'm watching that headland. Is that Mount Nephin beyond?

It is.

Well that's a coincidence. I was only over there last week. And it's making me think, anyway, I'm sorry for all you went through –

– Say no more –

– OK –

– We'll leave it at that.

I'll never mention it again, said Gary and he stood and followed me in.

We all sat down at the table and as the plates of food arrived to the table, Gary slowly bowed his head and said a prayer to himself. Desmond took no wine but water.

I was out there looking across at Nephin, Gary said.

You were, said Desmond and he started eating, without once looking up as if he knew the story. Da poured Gary a glass of Sauvignon Blanc. The meal continued in silence for a few minutes.

I was, said Gary. Do you want to know what happened me? he said turning to me. I met my mother in a village below that mountain for the first time last week.

What? asked Anna astounded. For the first time?

Yes.

I don't understand, I said.

You see she handed me up for adoption after I was born.

That's terrible, said Ma.

Well she had a reason.

What?

Well the reason is – she was a fortune teller, and this is what she told me – she looked at the cards and saw something bad would happen me if I stayed with her, so she handed me over.

Dear God, said Ma.

Yes.

It's unbelievable.

It was hard.

Christ.

Can someone else talk for a minute, said Gary, please.

We ate on in silence, till we reached the jelly and ice-cream.

And there a couple of months ago, Gary said, I at last got her name, my real mother's name after all these years, and I built up my confidence and went to see her to say Hallo.

– You did, said Desmond –

– I knocked on the door –

– And –

327

– And out she came –

– Dear God –

Da poured out more wine, and Desmond again refused a glass.

I have to drive.

I understand.

Just take the one.

No thanks.

Don't, I said.

I won't.

OK, said Da, Sorry, I understand.

– Yes, said Gary. At last I met her, and he blessed himself as the meal ended.

The men got up to go home, but Da said: – Look there's two beds down in the studio in the garden. You might as well stay the night.

What do you think? asked Desmond.

I'm on, said Gary.

Do, I said.

Right, so am I, said Desmond and he accepted a drink, then another and went out to the van and came back with a concert flute and played a couple of polkas. After each tune he'd pat the biscuits on the table and bow his head.

It's nice, he said – that after all that – we got here.

True, said Gary. And that we got to see Mrs Adams of Dromod House. A fair independent spirit.

True, said Ma, nodding with a distant smile.

Go raibh maith agat, he said, nodding to me.

Anna went down the garden to make the beds. Gary again walked the beach alone in the dark. Desmond went off down to lock the lorry and the van. And Ma came in and turned to Da and said: That poor man Gary –

– It's hard to believe –

– And it happens –

– It does –

– And by the way –

– Yes? –

– On a different subject – before I forget –

– Fire away –

– That woman Miss Jilly is infatuated with you, and she sniggered. Chimes, she said –

– Chimes, yes–

– I see –

– And maybe eagles. She mentioned an eagle this evening –

– Did she mention divorce? asked my mother.

– Not yet. I'll let you know –

– Oh do. Soldiers and trees, she said and she shook her head. Then she stopped smiling and put her head in her hands. Christ it has been a sad evening, hasn't it Philip?

Yes, I said.

I never heard the likes.

Say no more, said Da.

The gang came back and gathered again at the table, and another bottle of Rioja was opened. Then Gary headed out to the van and came back in his Australian sombrero.

I missed my hat, he said, during all that chat.

Chapter Thirty-Five

Squaring the Circle

After dinner Da suddenly decided to take the men down to Joejoe's to listen to him playing the box.

A while passed. Myself and Anna were first watching the end of *The X Factor*, then *The Best Albums of All Time* on the other box. There was a sharp fast knock on the door. Gary was standing there a little breathless with these set hard eyes. I looked round to see who was with him. He was alone but Cnoic was at his feet.

I let him in and he sat down and smiled.

Tea? said Ma raising the iron of the ironing board.

Aye.

We sat there a while.

Did you enjoy yourself?

Your man Tom Feeney speaks a myriad.

You didn't understand him.

It's like being on a site with men from all over the world. I thought he was from round here, but the truth is he is a global local.

Aye.

On site we are all foreigners.

Got ya.

I don't mind working on a site, but you know what you have to learn?

A new language? asked Anna.

Yes, but not the language you think, and you have to get it right and I mean right, you can get it wrong and if the wrong word travels down the line, well you're in trouble, and you have to row gentle as you can go back to where you were when the first command was given wrong.

It's the same in the hospital, said Ma, ironing the sleeve of a shirt.

Is that so?

The arguments are something shocking. It's like a form of bullying. It would depress you. She rose the shirt in the air to look at it. And worst of all it happens in English.

Well there's another way of doing things, another language – I saw it first and learnt it down in the timber yard.

What's that?

Sign language. Sign language is the boy.

Aye, said Ma, folding a trouser leg, if you can get it right.

Now you're talking.

Yes, said Anna, here we are talking of sign language.

True, now tell me how do you square the circle? Gary asked.

Excuse me?

I'll explain. I made a mistake down in your granduncle's. I said to him: Your accordion is out of tune.

– Oh, said Ma, that was a bad move –

– I believe someone said that to him forty years ago, I said, and he was not pleased then either –

– And then he said to me, continued Gary, go out and square the circle –

And where are the others? I asked.

They're coming soon, and he bowed quick-like. No bother. We made tea.

That man your granduncle is some character.

He's a terror, I said.

I never met a man who knows so many dates off by heart.

You see he can't read.

Ah!

So he has to remember, said Anna.

Oh.

Yes. Every last date.

But he can forget certain things, I said.

Do you tell me?

The phone rang.

Is your man Gary with you? asked Da.

He is, I said.

Is he all right?

Yeh.

Right, say nothing, OK? and he rang off.

You will have a great garden out there when it's finished, said Gary.

I will.

It's a good class of earth.

Yes, said Anna. And myself and Philip there intend to set everything under the sun. Do you mind me asking you something?

Fire away.

Why did you leave the house below ahead of the others?

It's like this. I had to square the circle.

Please explain, I asked.

Well your Granduncle Joejoe whispered to me; would you square the circle please and go out and see is there a fellow at the gate. Who? Someone, he said. I stood outside the door but I could see no one. I went on out onto the road for a look around and there was nobody, nothing, so I just said to myself I'd not go back into the cottage, I'd take a walk, and then I said I'd head up back to here.

Ah.

Square the circle – what does he mean by that?

He means go the full jaunt, I said.

Aye, I can understand that.

And do the impossible, said Anna.

OK.

And make sense of it all.

And then arrive to the finish, said Anna, in the walk.

Yes, I have you there, but there's something else, isn't there?

Is there? I asked.

What about the fellow at the gate?

That's a different story entirely, agreed Ma.

Got ya! So, there's no one there? he said, leaning down to pet Cnoic.

No, she answered slowly.

It's just a saying of his – then.

Yeh, said Ma carefully.

But . . . he is expecting someone?

That's right. He is. He always is.

Who?

I don't know. Someone . . . he once was . . . maybe.

I see. Does it run in the family?

I suppose it does, said Ma, on their side, she added, as she ran the iron down the seam of a vest.

Soon after that Da came in with Desmond. They shook their coats in the hall and Da sat uncomfortably into the settee and began eyeing Gary.

Are you all right?

I am.

Well you had us moidered. Being so close to the sea and all that. And there's a storm gathering.

I'm sorry.

The vodka got to him, said his companion, laughing.

It did, said Gary. I think I'll go to bed.

Right, said Desmond.

They went down to the studio and I lit their way with the torch. The studio had started out as a caravan years ago and then my father had built a two roomed wooden shed round it, then he took the caravan apart. I put on the light for the men; the two beds were immaculate. They came outside and stood on the wooden porch with the dog leaping up my trouser leg. The sea was thundering. And the wind was thrashing. The Plough was over our heads and an aeroplane was ticking red-white-red up there in the dark. The horse was running in the field against the sky line while the ass stood by the wall, staring ahead.

The dog brushed up against me.

All right boss, goodnight lads.

Oiche mhaith, said Gary.

Good night, Desmond called and closed the door.

I steadied myself and found Anna at my side.

I better go.

OK.

She gave me a hug and we sat into the Fiat and I drove her home slowly in rain that began pelting in from the east.

When I got back Ma and Da were sitting on the sofa watching the box.

So you asked Mister Gary, I hear, said Da, about what happened below.

No, I didn't.

I did, said Ma.

I thought I told Philip not to.

I did not know that, and anyway, I only mentioned it in passing.

He's a mystery man is Gary. Well, from the moment he came in the door below he kept a beady eye on Joejoe, and was nodding at everything he said but funny enough Joejoe didn't speak one word in his direction, started a tune and then just gave this one whisper into his ear and your man was gone like a shot. Just like that. He leaped up and said *I'll be back in a minute*. We were kinda left wondering, and we were waiting but he never showed.

He filled out a final glass and cupped it and swirled it.

Joejoe must have said something shocking to him, he said and drank.

Wrong there, Da.

What do you mean?

He told him to go check the gate, said Ma.

You're joking me.

Aye, to see if there was anyone there.

Oh fuck, he said to himself, it's starting again. The whole thing is starting all over. We're back with the man who does not exist.

It's time for bed, said Ma, I think.

Next morning at eight the Animal Removal wagon arrived and drove into the meadow and hoisted the cow into the back as Da and myself watched. He whacked my shoulder and looked away, then at the gate he paid the driver, and drove on down to the site.

At nine the truck came backing up the lane. The clay piles spread like small hills. I drove the dumper over and back, and Ma spread seaweed I'd taken up from the shore. There was no sign of Joejoe so I took a walk down to the house and knocked on the door.

He was inside lying on the armchair.

Good morning . . . Grandda, I said. There was a storm last night.

A storm? What storm! I heard nothing.

The sand is across the fields.

Are there stones up?

No.

It was no storm. You think it was a storm. Is the barrel still under the downpipe?

Yes.

Well then. If the barrel is there then the water never rose. Last time, October 12th sixty-nine, the barrel was gone. She

335

was off to the west. The cows were crowded on the alt. The General was floating. Storm me arse. He waved a hand at the other seat. Sit down and rest yourself.

I have to go, I'm working.

Well then don't let me stop ya Mister Psyche.

There's a load coming.

There always is.

What's wrong?

The fucking midges got me, and he pulled up his trouser leg, look it! His shin was peppered with spots, he hauled his shirt to one side and there they were red wheals all over his neck, and then he tapped his forehead that was covered with bites.

Now do you see, he said, what I get for stepping outside yesterday.

I'll ask Ma for some cream.

Say nothing. You see it starts with the itch, he said, that's where it begins. Say not a word. The itch son is the beginning of the end.

The sick cow died.

Ah God.

I got up on my motor and spread the new loads that had arrived. At dinner time the two men ate with us, while Da ate at the site with Miss Jilly. Ma made banana curry with lamb off the mountain. Then she went down the garden with the rake, drawing the earth along the edge of the fields.

She's hardy, said Gary.

She's into the work, I said.

He strolled down to watch Ma.

You're tough, he said.

You have to be tough, said Ma.

They headed off and returned over the afternoon with seven loads, then finally near nightfall they came up the lane reversing with the final pile of the day. After them came the Volkswagen dunting along. A blinding mist was blowing off the sea. The new garden looked kind of crazy. Miss Jilly walked across the soft piles of earth, and inspected the earth, much like my granduncle had done, then she sat on the seawall, patting her knees.

Mister Psyche, she said.

Yes Miss Jilly.

What are you going to set first?

Leeks, I believe, first thing next year.

Good. Very appropriate. Here, she said, and she handed me a packet of Gauloises for 'Joejoeing'. I went into the toilet and searched for something for the itch and found a jar of cream and went down and did Joejoe's skin while he stood staring straight ahead of him with the French cigarette aloft.

Chapter Thirty-Six

Stepping into our Finery

There were steaks on the pan.

Da rose a glass of water.

Good luck, he said.

By the fire the fluter began to play. Between tunes Gary spoke again of entering the room near the mountain where he met his mother for the first time. She spoke little, he said. When I finish this job I'm going to Berlin to start a new life.

Will you see her again, I asked.

I don't know. I'm learning German. I enjoyed coming here, he said.

It's a great place to get lost in, agreed Desmond.

You were wary of Joejoe last night, said my father.

No, said Gary. The fear comes down on me and I go away.

The fear of what?

I don't know.

He's had it all his life, said Desmond.

Did your mother say she was glad to see you when you met her? I asked.

You're getting personal, said Ma.

Not at all, he's not, said Gary.

Did she say she was glad? – she did. Oh she did, but that doesn't mean she was glad. I wasn't hers, if you see what I mean. I might be hers another time, maybe, but not that day, no. Good luck, he said.

Good luck, said Da.

I started putting on me jacket.

Are you going downtown, asked Da.

No, I don't have to go to the shop. He has what he needs.

Good. You see since that boy left school he has taken on a full-time paid job looking after his old uncle.

Gary, said Desmond.

Yes.

Let you go and drive the young fellow down.

That's a good idea, sure thing – do ya mind?

No, but you see I'm going to take a ride on my bike.

Well I'll walk part of the way with you.

If you want.

You see that man Gary likes to wander, said Desmond.

I do.

I took me bike and walked Gary down the lane. The sea was clashing hard. The stars were out.

Have you a hero, he asked me.

I have.

Who?

Myself, I said.

By God.

I knocked on Joejoe's door. Yes, came the reply, come in.

Hallo there, he said looking at us.

This man came down for the walk with me.

And why wouldn't he. How do you do?

Fine.

I see you got back your voice.

Ah now.

Last night he lost his voice. I think something happened to you.

Not really, said Gary.

That cream worked a little Mister Psyche, but I still have the boys.

Will you not let me ask Ma?

No.

Sit down.

I'm off for a ride on me bike.

Well why don't you sit down? he said to Gary.

Ah no, it's all right, said Gary.

Sit down out of that.

Do and I'll go on, I said.

Are you sure?

Stop where you are, will ya.

Good enough.

I'll call on me way back.

And thanks for not forgetting me, said Joejoe.

I will not.

I'm gasping. Gasping.

Is there something wrong? asked Gary.

Fags, I said.

You see I have run out.

Joejoe you have not run out.

What are ya talking about?

You have fags.

What do you mean! he snarled.

Look round you.

Excuse me, I'm lost, said Joejoe, and he stood and took off his jacket and searched the pockets, took off a boot and looked into it.

I have you, I said.

Where was I, he said.

There, I said pointing at the strange box of cigarettes on the mantelpiece, and he lit up immediately, and sank into the chair.

I could not recognise the label, he explained, as he studied the blue packet.

Outside the sea fog covered everything. Even looking up there was nothing. I mind a biscuit box still in some sort of Christmas wrapping nestling by the pier of a gate. Tins of lager rustling. I headed on. Along the way I had to stop as the road ahead disappeared. The light of the bike picked out a thin fox, swinging her tail, who came out of a hedge in her best and glanced at me in passing. A light came up and went by. Then another. The mist raced into my face. I got off the bike and strolled the last few hundred yards. It was a dream walk. The sea rose up like smoke from a chimney at the blowhole. Outside the pub two tractors were parked with their engines running. A ghost was standing outside smoking.

Sweet John's niece in the bar was reading Ireland's Eye to one side, and doing Sudoku in a daily paper on the other.

Mick McSharry downed a half-one, his son downed another; they left. I got a packet of crisps, and headed back pushing the bike up the hill by the church. Outside Frosty's a crowd of geese followed me. Go home, I said. Three shovels stood against an electric pole. I could find the cold on my knees. I came to Joejoe's gate, knocked and threw open the door.

Hallo, I said.

Good man yourself.

I looked round me. Where's your man?

He left here ages ago, just after you went.

Is that so.

Sit down there and take the weight of your feet.

I think I'll go on up.

Whatever you want. There's no one in talking mood this evening, no, but thank you for the fags, certainly. And if you see that man Gary tell him I send my regards. Do please, for you see he sat there, without talking. The more I spoke, the less he said.

And he left?

He left. That's your Gary for you. He looked at me a long time, and then put a finger to his bottom lip. He never spoke a word. It unnerved me. Be careful, I said to myself. But I did not

341

put him out. I did not. We had a few quiet words. He was where you are. Then he suddenly stood. What's up, I said. Nothing, he said, I'll go above. Thank you.

Did you frighten him . . . Granddad?

I did not. Swear to God Mister Psyche. I've been thinking about it. There's been some misunderstanding. I think it was him that frightened me.

He indicated the door.

– Just out, he went –

– OK –

– But why I don't know.

So I said to myself well he's gone home again and headed off down the beach. There was an almighty whack of sea from the blowhole, then a loud spill breaking in the distance. The crack from the blowhole again split the air. And in the fog you were breathing in the sky. I took my time, as I climbed to where I thought home was, and then there on the bank of blue stones by the seashore I saw this shape still standing as the fog drifted by.

Hallo, I shouted. Hallo, I shouted again.

The figure turned.

You live in a wild place, Gary said. I was just thinking about you.

A few yards away from him the gravel was shifting.

Come on up, I said.

He walked behind me to the house, stopping ever so often as if he was entranced; he touched the torn leaves of the wild hollyhocks; then we went up the back field to the fence overlooking the sea, and there we stood a while with the horse and the donkey at our side. The sea was fetching over the lava rocks below. To one side sometimes the distant lights of Killybegs would appear, then to the other side the lights of Easkey would bounce into view as the fog moved on.

It was like looking out on a litany of questions – a map that would never be finished.

He touched my shoulder.

I made another mistake, Gary said. I mentioned fairies in a kinda light-hearted way. I think he took offence. He said to me: You can't play with history.

We headed down. At the kitchen table Da and Desmond were playing Patience.

Next morning it was go, go, go. In the late afternoon the truck left for the final load of earth. Joejoe held up his hand at the gate, and hauled himself into the front to accompany the men to Dromod. An hour later they returned; and the last earth was scattered. It seemed that the two men would soon disappear out of our lives. But they started to help me spread the earth; they dug in like soldiers, as Joejoe oiled the fenders of the lorry.

Salt, he said. You have to watch the salt and then he oiled the hinges on the doors of the van.

A while later Da appeared home with the digger, and behind him came Miss Jilly in her Volkswagen.

The two walked into the garden, and Da stood aside smiling.

You are all invited this evening for supper to Dromod House, she said. And I mean everyone, she said looking at Joejoe and the two lads.

Can I take my friend Anna?

Of course you can.

Then she took off.

We'll have to go to town to get dressed up, said Desmond.

Well, said Da, you're finished here.

Da paid Gary, and the two lads washed themselves under the outside tap, then drove off to town in the van and the lorry to get their gear. I rang Anna. Anna, would you like to eat out in Dromod House? You're joking, she said. No, for real, I said. Sure thing Philip, I'll see you. Da spread the remaining earth with the JCB, I drew buckets of seaweed from the shore, scattered them into the earth as Ma followed behind me shovelling.

I went in to see the Bird, she said. He was asking for ye all.

How is he?

The man in the next bed to him has died.

The man who did the crosswords? I asked.

Yes, she said.

I saw him in my mind's eye searching the tightly folded newspaper. I saw him again study the clues, and suddenly write in the answers. Watched by the donkey I laid a path of sea-stone flags through the new garden while Ma set a few daffodil and snowdrops for the spring, then we all went indoors to step into our finery.

Chapter Thirty-Seven

Supper

After locking up the dogs in Joejoe's we set off in Ma's car, and stopped for Anna who stepped into the car in a wide blue dress carrying a basket of assorted flowers.

The two men were waiting at the gate of Dromod in the van, and so we headed up the avenue together. Gary stepped out wearing his wide hat and flapping dungarees. Desmond was in a sports jacket. At the door of the big house was a man in a grey-striped suit standing beside Miss Jilly with a tray of drinks.

This is Mister Lundy, she said. He did not speak but nodded as Ma took her glass of white wine, and Da his brandy, just the one, he said; and Gary helped himself to a cold bottle of Miller's beer with lime in the spout.

Then there was sparkling water and lemonade for myself and Anna and Desmond.

Anna presented her with the basket of flowers, and Miss Jilly bowed. It's so kind of you to invite me, said Anna. It's an honour, said Miss Jilly. And, finally, a glass of Malibu for Joejoe.

Miss Jilly had done her homework.

Cheers, she said, lifting a sherry in the air.

Good luck, said Joejoe, and he immediately took off to the glasshouse to inspect the tomato plants, smell the herbs, the basil and rosemary while we watched him from afar. He returned like a man entranced.

So, she said, so I just want to welcome you all.

There you go, said the gentleman, then, tray in hand, he sat inside on a low stool behind the front door while she led us

345

into the entrance hall. Joejoe walked around talking to himself as the rest of us made small chat. The gentleman sat in the distance looking out the front door like a man considering his hand in a game of poker. Joejoe felt the backs of the chairs wrapped in sheets; he studied the Indian, then headed for the stairs, and stopped on each step to gaze at the old faded whites of the ice and snow, the illuminated cloths of linen, the old bearded floating figures.

He put down his glass on the top banister and headed off across the landing on the first floor.

Uncle Joejoe, Ma called up.

Let him continue, said Miss Jilly.

She led us to the door of the drawing room and with a gesture invited us in, then went off up the stairs to join our Joejoe on his travels. Our waiter arrived with a fresh tray of drinks and put them on the round table; then stood a moment by the window looking out, and left the room. Da, sparkling water in hand, looked up the chimney and whistled. In the grate the makings of fire was set with paper knots, and twigs, and branches.

Who is Mister Lundy, whispered Ma.

He's a famous architect, said Da.

And he's gay, said Desmond, is Mister Lundy.

Now, said Gary.

A complete recluse, explained Da. Mister Lundy lives on the mountain. He is the only visitor she ever gets, maybe twice a year. He is an admirer of the house, and has done some restoration for her in the past. It was him apparently suggested the plans for the removal of the earth. He looked toward the door. I think I'll go see if I can give him a hand.

Ma's mobile rang, she searched her bag; Yes, she said. Well please let me know, thank you. She looked around.

They may be moving Tom Feeney soon, she said.

A quick shower of rain fell. Overhead we heard a gong sound. Then another. I wondered had Joejoe and Miss Jilly reached the ferrets. Anna unearthed a number of old books and sat perched in an armchair reading about pollution in the North Pacific Ocean, a life of Countess Markievicz, sparrowhawks and the First World War. Desmond and Gary sat like two little boys on the couch. Ma sat on a stiff chair touching her cheeks. Around the table were nine chairs facing mats decorated with pictures of may bushes.

Da came back with knives and forks and set the table.

Mister Lundy brought in a bowl of salad then he lifted a large box of matches from the mantelpiece and lit a sheet of paper in the grate. With a whoosh the fire took. We heard the other old pair chattering in the hallway, there was a burst of laughter and Joejoe my pretend Grandda sauntered in wearing a small cowboy's hat belonging to a child from long ago. Then Miss Jilly entered lightly tapping her chest with her two hands, and handed Anna a violet tube of nail varnish and a small nailbrush. The very best from France, she said and sat at the table and opened her arms to us. Thank you, said Anna. Grandda took off his cap and slowly lowered himself into a chair to her side. Gary nodded, lifted the cap, tried it on then put it down on the side table beside his sombrero. We all sat down surrounded by portraits of people from another time on the wall. Mister Lundy reappeared with a large plate of fish, followed by Da carrying a bowl of potatoes. All were placed in front of Miss Jilly, then Mister Lundy handed her a plate from the pile sitting in front of her, and she began meticulously laying out the food.

Chives, iceberg lettuce, rocket, parsley and dill, she announced, and spooned out a section.

Wonderful, said Ma.

And next we have apple and celery. All from the garden. We have the hippies to thank for the weeding.

I met them, said Anna, Aaron and Angela and . . .

Tommy, I added.

And Tommy, said Grandda, *yes*, they are very tidy people.

Potatoes and spring onion, Miss Jilly said, and then sliding her fork under each portion, she added: and finally crab claws and a taste of mussels.

Da took each plate of food and handed them round to us. He had entered a new dimension. I had never been served at a table before by my father. He sat down with a sort of whimsical glance up at the ceiling as Ma took a long drink of wine and had her glass refilled.

Thank you, she said. Thank you for training in my husband.

I am delighted, said Miss Jilly. Such joy has no equal. Love makes lovers equal, as the musical goes. Who was it that said: *If you really love me then you should stop loving me.*

It would bring a tear to your eye, said my Grandda

Oh . . . *Joejoe*, said Anna.

Are you romantic or sentimental? Miss Jilly asked Anna.

I am . . .

. . . Which?

Both.

And very honest – to boot – I can see.

And just then Gary bowed his head and blessed himself, as Miss Jilly paused with a fork to her mouth. Mister Lundy popped a new bottle of wine, took the last chair and the space closed in around him.

Outside the sky darkened even more as the rain stopped.

You are all welcome, Miss Jilly said, and her accent took on a hunting sound as she leaned down to take the first bite. This is my first supper with visitors in years. A thousand thanks. I recall meals at this table when I was very young– it was like a puppet spectrum. A group of people filled with long, pleasant complaints. Then the tea dances. Feather was a very good girl, wasn't she Joejoeing?

Yes.

Yes, said Miss Jilly, but on the breath at the end of the word yes the sound only stretched in half-agreement; there was another alternative coming into view, Yes, she continued, Feather was my sister. She had lots of doubt, anger and cherries. She is out in the New Forest now.

Mister Lundy rose and filled our glasses. Da moved onto lemonade. Suddenly away in the distance there was a great roll of thunder.

Do you know what your granduncle the cowboy wanted to do upstairs in the children's room Mister Psyche? and she looked across at me, with her eyebrows raised. I will not hold you in suspense. The tinker wanted to ride a child's tricycle across the floor. I ask you.

I lost the run of myself walking through the house, said Joejoe.

Did you let him, asked Gary, take a spin.

It was far too small for him. She glanced at the fire. Thank you for cleaning my chimney.

No problem, said Da.

We ate for a while.

You intend to build a tomb, enquired Ma.

Not quite, said Miss Jilly, and she looked childishly at Mister Lundy. I think I used the wrong word.

Is it to be a gallery?

No. Just a ring of stone. In fact, she said, still staring at Mister Lundy, what I have in mind is a small mausoleum.

Oh, said Anna.

And there was a silence.

Let us drink to a man who is not here, Miss Jilly said.

We all sat waiting, wondering.

And I hope that gentleman is himself having a drink at this very moment. This morning I brought him in a bottle of champagne and told him we would be seated at this table here at eight o'clock and that he was to raise a glass on the hour.

349

Before I left I popped the cork. Then she rose her glass and said: To the Bird!

We all stood and drank in salute.

To the Bird! we all repeated.

Who is he? whispered Gary in my ear.

A neighbour.

Oh, thank you.

Overhead the thunder rolled as everyone sat. Then the sky started to light up as the storm flew overhead. And again came another roll of thunder.

Nature, said Miss Jilly, is upset.

Maister Gaoithe, said Desmond.

Oh translate please.

The churning wind, said Gary. Then there's the leap of the mare, and the whin bush.

Very nice. And Mister Thomas Feeney said that in his hospital bed he had been riding high next the sister of sorrow. I thought for a while on his words. Then I said: Mister Feeney you are making sense. And he said: if I am making sense, I am getting better. And he pointed sadly at the empty bed beside him. Then he said – Prepare yourself, do you hear that step in the corridor, you can always tell a doctor's step, wait for it – and into the ward stepped a doctor.

No, said Anna, just like that?

Yes.

Unfortunately, in a hospital you get to know the sound of the bosses, said Ma, yes, you do after a while.

The jugglers, I said.

Cuckoo, said Joejoe, aping the bird.

And they will be moving him soon – probably tomorrow – into a nursing home, St Francis's, said Ma. A bed, I think, became available there yesterday.

Life gets cold, said Miss Jilly.

Outside the thunder pitched wildly. We ate like old friends

who were strangers. The crab was doused in butter and lemon. Joejoe picked at his teeth to unearth the parsley and chives. Anna's mobile rang – Absolutely, grand, like, she said, then came the pause, and next – Look, chat you later. *Absolutely, grand*, repeated Miss Jilly, it is extraordinary how the local ear picks up the pure genteel without knowing.

Mister Lundy and Da stood and gathered the plates, and a few minutes later swung through the door with two trays of desserts. We got these tutti-fruttis – made of blackberries, strawberries, raspberries and apple juice. Anna looked at me and Joejoe, and pointed at both of us.

This is the second time in two days that pair have been served by a waiter, she said.

Oh, said Miss Jilly. We all have our own factotum. I had a servant once. My husband was a military man. He was my master. My master is dead.

Ma looked startled.

I'm sorry, said Grandda. He died on October 10th 1990.

Correct. You have an incredible memory Joejoeing –

– But I cannot see colours –

– And there are his ashes, and Miss Jilly pointed with a dessert spoon to the small vase positioned in the corner of the room on the small table, the same vase she had cradled to her chest the day we did the chimney. I have stood for years wondering where to put them, she continued, I must have stood in a thousand places, then as the earth began to leave here over the last few days, I thought out there, where the earth once was, facing the bay, they should sit ... in a small mausoleum ... where I can join him in time. You were digging a grave, gentlemen, she said to the two men.

Ah – it's no wonder we got lost, said Gary.

Pray?

On our way out.

351

We were going round in circles, said Desmond.

And circles –

– Till finally –

– We hit Ballintra.

And then landed in Meenagorp, said Desmond.

Translate, please?

A smooth place of the dead, said Gary.

Thank you. The dead each year sprout out of the ground like daisies. That's why I'd like to have a chime. When I was a young woman I found a dog walking the road, and knew it belonged to our house in another generation. It was a tall dog of a type I knew from a previous existence, so I said the words and it followed me up the avenue. And the dog lived till he was eighteen. You remember his name?

Tonto, I said.

Correct. She turned to our granduncle. And who buried him?

I did, said Joejoe.

Forgive my morbidity. When I wine and dine I grow sad and always blame someone.

And I look for signs.

Now it's time I kept my promise, she said, and as the thunder rolled again we followed her upstairs to the Watch Room where all of us took a look up through the telescope at the lightning in the sky. And immediately into my head stepped the Russian sailors looking up at the ocean as Joejoe pondered the heavens. Then downstairs again Anna painted her nails a wild violet as Mister Lundy turned on a tape under instruction from Miss Jilly and on came *The Pirates of Penzance*, then later an old gent called Perry Como, singing, while the fire in the chimney roared; then the architect and the lady saw us to the door; the van went to town with Gary waving like a man demented, and Da sat in soberly behind the wheel of Ma's car and drove us all home.

Chapter Thirty-Eight

My Story

I woke at five o'clock in the bed, and bit by bit the crew of my dreams reluctantly left me, then they were gone completely and I got up to find a low white haze over the fields. A cow stood looking through the mist with two calves at her udders, in the next field the horse was running in circles.

Then the mist grew deeper till there was nothing to be seen. All you could hear outside was the lewing cow. The sea went, and all that came in was the sound. I sat among the montbretia and watched them shake their red veins. The wild hollyhock was gone old and brown. The stiff rods of the arum lilies stood stiffly up in the air like a choir of gnarled heads. The white flowers were long dead. The branch of a poor sycamore, driven helpless by wind, looked at me like a woman's head. The empty rose bush shuffled. I leaned down to look at the two purple heads of hydrangea that had survived the winds. Then the mist flattened and began to lift with just the slightest urge of a breeze. What was out there? I walked down the road to the pier and touched the wall, and found my way down to the boat. I sat there for an hour at the wheel watching the white world sifting past.

Then I made my way back up the road, and into bed, and did the crossword, and did the other one, then at last at seven I got up and put on the kettle. Ma came into the kitchen.

I called your father, she said, but not a budge.

Da, I called up the stairs.

Ma was on duty for just half a day; she had porridge and headed off into the mist. I put the hedge cutters and the strimmer in Da's boot and waited. At last he appeared in his fishing gear.

I'm going to take out the boat for a run before the weather breaks, he said, where have I to bring you?

The Judge's.

Oh yeh.

We set off in second gear. The road ahead was like one we had never been on before, but as we went inland the mist began to lift and he dropped me off at the Judge's house where I did his lawns with his mower, and chopped timber, then cleared the tall weeds along his walls.

How is your uncle?

I have not seen him in a couple of days, but he seems OK.

Good.

He left me down to Miss Constance's where I cut the weeds each side of the lane to her house. At twelve I stepped across the road and washed Miss Gurn's windows and weeded her garden.

The sun was high in the sky. The sound of mowing was everywhere.

It grew hotter and hotter.

I did Father Grimes's hedges. The roads were filled with tractors drawing hay. It was the second cut. Then I got a lift home in a tractor and trailer. As I entered the house the phone rang off. I looked out to sea and saw Da's boat out towards the island.

The hare walked out the rocks and sat – ears up beside the heron – looking out to sea. Why does the hare go out the rocks? I once asked Joejoe. Because he is enchanted, he said. The hare is enchanted. He likes his salt. Then I worked the garden, laying more flags to make a path that would form an X that would run from corner to corner. Then I went to weed the potato and the carrot beds.

When Ma arrived home in the afternoon I was sitting in the studio going through a book of stamps that had travelled through the family. She looked in.

Hi, I said.

Hi! I have news. This morning I went up to see the Bird with a clean set of clothes and found his bed empty. I waited a while thinking he was at the toilet, then nurse Jean came along to say they had just moved him to St Francis's Home for old folk.

Does that mean he won't be coming back home?

I'm afraid so, for the time being. I just called to him on my way out. He is in ward Male 2.

How was he?

Discontented, she said, but there again he had a certain request.

For what?

Champagne, yes, champagne, she said.

She changed her clothes and took up a rake and started to filter the clay. I set off down to the Bird's house with a cardboard box. I dropped in to say Hallo to Joejoe and Cnoic raced out and joined me. I opened the door of the Bird's and went to the toilet; the dog ran into the house, and started barking wildly, then ran out again. I filled the cardboard box, then stepped down to the pier and waited for Da to return.

About half an hour later Da landed, with two pollock and fourteen lobsters, and we drove off and dropped them at the Sea Café, then headed to the Nursing Home.

Outside St Francis's a man was standing propped on his walking stick and beyond him was a wren singing sweet on a leafless tree. Flowers filled the sills. Gentlemen and ladies felt their way along the corridor as we went looking for Male 2. A scream was repeated as we walked along.

What have you got in the box, asked Da.

A present.

I see.

Then we reached the Male 2 that had eight beds. At the furthest remove below the window the Bird was in an armchair with his cap on his head and his eyes closed.

Tom, said Da.

Well?

Tom, repeated Da.

Aha Mister Feeney, he said wakening with a smile, and how is Mister Psyche?

Very good sir.

Did you get the dog?

I did.

Where is he now?

In Joejoe's.

Aha, he said contentedly.

Just then a man entered the ward dressed in a shirt and trousers and bare feet. He came along to the Bird's bed and sat on it. He looked at the three of us quizzically, as if we were in the way, or people he should have known, then, in one quick move, he took off his trousers.

Excuse me, said Da.

Is there something wrong? the man asked him, as he climbed into Tom's bed and lay back beneath the sheets.

I think you are in the wrong place.

Pardon?

Please get up.

What do you mean?

That is my bed, said the Bird quietly, Mister James.

It's my bed, he said, and he pulled the sheets to his chin.

I'm afraid you are making a mistake, said Da.

This has already happened today, explained Tom in a quiet voice. This morning he nearly climbed in beside me.

You're joking.

No, I am not.

What are you saying about me?

The other men in the ward who were awake watched us with a great sense of finality.

Will I get the nurse? asked Da.

Say nothing, said the Bird.

My wife's birthday, said the man, was a Holy Day of Obligation. Now it's not. Pope John said there was no Philomena. That she never existed. That there was no such thing. I was ashamed for my wife, and when she was young she had nothing but miraculous medals pinned to her. And my wife Philomena is in the women's ward. But they won't let me go to see her.

Just then the nurse raced to the door, bowed her head, came down and took the man's hand.

Jim?

Yes sister.

Come on Jim, she said.

Where are we going?

Back to your room.

Was it a man or woman came round this morning with communion?

A woman.

I thought that.

He looked at us and got out of the bed, and climbed into his trousers. He sat a moment as she rubbed his hands.

It was good of you to call folks, he said.

Sorry, she said, fixing the sheets, then off he went with her.

When they were gone, the Bird explained: It seems he is in the next ward to this one, and in a bed placed exactly where my one is. So every time he goes to the toilet he's inclined to wander looking for his wife and he ends up here.

It's sad, I said. Why will they not let him see his wife?

I don't know.

That's strange.

Maybe she's not here.

Oh Christ.

What have you got there?

Something for you, I said.

I opened the box and slowly placed the six bottles of perfume – one after another – on his side table. He watched me with grateful eyes, then with his good hand he lifted one bottle, handed it to me and so I undid the cap, and he held the perfume to his nose, and he smelt it, and closed his eyes.

I placed the other bottles out of sight in the locker with the caps loosened. Thank you sincerely, he said.

And Da looked on in wonder as the Blackbird squirted a swish of perfume onto his neck, chest, wrist and with a tortuous reach under the sheets did his knees. Then the final bottle disappeared into the locker and he took the dudeen out of the pocket of his pyjamas and placed it on his side table.

You brought me the very things I wanted, he said. I'm glad I gave you the key.

I didn't want it to look like I was breaking a secret, I said, but I thought you'd like them.

And I was afraid to ask you. He looked at me cautiously. There's a few secrets in that house.

There is, I said.

He nodded. And so now I have my perfumes and you have my dog. Aye. There's a certain relief in that. You see they say I might not see home again.

Is there anything we can do? asked Da.

No, son. This is it I think. As they say in the airport my flight is now closing. The brain has taken a beating. And he looked around him at the silent beds, the nodding heads. I'm back on the ground floor again, he said. Then his voice dropped to a whisper – Do you see that man over there – in the blue top – a young couple came to see him and they were all speaking English with a Dublin accent – then they slipped into another language from somewhere out there in the world and then suddenly they were back in English. They had flown from far away to see him. And I wanted to ask where they came from. And then I thought I won't. I won't ask. I'll leave it as a mystery, and they were gone, just like that. I'm not too sure what I'm going to say next. Except to say I lost my singing nurse.

Bimbo.

The very man. But now I know what I want to say – How is Joejoe?

He has a very tidy house.

Do you know what it is – you stay at a certain age in your head. Going back I met the man coming, the man I was then. Everywhere I went I met myself, and other forgotten voices kept breaking in. I do not want those voices. I want the silence. The voices grow, and along comes the same song over and over, till I'm demented with the repetition of the words. It could be 'The Auld Triangle' today, and 'They Shot Henry Mountjoy' tomorrow I'll be singing. And it will be the same three lines. I'm there and here, and I'm fast approaching the horror again. I have something in my past is troubling me. Yes. Yes. By the way do you know who was sitting in that chair first thing this morning?

Who?

He leaned down and opened the locker and with his good hand took out a paper bag, and put it between his feet, and out of the bag he took a small bottle of champagne with a tissue in the top.

Miss Jilly, I said.

Yes sir. She went to the general hospital and they directed her here. And she pulled the cork, and filled me out two glasses. But I think that woman is very low, he whispered.

Do ya, asked Da.

Yes.

Well she has plenty of plans, said Da.

As Joejoe would say, it's a sign.

Well from now on she'll have a clear view of the sea from her drawing room.

That's good.

Yeh, said Da.

And we sat in silence.

The Bird looked straight in front of him.

You are the second generation, he said. It will come to you. As it did to us, and then to you, and you are the third generation, you Mister Psyche are like my father, the same sane eyes. He left me when I was young and I sought him out, then as I grew old he tried to find me. The rejection went both ways in the long run, with my mother looking on. He died unhappy. I got my revenge, and now he – as I grow old – is having his revenge on me. I want to make this clear Tommy Feeney. Love travels on the same journey as hate. Isn't that right Mister P?

Yes.

I am here because of a wrong I did. Then he turned to Da, and said: Do you know you are my son?

What?

That's why you hate me.

I don't hate you.

We are not saints, said the Bird. That's why we have the same name.

Tom.

Yes.

You are not even related to me.

I am your father!

A nurse appeared at the doorway and walked the ward silently towards us.

Is there something wrong Mister Feeney? she asked.

No, said the Bird.

Is there anything I can do for you?

I'm up in the air and running, running out of breath, he said.

Excuse me, she said to Da, I take it you are a relation.

He is a relation! said the Bird.

Let's put it like this – we share the same name.

Can I speak to you for a moment? she asked, please.

Shaking, Da followed her out of the ward and the Blackbird closed his eyes. He rose his right hand round his head like he was looking for forgiveness, but really he was trying to wake himself up. Not a word was said till Da returned about ten minutes later by himself. He took a see-through plastic bag of the Bird's clothes off the floor. We're taking his washing home, he whispered. We sat waiting. Da nodded at the door and watched me.

Am I your son as well, I asked the Blackbird.

Indeed you are Mister Psyche, and he suddenly opened his eyes and stared straight ahead into an empty space till slowly we returned into view. I can make small talk, he said slowly, I can do that but out of the corner of my eye I can see the dark approaching.

He looked at us and then he touched the tips of the fingers of his left hand with his right hand, and shook hands with himself, then the left hand fell back down into the sling.

You can go now, he said.

We shook hands.

Sin-é, he said. Good luck.

We stepped along the corridor without speaking, and as we drove the road to Ballintra we passed Anna running for home.

That night myself and Anna and Ma and Da went up to Mister John's to take part in a quiz where all the monies made were being donated to cancer. There were free sandwiches and crisps and tea and coffee.

361

About forty people arrived. To take part we all paid fifteen euro per person, so 600 euro went into the kitty.

The four of us were joined by Anna's father to make up a table of five.

He took the questions on sport, Lala answered the ones on Pop, Geography and Natural History; Da took on the political ones and traditional music; Ma answered the current affairs and films; and I was left with History and Irish Mythology. The answers – in the long run – included Michael Collins; wild celery; Churchill; the sandpiper; the Far East; County Kerry; The Chieftains; *The Quiet Man*; Donal Lunny; Jack Lynch; nectar; Maureen Potter; Schillaci, Red Hot Chilli Peppers; John Cleese; Tullamore; *The Godfather*; Easkey; 'Ruby Tuesday'; Diarmuid and Grainne; Britney Spears; the Brent geese; Buddy Holly; and a lodestone.

We came third.

On the way back I stepped into Joejoe's. The remembrance candles were fluttering on the windows.

He handed me the book of Psalms that fell open at Matthew.

I read:

And when they were come to a place called Golgotha, that is to say a place of a skull,

They gave him vinegar to drink mingled with gall: and when he had tasted it thereof, he would not drink.

The place of the skull, Joejoe said; and he tapped his forehead. He looked at me. Is that right?

Yes.

And he would not drink.

No.

No, he agreed with a nod.

I could see blue lines gather on his face.

Are you all right?

No.

Will I fill you a glass?

Do.

He sat back in the armchair. Cnoic was at his feet and Timmy was in his chair and both were watching the old man. He took the glass and held it with both hands in his lap. Rain started pelting on the galvanised roof. The front windows echoed with splashes.

We go round in circles, he said.

We do.

Circles, he said.

Aye.

Like Mister Gary said. Unless you have a place away in the heights ahead of you that you can see. That's why they put the forts on the hills – so that you could find your way. But then – what happens – you come back!

You do.

And what do you do – you head off again, he said, shaking his head.

He drank. The rain threw another clout at the windows.

We're back in February of eighty-seven. You'll be drenched. Take the auld umbrella with you.

I will.

And don't be worrying son.

I won't.

Good man. Spell the word mystery.

M–y–s–t–e–r–y.

One night here you know what that man Gary said; he said the whole thing was a mystery, and then he asked me what the word *mystery* sounds like, and I said I don't know, and he said it sounds like *my story*.

I took the auld black umbrella, and he stood behind the door, opened it a fraction and the rain beat in, then I dived out and hoisted the umbrella and the door crashed closed behind me.

BOOK SEVEN

The Signs

Chapter Thirty-Nine

Diamonds

I opened my eyes, got up and Grandma followed me across the room. She was in black, and then I heard the Bird singing 'I Wish, I Wish in Vain' over and over so I dressed as quick as I could, and ran downstairs.

The house was empty and the sun streaming through the windows.

There was a note on the floor inside the front door.

Can you give us a hand today, yours, Joe Lenihan, it read.

I headed off on the tractor with bales of hay from Lenihan's fields to Laird's Barn. The humming trawl of the mowers was everywhere. Steam was rising on the road. The rushes were bent and swishing. Montbretia was swaying its lucifers, and here and there were the last of a few harebells and the torn ends of what was once the wild woodbine. A storm was due on the morrow, so the final cut had to be done and finished today. There were four of us lads going back and forward till night fell, then the lights were switched on and we continued in the dark.

The last bale was dropped at ten. Joe paid me 100 euro. I was coated in straw when I stepped into Joejoe's that night.

Sit down there, son, he said. You look like a scarecrow.

Do you know what a straw man is? I asked

Continue.

He is a lie. He is pretending.

Well last night, he said, I saw another lie. I saw the Bird in my sleep. We were back at the Stations, and the Bird was choking on his communion.

Jesus. I had a dream last night too.

You had.

I dreamt that my Grandma had just died yesterday.

Dear God.

And she had died long before I was born.

He looked at me with astounded eyes, and felt his neck, and then he patted my knee. Aisy son, he said.

Why did I dream her?

Because you never met her. The dead you never met die a little bit every day in your head.

I looked at the photo of herself and Grandda, and Granduncle Joejoe that sat on the third shelf of the dresser, along the way from the Wayward Lad. She was seated. Joejoe and Grandda were standing. She was in black, with glasses, not posing but studying herself in the eye of the camera. I took down my drawing pad and pencil, moved the photo to the table and began to draw her. Beside me the oil lamp blazed on the window. I got her shoulders, I got the dark twist of hair, and then I waited on the eyes and the cheeks to appear, but the face remained empty.

Joejoe looked over my shoulder.

Aye, he said, and he placed a lit candle on the table and went back to his chair.

I sat carefully dressing the cheeks and the ears, and then I brought the rim of the glasses round the eyes. I tried to get the puzzle into the pupils. Then I saw Grandda's hand on her shoulder and I followed his arm back up to his shoulder and stopped there. I wanted to get that touch of his hand on her black woollen jumper. I curved the threads and straightened the neck line. And then went after the slight bow, that questioning nod.

I tapped the nostril. Put in the only wrinkle.

I looked at the face a while. I looked at his hand on her shoulder. I put in the fingers nails, the knuckles and the bent thumb.

Are you done son?

The best I can do.

I handed him the drawing book.

Dear God, he said, and he stared at me nearly in anger, then smiled, and closed the copy book and handed it to me. I turned another page, and started drawing him, trying to get his eyes, but he closed them, then I stopped and put the book back on the shelf, and made tea.

He came over and beat the straw off the back of my jacket.

Did you ever hear of the boys from the Andes? The Incas were tough. Tough out! And the Aztec from Mexico was a hard man. He stopped work at twenty to twelve every night.

And we're standing here at the same time.

It's a strange world Mister Psyche.

It is.

Timmy came up and looked at him. Right, he said, and he lifted the bag, and as he poured the nuts into the dog's bowl, Timmy kissed his hand while Cnoic, with a backward eye, quietly waited his turn.

So read us the news, he said.

I lifted the local journal, and read various lines from small extracts:

On the Bank holiday weekend, an elderly man was fatally injured at the Cross at Binn. Meanwhile a Latvian lorry driver died when his milk tanker ploughed into a bog. And sadly a fisherman fell overboard as he reined in lobster pots off Carn.

Dan Herrity won the singing contest at Leyden's in a rendition of an old McCormack favourite.

2000 euro was collected for cancer in the 30 mile run. 400 people took on the run, including a class of girls from St Ann's.

Good lassies, he nodded, and I put away the paper and he lifted the remote and turned on the weather on *Russia Today* news.

*

369

The thundering rain started at midnight. I got drenched on the road up home. The dark was swinging round the blowhole. Da and Ma were seated at the table playing poker.

You were busy today.

I was.

Will you take a hand?

I will.

I joined the game and we played till one o'clock when the telephone rang.

Ma took it.

Yes, she said, that's me. Yes, she said looking at us. Oh dear. What time was that at? I see. OK, thank you.

She came back to the table.

Is it bad news, asked Da.

No.

What happened?

The Bird was caught trying to climb out a window.

What?

He said he was only trying to get some air. If he does it again he'll be in trouble, she said. What's trumps?

Diamonds.

Late the following afternoon myself and Ma went to shop in Lidl's on the far side of town. We filled the boot with toilet rolls, sugar, tins of tomatoes, white wine, McAllister's Shortbread, Mister Choc's Choco Caramel, balti sauce, mint-chocolate biscuits; rashers, sausages, a saw, a lamp, Tayto Crisps, an apron, Italian apples, and Spanish oranges; stopped off down the road for a McDonald's salad hamburger and chips, and sat in the car watching a group of jackdaws and crows attack a dustbin, and scurry across the pavement like monks in dark wind-blown shawls; then we drove to the Garden Centre where Anna worked.

She was alone in the huge glasshouse watering plants.

I just want to get a few things.

It's so late in the year, it's not a good time for setting, Anna said but she brought us round to the coastal plants and we bought camellia, sea buckthorn, and sea holly.

Next spring you can tell us what to do.

I will.

See you Anna.

See ya.

Wait a minute. Can you get off for a half an hour, we are on our way to see the Bird.

I'll ask, and she was given an hour off.

And so we went to visit Thomas Feeney.

There was an empty bus at the door of St Francis's Home. In the foyer the old folk sat facing the door. A woman stood and pointed her stick at me.

Are you over twenty-one? she asked.

No, I said.

Well don't do it again, she said, and sat back into her armchair laughing and reached out to her ice-cream.

Are you all right? asked Ma.

I'm waiting on my hairdresser, sister, the woman explained. My son set up the appointment. I have to get my hair done as I'm going to Lourdes on Friday.

Good for you.

A man inched forward on his walking frame down the long corridor and we walked behind him past the empty church, the care assistants sorting clothes, till we reached Male 2. The Bird was seated by his bed, the cap on his head, the face lowered, and the hands joined.

Tom, said Ma.

Ah Mrs Feeney, he said waving, and Psyche and Miss Anna Conan. He laughed.

He lifted up his arm to show the blue band around his right wrist that had a little bubble at the centre.

You see they have me handcuffed, he said.

We heard you were going on a journey, said Ma, as she took his clothes for the wash and put them in a plastic bag.

Is that what they are saying?

Yes.

Well let them.

Tom.

Yes.

Relax.

Well listen to this. A doctor came in here a while back, said the Bird, and I said *I'm hungry*, and he said *why are you angry?* I got angry then, and roared *I'm hungry*. And he said *Cool down, Mister Feeney*.

Oh dear.

My anger is my own, Mrs I must get rid of it. But I'm not in the humour for jokes. Yesterday my pension arrived here to the hospital. So this is home now. It all started before school. I saw it written in my face. Then at school it got worse, and worse. There was no let-up. And do you know what my problem was – and he called Anna's ear to his lips – *good looks*, he whispered smiling.

Oh you poor fellow, she said.

It's great to tell lies, he said nodding.

In the next bed a man that was lying under the sheets with his legs crossed suddenly jerked up and made a small tent with his knees. Tom shook his head, lifted the dudeen and put it in his mouth and took a long breath with his eyes closed.

That pipe could give you an infection, said Ma.

The nurse washed it out for me.

Oh.

Lovely, he said.

Ma put an unopened packet of Major cigarettes on his bedside table.

He opened his eyes and looked at the fags. A drowned man is never found on his back, he said.

Is that it?

Yes, the sea turns you over.

All of a sudden the TV overhead raced up a notch as the camera honed in on a bar in Australia. The Bird put down the pipe.

I'm in a house of endless soaps, he said.

I know.

And you grow tired after the elation.

Is that why you wanted out? asked Ma.

Sh! he said, and put a finger to his lips. You see I cannot stand the noise. Now Psyche. I have a request. Will you turn down the sound?

I'll do it, said Ma and she went off to find the remote.

He pointed at a man in the first bed to the right and whispered: He fell in a bowling alley.

All of a sudden I got the smell of the perfumes as the Bird got up and looked over towards the window. Are there still daisies in the ditches?

There is, Anna said.

Have the blackberries come?

Up your road they're ripe, I said.

Will you bring me in some on your next visit, please?

I will.

He lifted his good hand with the band up in the air and pointed at the yellow line drawn across the floor.

If I was to cross that line to touch that window, the . . . he said and then he sat down immediately, as a nurse and Ma stepped into the ward and walked slowly towards us.

Don't do it, the nurse said.

Do what? asked the Blackbird.

You know what I mean. Don't cross that line. You'll set off the alarm. You know what he's at – he's looking for attention, she said and then she lifted the remote off the window sill and turned down the sound.

*

The cement mixer shook and roared under the trees at Dromod House. Myself and Da were placing the last square stones from the old monastery shed in the foundation and walls of the mausoleum.

Miss Jilly was not there to greet us.

Da looked at Mister Lundy's drawing.

We go up four feet in stone, said Da, and one foot in brick.

Right.

And she is to be five foot long.

So we did the measuring and went in tight, standing back to look without another word. He put the drawing back inside the car on the driver's seat. It was a square we were making. No curves. And the cement was not to appear to the eye, but be pushed far in. Not a trace was allowed.

Mister Lundy had written: *The trick is to let it appear like a drystone wall.*

We dug in the bed of cement, and following the twine dropped in the first layer of rock and he fed in the cement as I started on the second layer. When we reached the beginning of the fifth foot I took over the cement and Da started laying the red bricks that had come from an old caved-in house on the estate.

I saw Miss Jilly at the window looking down as I placed the round sea stones into two small circles onto the shingle floor of the mausoleum. In them the two urns would one day sit. By that evening the four walls were done with an opening in the north wall that was three foot high and two feet wide. It was facing the sea. The door for the opening was made from timber taken from the trees that had fallen over the years – birch wood. The electric saw rang throughout the estate as Da shaved the wood into short thick panels that I painted with three goes of undercoat, and then the following morning I'd give them a coat of dark brown.

I put the wood under the trees to save them from getting wet.

That night we dropped in to the Blackbird but he was fast asleep in the bed.

Tom, whispered Da.

There was no reply.

Tom, he whispered again into his ear, then he looked at me and jerked his eyes towards the corridor, so we did not wake him but went on down to the nurses' desk.

How is Tom Feeney? Da asked.

You are a relation?

Yes.

He is very tired in himself these last few days. We may have to return him to the General Hospital for further tests.

I see. Thank you.

Good night.

Good night.

Next day Da put a round window frame into the door, and the wood panels were placed in a circle so that they came down in a radius at the end. He then fitted in a pane of double-glazed glass one foot in diameter.

The porthole, he called it.

Dandelion clocks were blowing in the wind.

We began the roof. We hammered the longer planks of birch onto a bed of pine to make the support. Towards the middle we chiselled in a hole for the wind chime, and then laid the yellow flagstones – that were laid in a neat pile after the dig – across the top in star shapes working back to the ring in the centre.

Then the door, with an all-weather lock and handle, was hung on plastic coated hinges in the entrance.

I looked down into the window.

It felt like I was looking up into the telescope.

Well, said Da.

It looks good.

We stepped back to the trees, and sat there looking out to sea. The little house of stone was standing there on a grim patch of ground, without a blade of grass on any side, in a half an acre of cold tattered earth and long swoops of clay flattened by the machine. Miss Jilly had already scattered thousands of flower seeds for the coming year, and piles of horse dung had been drawn in, and buried; but the place looked abandoned, even by weeds.

I wonder should we give her a knock, asked Da, then No, no, he said to himself, best leave it.

We were gathering our tools when Mister Lundy pulled in with the last item. He put the wind chime in the centre and we sealed the hole with cement. He stood by the mausoleum and first looked out to sea, and then he stood to one side and looked back to the house. He turned and gave us the thumbs-up.

Don't go yet, he said.

He went into the house, and Miss Jilly appeared with him a few minutes later, with the flowers Anna had given her.

They walked towards the mausoleum. The wind chime had begun to hum.

She placed the pots of flowers on the ground. Forgive me for hiding, said Miss Jilly; Not at all, said Da, and he leaned down and opened the door, then stood aside. She carefully knelt and touched the glass then felt both sets of round sea stones, and stood and smiled. Mister Lundy closed the door, and turned the key, and handed it to her.

At last, she said.

Chapter Forty

Three Black Ties

Early next morning the phone rang.

Ma took the call.

I could hear her speaking and then she ran up the stairs and shouted Tom! Tom!

I got up into my shirt and trousers and stepped out onto the landing, at the same moment as Da in a dressing gown came out of his bedroom door. We locked eyes for a split second. Ma was standing in her slip on the bottom step of the stairs listening.

Thank you, she said, and she put down the phone.

She looked at us.

Yes? said Da.

The Bird is dead, she said.

We sat in the kitchen as the winds plucked the windows.

Ma turned on the kettle and faced the wall alone. I rang Anna to tell her the news. Ma lit a candle and put it in the window, got into her slippers and walked out the front door in her pyjamas into the wind. Da went upstairs and came down dressed. He sat down and laced his shoes. Ma arrived back in with strands and strands of wild mint and a few blackberries. The berries were placed centre table in a saucer. She washed the mint and threw it into a bowl. She poured the boiling water over the leaves, spooned in some honey and stirred the brew.

We dipped our glasses into the wild tea and drank.

I picked a head of blackberry and bit into it.

*

At 7.30 Ma rang the hospital to say she would not be at work today, or tomorrow, or the day after, and Da got on the phone and rang all the numbers on the list I'd found in the Bird's house but again he got nowhere. We got into the car. The windscreen was covered in salt. Da threw three buckets of water onto the glass and drove to Tom Feeney's to get his good suit, and search the house for other phone numbers and addresses. I opened the door and Da went straight to his bedroom. He was standing there with the rifle in his hands when I looked in.

What's the meaning of this?

It's Joejoe's, I said.

How did it get here?

The Bird took it away from him.

Oh Christ, he said and he went out and put it in the car.

Then we went through all the drawers, searching, searching. We found a few more names and telephone numbers written in notebooks, on the back of bills, and on envelopes. Ma picked out a shirt, and found an old-fashioned brown suit in the wardrobe. She came across a pair of good shoes. I swept out the living room, and cleaned the kitchen, and Ma went back up to the house to iron the suit and shirt while Da brought up the rifle, and said he would call Tom Feeney's sister Lilly in Luton, and other people in England, and Scotland and Ireland.

When they came back he said it was the same as before, wrong numbers, he spoke to people who had no notion of who Tom Feeney was; nobody knew him; but then he found one young man who said he was a nephew, and he told Da that Tom's sister – his own mother Lilly – had died years ago. His name was Jer Feeney, and he had taken down the details of the funeral, but did not know whether he could make it over, but he would try his best.

He has no one, said Da; no one but one nephew.

We began another search, but came up with nothing. Then we sat into the car and at last stopped off at Joejoe's.

A man on the pier stood by a telescope looking out at the island.

We sat a while wondering who should go in, then we all got out, and faced the door.

Da knocked. Cnoic barked a terror within.

Come in, shouted Joejoe as he turned the key in the door.

He looked at the four of us as we entered the kitchen.

Don't tell me, he said. He was in his shirt and long johns.

I'm sorry Joejoe, said Ma.

Is it the Bird?

He passed away at six this morning.

He turned and went back into his bedroom.

Psyche, he called.

I went in and he closed the door.

I cannot go on without him, said Joejoe. If the Bird is gone then I should be gone too.

Joejoe, I said.

He pulled on his trousers.

Do you want to come into the hospital with us?

No. But will you do me a favour?

I will.

There's a certain item called for.

Right.

Now, he said, and he handed me two twenties, and a tenner, and opened the door. Inside Da was putting a match to the pile of twigs and paper he had built up in the grate. A cup of tea and toast was on the table.

I'm really sorry, Joejoe, said Ma.

I know, daughter. He stepped outside and cleared the seashells from the window sills into a plastic bag, came in and sat into his armchair with a cup of tea.

His hair was standing.

Ma petted his head.

Now, said Da, throwing in a shovelful of coal. Can you help us out – do you know any of Tom's relations?

No.

Now, what are we going to do? Will we have him brought out for a wake in his house?

Whatever you decide, said Joejoe.

We'll let it be your decision.

I would not like to see him in a corpse house.

Well then we should have a wake, said Ma.

Whatever you think.

OK. We'll go on to make the arrangements, said Da. Will you be all right?

I will.

All right, said Da, we'll be back in a couple of hours.

He dropped myself and Ma at St Francis's, and drove on to the undertakers.

Ma, with the suit on a hanger, spoke to the receptionist who did not know us at the desk.

I have brought in Tom Feeney's clothes.

Are you relations? she asked.

No, said Ma, but we were responsible for Mister Tom Feeney. Most of his family are abroad.

Could I have you and your husband's name?

Geraldine and Tom Feeney.

The woman looked up.

That is the name of the deceased.

Yes.

Oh, she said, bewildered at hearing the same name twice, and she again checked her file.

Oh, she said, I see, then nodded. Please accept our condolences on your loss. I will have someone to talk to you in a moment.

Thank you.

Ma sat.

I went on a wander. I looked into the empty church. I heard a scream from the TV room. I reached the door into Alzheimer's, turned, and saw all the sleeping eyes in Female 2. I saw the familiar faces in Male 1. Food was travelling on trolleys. Tea was being poured. I went down into Male 2. The men watched me as I walked to the empty bed. It had already been changed for the next man in line. New sheets. New eiderdown. I stood a moment, and then I opened his bedside locker and it was empty.

I came back to the desk.

Where are Tom Feeney's things? I asked.

In storage, the receptionist said.

Well can I have them?

Yes, in a moment, and she took another call on the phone, then a few minutes later Tom's gear, well-tagged, appeared. I filled the bag I'd brought with his perfumes and clothes. The dudeen and fags I put in my shirt pocket.

Ma was speaking to a male nurse.

You wait here, she said, and she went off to the morgue to dress the Bird. I sat in the foyer among the old. The men and women sat facing the front door as if they were watching an old silent movie.

When everything had been arranged Da rang round the neighbours, the undertaker had already informed the local radio station, and inserted a death's notice in the *Irish Independent*.

Da had bought three black ties – one for himself, one for me and one for Joejoe. That evening we drove out behind the hearse, round Cooley Lane and stopped at the Bird's house. Frosty was standing at the gate, and himself, the undertaker and myself and Da carried the coffin in, and sat it on four chairs placed against the wall in the bedroom. The bed was newly made with crisp white sheets. The pillow was spotless, the blankets and eiderdown a light blue.

Each window had a vase of montbretia on the sill.

The two mirrors in the house had been turned to the wall.

The undertaker undid the screws and took the lid off the coffin and there the Blackbird lay alone in his brown suit and shirt, hands crossed, eyes closed, looking into the distance, with a hint of a smile.

Anna came in with a pot of lamb stew.

Thank you so much, said Ma.

It's nothing.

She touched the Bird's forehead, then she took my hand.

I'm sorry Philip.

I know.

She went off and lit the fire in the living room.

Ma brought in a few bottles of beer, and one bottle of whiskey and one of Harvey's Cream Sherry, and placed plates of sandwiches on the table. I put the bottle of Malibu in a safe place and then I placed the perfume bottles on a silver tray on a table at the head of the coffin, and sprayed his neck and wrists and ankles. I went out and walked up the lane and began picking blackberries. A pool of blood lay scattered on the road under the dripping fuchsia bush. The starlings were swooping over and back in a ball away in the distance, and nearer home sea gulls flashed as they flew over a newly cut field.

Then at the foot of the lane Joejoe appeared.

Psyche, he said.

I walked alongside him to the house.

He stalled in the kitchen to take stock and went into the bedroom by himself for a minute. There was a long silence and then he came into the living room and sat down in the Bird's armchair. He ran the fingers of his right hand across the back of his left hand.

Yes, he said, and he bent forward and stirred his feet like a bee feeding.

Not long after the first local souls began arriving for the wake; and as talk of Tom Feeney's family began it became clear that there was not a living relation of his in the room. The Bird was a stranger. They went over the story of how his father had died here in Cooley when the Bird was young, and how, the following year, the death of his mother took place. Now Da told the news that his sister Lilly was dead. There were no cousins in the locality. As more mourners came to the wake house all the time the mystery grew.

And Joejoe said not a word.

At one o'clock seated round the coffin was Frosty and Mister St Patrick and the General; at two o'clock there was Frosty and Sean Caraway, Freddie Hart, while out in the drawing room was Da, Joejoe, Mister and Mrs Conan, Mick Doyle, Stefan, and the General; in came Mister Awesome; Ma and Anna, like the night of the Stations, kept going to and fro with the stew and the sandwiches; then round three, Frosty sang and Joejoe accompanied him on his fingers.

He sat there till dawn broke.

Then he went to the bedroom and tipped a handful of sea shells into the coffin.

We all went home to bed for a couple of hours, then got up to dig the grave. The crew from the night before were there waiting at the gate of the graveyard with shovels and spades. Da and the General began the dig in front of the tombstone erected in memory of Johnny and Catherine Feeney.

Then myself and Frosty took our turn in the grave.

As we reached about four feet down we hit a few bones of the ancestors.

Frosty looked me in the eye, and nodded, and we dug another hole deeper down, and buried them.

*

Before the removal that evening we all sat round in the bedroom till the undertaker came. The smile on Tom Feeney's grey face began to tighten, and the lips straightened. I put the dudeen in his top pocket. Joejoe leaned in and stirred the shells. The lid was closed and the Bird was moved to the local church. We carried him up the aisle to the front, and the rosary was said by the priest and a few locals. It was there he spent his second night, on a trolley just below the altar.

Next morning the four front rows to the left of the altar where relations would sit at a funeral Mass were empty.

Our family kneeled in the fifth row behind, with Joejoe, in his old black suit and new black tie, seated next the aisle. And scattered round the nearly empty church behind us there were a few mourners. Anna came in and sat beside me. To my right-hand side I saw the three hippies enter and kneel. Angela had her hands joined in front of her face. The priest looked at the empty seats to the front and slowly began the Mass. Just then a man in his twenties appeared, walked up the middle of the church, and, with a great sense of unease, sat alone in the front row. The priest made no speech but just offered up the service in memory of the soul of the bachelor Tom Feeney, late of Cooley, then he shook incense on the remains, and turned and shook Joejoe's hand, then shook the young man's hand.

The family would like to invite you all after the burial to a meal in the Sea Café, he said.

Go in peace, he said, the Mass is ended.

The man looked back at us; and as we rose he came over and said he was Jer Feeney, Tom's nephew. We shook hands; then he followed us at the head of the queue of mourners as we carried the coffin on our shoulders to the graveyard, and lowered it on lengths of rope into the open grave. Anna threw in a handful of blackberries. We took our turns with the shovels at the filling-in as the priest said the Five Holy Mysteries. Joejoe stood with his cap to his chest beside Jer. With each clash of earth on the coffin it felt like we were burying two men, one a stranger and one a friend. I saw Jer stiffen with each clout of clay. It was Frosty, Terence MacGowan, and Mister McSharry threw in the first round of shovelfuls. Then, we tapped them on the shoulder and they stood aside and now it was myself, Da and the General digging into the pile of earth.

The widows stood chanting the responses as rain fell.

And just as the grave was near full a taxi pulled up at the gate of the graveyard and Miss Jilly got out and stood at the gate and watched and listened to the final prayers, then she got back into the taxi and took off. Mrs Currid, in her feathered cap, looked me in the face and said: Wonders will never cease, Philip.

Chapter Forty-One

Passing the Time

The last layer of earth was flattened; the wreaths were spread, and we stood in silence a moment, then suddenly Jer shook Joejoe's hand, waved to us and crossed the graveyard alone.

Where is he going? asked Ma.

He has to catch a flight from Knock, said Joejoe.

Ah dear.

Sir, said Angela and she kissed my granduncle's cheek, I am sorry you lost your friend.

Mister Feeney, said Tommy and Aaron together, and they shook hands.

We started down the path and on the way Joejoe took off his cap as Da knelt at Grandma's and Grandda's tombstone, then we went on.

Now we'll head to the Sea Café, said Da at the gate. Everyone is invited.

I'll not go, whispered Joejoe to me.

OK, Joejoe, I said.

Outside the graveyard the crowd were getting into their cars and Da stood waiting by the Volkswagen with the front passenger door open.

Now Uncle Joejoe, step in, he said.

He does not want to go, Da.

What?

Look, said Ma, I'll take him home.

Myself and Joejoe and Anna climbed into the Fiat.

Ma looked into the rear-view mirror.

Will you not change your mind, Joejoe?

No, Nurse.

And so Ma drove us back to his cottage, while Da sat in – with the General beside him – to lead the cortège to the restaurant.

There was not a word in the car till we pulled in at Ballintra.

Enjoy yourselves, Joejoe said, stepping out.

I better stay with him, I whispered into Anna's ear, on instinct, and I got out as well.

And are you not coming with us? asked Ma.

I'll stop with him, I think.

Ma sat a few seconds without moving while we stood by the gate, then she let down the window and said: Are you sure Joejoe? – while she looked at me. Yes Ma'am, he said, so reluctantly she turned the car around to face inland, and slowly they went up the road.

Immediately they were gone I released the dogs and Joejoe began his jaunt.

For the first hour he was up and down the road outside his house.

I walked him up; I walked him down while the two dogs went before us and behind. Everywhere the fuchsias were shedding their leaves and the clocks were scattering. The montbretia were being shredded down to their veins as the gusts from the Atlantic struck inland.

And the rowan berries were growing a more violent red by the minute, a sign, said Joejoe, of a bad winter ahead.

We went out on the battery wall with our clothes being torn apart by the wind; and he sat in his place for a while on the giant sloping rock; then it was off walking again, up to Cooley and back as if he was following the Bird's litany ... *Up Cooley and across Poll an Baid. Poc Awokatche. Culleens. Culleens. Poll and Saggart. Through the Bent. The Night Field. The raven. Dromod. Through the willows. Take a left. Onto the New Road.*

387

Jer, he said.

Then there it was, without a word being said, the same mantra I heard in my head as we took off again . . . *Into the quarry. Hens. Ballintra. Ballintra. Cooley. Hens. I was reared under their wings. Sea holly. The long squares. Christ's tears. Sally Anne. Culleens.*

The poor man, he said.

Off again . . . *The blooming General. Culleens. Cooley.* Then suddenly the Merc appeared before us on the road and at last Joejoe stopped.

Dido and the ambassador got out smiling with a bare questioning look.

How are you sir? asked the ambassador.

I am fine.

Chest! said Dido.

You gave my friend here and his wife a wonderful night.

Yes, said Joejoe, staring ahead, with his feet thrashing. Last Friday, three weeks ago, and he started to beat his chest with his hands.

Is something wrong? the ambassador said turning to me.

We are just back from a funeral, I explained.

I am sorry, and he translated for Dido, who bowed.

We go now, said the ambassador.

Do widzenia, said Dido, and he said something else in Polish, and the ambassador translated and said: He says goodbye and he says he will sing for you again sometime, and they got into the car and drove down to the pier; then seeing the state of the ocean they sat looking out; and at last turned and passed us on the road as myself and Joejoe headed off on another search. Dido held up the palm of one hand in a blessing, then it was the journey of . . . *The foxgloves. St John's Eve. Cooley graveyard. Childer, Childer. The long awns. The moon. The urchin. The rake. Hens flying in the rafters. Sea pink. Sea pink.*

A woman in a builder's jacket went by power-jogging followed by a spaniel she had tied to her wrist. Overhead the chopper flew in a circle. We ended up outside the Bird's house. The starlings were lined up on the electric wires overhead ready to take off with a whoosh.

I have lost a friend, said Joejoe, like you did.

Yes, Joejoe.

I unlocked the door and Cnoic leaped in and went round every room barking as Joejoe sat in the Bird's armchair.

Psyche, is there a tipple left?

I found a half-bottle of whiskey with a tincture remaining, and poured him a half-one.

He whisked the glass round and round in his hand then leaned forward and shot the full drop into the grate.

Good luck, he said.

I put the perfume bottles in a little box and led him home. The sheep above on the hill were lying in a long straight line along the ditch in Ewing's field. In the far distance a new storm was throwing her skirts in the air. The Apostles were gathering. The yellow and red marigolds were dipping their heads. Timmy and Cnoic ran and rose onto their back legs at the door. We let them in, and they flattened on the floor, shivering.

I filled the grate with paper and timber and turf and struck the match.

He stood and shook the old draper's bell.

Cuckoo! he said and Timmy whined. Our shadows went round the walls followed by the flames.

We sat by the fire in his house till darkness fell and slowly he returned from wherever he'd been. I filled him two glasses of poteen.

His phone rang.

I picked it up and said Hallo and the phone rang off.

Who was that, he asked.

No one.

That's going on all the time, he said.

He turned on the small portable TV and we watched ten minutes of a film set in Vietnam. As the soldiers shot into the forest he pointed the remote at the screen, said April 1965, and turned it off; *You were some bird when you left Raspberry hill*, he sang to himself, *you were, you were*; then he moved on to *The crows are alive on the trees, like honey bees*; then he moved on to the song 'Black is the Colour of My True Love's Hair'; and he sat, doing that mad movement with his feet, the tap then the pawing and the kick-back in rhythm to a tune inside his head. On to the song 'All around the bloomin' heather, will you go lassie go'. Then he oiled the saw and the blades. He oiled the lock on the front door and then fell asleep in the armchair.

There was a small knock on the window. I opened the door and Miss Jilly entered under an umbrella; said Excuse me, as she downed it.

Is he asleep?

Yes Ma'am.

I hear a voice I know, he said, without opening his eyes, who is it?

Miss Jilly, she said and she went over and shook Joejoe's hand.

It was in your house, he said, that I saw my first tomato and I carried it home like it was a marvel. Now for you. That's how I got to know tomatoes.

I used to see you always wandering about at all hours in the glasshouse.

Yes, and up and down the stairs in the main house cause I loved the carpets. I asked your father once what he would like most in this world and he said he would like to hear again. He had gone deaf.

Yes. And that was me on the phone, she said, a few minutes ago but I could not speak.

Sit yourself down.

I'm sorry, Mister Psyche, she said and she shook my hand. I could not enter the graveyard.

Please stay a while.

No, I am only infringing.

Just then through the open door we heard a car pulling up and Anna came in with two bags of fish and chips, a box of mushy peas and a cold bottle of Chablis.

Oh Anna, said Miss Jilly, and she hugged her.

Lala will chat you later, said Anna.

I followed her out to the car.

How is he, said Ma.

He's not so bad.

Is there anything we can do, asked Da.

It's all right.

Jesus son, I'm sorry for putting all this on you, and he shook his head.

It's OK, Da. It's OK. Miss Jilly has just arrived.

I know – we saw the car at the pier, that's why we did not go in.

I'll be up soon.

Right son.

They took off and I waved them away.

Anna held both my hands, put her head down, and followed me into the house. Inside Miss Jilly had sat alongside Joejoe. She would not eat, so myself and Joejoe ate out off our laps by the fire. He ate every last chip and every morsel of cod. Then I made tea in the dark scullery and the ladies accepted a cup. He lit a candle and asked me to read and I searched through the Psalms trying to find a piece that did not speak of death or murder till I came to Revelations 16 and I found these words:

Behold I come as a thief. Blessed is he that watcheth and keepeth his garments, lest he walk naked and they see his shame.

And he gathered them together into a place called in the Hebrew tongue Armageddon.

And the seventh angel poured out his vial into the air, and there came a great voice out of the temple of heaven, from the throne, saying, It is done.

And there were voices and thunders and lightnings –

– Yes, he said, the signs –

– Beautiful, Anna said –

– They are always there –

– They are, said Miss Jilly, Just yesterday I put my husband's urn in the mausoleum –

– Read on, he said –

Psalm 50 –

I will take no bullock out of thy house, nor the goats out of thy folds.

For every beast of the forest is mine, and the cattle upon a thousand hills.

I know all the fowls of the mountains: and the wild beasts of the field –

A belt of rain pelted down on the roof. I stopped, put the Psalms next to the Wayward Lad on the dresser.

Would you people like to be on your own? Miss Jilly asked.

I am on my own, said Joejoe. Stay a while longer. It will pass the time, and he stood and patted my shoulder.

I opened the bottle of wine and poured out four glasses.

Good, good, he said.

It's French.

We touched glasses and drank.

You'll get that, he said.

You will, said Anna.

Miss Jilly looked at him, turned away and stood silently a moment then she flung the long black scarf back round her neck.

How are you? she asked.

I know I'm here but I'm inclined to wander.

Are you sad?

No. That would be the wrong word. I'm in a hurry, he said.

A hurry?

Aye.

Well wait for me.

I will.

I'm glad I called, she said, cheers.

Good luck.

Thank you Mister Psyche.

Again, another belt of rain thrashed the galvanised roof and steam poured from the fire. And just as quickly the battering stopped. Then a minute later the showers began drumming across the roof again in earnest.

There's a hurricane out there somewhere, he said. The sea wrack will be up the beach on the morning.

I poured another few glasses. He suddenly tore at his back, and then settled down.

I felt the loss coming, he said, but the real thing brings on the guilty plea – the selfishness.

There is no such thing as remorse, said Miss Jilly, only alleviation. It is best, perhaps, said Miss Jilly, to say goodbye privately.

Yes, he said, and then he said *Apples*. Apples I love, but not the skins. He stared at the ceiling. His eyes never flinched. He smiled quietly to himself.

Can I admit something Anna? said Miss Jilly –

– Do –

– I abhor sentiment because I indulge in it –

– Oh –

– while pretending I don't. The strict face has a tear blocking its view.

Indeed you're right Ma'am, said Joejoe.

I stood and opened the Blackbird's box of perfumes.

Pick a bottle, Madam, I said.

Miss Jilly reached in and lifted a dark bottle, undid the cap and smelt in.

My God, he said, it's him.

It's yours. They were Tom Feeney's private collection.

That is so thoughtful of you.

I had better go, I said. They are waiting for me above.

And we'll go with you, said Miss Jilly.

Joejoe stepped out the door with us and we all looked at each other as the dogs circled us. The sky was a ball of black. The clouds were at war, stalking the map of the heavens. Miss Jilly unfurled her tall blue umbrella.

Goodbye Miss Jilly and Miss Anna, he said, thank you for calling. Say Hallo to the family, Mister Psyche, he said. C'mon in lads.

The dogs went in. The door closed. He blew the candle out. There was only the odd flash of the flames in the house as I looked back. We walked Miss Jilly to her car in the dark. She put her hand on the back of my hand.

Thank you, she said, for everything. Will you take a lift?

No, I'll walk, said Anna.

Miss Jilly drove off. I looked south. The lights of dozens of houses were twinkling on another shore. Then I smelt the perfume Miss Jilly had rubbed into my skin. Smell that, I said. Anna let my hand go and headed home walking in her black coat and shoes. I watched her till she went out of sight

The gang were round the table.

I thought you would never come, said Da.

How did the meal go?

First that man Jer left, the meal without him was wrong. The meal without Joejoe was worse. We should have just come home. I never felt so lonesome in my life.

It was sad, said Ma.

I can get nowhere with that man, said Da, or without him. He should by right move in with us.

He's in mourning.

I know. I know.

Da cut the pack of cards that sat on the table, then put them back in their place.

We have been given a warning, he said.

Easy Tom.

Geraldine, sorry, I can't stop myself.

The fish and chips were perfect, I said. He ate every last bit.

Good, said Ma.

And I had four glasses of Chablis.

Now. Good for you – remember you missed the college party in town.

I think I didn't want to go.

You did very well Philip, said Ma.

I did OK.

I'm being utterly selfish, said Da, with all that's going on I never thought to raise a glass to my son. Here, said Da, and he poured me a gin and tonic. Good luck.

Good luck.

A quick silence passed.

Well, yes, everyone was sitting there looking at us wondering where Joejoe was, said Da. Where is Joejoe? Where is Joejoe? Why did he not come?

But they understood, said Ma.

Tell me this son, what did he say to you when he called you into the room the day we told him the Bird had died?

He asked me to get a bottle of Malibu.

I see. And that was all?

Yes, I lied.

He studied me then shook and boxed the cards. OK, let's have one game before bed. And he cut the pack into two halves and laid them in front of me. I touched the half to the right, and he dealt out a few hands. When the game was over he went down to the studio alone. The light was on till all hours.

Chapter Forty-Two

The Dark Saying

Next morning Ma on her way to work found Joejoe about half a mile away from his cottage. She drove him home and rang Da. We went down, and as I lit the fire Da sat facing his uncle.

It's not right, said Da.

What do you mean?

At your age.

Look I needed a breath of fresh air, explained Joejoe. That's all.

OK, OK.

Da took off to the site.

I made vegetable soup, and we ate at the table.

When we were finished he said: Thanks for the dinner.

No problem.

Read us a little.

The book fell open at Psalm 49.

I will incline mine ear to a parable: I will open my dark saying upon the harp.

Yes, said Joejoe, lifting up a hand. That is it. Everything is fine, you need not sit around here, go and do what you have to do.

You'll be all right?

I will.

I put the Book of Psalms back on the shelf.

Don't you worry Mister Psyche, I might meet someone on the other side.

What do you mean?

The less said the better, and he touched Timmy's ear.

I went off and stood on the battery wall and studied the cottage. It was like the morning I was waiting on the Judge at the pier after the Bird entered Joejoe's. A black tirade of smoke suddenly rose from the chimney. He must have thrown on more logs. I headed up and dug in some seaweed into the garden. I got four lobsters then I took in each lobster pot and stacked them at the back of the house. It was the end of the season. I groomed the horse and took him for a walk on the beach. Out to sea the huge coal boat from Poland was waiting for the high tide. I filled in some of the potholes the machine had made on the road with sea stones. Then I took a lift with Joe Lenihan and up at his place we cut enough timber to fill sixty cement bags.

He dropped me back at the gate around six. I went down the path. I knocked, no answer but a bark. I turned the handle. Joejoe's door was open.

Hallo, I called. Hallo.

There was no reply.

I went through all the rooms. The cottage was empty. The two dogs were in the front room watching my every move. I went round the back, walked through the garden, then went and stood on the battery wall, I searched the boat, went down the beach. I went to the Bird's. I went back through the fields. He was not to be seen anywhere.

I rang Ma.

Joejoe's gone, I said.

Oh Jesus Philip.

Ma I can't find him.

Philip! He's bound to be someplace.

I'll go looking again.

Right, right, don't worry.

OK Ma!

I headed off up the road. Da rang me.

He's not in the house?

397

No. He's gone.

What?

I can't find him.

I'm on my way, he said.

I headed up towards the crossroads looking over ditches, into the fields, and then I headed back and ran round the back of the house at Ballintra and searched the drains.

Joejoe, I screamed. Joejoe!

The dogs ran at my heels as I headed up the road again, and then suddenly Da rang me to say he had found him wandering up by the fort.

He's OK.

Thanks beta God.

I've taken him for a drink to Mister John's.

I'll come up.

Are you at the cottage?

I am.

Stop where you are.

I let the dogs back into the house, fed them and Da came down and collected me.

Mister John was standing inside the door of the pub on guard.

At the bar Joe was sitting alone with a glass of whiskey in his hand. He was breathing hard, with his head down.

Joejoe, are you all right? asked Da.

Yes.

It's you, he said to me.

It is.

Come on, I'm going to step out to the glasshouse for a smoke.

I went out with him and we stood together while he lit up and stared straight ahead.

You gave me a fright, Joejoe.

I'm sorry son.

I didn't know what happened.

I'm sorry. You see the walk is in the blood. It's in all our blood. I had to get out of the shop.

I looked everywhere for you.

I wasn't thinking son. I was acting selfish. I can see you're upset.

I can't help it.

Relax. Everything we do is wrong even when it's right. Look! He watched the last of the swallows dive past. Up the lane they skimmed and tossed fast like leaves torn from the wind-struck trees. They are after the blasted midges, he said, my cursed enemies.

He touched the flower heads and started to shake.

Soon the geese will be coming. Memory, said Joejoe, is a scourge, a scourge. You boys can write it down, but we have to remember it always. You see the Bird is down there in that house of mine. He threw the butt away. I don't believe in God Philip.

That means you do, Joejoe.

Is that so?

Otherwise you wouldn't have to say it.

I'll mind that in future, he said, and we shook hands, and stepped inside again, and the shaking started, then stopped as he looked round his old empty haunt. He studied the photos of the old timers; wandered the lounge that looked out on the sea; and stepped into the toilet. Da ordered another round. Anna saw our Volkswagen at the door as she ran past. She came in and we shot a game of pool. Joejoe threw a few darts. Frosty waltzed in and put his tongue in Joejoe's ear.

It's great to see you, he said.

Ah, Mister Frosty.

I'm sorry Joejoe.

I know. I see there are still marigolds growing out the back.

Flowers are funny, said Frosty.

A local couple and their two children arrived. The son dropped to the floor and keeping time with his knees he shouted Daddy! Daddy! The pair of kids began laughing like mad birds and Joejoe shook his cap.

The mother said to the daughter: What is your first name? Name?

Yes, name, she said.

Cow.

Cow is all right. But the cow is in the field. Name, please? Fido.

No, that's him, your father, you – who are you?

Me?

Yes, you! Name?

The child shook her head and sipped her straw. She began jabbing her fingers each side of her eyes, like in some sort of rhythm.

No name, she said.

And she shook her head again, and smiled.

It's to do with the echo, said Joejoe, not the yoke that makes the echo.

Please? said the mother. Please, I would like to know what you mean?

The echo is the key.

Explain Joejoe, said Anna.

The rule is – he said looking at the child – is that you go out the door you came in.

Louise, said the girl smiling.

Hallo, he said.

Thank you, the mother said with a nod.

More folk started arriving; a night of waltzing and jiving was ahead. In came a crowd of my mates who were just back after a weekend in Amsterdam and they all gave me the thumbs-up. Philip, said Tom Brady, it's good to see you out and about again.

Good to see you Tom.

How are things?

Not so bad.

I heard you did all right in the Leaving.

Not so bad.

You're sound, Philip – can I get you a drink?

No, I'm all right. Some other night. You see Joejoe over there – he's upset since the Bird died and we're having a few.

Got ya. Do what ya have to do, and give us a ring and we'll meet.

We shook hands and he went over to Joejoe and said: I'm sorry to hear you lost a friend, then he went off and joined the gang.

Who was that? asked Joejoe.

Tom Brady, Mickey's cousin.

Ah, I see.

A nice lad.

The best.

Da called another round. More locals started arriving. The widows chimed in and took their glasses of sherry and sat to the side. Mister John threw a board and cloth across the pool table and swept the dance floor.

The band took to the stand and started to plug in. The drum kit landed, the microphones were set up.

One, two! said the lead guitar man into the mike and his voice echoed down the lounge.

One, two! said the bass and the words boomed.

Stop! said Joejoe.

One two, said the singer.

One, two, repeated Joejoe, that's enough, that's it, and he threw back his drink just as the music started, then suddenly he stepped out alone onto the dance floor and began to waltz with a woman who was not there; as everyone watched – not knowing whether to laugh or cry – he held her back, he held her hand high, he swung her to the side, and gave a quick few steps, then in a great mime he swung the ghost lady to the other side; then suddenly into his arms stepped one of the widows Sadie Gillen; You wanna boogie? she asked; Sure thing, he said; and together they sailed off across the dance floor.

Jesus, said Anna, he can dance.

He can, said Da.

When the break came Sadie led Joejoe back to the bar. He sat down and let a whack of air out of his lungs.

You're good, I said.

It's been years, he said. That was Bridie I had in my arms. We'll have one for the road.

Next thing I found myself in Anna's arms as Joejoe stood clapping at the bar.

Round eleven o'clock we dropped off Anna and drove Joejoe home. We dressed him for bed and my father pocketed the key of the cottage and said: I have to take it Uncle Joejoe, I can't trust you not to open the door, and head out into the night; you know what I mean. His uncle looked away, and shouted: Leave that key where it is!

All right, but please don't go wandering.

Can't a man go for a walk?

I suppose so.

Well then, leave me be.

We headed back to our house.

He could get knocked down, said my father.

Aye.

He can't be left down there alone.

What do you want us to do? I asked.

I don't know. He's at risk.

He is.

Anything might happen him, said my father, anything.

Aye.

The waves pounded by. Out beyond the sea was doing a murder, and the smell of slurry was spreading across the fields after the last cut of the season.

Chapter Forty-Three

A Jacket and Shoes

A few strange days passed. Sunsets tumbled into storms. When the calm came the boats were hauled out of the water onto the pier. Another storm arrived. The following morning I came across a donkey jacket hanging from the wooden stake next the pier. I looked about. Not a soul. No one.

Joejoe's door was unlocked. He's gone on a walkabout I thought, and back came the panic. I looked in expecting to find the house empty, but the dogs were in the kitchen, and he was still in bed. He'd taken to the bed with the itch. I lit the fire and took him in tea and toast.

I'm destroyed, he said.

Can I get you something?

No. Say nothing, tell no one. Your mother was in that door first thing this morning. Say nothing.

Right.

If they hear I have the itch they'd have me put away. Yes.

I set off for home in the storm and again I saw the coat swinging in the wind. It was one of those leathered-shouldered dark blue labouring jackets, hanging there as if the man who owned it had taken it off and said: *Enough, enough of that*, and gone for a long walk. Now there it was flapping demented. I waited around a while just to see who it was that owned the coat. The beach was empty. I said to myself well he'll be back, whoever you are you'll be back, and I went on.

Well how is Joejoe? asked my father.

He's all right.

Is he in the house?

He is.

I think I'll go down and give him a shout.

Next day I had forgotten all about the jacket and then I came upon it again.

This time the wind had died down, and there it hung, not moving now, exactly at the height of a grown man's head, and looking fierce human on the edge of the pier. He must have taken it off, reached up and fastened it tight to the knob of the stake. And he must have fastened it well for it to survive the storms. The stake was blistered black by the constant wind. The wire had rusted a deep brown. Even the nettles in the ditch had gone black. A good enough coat. Yes, he must have taken it off, reached up and said: There.

There now.

Maybe he had work to do somewhere. Maybe he was hot and clammy at the time and went on and forgot it.

Anyway there it was, and the day after, a coat that had years ahead of it if it had been looked after. Another man might have taken it down, but I didn't. If I was lost I might have put it on but at the time I knew where I was. I headed on to Joejoe's and came in to find him standing in the scullery in his vest and pants, barefooted, at the back window. He was salting a basket of mackerel on the sink.

I'll have tay, said Joejoe. Thank you.

Right.

And a slice of bread, thank you.

I'm making it.

And what has yon fellow above to say?

He says you should move in with us.

Tell him no.

I told him.

Joejoe tiptoed into the sitting room and slowly dropped into a blanketed chair.

But he wouldn't listen, would he, he continued.

No.

I knew it. That man is a bad actor. He suddenly shook himself. Oh dear Jesus.

He leaned forward and lifted his vest at the back. The wheals were bloody.

You see?

I do Joejoe.

I'm destroyed. Ever since Cnoic came into this house the itch has grown worse.

It looks bad.

Will you scratch my back?

I will.

There, just there, aisy.

Yes.

Yes, nice and cushy, good man. And don't tell anyone.

No.

Just let me go.

A few days later I came upon the shoes, the heel of one on the toe of the other, sitting on the gravel next the bank.

They were down the strand, some distance from the coat; but it was the same thing only different, I got the same feeling when I came upon the pair of men's shoes as I did when I came upon the coat. I didn't see them immediately. I was searching for buoys which might have come in the storm. The storm had been blowing nonstop and the land was plastered with salt. The dunes had gone back yards. The wreck of a small boat had appeared bit by bit over the few days. They say it was a butter boat.

First the gunwales came, then some boards, a part of the keel. Then the name of the boat – the *Lagoon* – drifted in.

I found a buoy attached to a long green rope. The buoy itself was a soccer ball. As I lifted it up I saw the shoes. They had been parked there out of the wind by someone. They could have been a pair of shoes that would have suited a pony man. The laces were undone in a tidy manner. He'd tipped out neat whoever he was. The brown leather well kept, polished.

The shoes were placed well back from the floods. No one was out swimming. No boats, only a wreck. Myself and the buoy and the shoes. A tidy man. I sat down and looked out at the water and then I looked at the shoes. Around size 9. I didn't know him. He was a stranger to me. One quick step and away. A man about to take a leap.

They were sad shoes.

Next day, as with the coat, the shoes were still there. And the day after. The leather turning white and the toes rising.

I resisted the attempt to step into the shoes and try them for size. I thought of moving them further back to the pier to keep them safe for the stranger, but then he put them there whoever he was and it was not for me to move them.

I said to Joejoe who had not stirred out of the house in days that I'd seen a coat hanging from a stake by the pier.

Did ya?

I did.

Now then. Well?

Well what?

And who owned it?

No one.

Oh.

Very good, he said.

And then I saw a pair of shoes down the strand.

He looked at me rheumy-eyed. He wet his lips.

And no one about?

No.

No, and he nodded as if he understood. Not a soul?

No.

It's bad, he said. It's a bad sign.

He stirred himself, took his coat off the back door, put it on and sat. Suddenly he knocked the wood rest of the chair with his knuckles and looked at me as if he was demanding something.

You're too young, he said bitterly.

Too young for what?

For the whole shebang. You know nothing. And by the time you know it'll be all over.

I don't know what you're talking about.

That's what I mean!

Stop being cross!

What are you talking about!

Stop shouting!

All right, I'm sorry, he said. I don't hear myself shouting. He got up and lifted the photo of himself with Grandma, and Grandda, looked at it a while and put it away.

We sat there a while.

Tell me this, he asked.

What.

Do you think the shoes and jacket might have belonged to the one man?

I didn't think about that.

Ha-ha!

I said nothing.

Are you thinking about it now?

I am.

And what do you say?

No. They were two different men.

You could be right, he said. Two different men. Yes indeed. All right, two different men . . . but on the same journey.

Maybe, I said.

Aye.

*

A coat and a pair of shoes.

I can see them still. Someone had worn them, then left them behind, and set out. The next day I was passing where the coat was and it was gone, and then I went and looked for the shoes and they were gone too.

Just a pile of ash there as if someone had burnt them.

That was it. I sat with Joejoe a while, told him the story; and then he suddenly got up and rang the house above.

Hallo, he said, it's Saturday, why don't ye go into town? Yes, give yourselves a break! I'll not budge, I promise ya. Aye, he's here with me.

And so a few minutes later Da pulled in. It was Cnoic's first time in a car and he buried his snout into Timmy's neck in the back seat as they perched each side of me. All the clouds were a wild stormy red as the Volkswagen left Ballintra and the red grew huge above the hills as we took the mountain road. In the distance the whole town looked volcanic. Da drove round the streets slowly, and then pulled in at the usual spot.

Da went up Main Street to step into his usual doorways and watch the passing crowds.

We listened to the radio; then I got out and walked the dogs around the monastery, and along the river. Strips of clouds on fire drifted upstream. Quickly, the new night began to fall. I went and bought Joejoe his packet of Major. The town sounded like a muffled shout as we sat in the car.

Do ye want to go for a walk, asked Ma, round the streets?

No, I said.

Ma switched the radio off. Then, after sitting there for maybe an hour Da came back, and sat in.

Will we go home?

Yes, said Ma.

He turned the key.

It's not the same, he said.

*

409

At Ballintra we found Joejoe standing by the gate of the house in the dark. The dogs jumped out of the car and landed at his feet.

You're home fierce early, he asked, leaning in the window.

The town was quiet.

Did you not trust me?

I did, Uncle Joejoe, said Da, I did.

Good night, all, he said.

Here you are, I said, and handed him his fags.

Thank you son, and he headed in, turned and said: Do you get the pong of shit? The slurry is something else.

Chapter Forty-Four

The Cure

The next day I went out and dug up the last of the shallots, scullions, potatoes, and onions, then got the wok, put in the oil, pepper and salt, and put her on low. Cut the onions into pieces and left them frying as I went back out to the garden and collected the last of the wild marjoram, oregano, chives, parsley and sage; added them to the onions, and in with the red pepper, the pine nuts, the basil, then the mince; and lastly the tins of tomatoes, and pesto.

Next I took the leavings of the chicken from the fridge, cut it into little pieces and boiled some water in the saucepan; in with the salt and pepper; added the onions, then the chicken and the juice of two oranges; and back out to the garden for wild thyme, more chives, parsley, celery leaves, and picked the final two carrots and one leek, and added all to the chicken, with a touch of turmeric.

The job was done. Dinner was ready.

I went on down with two portions for himself.

He was seated by the fire, his blue head high in the air, and he tearing at himself.

God give me patience, he said, but I'm destroyed. Do you see the other day?

Yes.

Well I could have died. Your Da looked in last night, and there he was first thing this morning, he has me haunted, and there I was – wanting to scratch – and not being able to scratch, if you know what I mean.

I do.

Did you see that?

I did.

I thought I'd die. There was mice darting up and down my trousers, and I couldn't even go near them, Jesus!

He called me over with his forefinger.

Do you see my hair?

Yes.

My very hair is piercing me, and he nodded vehemently. Meeee, he said.

I'm sorry Joejoe.

Jesus.

Jesus, I said.

I'm destroyed, you hear, destroyed.

Can I not get you something?

There's nothing for it. Nothing works.

There must be something.

No. And there's something else I should add.

What's that?

He pointed at the front door.

What's that item over there?

It's the front door . . . Grandda.

Exactly. I want to be always able to walk out my own front door. You hear?

– I hear you, Joejoe –

– Do you? –

– You're shouting! –

– And so are you! –

– Please! –

– I do not want to be locked in –

OK.

I want in the . . . in the middle of the night to get the cool air on my skin. You see what I do each night?

What.

I step out through that there door at two in the morning in my skin and stand there in the rain. That is my comfort and no man is going to take that away from me. You hear?

I hear you.

He drew the nails of his hand down the lower part of his neck and then looked at his nails.

Jesus, he said. The pain, the pain. And you know what?

What Grandda?

While the earth remaineth . . . day and night shall not cease. Have you got that?

I have, I said.

He nodded and slowly smiled as if he was recognising someone from the past as I placed the soup and the pasta before him and he ate like the man doing the crossword. You are a good friend Mister Psyche, he said.

I rang Ma who was on night duty at the hospital.

Do you have anything for the itch?

There are certain creams.

Can you get me the best?

And who is it for?

Joejoe.

I thought so. Is he bad?

The worst.

It sounds like psoriasis. You know something – the very dogs he loves could be doing him a disfavour.

Can you get me something?

I will.

But don't let on I told you.

I won't, but why?

He thinks the itch is a sign.

A sign of what?

Dying.

I've heard that. Lots of the old folk believe that. But . . .
Yeh?
. . . Anyway.
Chat ya. It's great to have a mother who is a nurse.
Ta Philip.

There was a faint knock on my door next morning and Ma came with the tube of cream.

This is the best stuff on the market, she whispered. Now what you do is rub it in, and change his clothes entirely afterwards. Clear the bed of sheets and pillow cases, and bring all them to me and we'll give them a great wash OK? And here is a whole new set of sheets and pillow cases. Your Da's shirt, and underpants and vest and a clean pair of socks.

OK.

I had the breakfast and went down. He was sitting by the unlit fire in the dark kitchen with Timmy in his chair and Cnoic at his feet.

What do you want!

I have the cure.

Oh, is that so.

Yes Joejoe.

I have not slept in days, do you hear me.

Take off your clothes.

Right, he said.

And I'll light the fire.

He took off his jacket, his shirt, his vest, his trousers, his socks, his underpants. And as he stood there nude I pumped the cream onto my palms. He stood erect and closed his eyes. I began with his scalp. Then his back. Then his neck, his waist, his arse, his knees, the backs of his legs. He turned in the half light. I did his neck, his chest, his stomach, his balls, his mickey, his elbows and lastly his knees again. Then I reached his feet, and was amazed to find that his toes were not old.

They were like a child's.

He stood by the fire glistening.

He opened his eyes.

Are you still there, he whispered.

I am.

Ah good.

Wait till it dries in.

I will, I will.

And you can't go back into the same clothes, I said.

Right, son.

I put on the kettle and filled a basin and washed and dried his hair.

He stood naked by the roaring fire as I dressed him in clean underpants, vest, socks and shirt, and a pair of trousers. I brought out his Christmas jacket. When he was dressed in his best, he sat into the chair. I put on the socks. He stepped into his shoes.

Man alive, he said, I never felt better.

I took all the old bedclothes and packed everything in a bag and then I made up a fresh bed with the new sheets and pillow slips.

I took the towel to his scalp again.

He got up and brushed his hair.

Are we going to a party? he asked.

Yes, Joejoe.

That's better, he said, you have given me great peace son, then he went quiet and patted his forehead and wandered off into prayer.

The meal was lovely, especially the soup, said Ma.

There's something wrong down in that house, said Da.

He is all right, I said.

No, he's not all right, the whole thing is getting to him. I'll go down and take a look.

He stepped off into the night.

Did you do the job, Ma whispered to me.

I did.

She threw Joejoe's clothes into the washing machine.

Well now, what would ye like to do son?

I'd like a game of pool, I said, with my dear friend.

And so she collected Anna and drove us up to Mister John's. We had two cans of cider, and Ma had a gin and tonic. When she went to pay for them, Mister John nodded at Frosty who was sitting alone in a chair.

His honour bought them.

Thank you sir.

No problem, Missis.

Anna broke, and knocked in a red, and tipped four more down in quick succession.

Do you like girls with caps, she asked me as I lined up for my shot.

I don't know.

I was only asking.

I missed my shot on yellow and she won the game and Frosty clapped.

Don't laugh, I said.

Why? asked Anna.

Never laugh if you can help it.

Never?

Never.

Can I smile, Jeremiah?

Yes, Lala.

You see I want to smile at you.

OK.

And she lined up the next game, as Ma did the Sudoku at the bar. Then Da stepped in.

I walked up.

Everything all right?

Fine, and he threw me a look, then bent his head and breathed out. As a matter of fact I have never seen Joejoe so peaceful. A pint of Smithwicks please, he said to Mister Sweet John.

As we were preparing for bed that night, the phone rang. After three rings, it stopped.

I'll go down, I said.

I tipped down the lane on a wing and a prayer. The sky was peppered with stars. The half-moon had a rugged edge, and below was a cloud like a hawk rising. Then as the haze of cloud lifted the half-moon turned into the face of an old white bearded man looking up into the heavens. There was a candle fluttering in the bedroom window. I looked in. Joejoe was lying, the hands flat out each side of him, and his eyes glued to the ceiling. I sat down under the sill and watched the peninsula. What I thought of was suddenly sucked out of my head. *While the earth remaineth day and night shall not cease.*

After a while I heard him pull on the front door.

Then I heard my granduncle Joejoe shout.

It was a terrible roar.

Like the roar I heard once of a man going mad in a church. I was going to say something to him, then I stopped myself. I backed away and stood against the gable. The two dogs began barking into the night. Then all of a sudden without a stitch on him Joejoe stood at the gate waving his arms, then went in and closed the door without a sound, and climbed back into bed, and lay there, listening.

417

Chapter Forty-Five

The Second Fall

Next morning Da came running into the kitchen in the house.

C'mon, he said. I think we are in trouble.

What's wrong?

He can't open the door. Something is wrong.

We drove down to Joejoe's. Da knocked.

Joejoe, he called.

I hear you, said my granduncle and his distant voice was thin and weary.

I came down to see you.

You're welcome.

My father smiled oddly. And how are you? he asked through the door.

I'm fine.

Well let us in.

In a while, he said.

What are you saying?

In a while I said.

The father looked at me and went to the middle room window. He could see nothing. He tapped on the window.

Joejoe, he called.

Yes.

Will you let us in?

I'm trying son, he called, I'm trying.

Joejoe.

Dear God, I'm trying I said. I really am.

There's something wrong, my father said. He bounced his shoulder off the front door but there was no give. He went to

418

the window of the bedroom and brushed away the salt from the storm that had lashed the house.

He's not in bed, he said.

He went to the kitchen at the back of the house and tried the back door. It was locked tight. He came back to the front door.

Uncle Joseph, he said.

Yes, said my granduncle and this time his voice was closer to us.

Where are you?

I'm in bed.

No you're not.

Yes I am.

You're not in the bed.

I am, and I'm trying to get up to let you in.

Joejoe, my father said, stay where you are.

All right.

Just stay there.

All right so, and his voice was disappearing.

I fear he's down, said my father. He went back to the bedroom window and tried the sash. He got a stick and levered it between the jambs and the top of the window opened. He put his head in.

That bed has not been slept in, he said.

He turned to me.

Now, he said, it's up to you.

I climbed up onto the sill and turned to the side and lifted one leg in; but I could not draw the rest of my body after it. So head first I went into the small window while Da held my two feet up and pushed me on bit-by-bit as I edged forward on the palms of my hands across the sill, making sure I did not slit myself with the window catch, then I reached onto the table, past the shaving gear and plaster cast of Jesus, and slowly I drew one foot in then the other and lay there.

I dropped to the floor and went into the middle room. Joejoe was lying on his back in a pool of piss between the doorway to the kitchen and the doorway to the bathroom. He was in his long johns. His brown eyes were wide open and he was staring at the ceiling. He had his hands wide open on the ground each side of him and he was trying to push himself up. I knelt down beside him.

Grandda, I said.

Atta boy, he said.

I let my father in.

Oh God, he said.

Joejoe went to get up.

Steady, Joejoe.

I'm all right son.

He came up into my father's arms like a child. We settled him on an armchair by the dead fire. My father stood in the scullery with the kettle on as I took off the long johns. I washed his thighs and put on another pair of pants. His breath was like a glass of whiskey. Then I removed the fags and money from the old trousers and when I tried to put the money into the new trousers, he pushed what might have been couple of hundred euros into my hand. Take it, he whispered, and winked, I have no use for it.

As I was pulling down his shirt over an arm that was peppered with spots, Da came in and looked at Joejoe.

Are they sore? he asked.

Are what sore? Joejoe asked from within the shirt.

The bites.

Ah the cursed midges.

Yes.

Not any more, I got the cure, and his voice began racing. I've never known such peace in days.

Then his head fell forward and I grabbed him. And steered him back into the armchair. His two eyes were filled with terror.

Joejoe, I said, Joejoe.

My chin! My chin! he shouted. I'm cursed, Psyche.

Da lifted the phone and rang an ambulance.

Ballintra, he said, second last house by the sea, Feeney, Joejoe, then he gave the phone number. He rang Ma and whispered the news.

Slowly a small burst of power returned to Joejoe.

He whistled and clicked his tongue.

Where's me dogs? he asked me, holding himself.

They must be out.

And how did they get out?

I don't know.

They musta took them.

Who?

Those boys, and he sat up straight, go out and call.

I went outside and whistled but there was no sign. I looked down the beach but saw no dogs.

I came in the door. My father was building a fire. The kettle was boiling with a loud sound. My granduncle felt his head for his cap then he saw me.

Did you get them?

No.

He shook his head.

You whistled?

I did.

That dog Timmy has never once left my side.

He'll be back.

No, he'll not, he said, Timmy's gone. The dogs know when things are bad. The dog knows what I don't want to know.

He thought a while.

It's that crowd are to blame, he said.

My father took the tongs and stirred the turf. We waited for Joejoe to explain but he said nothing else.

421

Who, my father asked.

Who is right! You see this tea?

I do.

Well I offered them tea. And did they take it?

Well did they?

They did. Without a word.

And who were they?

Strangers.

And you let them in?

I did, he smiled.

How often have I told you to keep that door closed. Who were they?

I don't know.

Did they threaten you?

No. They said nothing. They were men who don't speak.

I see.

Yes indeed. And see where you are sitting now?

Yes, said my father.

Well that's where they were sitting.

You should not have let them in, he said.

I thought they were neighbours.

Was it them that knocked you down?

I don't know. But I'll tell you this. If they'd spoken to me the once I wouldn't have fallen.

Why did they not speak? I asked.

Because they stayed silent, he said. Two men who would not speak, maybe three. They came knocking at one and I let them in. And in they came. Not a word. Sat down. Not a word. And sat there till three, where you are now, maybe four, just looking at me, and nodding. I tried all kinds of conversation. But nothing.

Jesus, said my father.

That's the story, said Joejoe. Say hallo to Miss Conan for me.

I will, I said.

And just then the phone rang.

Right, said Da. They're coming.

No! said Joejoe.

Please, said the ambulance man, Mister Feeney.

No! I want to stop here, he said, and I saw the blue lines form on his cheeks and over his eyes. I saw his eyes wander.

I need a breath of fresh air, he said.

Joejoe, please.

I don't want to see my name on another man's lips ever again. Right?

Right.

Give us a break will ye.

OK.

The less said the better. Can I have one last fag?

Yes, you can.

He lit a Major from the turf in the fire, took a few draws, then threw it into the grate.

Once a man, twice a child, said Joejoe as he was hoisted onto a stretcher and lifted into the back of the ambulance.

Da sat opposite him.

Please lie down, Mister Feeney, said the ambulance driver.

Find – my – dogs – Mister – Psyche, said Joejoe in five long breaths, before they closed the doors.

Chapter Forty-Six

The Search

I met a ball of salt as I went down the winkled rocks. I rang Anna but could get no signal. The yellowed bones of a dogfish sat below. The flesh had been torn off his body but the bones of his head and long tail were perfectly intact. The white teeth glinted. The gulls were shaking their shawls as they sat looking out. I called for Timmy. I went under the cliffs to the caves. The echo of my call came back but no barks. Then I crossed the whin beds.

Timmy, I called.

Cnoic! I called.

I rose curlews and a flock of long-billed snipe. I reached Joejoe's again and walked the flooded fields with no luck. A lone cormorant flew over. Two ESB poles stood in pools of water. The high tide was going out across the beach without a sound. These great purple clouds were pushing in from the sea. When they crossed, the blue sky opened up and the sun shone down with a great sweep of heat. The heron was out on his rock with the tide splashing through his legs. At times I thought I saw the dogs but I was always mistaken. A small bush became Timmy.

A bunch of dry grass was racing towards me. A pair of ears rose in the bog. A hawk jerking from side to side flew up the lane.

I walked back to the beach. It was strewn with shells. The hare raced by and headed out the rocks for a taste of salt. Annie-John, the winkle picker, in men's boots and a man's overcoat went by with an empty bucket.

Did you see Timmy? I asked her.

No. Did he get out?

He did.

Hah haw!

She nodded and went on. I continued the search for if I found the dogs then what my granduncle feared would not happen. A couple of hours passed. The tide was now well out. I walked the lava rocks; I went round the blow hole and stood a long time on the battery wall. A group of bird-watchers, with cameras slung round their necks, headed round Shell Corner. The Japanese fisherman drove up the lane, waved and crossed the rocks towards the fish pool.

Timmy, I yelled.

Cnoic! Cnoic! I roared as I crossed the Night Field. I searched Gillen's; went up Ewing's; back by Pockawockida. The sun arrived in brave wild spurts. The divers were leaping into the waves. Out the rocks the hare was now sitting by his friend the heron looking out to sea. They never moved, but stayed side-by-side with their eyes fixed on the island. Sea gulls were thrashing next to Joejoe's, and now the sound of the baler crossed the field as the wandering windrows of clipped grass were fed into the square black bales with a loud, piercing zip.

Every field on all sides was on the move.

In the cut fields the smell of slurry rose.

I went back to the walk I'd taken with Joejoe, up past Ballintra, and the mantra continued as I turned round the corner at Cooley Lane, and there I found them. The two dogs were sitting outside the Bird's house, flat on their stomachs, with ears raised among the last blues of the scattered periwinkles.

C'mon lads, I said.

They looked at me.

C'mon!

Timmy rose slowly as if the years were telling. Cnoic jumped to attention and smelt my shoes. They stepped out in front, uncertain as to who should take the lead; Cnoic gave a pretend bark at a stranger who was not there, tossed his tail like a lasso, while Timmy stayed perfectly silent with an odd look behind him from a pair of dark questioning eyes. When we reached Joejoe's cottage at Ballintra they went fast past the open gate and ran on up the lane to our house, looking backwards, then jaunting ahead.

Ma's car was outside our house behind Da's. When I went in they were sitting at the kitchen table with Anna. They all stood and looked at me.

Cnoic and Timmy shot in alongside my feet, and lay down.

I found the dogs, I said.

Philip.

Yes Ma.

We have something to tell you.

She looked at Da.

Something bad happened.

What?

I hate having to tell you this – Joejoe died on the way to the hospital.

Jesus Christ, Da.

He had a heart attack.

Ah no.

Son, I'm sorry.

Philip, said Anna and she took my hand and squeezed it. The room swam before my eyes.

Look it, I said, I'll just step out for a moment.

Followed by the dogs I went through the front door.

I leaned over the new wall.

Outside in the sky the clouds made waves. The sky was reflecting the sea. I saw the shape of the Connemara pony on the hill as he fed on a clump of weeds, and beyond him the ass was looking at nothing, with a great ancient gaze. My head was tormented by words.

I lay against the stones from the old monastery. I started this shivering. A shadow appeared behind me. It was like the old stonewall builder was approaching me. I turned, and there was Da.

He reached out a hand.

I'm sorry son. Come in when you're ready, and he stepped away.

I never felt as selfish as I did standing at that wall, then I looked down towards Joejoe's. There was another job to be done. I went back into the house and said OK, Let's do it.

I'm with you, said Anna.

Let's go, Da said.

We headed down to Ballintra and swept out all the rooms, and arranged again another four chairs in the bedroom to take the coffin. The rifle was hung back in its old place above the bedroom door in the living room. To the side of the dresser I found the rat trap in place with a sausage pinned under the spring. I threw it into the dustbin. Fuchsia and a few last threads of ancient yellow montbretia were placed in jars on the mantelpiece.

I put all his books on show on the second level of the dresser.

The same routine continued as before – Da headed off again to the undertakers in town; Ma and Anna spent all evening sorting out food. Eventually I walked Anna home and Mister and Mrs Conan brought us into their living room and we sat a long time together. I headed home. Ma and Da were waiting. We all climbed the stairs to bed. Out of habit I stopped and listened for the phone to ring, then closed the bedroom door. Somewhere during the night as I climbed the family tree I found myself shouting at the ceiling, but no sound came out of my mouth. I was speechless.

I lay there eyes closed.

Then slowly I touched the pillow and the sheets with my finger tips. I moved my toes. The next morning we dug the grave alongside Grandma's and Grandda's. The earth was tossed up by the same crew as dug the Bird's.

Joejoe that afternoon arrived home in a coffin, the lid was taken off and he lay there like a man who had kept his word.

I put *Moby Dick* in his joined hands. We sat all night with him at the wake in Ballintra.

In came the widows; the Germans; the French, the Belfast crew; the Judge and his wife; Sweet John who arrived with boxes of cans of beer then took off again, Mrs Flynn, J. D. Moffit, Mrs Hart, the Mannions, Joe Foran, Paul Donlon, Don Herrity; the coalman Mister Awesome, Barney Buckley, Jim Simpson, Miss Currid, Terence MacGowan and Joe and Marie Conan and Anna, Aaron, Tommy and Angela. In came Mister and Mrs Tingle, and again for a moment I climbed up the rungs at the pier, reached out for the rope, and the rope gave. Our relations kept coming through the door to stand at the bottom of the coffin staring at Joejoe. I went outside and stood trying to get my bearings.

My mobile rang.

Hallo, I said.

This is Stefan. I hear the news. I am sorry.

I know.

And I never brought him for the drive.

Not to worry.

I will see you soon.

Goodbye, Stefan.

I went back in and more figures out of the past appeared. Through the door came Gary and Desmond, and Gary stood for an age by the coffin, wandering, with his lips moving constantly in some refrain, then he pumped my hand.

And never once, said Da, did he relent from the story about the visitors who did not speak.

And then we became them – the people who did not speak. They had come again to call as we sat around the bedroom for long periods without a word being spoken. Conversations would start and then stop. In came Mick Doyle and Stefan. Frosty was like a man haunted. He kept looking in at Joejoe's face, and backing off to study his thumbs. Nobody sang. Frosty was tormented.

They were visited, he said –

– They were –

– Well they were not strangers –

– I'm only saying –

– You are –

– I'm only saying –

Anna went out the front door to leave Miss Gillen to her car and when she came in she cupped her hands.

– Lala said Lala –

– I said Doras –

– And she said Fuinneog –

– Frosty said Psyche –

– Look said Anna –

– And he said she's dark –

– She is –

– I'm only saying –

– What's going on, asked Aunty Eilish –

Look! said Anna, and she put her hand, palm-up in front of Gary, I found a Man Keeper on the path.

He drew back.

He looks like a lizard, said Gary.

He's a newt, actually, said Miss Hart. They are local lads.

But he's still a mystery, the same boy, said Frosty. Get rid of him quick, if that fellow jumps into your mouth, you'll be sorry.

Lick his belly, and you'll have the cure for the burn, said the old lady.

Draw him for me, will you Philip, said Anna, please.

I got a pencil and drawing book down off the dresser and drew the Man Keeper who stayed perfectly still as he lay on her palm. Only once did he stir his two back legs. The wee turn of the tail was hard to get because at first it looked easy. First time I drew it the turn and the sweep was too long. Then I followed its dark curved shape along the lines for memory and forgetfulness that crossed the palm of my friend's hand.

He feels like nothing on earth, she said.

Done, I said.

She brought the newt back outside to place him back on the wet flags and came in, washed her hands.

Can I see that, asked Desmond. He studied the page and said nothing. Then he handed it on to Gary who held his face away back.

He's like a question mark, he said.

Lala took the copy book and placed it on the window sill.

Thank you, Philip.

Is there any of you fit to sing? asked Mrs McSharry, it would be befitting for you all know Joejoe was a musical man.

No one answered. Da looked at the old violin on the wall, the squeezebox sitting by the armchair, and gave one last glance at the rifle hanging above the door into the bedroom, and closed his eyes.

I wonder is the disc still there, asked Aaron, pointing at the dresser.

What disc is that?

The opera singer.

Christ I forgot all about it, and I went and searched.

Any luck?

And there it was, next the Wayward Lad.

Yes, I have it.

Tommy went out to the van and came back in with his CD player.

Who is going to sing, pray? asked Ma.

Dido, I said; the man whose car you started.

Oh, the *chauffeur*, she said, giving the sound a French purr in a long memory sound as she lowered her head.

Tommy read the wording on the tape: *The Great Theatre, Poznan*, he announced, and tapped the play button; and as the chords struck and the voice began St Patrick and the General stepped in and stood by the bedroom door to listen to a man they did not know sing a song that nobody knew the meaning of, then the widows and Mick, Frosty, the cousins and aunts, and Da and Ma all stood with smiles or furrowed brow and questioning looks, that turned to quiet listening as the lone lover again was arguing the rights and the wrongs and then he went away outside, nearly out of earshot as Anna stared through the bedroom door at where Joejoe was laid, and slowly the voice began returning and then stopped somewhere near us and went away again; and when we reached the part where the CD had suddenly stopped that night at the party the voice travelled on by into another series of repetitions, and questions; and sang outside; the football flew again in the air in the Night Field, and then the violin took over and the song went into a harsh whisper, and ended.

There came this long applause that grew louder and louder as the people in the audience came to their feet in the distant hall.

You could hear the tumble of chairs, and the echo of the clapping went to and fro, then silence.

And into my head came the last line I had read from the Psalms to Joejoe: *I will open my dark saying upon the harp*, and for the first time I suddenly realised that when we buried the Bird we were putting Joejoe in the grave.

*

Mrs Tingle came to her feet and clapped.

Where were we? asked Frosty.

Poland.

Thank you Tommy, said Anna as he replaced the disc on the dresser.

In a man's tweed jacket, and her hair tied back like an elderly Indian, Aunty Eilish said: That was breathtaking.

It was beautiful, said Ma.

Well I'm bowled over.

I never – said Frosty, shaking his head – in all my life.

I got the drawing book down off the sill and flicked through the faces till I reached Grandma's face and Grandda's hand and there I found my last attempt at Joejoe's face. I had done his ears, his neck, his mouth but not the eyes.

Now I began another search and tried filling them in, but the wrong man came onto the page. I erased the pupils with a rubber and started again, but the look escaped me, so I went into the bedroom and drew him as he lay in the coffin and somehow I learned that the closed eye told something different from the open eye, the open eyes I'd drawn told a lie; and as the General and St Patrick sat stoically in their chairs against the wall, I tried to pencil in Joejoe as he was, laid out, with the last thoughts still travelling through his head, then he went beyond my reach; so I drew his shoes standing upright staring back at his face and closed the book; and sat on.

A few minutes later Ma led Mister and Mrs Brady quietly into the mourning room, and she went back to the drawing room, followed by the General and St Patrick. They left the three of us alone with Joejoe. Mickey's parents both gripped my shoulders.

Philip, Mrs Brady said, I'm sorry for you, and she shook her head, then petted Joejoe's forehead.

Easy son, said Mister Brady.

Thanks for coming.

I suppose this is not the time to mention it, but I heard you did well in the Leaving.

Thanks, I said.

They sat alongside me in silence for a few minutes with their heads down, then got up to go, and Mrs Brady held my hand as I walked them through the now silent house of mourners out to their car.

Good luck with the rest of your life, said Mister Brady and Mrs Brady leaned over and kissed my cheek.

I went back and sat by the coffin. Ma came in and said: We have a request.

Yes Ma.

We'd like you to read at the funeral Mass.

OK.

I sat on. Angela pressed a small envelope into my hand, and she and Tommy and Aaron went. I read a few lines then put it away in my pocket. There was a sudden chatter of voices in the living room, and then Anna led Miss Jilly and Mister Lundy into the bedroom. Holding a wreath of yellow and red marigolds they stood silently by the door while behind them the family and friends watched the lady.

Mister Psyche, she whispered.

She leaned in and petted Joejoe's cheeks. Mister Lundy placed a chair for her, and then he sat at the far end of the room and, as always, stared straight ahead.

With one hand on the edge of the coffin she lowered her head.

What was it Joejoeing? she said. What was it? And she tapped her forehead with her knuckles, tell me.

Are you all right? asked Mister St Patrick.

Yes. Help me, memory, she said, and then she threw back her head and said, Yes, yes, I have it – of course, coarse-cut –

– What? –

– He had a bitter tongue, you see –

– Excuse me? –

You've got me wrong, sir, she said – You know what he loved, Mister Psyche, she said, I have just remembered – the hard bits in marmalade. I love the legs, he used to say.

This great warmth travelled through Miss Jilly.

The legs, he called them. I love the legs! And she thumped the floor with her heels. Oh it had to be chopped fruit peel from then on, she said; rind and zest was the key. She laughed to herself and tapped the coffin: I like my jam bitter, he'd say, and she smiled and nodded at the General –

– He did, Ma'am –

– And so I put in heaps! –

– You did –

She clapped her hands as Da arrived in with a tray of whiskey.

We sat a while till the next in line arrived, then we gave up our chairs and in the sitting room Gary and Desmond rose, and went off into the night and Miss Jilly and Mister Lundy took their places.

Philip? said Miss Jilly, is that who you really are?

Yes, I said.

I see.

And I am Stepanon, said Stefan, but here – and he spun his right hand on an extended arm – they always call you by another name.

I know, she said. We are all rechristened in this part of the world.

St Patrick cut an onion in two and chewed. Then he cut another and his eyes cried. My mother filled out glasses from the remaining quarter-bottle of Malibu, and my aunt had a taste, and so did Stefan who said *Achiu!* and raised the glass to the tip of his forehead. More folk arrived and Miss Jilly got up to go and shook hands again with the General and St Patrick, and they and Ma and Da went to the gate to say goodbye. I accompanied Mister Lundy and herself to the old blue Volkswagen that was parked among many other cars at the pier.

She sat into the passenger seat, then got out, pulled the seat forward and lowered herself into the back, and then she pushed the seat forward, stepped out and got into the front while Mister Lundy sat impassively in the driver's seat with the engine running.

We are obsessed, Philip – she said – to our detriment, and she gave a polite, crazy nod then they slithered away in first. I waved goodbye and stood a while on my own. The sea was swooning and the lights in the houses to the south were flickering but the sky had its stars and their light did not budge. At intervals the cows lewed angrily, then in reply from a further field there came this long, soft moo.

Cnoic and Timmy appeared.

They circled me.

Good men, I said.

I led them up to our house, and fed them. Timmy was as yet allowed no chair to sit in, so the two lay in the corridor, below the steps, head to head, watching for the next move. Cnoic drew a sigh, Timmy a whinge. I pulled the door, and stood, thinking I had left something behind me. I looked at the beams of tractor lights as the balers went over and back through Lenihan's field. It felt like it was an Amusement Arcade, and I headed on back down to the pier. St Patrick came to my side, and lit a fag and said: Look at the white ducks out the rocks, and disappeared back into Joejoe's cottage that was surrounded by cars and bicycles. I went into the crowded house and took down the book of Psalms off the dresser, and the torch, and watched by Anna I stepped out the door again, and headed to Cooley corner, then straight on up the hill to the scene of the accident.

For a few minutes I stood there in the dark and then I walked on.

A car came up behind me. The General pulled in with Frosty seated beside him.

Do you want a lift?

I'm going up to Mister Sweet's.

Sit in.

I sat in.

I have a cow, he said, who has rejected her calf and we are going up to see how they are.

The poor calf is terrified, said Frosty, of his mother. It's a terrible sight to see.

I'll be going back down to Joejoe's in a while, said the General, if you want a lift.

No, I said, I'll walk.

Good man.

The smell of September slurry followed me.

The door of the pub was closed, and the blinds drawn. The lights were lowered to the front in honour of Joejoe. A single female pheasant trotted down the road; I went round the back and in the side door. Sweet John was in there alone looking at the racing pages of the Indo. A few low lights were lit. On the TV they were rolling back the years in silence.

Are you OK asked John.

I'll have a cider.

I sat in the corner under the light, took out the book of Psalms and tossed the leaves and let them fall open, and read to myself what I might read out at the funeral Mass on Joejoe's behalf; I closed the book. Yes, I said. Then I realised I had not marked the page nor knew the number of the psalm I'd just looked at, so I opened the book again and landed at Chapter 3 in Corinthians. As I read the lines I did not rightly understand them. It felt false reading them alone. I knew what the words meant, but I needed his reply. I had never read the book alone.

436

It was him who shared with me the sound that made sense of the words. Joejoe's absence suddenly emptied my head. I closed the book of Psalms, then heard a command, and tried one more time and reached Psalm 46, but then I thought *leave it, leave it son,* and I decided to just let the book fall open at random on the morning I had to speak from the altar.

Yes.

I ordered a glass of Malibu and played a game of pool against myself. Red won. I called another and set the balls up again.

My mobile rang.

Are you all right? asked Da.

I am, I said, I am.

Where are you?

Sweet John's.

Do you want us to come up and collect you?

No, I'm going to walk.

Here, he said, hold on – Anna wants to talk to you.

OK.

Philip –

– Anna –

– I just –

– Yes –

– I just wanted to let you know that some of your mates have arrived –

– I'll be down soon. I promise –

– Good man. Chat ya –

– See ya, Anna –

– OK Philip –

I put the mobile in my pocket and took out again the envelope Angela had given me. I stepped outside into the smokers' glasshouse, and read her writings of condolence. Each letter *L* swooped overhead in a loop, each *E* was like a bird cupping its head under her wings, and the *T*'s were like the chimneys of a gas station, cut across by short strokes of lightning. *Sorry for all your trouble,* she'd written. *We will see you down the line and . . .*

Round the back came the General and Frosty.

Jesus, said Frosty, seeing me. Did you ever feel haunted?

I did, I said.

You are some boy. He coughed and a long lookey fell out of his nose. Miss Jilly was fierce high, he said.

That's the way.

I put the letter away and followed them in, lifted the glass and drank.

– Cuckoo! I said –

– Cuckoo! said Frosty –

And I broke the balls, and played against myself again, the white flew off the table, twice, and I lost and won; and won and lost; then I went to the side door.

Have one for the road – it's on the house, called Sweet John, and we can all go down together.

No, thanks, see you below, I said.

Good enoughski.

Aye, the General repeated, nodding gravely, see you below.

Sound! said Frosty.

Goodnight Philip, called Mister Sweet John.

I said good night, and went out and took the Bog road, and started the walk, with the torch, through the smell of dung, back down through the cut fields, past the rushes and whins and grey shuffling reeds, to the Wake.